THE SOUND AND THE FURY

&

AS I LAY DYING

THE SOUND AND THE FURY

&

AS I LAY DYING

by WILLIAM FAULKNER

WITH A NEW APPENDIX AS A
FOREWORD BY THE AUTHOR

THE

MODERN LIBRARY

NEW YORK

This Appendix for *The Sound and the Fury*
was written for *The Portable Faulkner*, ed-
ited by Malcolm Cowley, and is used here
by permission of The Viking Press

Random House IS THE PUBLISHER OF

THE MODERN LIBRARY

BENNETT A. CERF · DONALD S. KLOPFER · ROBERT K. HAAS

Manufactured in the United States of America
By H. Wolff

The Sound and the Fury

THE SOUND AND THE FURY

APPENDIX

COMPSON: 1699–1945

IKKEMOTUBBE. A dispossessed American king.
Called "l'Homme" (and sometimes "de l'homme") by his
fosterbrother, a Chevalier of France, who had he not
been born too late could have been among the brightest
in that glittering galaxy of knightly blackguards who
were Napoleon's marshals, who thus translated the Chickasaw title meaning "The Man"; which translation Ikkemotubbe, himself a man of wit and imagination as well
as a shrewd judge of character, including his own, carried one step further and anglicised it to "Doom." Who
granted out of his vast lost domain a solid square mile of
virgin North Mississippi dirt as truly angled as the four
corners of a cardtable top (forested then because these
were the old days before 1833 when the stars fell and
Jefferson Mississippi was one long rambling onestorey
mudchinked log building housing the Chickasaw Agent
and his tradingpost store) to the grandson of a Scottish
refugee who had lost his own birthright by casting his
lot with a king who himself had been dispossessed. This
in partial return for the right to proceed in peace, by
whatever means he and his people saw fit, afoot or
ahorse provided they were Chickasaw horses, to the wild
western land presently to be called Oklahoma: not
knowing then about the oil.

JACKSON. A Great White Father with a sword.
(An old duellist, a brawling lean fierce mangy durable

3

imperishable old lion who set the wellbeing of the nation above the White House and the health of his new political party above either and above them all set not his wife's honor but the principle that honor must be defended whether it was or not because defended it was whether or not.) Who patented sealed and countersigned the grant with his own hand in his gold tepee in Wassi Town, not knowing about the oil either: so that one day the homeless descendants of the dispossessed would ride supine with drink and splendidly comatose above the dusty allotted harborage of their bones in speciallybuilt scarletpainted hearses and fire-engines.

These were Compsons:

QUENTIN MACLACHAN. Son of a Glasgow printer, orphaned and raised by his mother's people in the Perth highlands. Fled to Carolina from Culloden Moor with a claymore and the tartan he wore by day and slept under by night, and little else. At eighty, having fought once against an English king and lost, he would not make that mistake twice and so fled again one night in 1779, with his infant grandson and the tartan (the claymore had vanished, along with his son, the grandson's father, from one of Tarleton's regiments on a Georgia battlefield about a year ago) into Kentucky, where a neighbor named Boon or Boone had already established a settlement.

CHARLES STUART. Attainted and proscribed by name and grade in his British regiment. Left for dead in a Georgia swamp by his own retreating army and then by the advancing American one, both of which were wrong. He still had the claymore even when on his homemade wooden leg he finally overtook his father and son four years later at Harrodsburg, Kentucky, just in time to bury the father and enter upon a long period of being a split personality while still trying to be the schoolteacher which he believed he wanted to be, until he gave up at last and became the gambler he actually was and which no Compson seemed to realize they all were provided the gambit was desperate and the odds long enough. Succeeded at last in risking not only his neck but the security of his family and the very integrity of the name he would leave behind him, by joining the confederation headed by an acquaintance named Wilkinson (a man of considerable talent and influence and intellect and power) in a plot to secede the whole Mississippi Valley from the United States and join it to Spain. Fled in his turn when the bubble burst (as anyone except a Compson schoolteacher should have known it would), himself unique in being the only one of the plotters who had to flee the country: this not from the vengeance and retribution of the government which he had attempted to dismember, but from the furious revulsion of his late confederates now frantic for their own safety. He was not expelled from the United States, he talked himself countryless, his expulsion due not to the treason but to his having been so vocal and vociferant in the conduct of it, burning each bridge vocally behind him before he had even reached the place to build the next one: so that it was no provost marshal nor even a civic agency but his late coplotters themselves who put afoot the movement to evict him from Kentucky and the United States and, if they had caught him, probably from the world too. Fled by night, running true to family tradition, with his son and the old claymore and the tartan.

JASON LYCURGUS. Who, driven perhaps by the compulsion of the flamboyant name given him by the sardonic embittered woodenlegged indomitable father who perhaps still believed with his heart that what he wanted to be was a classicist schoolteacher, rode up the Natchez Trace one day in 1811 with a pair of fine pistols and one meagre saddlebag on a small lightwaisted but stronghocked mare which could do the first two furlongs in definitely under the halfminute and the next two in not appreciably more, though that was all. But it was enough: who reached the Chickasaw Agency at Okatoba (which in 1860 was still called Old Jefferson) and went no further. Who within six months was the Agent's clerk and within twelve his partner, officially still the clerk though actually halfowner of what was now a considerable store stocked with the mare's winnings in races against the horses of Ikkemotubbe's young men which he, Compson, was always careful to limit to a quarter or at most three furlongs; and in the next year it was Ikkemotubbe who owned the little mare and Compson owned the solid square mile of land which someday would be almost in the center of the town of Jefferson, forested then and still forested twenty years later though rather a park than a forest by that time, with its slavequarters and stables and kitchengardens and the formal lawns and promenades and pavilions laid out by the same architect who built the columned porticoed house furnished by steamboat from France and New Orleans, and still the square intact mile in 1840 (with not only the little white village called Jefferson beginning to enclose it but an entire white county about to surround it because in a few years now Ikkemotubbe's descendants and people would be gone, those remaining living not as warriors and hunters but as white men—as shiftless farmers or, here and there, the masters of what they too called plantations and the owners of shiftless slaves, a little dirtier than the white man, a little lazier, a little crueller—until at last even the wild blood itself would have vanished, to be seen only occasionally in the nose-shape of a Negro on a cottonwagon or a white sawmill hand or trapper or locomotive fireman), known as the Compson Domain then, since now it was fit to breed princes, statesmen and generals and bishops, to avenge the dispossessed Compsons from Culloden and Carolina and Kentucky, then known as the Governor's house because sure enough in time it did produce or at least spawn a governor—Quentin MacLachan again, after the Culloden grandfather—and still known as the Old Governor's even after it had spawned (1861) a general—(called so by predetermined accord and agreement by the whole town and county, as though they knew even then and beforehand that the old governor was the last Compson who would not fail at everything he touched save longevity or suicide)—the Brigadier Jason Lycurgus II who failed at Shiloh in '62 and failed again though not so badly at Resaca in '64, who put the first mortgage on the still intact square mile to a New England carpet-bagger in '66, after the old town had been burned by the Federal General Smith and the new little town, in time to be populated mainly by the descendants not of Compsons but of Snopeses, had begun to encroach and then nibble at and into it as the failed brigadier spent the next forty years selling fragments of it off to keep up the mortage on the remainder: until one day in 1900 he died quietly on an army cot in the hunting and fishing camp in the Tallahatchie River bottom where he passed most of the end of his days.

And even the old governor was forgotten now; what was left of the old square mile was now known merely as the Compson place—the weedchoked traces of the old ruined lawns and promenades, the house which had needed painting too long already, the scaling columns of the portico where Jason III (bred for a lawyer and indeed he kept an office upstairs above the Square, where entombed in dusty filingcases some of the oldest names in the county—Holston and Sutpen, Grenier and Beauchamp and Coldfield—faded year by year among the bottomless labyrinths of chancery: and who knows what dream in the perennial heart of his father, now completing the third of his three avatars—the one as son of a brilliant and gallant statesman, the second as battleleader of brave and gallant men, the third as a sort of privileged pseudo-Daniel Boone-Robinson Crusoe, who had not returned to juvenility because actually he had never left it—that that lawyer's office might again be the anteroom to the governor's mansion and the old splendor) sat all day long with a decanter of whiskey and a litter of dogeared Horaces and Livys and Catulluses, composing (it was said) caustic and satiric eulogies on both his dead and his living fellowtownsmen, who sold the last of the property, except that fragment containing the house and the kitchengarden and the collapsing stables and one servant's cabin in which Dilsey's family lived, to a golfclub for the ready money with which his daughter Candace could have her fine wedding in April and his son Quentin could finish one year at Harvard and commit suicide in the following June of 1910; already known as the Old Compson place even while Compsons were still living in it on that spring dusk in 1928 when the old governor's doomed lost nameless seventeen-year-old greatgreatgranddaughter robbed her last remaining sane male relative (her uncle Jason IV) of his secret hoard of money and climbed down a rainpipe and ran off with a pitchman in a travelling streetshow, and still known as the Old Compson place long after all traces of Compsons were gone from it: after the widowed mother died and Jason IV, no longer needing to fear Dilsey now, committed his idiot brother, Benjamin, to the State Asylum in Jackson and sold the house to a countryman who operated it as a boarding house for juries and horse- and muletraders, and still known as the Old Compson place even after the boardinghouse (and presently the golfcourse too) had vanished and the old square mile was even intact again in row after row of small crowded jerrybuilt individuallyowned demiurban bungalows.

And these:

QUENTIN III. Who loved not his sister's body but some concept of Compson honor precariously and (he knew well) only temporarily supported by the minute fragile membrane of her maidenhead as a miniature replica of all the whole vast globy earth may be poised on the nose of a trained seal. Who loved not the idea of the incest which he would not commit, but some presbyterian concept of its eternal punishment: he, not God, could by that means cast himself and his sister both into hell, where he could guard her forever and keep her forevermore intact amid the eternal fires. But who loved death above all, who loved only death, loved and lived in a deliberate and almost perverted anticipation of death as a lover loves and deliberately refrains from the waiting willing friendly tender incredible body of his beloved, until he can no longer bear not the refraining but the restraint and so flings, hurls himself, relinquishing, drowning. Committed suicide in Cambridge Massachusetts, June 1910, two months after his sister's wedding, waiting first to complete the current academic year and so get the full value of his paid-in-advance tuition, not because he had his old Culloden and Carolina and Kentucky grandfathers in him but because the remaining piece of the old Compson mile which had been sold to pay for his sister's wedding and his year at Harvard had been the one thing, excepting that same sister and the sight of an open fire, which his youngest brother, born an idiot, had loved.

CANDACE (CADDY). Doomed and knew it, accepted the doom without either seeking or fleeing it. Loved her brother despite him, loved not only him but loved in him that bitter prophet and inflexible corruptless judge of what he considered the family's honor and its doom, as he thought he loved but really hated in her what he considered the frail doomed vessel of its pride and the foul instrument of its disgrace; not only this, she loved him not only in spite of but because of the fact that he himself was incapable of love, accepting the fact that he must value above all not her but the virginity of which she was custodian and on which she placed no value whatever: the frail physical stricture which to her was no more than a hangnail would have been. Knew the brother loved death best of all and was not jealous, would (and perhaps in the calculation and deliberation of her marriage did) have handed him the hypothetical hemlock. Was two months pregnant with another man's child which regardless of what its sex would be she had already named Quentin after the brother whom they both (she and the brother) knew was already the same as dead, when she married (1910) an extremely eligible

young Indianian she and her mother had met while va-
cationing at French Lick the summer before. Divorced
by him 1911. Married 1920 to a minor movingpicture
magnate, Hollywood California. Divorced by mutual
agreement, Mexico 1925. Vanished in Paris with the
German occupation, 1940, still beautiful and probably
still wealthy too since she did not look within fifteen
years of her actual fortyeight, and was not heard of
again. Except there was a woman in Jefferson, the county
librarian, a mousesized and -colored woman who had
never married, who had passed through the city schools
in the same class with Candace Compson and then spent
the rest of her life trying to keep *Forever Amber* in its
orderly overlapping avatars and *Jurgen* and *Tom Jones*
out of the hands of the highschool juniors and seniors
who could reach them down without even having to tip-
toe from the back shelves where she herself would have
to stand on a box to hide them. One day in 1943, after a
week of a distraction bordering on disintegration almost,
during which those entering the library would find her
always in the act of hurriedly closing her desk drawer
and turning the key in it (so that the matrons, wives of
the bankers and doctors and lawyers, some of whom had
also been in that old highschool class, who came and
went in the afternoons with the copies of the *Forever
Ambers* and the volumes of Thorne Smith carefully
wrapped from view in sheets of Memphis and Jackson
newspapers, believed she was on the verge of illness or
perhaps even loss of mind) she closed and locked the library in the middle of the afternoon and with her handbag clasped tightly under her arm and two feverish spots
of determination in her ordinarily colorless cheeks, she
entered the farmers' supply store where Jason IV had
started as a clerk and where he now owned his own busi-

ness as a buyer of and dealer in cotton, striding on through that gloomy cavern which only men ever entered —a cavern cluttered and walled and stalagmitehung with plows and discs and loops of tracechain and single-trees and mulecollars and sidemeat and cheap shoes and horselinament and flour and molasses, gloomy because the goods it contained were not shown but hidden rather since those who supplied Mississippi farmers or at least Negro Mississippi farmers for a share of the crop did not wish, until that crop was made and its value approximately computable, to show them what they could learn to want but only to supply them on specific demand with what they could not help but need—and strode on back to Jason's particular domain in the rear: a railed enclosure cluttered with shelves and pigeonholes bearing spiked dust-and-lintgathering gin receipts and ledgers and cottonsamples and rank with the blended smell of cheese and kerosene and harnessoil and the tremendous iron stove against which chewed tobacco had been spat for almost a hundred years, and up to the long high sloping counter behind which Jason stood and, not looking again at the overalled men who had quietly stopped talking and even chewing when she entered, with a kind of fainting desperation she opened the handbag and fumbled something out of it and laid it open on the counter and stood trembling and breathing rapidly while Jason looked down at it—a picture, a photograph in color clipped obviously from a slick magazine—a picture filled with luxury and money and sunlight—a Cannebière backdrop of mountains and palms and cypresses and the sea, an open powerful expensive chromiumtrimmed sports car, the woman's face hatless between a rich scarf and a seal coat, ageless and beautiful, cold serene and damned; beside her a handsome lean man of middleage in the ribbons and tabs of a German staffgeneral—and the mousesized mousecolored spinster trembling and aghast at her own temerity, staring across it at the child-less bachelor in whom ended that long line of men who had had something in them of decency and pride even after they had begun to fail at the integrity and the pride had become mostly vanity and selfpity: from the expatri-ate who had to flee his native land with little else except his life yet who still refused to accept defeat, through the man who gambled his life and his good name twice and lost twice and declined to accept that either, and the one who with only a clever small quarterhorse for tool avenged his dispossessed father and grandfather and gained a principality, and the brilliant and gallant gover-nor and the general who though he failed at leading in battle brave and gallant men at least risked his own life too in the failing, to the cultured dipsomaniac who sold the last of his patrimony not to buy drink but to give one of his descendants at least the best chance in life he could think of.

'It's Caddy!' the librarian whispered. 'We must save her!'

'It's Cad, all right,' Jason said. Then he began to laugh. He stood there laughing above the picture, above the cold beautiful face now creased and dogeared from its week's sojourn in the desk drawer and the handbag. And the librarian knew why he was laughing, who had not called him anything but Mr Compson for thirty-two years now, ever since the day in 1911 when Candace, cast off by her husband, had brought her infant daughter home and left the child and departed by the next train, to return no more, and not only the Negro cook, Dilsey, but the librarian too divined by simple instinct that Jason was somehow using the child's life and its illegitimacy both to blackmail the mother not only into staying away from Jefferson for the rest of her life but into appointing him sole unchallengeable trustee of the money she would send for the child's maintenance, and had refused to speak to him at all since that day in 1928 when the daughter climbed down the rainpipe and ran away with the pitchman.

'Jason!' she cried. 'We must save her! Jason! Jason!'—— and still crying it even when he took up the picture between thumb and finger and threw it back across the counter toward her.

'That Candace?' he said. 'Dont make me laugh. This bitch aint thirty yet. The other one's fifty now.'

And the library was still locked all the next day too when at three oclock in the afternoon, footsore and spent yet still unflagging and still clasping the handbag tightly under her arm, she turned into a neat small yard in the Negro residence section of Memphis and mounted the steps of the neat small house and rang the bell and the door opened and a black woman of about her own age looked quietly out at her. 'It's Frony, isn't it?' the librarian said. 'Dont you remember me—— Melissa Meek, from Jefferson——'

'Yes,' the Negress said. 'Come in. You want to see Mama.' And she entered the room, the neat yet cluttered bedroom of an old Negro, rank with the smell of old people, old women, old Negroes, where the old woman herself sat in a rocker beside the hearth where even though it was June a fire smoldered—a big woman once, in faded clean calico and an immaculate turban wound round her head above the bleared and now apparently almost sightless eyes—and put the dogeared clipping into the black hands which, like the women of her race, were still as supple and delicately shaped as they had been when she was thirty or twenty or even seventeen.

'It's Caddy!' the librarian said. 'It is! Dilsey! Dilsey!'

'What did he say?' the old Negress said. And the librarian knew whom she meant by 'he', nor did the librarian marvel, not only that the old Negress would know that she (the librarian) would know whom she meant by the 'he', but that the old Negress would know at once that she had already shown the picture to Jason.

'Dont you know what he said?' she cried. 'When he realised she was in danger, he said it was her, even if I hadn't even had a picture to show him. But as soon as he realised that somebody, anybody, even just me, wanted to save her, would try to save her, he said it wasn't. But it is! Look at it!'

'Look at my eyes,' the old Negress said. 'How can I see that picture?'

'Call Frony!' the librarian cried. 'She will know her!' But already the old Negress was folding the clipping carefully back into its old creases, handing it back.

'My eyes aint any good anymore,' she said. 'I cant see it.'

And that was all. At six oclock she fought her way through the crowded bus terminal, the bag clutched under one arm and the return half of her roundtrip ticket in the other hand, and was swept out onto the roaring platform on the diurnal tide of a few middleaged civilians but mostly soldiers and sailors enroute either to leave or to death and the homeless young women, their companions, who for two years now had lived from day to day in pullmans and hotels when they were lucky and in daycoaches and busses and stations and lobbies and public restrooms when not, pausing only long enough to drop their foals in charity wards or policestations and then move on again, and fought her way into the bus, smaller than any other there so that her feet touched the floor only occasionally until a shape (a man in khaki; she couldn't see him at all because she was already crying) rose and picked her up bodily and set her into a seat next the window, where still crying quietly she could look out upon the fleeing city as it streaked past and then was behind and presently now she would be home again, safe in Jefferson where life lived too with all its incomprehensible passion and turmoil and grief and fury and despair, but here at six oclock you could close the covers on it and even the weightless hand of a child could put it back among its unfeatured kindred on the quiet eternal shelves and turn the key upon it for the whole and dreamless night. *Yes* she thought, crying quietly *that was it she didn't want to see it know whether it was Caddy or not because she knows Caddy doesn't want to be saved hasn't anything anymore worth being saved for nothing worth being lost that she can lose*

JASON IV.   The first sane Compson since before Culloden and (a childless bachelor) hence the last. Logical rational contained and even a philosopher in the old stoic tradition: thinking nothing whatever of God one way or the other and simply considering the police and so fearing and respecting only the Negro woman, his sworn enemy since his birth and his mortal one since that day in 1911 when she too divined by simple clairvoyance that he was somehow using his infant niece's illegitimacy to blackmail its mother, who cooked the food he ate. Who not only fended off and held his own with Compsons but competed and held his own with the Snopeses who took over the little town following the turn of the century as

the Compsons and Sartorises and their ilk faded from it
(no Snopes, but Jason Compson himself who as soon as
his mother died—the niece had already climbed down
the rainpipe and vanished so Dilsey no longer had either
of these clubs to hold over him—committed his idiot
younger brother to the state and vacated the old house,
first chopping up the vast oncesplendid rooms into what
he called apartments and selling the whole thing to a
countryman who opened a boardinghouse in it), though
this was not difficult since to him all the rest of the town
and the world and the human race too except himself
were Compsons, inexplicable yet quite predictable in that
they were in no sense whatever to be trusted. Who, all
the money from the sale of the pasture having gone for
his sister's wedding and his brother's course at Harvard,
used his own niggard savings out of his meagre wages as
a storeclerk to send himself to a Memphis school where
he learned to class and grade cotton, and so established
his own business with which, following his dipsomaniac
father's death, he assumed the entire burden of the rotting family in the rotting house, supporting his idiot
brother because of their mother, sacrificing what pleas-
ures might have been the right and just due and even the
necessity of a thirty-year-old bachelor, so that his
mother's life might continue as nearly as possible to what
it had been; this not because he loved her but (a sane
man always) simply because he was afraid of the Negro
cook whom he could not even force to leave, even when
he tried to stop paying her weekly wages; and who despite all this, still managed to save almost three thousand
dollars ($2840.50 as he reported it on the night his niece
stole it; in niggard and agonised dimes and quarters and
halfdollars, which hoard he kept in no bank because to
him a banker too was just one more Compson, but hid

in a locked bureau drawer in his bedroom whose bed he made and changed himself since he kept the bedroom door locked all the time save when he was passing through it. Who, following a fumbling abortive attempt by his idiot brother on a passing female child, had himself appointed the idiot's guardian without letting their mother know and so was able to have the creature castrated before the mother even knew it was out of the house, and who following the mother's death in 1933 was able to free himself forever not only from the idiot brother and the house but from the Negro woman too, moving into a pair of offices up a flight of stairs above the supplystore containing his cotton ledgers and samples, which he had converted into a bedroom-kitchen-bath, in and out of which on weekends there would be seen a big plain friendly brazenhaired pleasantfaced woman no longer very young, in round picture hats and (in its season) an imitation fur coat, the two of them, the middleaged cottonbuyer and the woman whom the town called, simply, his friend from Memphis, seen at the local picture show on Saturday night and on Sunday morning mounting the apartment stairs with paper bags from the grocer's containing loaves and eggs and oranges and cans of soup, domestic, uxorious, connubial, until the late afternoon bus carried her back to Memphis. He was emancipated now. He was free. 'In 1865,' he would say, 'Abe Lincoln freed the niggers from the Compsons. In 1933, Jason Compson freed the Compsons from the niggers.'

BENJAMIN. Born Maury, after his mother's only brother: a handsome flashing swaggering workless bachelor who borrowed money from almost anyone, even Dilsey although she was a Negro, explaining to her as he withdrew his hand from his pocket that she was not only in his eyes the same as a member of his sister's family, she would be considered a born lady anywhere in any eyes. Who, when at last even his mother realised what he was and insisted weeping that his name must be changed, was rechristened Benjamin by his brother Quentin (Benjamin, our lastborn, sold into Egypt). Who loved three things: the pasture which was sold to pay for Candace's wedding and to send Quentin to Harvard, his sister Candace, firelight. Who lost none of them because he could not remember his sister but only the loss of her, and firelight was the same bright shape as going to sleep, and the pasture was even better sold than before because now he and TP could not only follow timeless along the fence the motions which it did not even matter to him were humanbeings swinging golfsticks, TP could lead them to clumps of grass or weeds where there would appear suddenly in TP's hand small white spherules which competed with and even conquered what he did not even know was gravity and all the immutable laws when released from the hand toward plank floor or smokehouse wall or concrete sidewalk. Gelded 1913. Committed to the State Asylum, Jackson 1933. Lost nothing then either because, as with his sister, he remembered not the pasture but only its loss, and firelight was still the same bright shape of sleep.

QUENTIN. The last. Candace's daughter. Fatherless nine months before her birth, nameless at birth and already doomed to be unwed from the instant the dividing egg determined its sex. Who at seventeen, on the one thousand eight hundred ninetyfifth anniversary of the day before the resurrection of Our Lord, swung herself by a rainpipe from the window of the room in which her uncle had locked her at noon, to the locked window of

his own locked and empty bedroom and broke a pane
and entered the window and with the uncle's firepoker
burst open the locked bureau drawer and took the money
(it was not $2840.50 either, it was almost seven thou-
sand dollars and this was Jason's rage, the red unbearable fury which on that night and at intervals recurring
with little or no diminishment for the next five years,
made him seriously believe would at some unwarned instant destroy him, kill him as instantaneously dead as a
bullet or a lightningbolt: that although he had been
robbed not of a mere petty three thousand dollars but of
almost seven thousand he couldn't even tell anybody; because he had been robbed of seven thousand dollars instead of just three he could not only never receive justification—he did not want sympathy—from other men
unlucky enough to have one bitch for a sister and another
for a niece, he couldn't even go to the police; because he
had lost four thousand dollars which did not belong to
him he couldn't even recover the three thousand which
did since those first four thousand dollars were not only
the legal property of his niece as a part of the money supplied for her support and maintenance by her mother
over the last sixteen years, they did not exist at all, having been officially recorded as expended and consumed
in the annual reports he submitted to the district Chan-
cellor, as required of him as guardian and trustee by his
bondsmen: so that he had been robbed not only of his
thievings but his savings too, and by his own victim; he
had been robbed not only of the four thousand dollars
which he had risked jail to acquire but of the three thousand which he had hoarded at the price of sacrifice and
denial, almost a nickel and a dime at a time, over a period
of almost twenty years: and this not only by his own vic-

tim but by a child who did it at one blow, without pre-
meditation or plan, not even knowing or even caring how
much she would find when she broke the drawer open;
and now he couldn't even go to the police for help: he
who had considered the police always, never given them
any trouble, had paid the taxes for years which supported them in parasitic and sadistic idleness; not only
that, he didn't dare pursue the girl himself because he
might catch her and she would talk, so that his only re-
course was a vain dream which kept him tossing and
sweating on nights two and three and even four years
after the event, when he should have forgotten about it:
of catching her without warning, springing on her out
of the dark, before she had spent all the money, and
murder her before she had time to open her mouth) and
climbed down the same rainpipe in the dusk and ran
away with the pitchman who was already under sentence
for bigamy. And so vanished; whatever occupation overtook her would have arrived in no chromium Mercedes;
whatever snapshot would have contained no general of
staff.

And that was all. These others were not Compsons.
They were black:

T P.   Who wore on Memphis's Beale Street the fine
bright cheap intransigent clothes manufactured specifi-
cally for him by the owners of Chicago and New York
sweatshops.

F R O N Y.   Who married a pullman porter and went to
St Louis to live and later moved back to Memphis to
make a home for her mother since Dilsey refused to go
further than that.

LUSTER. A man, aged 14. Who was not only capable of the complete care and security of an idiot twice his age and three times his size, but could keep him entertained.

DILSEY.
They endured.

APRIL
7
1928

THROUGH THE FENCE, BETWEEN THE CURLING FLOWER spaces, I could see them hitting. They were coming toward where the flag was and I went along the fence. Luster was hunting in the grass by the flower tree. They took the flag out, and they were hitting. Then they put the flag back and they went to the table, and he hit and the other hit. Then they went on, and I went along the fence. Luster came away from the flower tree and we went along the fence and they stopped and we stopped and I looked through the fence while Luster was hunting in the grass.

"Here, caddie." He hit. They went away across the pasture. I held to the fence and watched them going away.

"Listen at you, now." Luster said. "Aint you something, thirty-three years old, going on that way. After I done went all the way to town to buy you that cake. Hush up that moaning. Aint you going to help me find that quarter so I can go to the show tonight."

They were hitting little, across the pasture. I went along the fence to where the flag was. It flapped on the bright grass and the trees.

"Come on." Luster said. "We done looked there. They aint no more coming right now. Lets go down to the branch and find that quarter before them niggers finds it."

It was red, flapping on the pasture. Then there was a bird slanting and tilting on it. Luster threw. The flag flapped on the bright grass and the trees. I held to the fence.

"Shut up that moaning." Luster said. "I cant make them come if they aint coming, can I. If you dont hush up, mammy aint going to have no birthday for you. If you dont hush, you know what I going to do. I going to eat that cake all up. Eat them candles, too. Eat all them thirty-three candles. Come on, let's go down to the branch. I got to find my quarter. Maybe we can find one of they balls. Here. Here they is. Way over yonder. See." He came to the fence and pointed his arm. "See them. They aint coming back here no more. Come on."

We went along the fence and came to the garden fence, where our shadows were. My shadow was higher than Luster's on the fence. We came to the broken place and went through it.

"Wait a minute." Luster said. "You snagged on that nail again. Cant you never crawl through here without snagging on that nail."

Caddy uncaught me and we crawled through. Uncle Maury said to not let anybody see us, so we better stoop over, Caddy said. Stoop over, Benjy. Like this, see. We stooped over and crossed the garden, where the flowers rasped and rattled against us. The ground was hard. We climbed the fence, where the pigs were grunting and snuffing. I expect they're sorry because one of them got killed today, Caddy said. The ground was hard, churned and knotted.

Keep your hands in your pockets, Caddy said. Or

they'll get froze. You don't want your hands froze on Christmas, do you.

"It's too cold out there." Versh said. "You dont want to go out doors."

"What is it now." Mother said.

"He want to go out doors." Versh said.

"Let him go." Uncle Maury said.

"It's too cold." Mother said. "He'd better stay in. Benjamin. Stop that, now."

"It wont hurt him." Uncle Maury said.

"You, Benjamin." Mother said. "If you dont be good, you'll have to go to the kitchen."

"Mammy say keep him out the kitchen today." Versh said. "She say she got all that cooking to get done."

"Let him go, Caroline." Uncle Maury said. "You'll worry yourself sick over him."

"I know it." Mother said. "It's a judgment on me. I sometimes wonder."

"I know, I know." Uncle Maury said. "You must keep your strength up. I'll make you a toddy."

"It just upsets me that much more." Mother said. "Dont you know it does."

"You'll feel better." Uncle Maury said. "Wrap him up good, boy, and take him out for a while."

Uncle Maury went away. Versh went away.

"Please hush." Mother said. "We're trying to get you out as fast as we can. I dont want you to get sick."

Versh put my overshoes and overcoat on and we took my cap and went out. Uncle Maury was putting the bottle away in the sideboard in the dining-room.

"Keep him out about half an hour, boy." Uncle Maury said. "Keep him in the yard, now."

"Yes, sir." Versh said. "We dont never let him get off the place."

We went out doors. The sun was cold and bright.

"Where you heading for." Versh said. "You dont think you going to town, does you." We went through the rat tling leaves. The gate was cold. "You better keep them hands in your pockets." Versh said, "You get them froze onto that gate, then what you do. Whyn't you wait for them in the house." He put my hands into my pockets. I could hear him rattling in the leaves. I could smell the cold. The gate was cold.

"Here some hickeynuts. Whooey. Git up that tree. Look here at this squirl, Benjy."

I couldn't feel the gate at all, but I could smell the bright cold.

"You better put them hands back in your pockets."

Caddy was walking. Then she was running, her book-satchel swinging and jouncing behind her.

"Hello, Benjy." Caddy said. She opened the gate and came in and stooped down. Caddy smelled like leaves. "Did you come to meet me." she said. "Did you come to meet Caddy. What did you let him get his hands so cold for, Versh."

"I told him to keep them in his pockets." Versh said. "Holding onto that ahun gate."

"Did you come to meet Caddy." she said, rubbing my hands. "What is it. What are you trying to tell Caddy." Caddy smelled like trees and like when she says we were asleep.

What are you moaning about, Luster said. You can watch them again when we get to the branch. Here. Here's you a jimson weed. He gave me the flower. We went through the fence, into the lot.

"What is it." Caddy said. "What are you trying to tell Caddy. Did they send him out, Versh."

"Couldn't keep him in." Versh said. "He kept on until they let him go and he come right straight down here, looking through the gate."

"What is it." Caddy said. "Did you think it would be Christmas when I came home from school. Is that what you thought. Christmas is the day after tomorrow. Santy Claus, Benjy. Santy Claus. Come on, let's run to the house and get warm." She took my hand and we ran through the bright rustling leaves. We ran up the steps and out of the bright cold, into the dark cold. Uncle Maury was putting the bottle back in the sideboard. He called Caddy. Caddy said,

"Take him in to the fire, Versh. Go with Versh." she said. "I'll come in a minute."

We went to the fire. Mother said,

"Is he cold, Versh."

"Nome." Versh said.

"Take his overcoat and overshoes off." Mother said, "How many times do I have to tell you not to bring him into the house with his overshoes on."

"Yessum." Versh said. "Hold still, now." He took my overshoes off and unbuttoned my coat. Caddy said,

"Wait, Versh. Cant he go out again, Mother. I want him to go with me."

"You'd better leave him here." Uncle Maury said. "He's been out enough today."

"I think you'd both better stay in." Mother said. "It's getting colder, Dilsey says."

"Oh, Mother." Caddy said.

"Nonsense." Uncle Maury said. "She's been in school all day. She needs the fresh air. Run along, Candace."

"Let him go, Mother." Caddy said. "Please. You know he'll cry."

"Then why did you mention it before him." Mother said. "Why did you come in here. To give him some excuse to worry me again. You've been out enough today. I think you'd better sit down here and play with him."

"Let them go, Caroline." Uncle Maury said. "A little

cold wont hurt them. Remember, you've got to keep your strength up."

"I know." Mother said. "Nobody knows how I dread Christmas. Nobody knows. I am not one of those women who can stand things. I wish for Jason's and the children's sakes I was stronger."

"You must do the best you can and not let them worry you." Uncle Maury said. "Run along, you two. But dont stay out long, now. Your mother will worry."

"Yes, sir." Caddy said. "Come on, Benjy. We're going out doors again." She buttoned my coat and we went toward the door.

"Are you going to take that baby out without his overshoes." Mother said. "Do you want to make him sick, with the house full of company."

"I forgot." Caddy said. "I thought he had them on."

We went back. "You must think." Mother said. *Hold still now* Versh said. He put my overshoes on. "Someday I'll be gone, and you'll have to think for him." *Now stomp* Versh said. "Come here and kiss Mother, Benjamin."

Caddy took me to Mother's chair and Mother took my face in her hands and then she held me against her.

"My poor baby." she said. She let me go. "You and Versh take good care of him, honey."

"Yessum." Caddy said. We went out. Caddy said,

"You needn't go, Versh. I'll keep him for a while."

"All right." Versh said. "I aint going out in that cold for no fun." He went on and we stopped in the hall and Caddy knelt and put her arms around me and her cold bright face against mine. She smelled like trees.

"You're not a poor baby. Are you. You've got your Caddy. Haven't you got your Caddy."

Cant you shut up that moaning and slobbering, Luster said. Aint you shamed of yourself, making all this racket.

We passed the carriage house, where the carriage was. It had a new wheel.

"Git in, now, and set still until your maw come." Dilsey said. She shoved me into the carriage. T. P. held the reins. "'Clare I don't see how come Jason wont get a new surrey." Dilsey said. "This thing going to fall to pieces under you all some day. Look at them wheels."

Mother came out, pulling her veil down. She had some flowers.

"Where's Roskus." she said.

"Roskus cant lift his arms, today." Dilsey said. "T. P. can drive all right."

"I'm afraid to." Mother said. "It seems to me you all could furnish me with a driver for the carriage once a week. It's little enough I ask, Lord knows."

"You know just as well as me that Roskus got the rheumatism too bad to do more than he have to, Miss Cahline." Dilsey said. "You come on and get in, now. T. P. can drive you just as good as Roskus."

"I'm afraid to." Mother said. "With the baby."

Dilsey went up the steps. "You calling that thing a baby," she said. She took Mother's arm. "A man big as T. P. Come on, now, if you going."

"I'm afraid to." Mother said. They came down the steps and Dilsey helped Mother in. "Perhaps it'll be the best thing, for all of us." Mother said.

"Aint you shamed, talking that way." Dilsey said. "Don't you know it'll take more than a eighteen year old nigger to make Queenie run away. She older than him and Benjy put together. And dont you start no projecking with Queenie, you hear me, T. P. If you dont drive to suit Miss Cahline, I going to put Roskus on you. He aint too tied up to do that."

"Yessum." T. P. said.

"I just know something will happen." Mother said. "Stop, Benjamin."

"Give him a flower to hold." Dilsey said, "That what he wanting." She reached her hand in.

"No, no." Mother said. "You'll have them all scattered."

"You hold them." Dilsey said. "I'll get him one out." She gave me a flower and her hand went away.

"Go on now, 'fore Quentin see you and have to go too." Dilsey said.

"Where is she." Mother said.

"She down to the house playing with Luster." Dilsey said. "Go on, T. P. Drive that surrey like Roskus told you, now."

"Yessum." T. P. said. "Hum up, Queenie."

"Quentin." Mother said. "Don't let"

"Course I is." Dilsey said.

The carriage jolted and crunched on the drive. "I'm afraid to go and leave Quentin." Mother said. "I'd better not go. T. P." We went through the gate, where it didnt jolt anymore. T. P. hit Queenie with the whip.

"You, T. P." Mother said.

"Got to get her going." T. P. said. "Keep her wake up till we get back to the barn."

"Turn around." Mother said. "I'm afraid to go and leave Quentin."

"Can't turn here." T. P. said. Then it was broader.

"Cant you turn here." Mother said.

"All right." T. P. said. We began to turn.

"You, T. P." Mother said, clutching me.

"I got to turn around somehow." T. P. said. "Whoa, Queenie." We stopped.

"You'll turn us over." Mother said.

"What you want to do, then." T. P. said.

"I'm afraid for you to try to turn around." Mother said.

"Get up, Queenie." T. P. said. We went on.

"I just know Dilsey will let something happen to Quentin while I'm gone." Mother said. "We must hurry back."

"Hum up, there." T. P. said. He hit Queenie with the whip.

"You, T. P." Mother said, clutching me. I could hear Queenie's feet and the bright shapes went smooth and steady on both sides, the shadows of them flowing across Queenie's back. They went on like the bright tops of wheels. Then those on one side stopped at the tall white post where the soldier was. But on the other side they went on smooth and steady, but a little slower.

"What do you want." Jason said. He had his hands in his pockets and a pencil behind his ear.

"We're going to the cemetery." Mother said.

"All right." Jason said. "I dont aim to stop you, do I. Was that all you wanted with me, just to tell me that."

"I know you wont come." Mother said. "I'd feel safer if you would."

"Safe from what." Jason said. "Father and Quentin cant hurt you."

Mother put her handkerchief under her veil. "Stop it, Mother." Jason said. "Do you want to get that damn loony to bawling in the middle of the square. Drive on, T. P."

"Hum up, Queenie." T. P. said.

"It's a judgment on me." Mother said. "But I'll be gone too, soon."

"Here." Jason said.

"Whoa." T. P. said. Jason said,

"Uncle Maury's drawing on you for fifty. What do you want to do about it."

"Why ask me." Mother said. "I dont have any say so. I try not to worry you and Dilsey. I'll be gone soon, and then you"

"Go on, T. P." Jason said.

"Hum up Queenie." T. P. said. The shapes flowed on. The ones on the other side began again, bright and fast and smooth, like when Caddy says we are going to sleep.

Cry baby, Luster said. Aint you shamed. We went through the barn. The stalls were all open. You aint got no spotted pony to ride now, Luster said. The floor was dry and dusty. The roof was falling. The slanting holes were full of spinning yellow. What do you want to go that way for. You want to get your head knocked off with one of them balls.

"Keep your hands in your pockets." Caddy said, "Or they'll be froze. You dont want your hands froze on Christmas, do you."

We went around the barn. The big cow and the little one were standing in the door, and we could hear Prince and Queenie and Fancy stomping inside the barn. "If it wasn't so cold, we'd ride Fancy." Caddy said, "But it's too cold to hold on today." Then we could see the branch, where the smoke was blowing. "That's where they are killing the pig." Caddy said. "We can come back by there and see them." We went down the hill.

"You want to carry the letter." Caddy said. "You can carry it." She took the letter out of her pocket and put it in mine. "It's a Christmas present." Caddy said. "Uncle Maury is going to surprise Mrs Patterson with it. We got to give it to her without letting anybody see it. Keep your hands in your pockets good, now." We came to the branch.

"It's froze." Caddy said, "Look." She broke the top of the water and held a piece of it against my face. "Ice.

That means how cold it is." She helped me across and we went up the hill. "We cant even tell Mother and Father. You know what I think it is. I think it's a surprise for Mother and Father and Mr Patterson both, because Mr Patterson sent you some candy. Do you remember when Mr Patterson sent you some candy last summer."

There was a fence. The vine was dry, and the wind rattled in it.

"Only I dont see why Uncle Maury didn't send Versh." Caddy said. "Versh wont tell." Mrs Patterson was looking out the window. "You wait here." Caddy said. "Wait right here, now. I'll be back in a minute. Give me the letter." She took the letter out of my pocket. "Keep your hands in your pockets." She climbed the fence with the letter in her hand and went through the brown, rattling flowers. Mrs Patterson came to the door and opened it and stood there.

Mr Patterson was chopping in the green flowers. He stopped chopping and looked at me. Mrs Patterson came across the garden, running. When I saw her eyes I began to cry. You idiot, Mrs Patterson said, I told him never to send you alone again. Give it to me. Quick. Mr Patterson came fast, with the hoe. Mrs Patterson leaned across the fence, reaching her hand. She was trying to climb the fence. Give it to me, she said, Give it to me. Mr Patterson climbed the fence. He took the letter. Mrs Patterson's dress was caught on the fence. I saw her eyes again and I ran down the hill.

"They aint nothing over yonder but houses." Luster said. "We going down to the branch."

They were washing down at the branch. One of them was singing. I could smell the clothes flapping, and the smoke blowing across the branch.

"You stay down here." Luster said. "You aint got no business up yonder. Them folks hit you, sho."

"What he want to do."

"He dont know what he want to do." Luster said. "He think he want to go up yonder where they knocking that ball. You sit down here and play with your jimson weed. Look at them chillen playing in the branch, if you got to look at something. How come you cant behave yourself like folks." I sat down on the bank, where they were washing, and the smoke blowing blue.

"Is you all seen anything of a quarter down here." Luster said.

"What quarter."

"The one I had here this morning." Luster said. "I lost it somewhere. It fell through this here hole in my pocket. If I dont find it I cant go to the show tonight."

"Where'd you get a quarter, boy. Find it in white folks' pocket while they aint looking."

"Got it at the getting place." Luster said. "Plenty more where that one come from. Only I got to find that one. Is you all found it yet."

"I aint studying no quarter. I got my own business to tend to."

"Come on here." Luster said. "Help me look for it."

"He wouldn't know a quarter if he was to see it, would he."

"He can help look just the same." Luster said. "You all going to the show tonight."

"Dont talk to me about no show. Time I get done over this here tub I be too tired to lift my hand to do nothing."

"I bet you be there." Luster said. "I bet you was there last night. I bet you all be right there when that tent open."

"Be enough niggers there without me. Was last night."

"Nigger's money good as white folks, I reckon."

"White folks gives nigger money because know first white man comes along with a band going to get it all back, so nigger can go to work for some more."

"Aint nobody going make you go to that show."

"Aint yet. Aint thought of it, I reckon."

"What you got against white folks."

"Aint got nothing against them. I goes my way and lets white folks go theirs. I aint studying that show."

"Got a man in it can play a tune on a saw. Play it like a banjo."

"You go last night." Luster said. "I going tonight. If I can find where I lost that quarter."

"You going take him with you, I reckon."

"Me." Luster said. "You reckon I be found anywhere with him, time he start bellering."

"What does you do when he start bellering."

"I whips him." Luster said. He sat down and rolled up his overalls. They played in the branch.

"You all found any balls yet." Luster said.

"Aint you talking biggity. I bet you better not let your grandmammy hear you talking like that."

Luster got into the branch, where they were playing. He hunted in the water, along the bank.

"I had it when we was down here this morning." Luster said.

"Where 'bouts you lose it."

"Right out this here hole in my pocket." Luster said. They hunted in the branch. Then they all stood up quick and stopped, then they splashed and fought in the branch. Luster got it and they squatted in the water, looking up the hill through the bushes.

"Where is they." Luster said.

"Aint in sight yet."

Luster put it in his pocket. They came down the hill.

"Did a ball come down here."

"It ought to be in the water. Didn't any of you boys see it or hear it."

"Aint heard nothing come down here." Luster said. "Heard something hit that tree up yonder. Dont know which way it went."

They looked in the branch.

"Hell. Look along the branch. It came down here. I saw it."

They looked along the branch. Then they went back up the hill.

"Have you got that ball." the boy said.

"What I want with it." Luster said. "I aint seen no ball."

The boy got in the water. He went on. He turned and looked at Luster again. He went on down the branch.

The man said "Caddie" up the hill. The boy got out of the water and went up the hill.

"Now, just listen at you." Luster said. "Hush up."

"What he moaning about now."

"Lawd knows." Luster said. "He just starts like that. He been at it all morning. Cause it his birthday, I reckon."

"How old he."

"He thirty-three." Luster said. "Thirty-three this morning."

"You mean, he been three years old thirty years."

"I going by what mammy say." Luster said. "I dont know. We going to have thirty-three candles on a cake, anyway. Little cake. Wont hardly hold them. Hush up. Come on back here." He came and caught my arm. "You old loony," he said. "You want me to whip you."

"I bet you will."

"I is done it. Hush, now." Luster said. "Aint I told you

you cant go up there. They'll knock your head clean off
with one of them balls. Come on, here." He pulled me
back. "Sit down." I sat down and he took off my shoes
and rolled up my trousers. "Now, git in that water and
play and see can you stop that slobbering and moaning."

I hushed and got in the water *and Roskus came and
said to come to supper and Caddy said,*

It's not supper time yet. I'm not going.

She was wet. We were playing in the branch and
Caddy squatted down and got her dress wet and Versh
said,

"Your mommer going to whip you for getting your
dress wet."

"She's not going to do any such thing." Caddy said.

"How do you know." Quentin said.

"That's all right how I know." Caddy said. "How do
you know."

"She said she was." Quentin said. "Besides, I'm older
than you."

"I'm seven years old." Caddy said, "I guess I know."

"I'm older than that." Quentin said. "I go to school.
Dont I, Versh."

"I'm going to school next year." Caddy said, "When it
comes. Aint I, Versh."

"You know she whip you when you get your dress
wet." Versh said.

"It's not wet." Caddy said. She stood up in the water
and looked at her dress. "I'll take it off." she said. "Then
it'll dry."

"I bet you wont." Quentin said.

"I bet I will." Caddy said.

"I bet you better not." Quentin said.

Caddy came to Versh and me and turned her back.

"Unbutton it, Versh." she said.

"Dont you do it, Versh." Quentin said.

"Taint none of my dress." Versh said.

"You unbutton it, Versh." Caddy said, "Or I'll tell Dilsey what you did yesterday." So Versh unbuttoned it.

"You just take your dress off." Quentin said. Caddy took her dress off and threw it on the bank. Then she didn't have on anything but her bodice and drawers, and Quentin slapped her and she slipped and fell down in the water. When she got up she began to splash water on Quentin, and Quentin splashed water on Caddy. Some of it splashed on Versh and me and Versh picked me up and put me on the bank. He said he was going to tell on Caddy and Quentin, and then Quentin and Caddy began to splash water at Versh. He got behind a bush.

"I'm going to tell mammy on you all." Versh said.

Quentin climbed up on the bank and tried to catch Versh, but Versh ran away and Quentin couldn't. When Quentin came back Versh stopped and hollered that he was going to tell. Caddy told him that if he wouldn't tell, they'd let him come back. So Versh said he wouldn't, and they let him.

"Now I guess you're satisfied." Quentin said, "We'll both get whipped now."

"I dont care." Caddy said. "I'll run away."

"Yes you will." Quentin said.

"I'll run away and never come back." Caddy said. I began to cry. Caddy turned around and said "Hush." So I hushed. Then they played in the branch. Jason was playing too. He was by himself further down the branch. Versh came around the bush and lifted me down into the water again. Caddy was all wet and muddy behind, and I started to cry and she came and squatted in the water.

"Hush now." she said. "I'm not going to run away." So I hushed. Caddy smelled like trees in the rain.

What is the matter with you, Luster said. Cant you get done with that moaning and play in the branch like folks.

Whyn't you take him on home. Didn't they told you not to take him off the place.

He still think they own this pasture, Luster said. Cant nobody see down here from the house, noways.

We can. And folks dont like to look at a loony. Taint no luck in it.

Roskus came and said to come to supper and Caddy said it wasn't supper time yet.

"Yes tis." Roskus said. "Dilsey say for you all to come on to the house. Bring them on, Versh." He went up the hill, where the cow was lowing.

"Maybe we'll be dry by the time we get to the house." Quentin said.

"It was all your fault." Caddy said. "I hope we do get whipped." She put her dress on and Versh buttoned it.

"They wont know you got wet." Versh said. "It dont show on you. Less me and Jason tells."

"Are you going to tell, Jason." Caddy said.

"Tell on who." Jason said.

"He wont tell." Quentin said. "Will you, Jason."

"I bet he does tell." Caddy said. "He'll tell Damuddy."

"He cant tell her." Quentin said. "She's sick. If we walk slow it'll be too dark for them to see."

"I dont care whether they see or not." Caddy said. "I'm going to tell, myself. You carry him up the hill, Versh."

"Jason wont tell." Quentin said. "You remember that bow and arrow I made you, Jason."

"It's broke now." Jason said.

"Let him tell." Caddy said. "I dont give a cuss. Carry Maury up the hill, Versh." Versh squatted and I got on his back.

See you all at the show tonight, Luster said. Come on, here. We got to find that quarter.

"If we go slow, it'll be dark when we get there." Quentin said.

"I'm not going slow." Caddy said. We went up the hill, but Quentin didn't come. He was down at the branch when we got to where we could smell the pigs. They were grunting and snuffing in the trough in the corner. Jason came behind us, with his hands in his pockets. Roskus was milking the cow in the barn door.

The cows came jumping out of the barn.

"Go on." T. P. said. "Holler again. I going to holler myself. Whooey." Quentin kicked T. P. again. He kicked T. P. into the trough where the pigs ate and T. P. lay there. "Hot dog." T. P. said, "Didn't he get me then. You see that white man kick me that time. Whooey."

I wasn't crying, but I couldn't stop. I wasn't crying, but the ground wasn't still, and then I was crying. The ground kept sloping up and the cows ran up the hill. T. P. tried to get up. He fell down again and the cows ran down the hill. Quentin held my arm and we went toward the barn. Then the barn wasn't there and we had to wait until it came back. I didn't see it come back. It came behind us and Quentin set me down in the trough where the cows ate. I held on to it. It was going away too, and I held to it. The cows ran down the hill again, across the door. I couldn't stop. Quentin and T. P came up the hill, fighting. T. P. was falling down the hill and Quentin dragged him up the hill. Quentin hit T. P. I couldn't stop.

"Stand up." Quentin said, "You stay right here. Dont you go away until I get back."

"Me and Benjy going back to the wedding." T. P. said. "Whooey."

Quentin hit T. P. again. Then he began to thump T. P.

against the wall. T. P. was laughing. Every time Quentin thumped him against the wall he tried to say Whooey, but he couldn't say it for laughing. I quit crying, but I couldn't stop. T. P. fell on me and the barn door went away. It went down the hill and T. P. was fighting by himself and he fell down again. He was still laughing, and I couldn't stop, and I tried to get up and I fell down, and I couldn't stop. Versh said,

"You sho done it now. I'll declare if you aint. Shut up that yelling."

T. P. was still laughing. He flopped on the door and laughed. "Whooey." he said, "Me and Benjy going back to the wedding. Sassprilluh." T. P. said.

"Hush." Versh said. "Where you get it."

"Out the cellar." T. P. said. "Whooey."

"Hush up." Versh said, "Where'bouts in the cellar."

"Anywhere." T. P. said. He laughed some more. "Moren a hundred bottles left. Moren a million. Look out, nigger, I going to holler."

Quentin said, "Lift him up."

Versh lifted me up.

"Drink this, Benjy." Quentin said. The glass was hot. "Hush, now." Quentin said. "Drink it."

"Sassprilluh." T. P. said. "Lemme drink it, Mr Quentin."

"You shut your mouth." Versh said, "Mr Quentin wear you out."

"Hold him, Versh." Quentin said.

They held me. It was hot on my chin and on my shirt. "Drink." Quentin said. They held my head. It was hot inside me, and I began again. It was crying now, and something was happening inside me and I cried more, and they held me until it stopped happening. Then I hushed. It was still going around, and then the shapes began. "Open the crib, Versh." They were going slow. "Spread those empty sacks on the floor." They were going faster, almost fast enough. "Now. Pick up his feet." They went on, smooth and bright. I could hear T. P. laughing. I went on with them, up the bright hill.

At the top of the hill Versh put me down. "Come on here, Quentin." he called, looking back down the hill. Quentin was still standing there by the branch. He was chunking into the shadows where the branch was.

"Let the old skizzard stay there." Caddy said. She took my hand and we went on past the barn and through the gate. There was a frog on the brick walk, squatting in the middle of it. Caddy stepped over it and pulled me on.

"Come on, Maury." she said. It still squatted there until Jason poked at it with his toe.

"He'll make a wart on you." Versh said. The frog hopped away.

"Come on, Maury." Caddy said.

"They got company tonight." Versh said.

"How do you know." Caddy said.

"With all them lights on." Versh said, "Light in every window."

"I reckon we can turn all the lights on without company, if we want to." Caddy said.

"I bet it's company." Versh said. "You all better go in the back and slip upstairs."

"I dont care." Caddy said. "I'll walk right in the parlor where they are."

"I bet your pappy whip you if you do." Versh said.

"I dont care." Caddy said. "I'll walk right in the parlor. I'll walk right in the dining room and eat supper."

"Where you sit." Versh said.

"I'd sit in Damuddy's chair." Caddy said. "She eats in bed."

"I'm hungry." Jason said. He passed us and ran on up the walk. He had his hands in his pockets and he fell down. Versh went and picked him up.

"If you keep them hands out your pockets, you could stay on your feet." Versh said. "You cant never get them out in time to catch yourself, fat as you is."

Father was standing by the kitchen steps.

"Where's Quentin." he said.

"He coming up the walk." Versh said. Quentin was coming slow. His shirt was a white blur.

"Oh." Father said. Light fell down the steps, on him.

"Caddy and Quentin threw water on each other." Jason said.

We waited.

"They did." Father said. Quentin came, and Father said, "You can eat supper in the kitchen tonight." He stopped and took me up, and the light came tumbling down the steps on me too, and I could look down at Caddy and Jason and Quentin and Versh. Father turned toward the steps. "You must be quiet, though." he said.

"Why must we be quiet, Father." Caddy said. "Have we got company."

"Yes." Father said.

"I told you they was company." Versh said.

"You did not." Caddy said, "I was the one that said there was. I said I would"

"Hush." Father said. They hushed and Father opened the door and we crossed the back porch and went in to the kitchen. Dilsey was there, and Father put me in the chair and closed the apron down and pushed it to the table, where supper was. It was steaming up.

"You mind Dilsey, now." Father said. "Dont let them make any more noise than they can help, Dilsey."

"Yes, sir." Dilsey said. Father went away.

"Remember to mind Dilsey, now." he said behind us. I leaned my face over where the supper was. It steamed up on my face.

"Let them mind me tonight, Father." Caddy said.

"I wont." Jason said. "I'm going to mind Dilsey."

"You'll have to, if Father says so." Caddy said. "Let them mind me, Father."

"I wont." Jason said, "I wont mind you."

"Hush." Father said. "You all mind Caddy, then. When they are done, bring them up the back stairs, Dilsey."

"Yes, sir." Dilsey said.

"There." Caddy said, "Now I guess you'll mind me."

"You all hush, now." Dilsey said. "You got to be quiet tonight."

"Why do we have to be quiet tonight." Caddy whispered.

"Never you mind." Dilsey said, "You'll know in the Lawd's own time." She brought my bowl. The steam from it came and tickled my face. "Come here, Versh." Dilsey said.

"When is the Lawd's own time, Dilsey." Caddy said.

"It's Sunday." Quentin said. "Dont you know anything."

"Shhhhhh." Dilsey said. "Didn't Mr Jason say for you all to be quiet. Eat your supper, now. Here, Versh. Git his spoon." Versh's hand came with the spoon, into the bowl. The spoon came up to my mouth. The steam tickled into my mouth. Then we quit eating and we looked at each other and we were quiet, and then we heard it again and I began to cry.

"What was that." Caddy said. She put her hand on my hand.

"That was Mother." Quentin said. The spoon came up and I ate, then I cried again.

"Hush." Caddy said. But I didn't hush and she came

and put her arms around me. Dilsey went and closed both the doors and then we couldn't hear it.

"Hush, now." Caddy said. I hushed and ate. Quentin wasn't eating, but Jason was.

"That was Mother." Quentin said. He got up.

"You set right down." Dilsey said. "They got company in there, and you in them muddy clothes. You set down too, Caddy, and get done eating."

"She was crying." Quentin said.

"It was somebody singing." Caddy said. "Wasn't it, Dilsey."

"You all eat your supper, now, like Mr Jason said." Dilsey said. "You'll know in the Lawd's own time." Caddy went back to her chair.

"I told you it was a party." she said.

Versh said, "He done et all that."

"Bring his bowl here." Dilsey said. The bowl went away.

"Dilsey." Caddy said, "Quentin's not eating his supper. Hasn't he got to mind me."

"Eat your supper, Quentin." Dilsey said, "You all got to get done and get out of my kitchen."

"I dont want any more supper." Quentin said.

"You've got to eat if I say you have." Caddy said. "Hasn't he, Dilsey."

The bowl steamed up to my face, and Versh's hand dipped the spoon in it and the steam tickled into my mouth.

"I dont want any more." Quentin said. "How can they have a party when Damuddy's sick."

"They'll have it down stairs." Caddy said. "She can come to the landing and see it. That's what I'm going to do when I get my nightie on."

"Mother was crying." Quentin said. "Wasn't she crying, Dilsey."

"Dont you come pestering at me, boy." Dilsey said. "I got to get supper for all them folks soon as you all get done eating."

After a while even Jason was through eating, and he began to cry.

"Now you got to tune up." Dilsey said.

"He does it every night since Damuddy was sick and he cant sleep with her." Caddy said. "Cry baby."

"I'm going to tell on you." Jason said.

He was crying. "You've already told." Caddy said. "There's not anything else you can tell, now."

"You all needs to go to bed." Dilsey said. She came and lifted me down and wiped my face and hands with a warm cloth. "Versh, can you get them up the back stairs quiet. You, Jason, shut up that crying."

"It's too early to go to bed now." Caddy said. "We dont ever have to go to bed this early."

"You is tonight." Dilsey said. "Your pa say for you to come right on up stairs when you et supper. You heard him."

"He said to mind me." Caddy said.

"I'm not going to mind you." Jason said.

"You have to." Caddy said. "Come on, now. You have to do like I say."

"Make them be quiet, Versh." Dilsey said. "You all going to be quiet, ain't you."

"What do we have to be so quiet for, tonight." Caddy said.

"Your mommer aint feeling well." Dilsey said. "You all go on with Versh, now."

"I told you Mother was crying." Quentin said. Versh

took me up and opened the door onto the back porch. We went out and Versh closed the door back. I could smell Versh and feel him. "You all be quiet, now. We're not going up stairs yet. Mr. Jason said for you to come right up stairs. He said to mind me. I'm not going to mind you. But he said for all of us to. Didn't he, Quentin." I could feel Versh's head. I could hear us. "Didn't he, Versh. Yes, that's right. Then I say for us to go out doors a while. Come on." Versh opened the door and we went out.

We went down the steps.

"I expect we'd better go down to Versh's house, so we'll be quiet." Caddy said. Versh put me down and Caddy took my hand and we went down the brick walk.

"Come on." Caddy said, "That frog's gone. He's hopped way over to the garden, by now. Maybe we'll see another one." Roskus came with the milk buckets. He went on. Quentin wasn't coming with us. He was sitting on the kitchen steps. We went down to Versh's house. I liked to smell Versh's house. *There was a fire in it and T. P. squatting in his shirt tail in front of it, chunking it into a blaze.*

Then I got up and T. P. dressed me and we went to the kitchen and ate. Dilsey was singing and I began to cry and she stopped.

"Keep him away from the house, now." Dilsey said.

"We cant go that way." T. P. said.

We played in the branch.

"We cant go around yonder." T. P. said. "Dont you know mammy say we cant."

Dilsey was singing in the kitchen and I began to cry.

"Hush." T. P. said. "Come on. Lets go down to the barn."

Roskus was milking at the barn. He was milking with one hand, and groaning. Some birds sat on the barn door and watched him. One of them came down and ate with the cows. I watched Roskus milk while T. P. was feeding Queenie and Prince. The calf was in the pig pen. It nuzzled at the wire, bawling.

"T. P." Roskus said. T. P. said Sir, in the barn. Fancy held her head over the door, because T. P. hadn't fed her yet. "Git done there." Roskus said. "You got to do this milking. I cant use my right hand no more."

T. P. came and milked.

"Whyn't you get the doctor." T. P. said.

"Doctor cant do no good." Roskus said. "Not on this place."

"What wrong with this place." T. P. said.

"Taint no luck on this place." Roskus said. "Turn that calf in if you done."

Taint no luck on this place, Roskus said. The fire rose and fell behind him and Versh, sliding on his and Versh's face. Dilsey finished putting me to bed. The bed smelled like T. P. I liked it.

"What you know about it." Dilsey said. "What trance you been in."

"Dont need no trance." Roskus said. "Aint the sign of it laying right there on that bed. Aint the sign of it been here for folks to see fifteen years now."

"Spose it is." Dilsey said. "It aint hurt none of you and yourn, is it. Versh working and Frony married off your hands and T. P. getting big enough to take your place when rheumatism finish getting you."

"They been two, now." Roskus said. "Going to be one more. I seen the sign, and you is too."

"I heard a squinch owl that night." T. P. said. "Dan wouldn't come and get his supper, neither. Wouldn't come no closer than the barn. Begun howling right after dark. Versh heard him."

"Going to be more than one more." Dilsey said. "Show me the man what aint going to die, bless Jesus."

"Dying aint all." Roskus said.

"I knows what you thinking." Dilsey said. "And they aint going to be no luck in saying that name, lessen you going to set up with him while he cries."

"They aint no luck on this place." Roskus said. "I seen it at first but when they changed his name I knowed it."

"Hush your mouth." Dilsey said. She pulled the covers up. It smelled like T. P. "You all shut up now, till he get to sleep."

"I seen the sign." Roskus said.

"Sign T. P. got to do all your work for you." Dilsey said. *Take him and Quentin down to the house and let them play with Luster, where Frony can watch them, T. P., and go and help your pa.*

We finished eating. T. P. took Quentin up and we went down to T. P.'s house. Luster was playing in the dirt. T. P. put Quentin down and she played in the dirt too. Luster had some spools and he and Quentin fought and Quentin had the spools. Luster cried and Frony came and gave Luster a tin can to play with, and then I had the spools and Quentin fought me and I cried.

"Hush." Frony said, "Aint you shamed of yourself. Taking a baby's play pretty." She took the spools from me and gave them back to Quentin.

"Hush, now." Frony said, "Hush, I tell you."

"Hush up." Frony said. "You needs whipping, that's what you needs." She took Luster and Quentin up. "Come on here." she said. We went to the barn. T. P. was milking the cow. Roskus was sitting on the box.

"What's the matter with him now." Roskus said.

"You have to keep him down here." Frony said. "He fighting these babies again. Taking they play things. Stay here with T. P. now, and see can you hush a while."

"Clean that udder good now." Roskus said. "You milked that young cow dry last winter. If you milk this one dry, they aint going to be no more milk."

Dilsey was singing.

"Not around yonder." T. P. said. "Dont you know mammy say you cant go around there."

They were singing.

"Come on." T. P. said. "Lets go play with Quentin and Luster. Come on."

Quentin and Luster were playing in the dirt in front of T. P.'s house. There was a fire in the house, rising and falling, with Roskus sitting black against it.

"That's three, thank the Lawd." Roskus said. "I told you two years ago. They aint no luck on this place."

"Whyn't you get out, then." Dilsey said. She was undressing me. "Your bad luck talk got them Memphis notions into Versh. That ought to satisfy you."

"If that all the bad luck Versh have." Roskus said.

Frony came in.

"You all done." Dilsey said.

"T. P. finishing up." Frony said. "Miss Cahline want you to put Quentin to bed."

"I'm coming just as fast as I can." Dilsey said. "She ought to know by this time I aint got no wings."

"That's what I tell you." Roskus said. "They aint no luck going be on no place where one of they own chillens' name aint never spoke."

"Hush." Dilsey said. "Do you want to get him started"

"Raising a child not to know its own mammy's name." Roskus said.

"Dont you bother your head about her." Dilsey said.

"I raised all of them and I reckon I can raise one more. Hush now. Let him get to sleep if he will."

"Saying a name." Frony said. "He dont know nobody's name."

"You just say it and see if he dont." Dilsey said. "You say it to him while he sleeping and I bet he hear you."

"He know lot more than folks thinks." Roskus said. "He knowed they time was coming, like that pointer done. He could tell you when hisn coming, if he could talk. Or yours. Or mine."

"You take Luster outen that bed, mammy." Frony said. "That boy conjure him."

"Hush your mouth." Dilsey said, "Aint you got no better sense than that. What you want to listen to Roskus for, anyway. Get in, Benjy."

Dilsey pushed me and I got in the bed, where Luster already was. He was alseep. Dilsey took a long piece of wood and laid it between Luster and me. "Stay on your side now." Dilsey said. "Luster little, and you don't want to hurt him."

You can't go yet, T. P. said. Wait.

We looked around the corner of the house and watched the carriages go away.

"Now." T. P. said. He took Quentin up and we ran down to the corner of the fence and watched them pass. "There he go," T. P. said. "See that one with the glass in it. Look at him. He laying in there. See him."

Come on, Luster said, I going to take this here ball down home, where I wont lose it. Naw, sir, you cant have it. If them men sees you with it, they'll say you stole it. Hush up, now. You cant have it. What business you got with it. You cant play no ball.

Frony and T. P. were playing in the dirt by the door. T. P. had lightning bugs in a bottle.

"How did you all get back out." Frony said.

"We've got company." Caddy said. "Father said for us to mind me tonight. I expect you and T. P. will have to mind me too."

"I'm not going to mind you." Jason said. "Frony and T. P. dont have to either."

"They will if I say so." Caddy said. "Maybe I wont say for them to."

"T. P. dont mind nobody." Frony said. "Is they started the funeral yet."

"What's a funeral." Jason said.

"Didn't mammy tell you not to tell them." Versh said.

"Where they moans." Frony said. "They moaned twc days on Sis Beulah Clay."

They moaned at Dilsey's house. Dilsey was moaning. When Dilsey moaned Luster said, Hush, and we hushed, and then I began to cry and Blue howled under the kitchen steps. Then Dilsey stopped and we stopped.

"Oh." Caddy said, "That's niggers. White folks dont have funerals."

"Mammy said us not to tell them, Frony." Versh said.

"Tell them what." Caddy said.

Dilsey moaned, and when it got to the place I began to cry and Blue howled under the steps. Luster, Frony, said in the window, Take them down to the barn. I cant get no cooking done with all that racket. That hound too. Get them outen here.

I aint going down there, Luster said. I might meet pappy down there. I seen him last night, waving his arms in the barn.

"I like to know why not." Frony said. "White folks dies too. Your grandmammy dead as any nigger can get, I reckon."

"Dogs are dead." Caddy said, "And when Nancy fell in

the ditch and Roskus shot her and the buzzards came
and undressed her." *shift*

The bones rounded out of the ditch, where the dark
vines were in the black ditch, into the moonlight, like
some of the shapes had stopped. Then they all stopped
and it was dark, and when I stopped to start again I
could hear Mother, and feet walking fast away, and I
could smell it. Then the room came, but my eyes went
shut. I didn't stop. I could smell it. T. P. unpinned the
bed clothes.

"Hush." he said, "Shhhhhhhh."

But I could smell it. T. P. pulled me up and he put on
my clothes fast.

"Hush, Benjy." he said. "We going down to our house.
You want to go down to our house, where Frony is.
Hush. Shhhhh."

He laced my shoes and put my cap on and we went
out. There was a light in the hall. Across the hall we
could hear Mother.

"Shhhhhh, Benjy." T. P. said, "We'll be out in a
minute."

A door opened and I could smell it more than ever,
and a head came out. It wasn't Father. Father was sick
there.

"Can you take him out of the house."

"That's where we going." T. P. said. Dilsey came up
the stairs.

"Hush." she said, "Hush. Take him down home, T. P.
Frony fixing him a bed. You all look after him, now.
Hush, Benjy. Go on with T. P."

She went where we could hear Mother.

"Better keep him there." It wasn't Father. He shut the
door, but I could still smell it.

We went down stairs. The stairs went down into the

dark and T. P. took my hand, and we went out the door, out of the dark. Dan was sitting in the back yard, howling.

"He smell it." T. P. said. "Is that the way you found it out."

We went down the steps, where our shadows were.

"I forgot your coat." T. P. said. "You ought to had it. But I aint going back."

Dan howled.

"Hush now." T. P. said. Our shadows moved, but Dan's shadow didn't move except to howl when he did.

"I cant take you down home, bellering like you is." T. P. said. "You was bad enough before you got that bullfrog voice. Come on."

We went along the brick walk, with our shadows. The pig pen smelled like pigs. The cow stood in the lot, chewing at us. Dan howled.

"You going to wake the whole town up." T. P. said. "Cant you hush."

We saw Fancy, eating by the branch. The moon shone on the water when we got there.

"Naw, sir." T. P. said, "This too close. We cant stop here. Come on. Now, just look at you. Got your whole leg wet. Come on, here." Dan howled.

The ditch came up out of the buzzing grass. The bones rounded out of the black vines.

"Now." T. P. said. "Beller your head off if you want to. You got the whole night and a twenty acre pasture to beller in."

T. P. lay down in the ditch and I sat down, watching the bones where the buzzards ate Nancy, flapping black and slow and heavy out of the ditch.

I had it when we was down here before, Luster said.

I showed it to you. Didn't you see it. I took it out of my pocket right here and showed it to you.

"Do you think buzzards are going to undress Damuddy." Caddy said. "You're crazy."

"You're a skizzard." Jason said. He began to cry.

"You're a knobnot." Caddy said. Jason cried. His hands were in his pockets.

"Jason going to be rich man." Versh said. "He holding his money all the time."

Jason cried.

"Now you've got him started." Caddy said. "Hush up, Jason. How can buzzards get in where Damuddy is. Father wouldn't let them. Would you let a buzzard undress you. Hush up, now."

Jason hushed. "Frony said it was a funeral." he said.

"Well it's not." Caddy said. "It's a party. Frony dont know anything about it. He wants your lightning bugs, T. P. Let him hold it a while."

T. P. gave me the bottle of lightning bugs.

"I bet if we go around to the parlor window we can see something." Caddy said. "Then you'll believe me."

"I already knows." Frony said. "I dont need to see."

"You better hush your mouth, Frony." Versh said. "Mammy going whip you."

"What is it." Caddy said.

"I knows what I knows." Frony said.

"Come on." Caddy said, "Let's go around to the front." We started to go.

"T. P. wants his lightning bugs." Frony said.

"Let him hold it a while longer, T. P." Caddy said. "We'll bring it back."

"You all never caught them." Frony said.

"If I say you and T. P. can come too, will you let him hold it." Caddy said.

"Aint nobody said me and T. P. got to mind you."
Frony said.

"If I say you dont have to, will you let him hold it."
Caddy said.

"All right." Frony said. "Let him hold it, T. P. We going to watch them moaning."

"They aint moaning." Caddy said. "I tell you it's a
party. Are they moaning, Versh."

"We aint going to know what they doing, standing
here." Versh said.

"Come on." Caddy said. "Frony and T. P. dont have to
mind me. But the rest of us do. You better carry him,
Versh. It's getting dark."

Versh took me up and we went on around the kitchen.

*When we looked around the corner we could see the
lights coming up the drive. T. P. went back to the cellar
door and opened it.*

*You know what's down there, T. P. said. Soda water.
I seen Mr Jason come up with both hands full of them.
Wait here a minute.*

*T. P. went and looked in the kitchen door. Dilsey
said, What are you peeping in here for. Where's Benjy.*

He out here, T. P. said.

*Go on and watch him, Dilsey said. Keep him out the
house now.*

Yessum, T. P. said. Is they started yet.

*You go on and keep that boy out of sight, Dilsey said.
I got all I can tend to.*

A snake crawled out from under the house. Jason said
he wasn't afraid of snakes and Caddy said he was but
she wasn't and Versh said they both were and Caddy said
to be quiet, like father said.

*You aint got to start bellering now, T. P. said. You
want some this sassprilluh.*

It tickled my nose and eyes.

*If you aint going to drink it, let me get to it, T. P.
said. All right, here tis. We better get another bottle while
nobody bothering us. You be quiet, now.*

We stopped under the tree by the parlor window.
Versh set me down in the wet grass. It was cold. There
were lights in all the windows.

"That's where Damuddy is." Caddy said. "She's sick
every day now. When she gets well we're going to have
a picnic."

"I knows what I knows." Frony said.

The trees were buzzing, and the grass.

"The one next to it is where we have the measles."
Caddy said. "Where do you and T. P. have the measles,
Frony."

"Has them just wherever we is, I reckon." Frony said.

"They haven't started yet." Caddy said.

*They getting ready to start, T. P. said. You stand
right here now while I get that box so we can see in the
window. Here, les finish drinking this here sassprilluh.
It make me feel just like a squinch owl inside.*

We drank the sassprilluh and T. P. pushed the bottle
through the lattice, under the house, and went away. I
could hear them in the parlor and I clawed my hands
against the wall. T. P. dragged the box. He fell down,
and he began to laugh. He lay there, laughing into the
grass. He got up and dragged the box under the window,
trying not to laugh.

"I skeered I going to holler." T. P. said. "Git on the box
and see is they started."

"They haven't started because the band hasn't come
yet." Caddy said.

"They aint going to have no band." Frony said.

"How do you know." Caddy said.

"I knows what I knows." Frony said.

"You dont know anything." Caddy said. She went to the tree. "Push me up, Versh."

"Your paw told you to stay out that tree." Versh said.

"That was a long time ago." Caddy said. "I expect he's forgotten about it. Besides, he said to mind me tonight. Didn't he say to mind me tonight."

"I'm not going to mind you." Jason said. "Frony and T. P. are not going to either."

"Push me up, Versh." Caddy said.

"All right." Versh said. "You the one going to get whipped. I aint." He went and pushed Caddy up into the tree to the first limb. We watched the muddy bottom of her drawers. Then we couldn't see her. We could hear the tree thrashing.

"Mr Jason said if you break that tree he whip you." Versh said.

"I'm going to tell on her too." Jason said.

The tree quit thrashing. We looked up into the still branches.

"What you seeing." Frony whispered.

I saw them. Then I saw Caddy, with flowers in her hair, and a long veil like shining wind. Caddy Caddy

"Hush." T. P. said, "They going to hear you. Get down quick." He pulled me. Caddy. I clawed my hands against the wall Caddy. T. P. pulled me.

"Hush." he said. "Hush. Come on here quick." He pulled me on. Caddy "Hush up, Benjy. You want them to hear you. Come on, les drink some more sassprilluh, then we can come back if you hush. We better get one more bottle or we both be hollering. We can say Dan drunk it. Mr Quentin always saying he so smart, we can say he sassprilluh dog, too."

The moonlight came down the cellar stairs. We drank some more sassprilluh.

"You know what I wish." T. P. said. "I wish a bear would walk in that cellar door. You know what I do. I walk right up to him and spit in he eye. Gimme that bottle to stop my mouth before I holler."

T. P. fell down. He began to laugh, and the cellar door and the moonlight jumped away and something hit me.

"Hush up." T. P. said, trying not to laugh, "Lawd, they'll all hear us. Get up." T. P. said, "Get up, Benjy, quick." He was thrashing about and laughing and I tried to get up. The cellar steps ran up the hill in the moon-light and T. P. fell up the hill, into the moonlight, and I ran against the fence and T. P. ran behind me saying "Hush up hush up" Then he fell into the flowers, laugh-ing, and I ran into the box. But when I tried to climb onto it it jumped away and hit me on the back of the head and my throat made a sound. It made the sound again and I stopped trying to get up, and it made the sound again and I began to cry. But my throat kept on making the sound while T. P. was pulling me. It kept on making it and I couldn't tell if I was crying or not, and T. P. fell down on top of me, laughing, and it kept on making the sound and Quentin kicked T. P. and Cad put her arms around me, and her shining veil, and I couldn't smell trees anymore and I began to cry.

Benjy, Caddy said Benjy. She put her arms around me again, but I went away. "What is it, Benjy." she said, "Is it this hat." She took her hat off and came again, and I went away.

"Benjy." she said, "What is it, Benjy. What has Caddy done."

"He dont like that prissy dress." Jason said. "You think

you're grown up, dont you. You think you're better than anybody else, dont you. Prissy."

"You shut your mouth." Caddy said, "You dirty little beast. Benjy."

"Just because you are fourteen, you think you're grown up, dont you." Jason said. "You think you're something. Dont you."

"Hush, Benjy." Caddy said. "You'll disturb Mother. Hush."

But I didn't hush, and when she went away I followed, and she stopped on the stairs and waited and I stopped too.

"What is it, Benjy." Caddy said, "Tell Caddy. She'll do it. Try."

"Candace." Mother said.

"Yessum." Caddy said.

"Why are you teasing him." Mother said. "Bring him here."

We went to Mother's room, where she was lying with the sickness on a cloth on her head.

"What is the matter now." Mother said. "Benjamin."

"Benjy." Caddy said. She came again, but I went away.

"You must have done something to him." Mother said. "Why wont you let him alone, so I can have some peace. Give him the box and please go on and let him alone."

Caddy got the box and set it on the floor and opened it. It was full of stars. When I was still, they were still. When I moved, they glinted and sparkled. I hushed.

Then I heard Caddy walking and I began again.

"Benjamin." Mother said, "Come here." I went to the door. "You, Benjamin." Mother said.

"What is it now." Father said, "Where are you going."

"Take him downstairs and get someone to watch him, Jason." Mother said. "You know I'm ill, yet you"

Father shut the door behind us.

"T. P." he said.

"Sir." T. P. said downstairs.

"Benjy's coming down." Father said. "Go with T. P."

I went to the bathroom door. I could hear the water.

"Benjy." T. P. said downstairs.

I could hear the water. I listened to it.

"Benjy." T. P. said downstairs.

I listened to the water.

I couldn't hear the water, and Caddy opened the door.

"Why, Benjy." she said. She looked at me and I went and she put her arms around me. "Did you find Caddy again." she said. "Did you think Caddy had run away." Caddy smelled like trees.

We went to Caddy's room. She sat down at the mirror. She stopped her hands and looked at me.

"Why, Benjy. What is it." she said. "You mustn't cry. Caddy's not going away. See here." she said. She took up the bottle and took the stopper out and held it to my nose. "Sweet. Smell. Good."

I went away and I didn't hush, and she held the bottle in her hand, looking at me.

"Oh." she said. She put the bottle down and came and put her arms around me. "So that was it. And you were trying to tell Caddy and you couldn't tell her. You wanted to, but you couldn't, could you. Of course Caddy wont. Of course Caddy wont. Just wait till I dress."

Caddy dressed and took up the bottle again and we went down to the kitchen.

"Dilsey." Caddy said, "Benjy's got a present for you." She stooped down and put the bottle in my hand. "Hold it out to Dilsey, now." Caddy held my hand out and Dilsey took the bottle.

"Well I'll declare." Dilsey said, "If my baby aint give

Dilsey a bottle of perfume. Just look here, Roskus."

Caddy smelled like trees. "We dont like perfume ourselves." Caddy said.

She smelled like trees.

"Come on, now." Dilsey said, "You too big to sleep
with folks. You a big boy now. Thirteen years old. Big
enough to sleep by yourself in Uncle Maury's room."
Dilsey said.

Uncle Maury was sick. His eye was sick, and his
mouth. Versh took his supper up to him on the tray.

"Maury says he's going to shoot the scoundrel." Father
said. "I told him he'd better not mention it to Patterson
before hand." He drank.

"Jason." Mother said.

"Shoot who, Father." Quentin said. "What's Uncle
Maury going to shoot him for."

"Because he couldn't take a little joke." Father said.

"Jason." Mother said, "How can you. You'd sit right
there and see Maury shot down in ambush, and laugh."

"Then Maury'd better stay out of ambush." Father
said.

"Shoot who, Father." Quentin said, "Who's Uncle
Maury going to shoot."

"Nobody." Father said. "I dont own a pistol."

Mother began to cry. "If you begrudge Maury your
food, why aren't you man enough to say so to his face. To
ridicule him before the children, behind his back."

"Of course I dont." Father said, "I admire Maury. He
is invaluable to my own sense of racial superiority. I
wouldn't swap Maury for a matched team. And do you
know why, Quentin."

"No, sir." Quentin said.

"*Et ego in arcadia* I have forgotten the latin for hay."
Father said. "There, there." he said, "I was just joking."

He drank and set the glass down and went and put his hand on Mother's shoulder.

"It's no joke." Mother said. "My people are every bit as well born as yours. Just because Maury's health is bad."

"Of course." Father said. "Bad health is the primary reason for all life. Created by disease, within putrefaction, into decay. Versh."

"Sir." Versh said behind my chair.

"Take the decanter and fill it."

"And tell Dilsey to come and take Benjamin up to bed." Mother said.

"You a big boy." Dilsey said, "Caddy tired sleeping with you. Hush now, so you can go to sleep." The room went away, but I didn't hush, and the room came back and Dilsey came and sat on the bed, looking at me.

"Aint you going to be a good boy and hush." Dilsey said. "You aint, is you. See can you wait a minute, then."

She went away. There wasn't anything in the door. Then Caddy was in it.

"Hush." Caddy said. "I'm coming."

I hushed and Dilsey turned back the spread and Caddy got in between the spread and the blanket. She didn't take off her bathrobe.

"Now." she said, "Here I am." Dilsey came with a blanket and spread it over her and tucked it around her.

"He be gone in a minute." Dilsey said. "I leave the light on in your room."

"All right." Caddy said. She snuggled her head beside mine on the pillow. "Goodnight, Dilsey."

"Goodnight, honey." Dilsey said. The room went black. Caddy smelled like trees.

We looked up into the tree where she was.

"What she seeing, Versh." Frony whispered.

"Shhhhhhh." Caddy said in the tree. Dilsey said,

"You come on here." She came around the corner of the house. "Whyn't you all go on up stairs, like your paw said, stead of slipping out behind my back. Where's Caddy and Quentin."

"I told her not to climb up that tree." Jason said. "I'm going to tell on her."

"Who in what tree." Dilsey said. She came and looked up into the tree. "Caddy." Dilsey said. The branches began to shake again.

"You, Satan." Dilsey said. "Come down from there."

"Hush." Caddy said, "Dont you know Father said to be quiet." Her legs came in sight and Dilsey reached up and lifted her out of the tree.

"Aint you got any better sense than to let them come around here." Dilsey said.

"I couldn't do nothing with her." Versh said.

"What you all doing here." Dilsey said. "Who told you to come up to the house."

"She did." Frony said. "She told us to come."

"Who told you you got to do what she say." Dilsey said. "Get on home, now." Frony and T. P. went on. We couldn't see them when they were still going away.

"Out here in the middle of the night." Dilsey said. She took me up and we went to the kitchen.

"Slipping out behind my back." Dilsey said. "When you knowed it's past your bedtime."

"Shhhh, Dilsey." Caddy said. "Dont talk so loud. We've got to be quiet."

"You hush your mouth and get quiet, then." Dilsey said. "Where's Quentin."

"Quentin's mad because he had to mind me tonight." Caddy said. "He's still got T. P.'s bottle of lightning bugs."

"I reckon T. P. can get along without it." Dilsey said. "You go and find Quentin, Versh. Roskus say he seen him going towards the barn." Versh went on. We couldn't see him.

"They're not doing anything in there." Caddy said. "Just sitting in chairs and looking."

"They dont need no help from you all to do that." Dilsey said. We went around the kitchen.

Where you want to go now, Luster said. You going back to watch them knocking ball again. We done looked for it over there. Here. Wait a minute. You wait right here while I go back and get that ball. I done thought of something.

The kitchen was dark. The trees were black on the sky. Dan came waddling out from under the steps and chewed my ankle. I went around the kitchen, where the moon was. Dan came scuffling along, into the moon.

"Benjy." T. P. said in the house.

The flower tree by the parlor window wasn't dark, but the thick trees were. The grass was buzzing in the moonlight where my shadow walked on the grass.

"You, Benjy." T. P. said in the house. "Where you hiding. You slipping off. I knows it."

Luster came back. Wait, he said. Here. Dont go over there. Miss Quentin and her beau in the swing yonder. You come on this way. Come back here, Benjy.

It was dark under the trees. Dan wouldn't come. He stayed in the moonlight. Then I could see the swing and I began to cry.

Come away from there, Benjy, Luster said. You know Miss Quentin going to get mad.

It was two now, and then one in the swing. Caddy came fast, white in the darkness.

"Benjy," she said. "How did you slip out. Where's Versh."

She put her arms around me and I hushed and held to her dress and tried to pull her away.

"Why, Benjy." she said. "What is it. T. P." she called.

The one in the swing got up and came, and I cried and pulled Caddy's dress.

"Benjy." Caddy said. "It's just Charlie. Dont you know Charlie."

"Where's his nigger." Charlie said. "What do they let him run around loose for."

"Hush, Benjy." Caddy said. "Go away, Charlie. He doesn't like you." Charlie went away and I hushed. I pulled at Caddy's dress.

"Why, Benjy." Caddy said. "Aren't you going to let me stay here and talk to Charlie awhile."

"Call that nigger." Charlie said. He came back. I cried louder and pulled at Caddy's dress.

"Go away, Charlie." Caddy said. Charlie came and put his hands on Caddy and I cried more. I cried loud.

"No, no." Caddy said. "No. No."

"He cant talk." Charlie said. "Caddy."

"Are you crazy." Caddy said. She began to breathe fast. "He can see. Dont. Dont." Caddy fought. They both breathed fast. "Please. Please." Caddy whispered

"Send him away." Charlie said.

"I will." Caddy said. "Let me go."

"Will you send him away." Charlie said.

"Yes." Caddy said. "Let me go." Charlie went away. "Hush." Caddy said. "He's gone." I hushed. I could hear her and feel her chest going.

"I'll have to take him to the house." she said. She took my hand. "I'm coming." she whispered.

"Wait." Charlie said. "Call the nigger."

"No." Caddy said. "I'll come back. Come on, Benjy."

"Caddy." Charlie whispered, loud. We went on. "You better come back. Are you coming back." Caddy and I were running. "Caddy." Charlie said. We ran out into the moonlight, toward the kitchen.

"Caddy." Charlie said.

Caddy and I ran. We ran up the kitchen steps, onto the porch, and Caddy knelt down in the dark and held me. I could hear her and feel her chest. "I wont." she said. "I wont anymore, ever. Benjy. Benjy." Then she was crying, and I cried, and we held each other. "Hush." she said. "Hush. I wont anymore." So I hushed and Caddy got up and we went into the kitchen and turned the light on and Caddy took the kitchen soap and washed her mouth at the sink, hard. Caddy smelled like trees.

I kept a telling you to stay away from there, Luster said. They sat up in the swing, quick. Quentin had her hands on her hair. He had a red tie.

You old crazy loon, Quentin said. I'm going to tell Dilsey about the way you let him follow everywhere I go. I'm going to make her whip you good.

"I couldn't stop him." Luster said. "Come on here, Benjy."

"Yes you could." Quentin said. "You didn't try. You were both snooping around after me. Did Grandmother send you all out here to spy on me." She jumped out of the swing. "If you dont take him right away this minute and keep him away, I'm going to make Jason whip you."

"I cant do nothing with him." Luster said. "You try it if you think you can."

"Shut your mouth." Quentin said. "Are you going to get him away."

"Ah, let him stay." he said. He had a red tie. The sun

was red on it. "Look here, Jack." He struck a match and put it in his mouth. Then he took the match out of his mouth. It was still burning. "Want to try it." he said. I went over there. "Open your mouth." he said. I opened my mouth. Quentin hit the match with her hand and it went away.

"Goddamn you." Quentin said. "Do you want to get him started. Dont you know he'll beller all day. I'm going to tell Dilsey on you." She went away running.

"Here, kid." he said. "Hey. Come on back. I aint going to fool with him."

Quentin ran on to the house. She went around the kitchen.

"You played hell then, Jack." he said. "Aint you."

"He cant tell what you saying." Luster said. "He deef and dumb."

"Is." he said. "How long's he been that way."

"Been that way thirty-three years today." Luster said. "Born looney. Is you one of them show folks."

"Why." he said.

"I dont ricklick seeing you around here before." Luster said.

"Well, what about it." he said.

"Nothing." Luster said. "I going tonight."

He looked at me.

"You aint the one can play a tune on that saw, is you." Luster said.

"It'll cost you a quarter to find that out." he said. He looked at me. "Why dont they lock him up." he said. "What'd you bring him out here for."

"You aint talking to me." Luster said. "I cant do nothing with him. I just come over here looking for a quarter I lost so I can go to the show tonight. Look like now I ain't going to get to go." Luster looked on the ground. "You aint got no extra quarter, is you." Luster said.

"No." he said. "I aint."

"I reckon I just have to find that other one, then." Luster said. He put his hand in his pocket. "You dont want to buy no golf ball neither, does you." Luster said.

"What kind of ball." he said.

"Golf ball." Luster said. "I dont want but a quarter."

"What for." he said. "What do I want with it."

"I didn't think you did." Luster said. "Come on here, mulehead." he said. "Come on here and watch them knocking that ball. Here. Here something you can play with along with that jimson weed." Luster picked it up and gave it to me. It was bright.

"Where'd you get that." he said. His tie was red in the sun, walking.

"Found it under this here bush." Luster said. "I thought for a minute it was that quarter I lost"

He came and took it.

"Hush." Luster said. "He going to give it back when he done looking at it."

"Agnes Mabel Becky." he said. He looked toward the house.

"Hush." Luster said. "He fixing to give it back."

He gave it to me and I hushed.

"Who come to see her last night." he said.

"I dont know." Luster said. "They comes every night she can climb down that tree. I dont keep no track of them."

"Damn if one of them didn't leave a track." he said. He looked at the house. Then he went and lay down in the swing. "Go away." he said. "Dont bother me."

"Come on here." Luster said. "You done played hell now. Time Miss Quentin get done telling on you."

We went to the fence and looked through the curling flower spaces. Luster hunted in the grass.

"I had it right here." he said. I saw the flag flapping, and the sun slanting on the broad grass.

"They'll be some along soon." Luster said. "There some now, but they going away. Come on and help me look for it."

We went along the fence.

"Hush." Luster said. "How can I make them come over here, if they aint coming. Wait. They'll be some in a minute. Look yonder. Here they come."

I went along the fence, to the gate, where the girls passed with their booksatchels. "You, Benjy." Luster said. "Come back here."

You cant do no good looking through the gate, T. P. said. Miss Caddy done gone long ways away. Done got married and left you. You cant do no good, holding to the gate and crying. She cant hear you.

What is it he wants, T. P. Mother said. Cant you play with him and keep him quiet.

He want to go down yonder and look through the gate, T. P. said.

Well, he cannot do it, Mother said. It's raining. You will just have to play with him and keep him quiet. You, Benjamin.

Aint nothing going to quiet him, T. P. said. He think if he down to the gate, Miss Caddy come back.

Nonsense, Mother said.

I could hear them talking. I went out the door and I couldn't hear them, and I went down to the gate, where the girls passed with their booksatchels. They looked at me, walking fast, with their heads turned. I tried to say, but they went on, and I went along the fence, trying to say, and they went faster. Then they were running and I came to the corner of the fence and I couldn't go any further, and I held to the fence, looking after them and trying to say.

"You, Benjy." T. P. said. "What you doing, slipping out. Dont you know Dilsey whip you."

"You cant do no good, moaning and slobbering through the fence." T. P. said. "You done skeered them chillen. Look at them, walking on the other side of the street."

How did he get out, Father said. Did you leave the gate unlatched when you came in, Jason.

Of course not, Jason said. Dont you know I've got better sense than to do that. Do you think I wanted anything like this to happen. This family is bad enough, God knows. I could have told you, all the time. I reckon you'll send him to Jackson, now. If Mrs Burgess dont shoot him first.

Hush, Father said.

I could have told you, all the time, Jason said.

It was open when I touched it, and I held to it in the twilight. I wasn't crying, and I tried to stop, watching the girls coming along in the twilight. I wasn't crying.

"There he is."

They stopped.

"He cant get out. He wont hurt anybody, anyway. Come on."

"I'm scared to. I'm scared. I'm going to cross the street."

"He cant get out."

I wasn't crying.

"Don't be a 'fraid cat. Come on."

They came on in the twilight. I wasn't crying, and I held to the gate. They came slow.

"I'm scared."

"He wont hurt you. I pass here every day. He just runs along the fence."

They came on. I opened the gate and they stopped, turning. I was trying to say, and I caught her, trying to say, and she screamed and I was trying to say and trying and the bright shapes began to stop and I tried to get out. I tried to get it off of my face, but the bright shapes were going again. They were going up the hill to where it fell away and I tried to cry. But when I breathed in, I couldn't breathe out again to cry, and I tried to keep from falling off the hill and I fell off the hill into the bright, whirling shapes.

Here, loony, Luster said. Here come some. Hush your slobbering and moaning, now.

They came to the flag. He took it out and they hit, then he put the flag back.

"Mister." Luster said.

He looked around. "What." he said.

"Want to buy a golf ball." Luster said.

"Let's see it." he said. He came to the fence and Luster reached the ball through.

"Where'd you get it." he said.

"Found it." Luster said.

"I know that." he said. "Where. In somebody's golf bag."

"I found it laying over here in the yard." Luster said. "I'll take a quarter for it."

"What makes you think it's yours." he said.

"I found it." Luster said.

"Then find yourself another one." he said. He put it in his pocket and went away.

"I got to go to that show tonight." Luster said.

"That so." he said. He went to the table. "Fore, caddie." he said. He hit.

"I'll declare." Luster said. "You fusses when you dont
see them and you fusses when you does. Why cant you
hush. Dont you reckon folks gets tired of listening to
you all the time. Here. You dropped your jimson weed."
He picked it up and gave it back to me. "You needs a
new one. You 'bout wore that one out." We stood at the
fence and watched them.

"That white man hard to get along with." Luster said.
"You see him take my ball." They went on. We went on
along the fence. We came to the garden and we couldn't
go any further. I held to the fence and looked through the
flower spaces. They went away.

"Now you aint got nothing to moan about." Luster
said. "Hush up. I the one got something to moan over,
you aint. Here. Whyn't you hold on to that weed. You be
bellering about it next." He gave me the flower. "Where
you heading now."

Our shadows were on the grass. They got to the trees
before we did. Mine got there first. Then we got there,
and then the shadows were gone. There was a flower in
the bottle. I put the other flower in it.

"Aint you a grown man, now." Luster said. "Playing
with two weeds in a bottle. You know what they going
to do with you when Miss Cahline die. They going to
send you to Jackson, where you belong. Mr Jason say so.
Where you can hold the bars all day long with the rest of
the looneys and slobber. How you like that."

Luster knocked the flowers over with his hand. "That's
what they'll do to you at Jackson when you starts bellering."

I tried to pick up the flowers. Luster picked them up,
and they went away. I began to cry.

"Beller." Luster said. "Beller. You want something to beller about. All right, then. Caddy." he whispered. "Caddy. Beller now. Caddy."

"Luster." Dilsey said from the kitchen.

The flowers came back.

"Hush." Luster said. "Here they is. Look. It's fixed back just like it was at first. Hush, now."

"You, Luster." Dilsey said.

"Yessum." Luster said. "We coming. You done played hell. Get up." He jerked my arm and I got up. We went out of the trees. Our shadows were gone.

"Hush." Luster said. "Look at all them folks watching you. Hush."

"You bring him on here." Dilsey said. She came down the steps.

"What you done to him now." she said.

"Aint done nothing to him." Luster said. "He just started bellering."

"Yes you is." Dilsey said. "You done something to him. Where you been."

"Over yonder under them cedars." Luster said.

"Getting Quentin all riled up." Dilsey said. "Why can't you keep him away from her. Dont you know she dont like him where she at."

"Got as much time for him as I is." Luster said. "He aint none of my uncle."

"Dont you sass me, nigger boy." Dilsey said.

"I aint done nothing to him." Luster said. "He was playing there, and all of a sudden he started bellering."

"Is you been projecking with his graveyard." Dilsey said.

"I aint touched his graveyard." Luster said.

"Dont lie to me, boy." Dilsey said. We went up the steps and into the kitchen. Dilsey opened the firedoor

and drew a chair up in front of it and I sat down. I
hushed.

What you want to get her started for, Dilsey said.
Whyn't you keep him out of there.

He was just looking at the fire, Caddy said. Mother
was telling him his new name. We didn't mean to get
her started.

I knows you didn't, Dilsey said. Him at one end of the
house and her at the other. You let my things alone, now.
Dont you touch nothing till I get back.

"Aint you shamed of yourself." Dilsey said. "Teasing
him." She set the cake on the table.

"I aint been teasing him." Luster said. "He was playing
with that bottle full of dogfennel and all of a sudden he
started up bellering. You heard him."

"You aint done nothing to his flowers." Dilsey said.

"I aint touched his graveyard." Luster said. "What I
want with his truck. I was just hunting for that quarter."

"You lost it, did you." Dilsey said. She lit the candles
on the cake. Some of them were little ones. Some were
big ones cut into little pieces. "I told you to go put it
away. Now I reckon you want me to get you another
one from Frony."

"I got to go to that show, Benjy or no Benjy." Luster
said. "I aint going to follow him around day and night
both."

"You going to do just what he want you to, nigger
boy." Dilsey said. "You hear me."

"Aint I always done it." Luster said. "Dont I always
does what he wants. Dont I, Benjy."

"Then you keep it up." Dilsey said. "Bringing him
in here, bawling and getting her started too. You all go
ahead and eat this cake, now, before Jason come. I
dont want him jumping on me about a cake I bought

with my own money. Me baking a cake here, with him counting every egg that comes into this kitchen. See can you let him alone now, less you dont want to go to that show tonight."

Dilsey went away.

"You cant blow out no candles." Luster said. "Watch me blow them out." He leaned down and puffed his face. The candles went away. I began to cry. "Hush." Luster said. "Here. Look at the fire whiles I cuts this cake."

I could hear the clock, and I could hear Caddy standing behind me, and I could hear the roof. It's still raining, Caddy said. I hate rain. I hate everything. And then her head came into my lap and she was crying, holding me, and I began to cry. Then I looked at the fire again and the bright, smooth shapes went again. I could hear the clock and the roof and Caddy.

I ate some cake. Luster's hand came and took another piece. I could hear him eating. I looked at the fire.

A long piece of wire came across my shoulder. It went to the door, and then the fire went away. I began to cry.

"What you howling for now." Luster said. "Look there." The fire was there. I hushed. "Cant you set and look at the fire and be quiet like mammy told you." Luster said. "You ought to be ashamed of yourself. Here. Here's you some more cake."

"What you done to him now." Dilsey said. "Cant you never let him alone."

"I was just trying to get him to hush up and not sturb Miss Cahline." Luster said. "Something got him started again."

"And I know what that something name." Dilsey said. "I'm going to get Versh to take a stick to you when he comes home. You just trying yourself. You been doing it all day. Did you take him down to the branch."

"Nome." Luster said. "We been right here in this yard all day, like you said."

His hand came for another piece of cake. Dilsey hit his hand. "Reach it again, and I chop it right off with this here butcher knife." Dilsey said. "I bet he aint had one piece of it."

"Yes he is." Luster said. "He already had twice as much as me. Ask him if he aint."

"Reach hit one more time." Dilsey said. "Just reach it."

That's right, Dilsey said. I reckon it'll be my time to cry next. Reckon Maury going to let me cry on him a while, too.

His name's Benjy now, Caddy said.

How come it is, Dilsey said. He aint wore out the name he was born with yet, is he.

Benjamin came out of the bible, Caddy said. It's a better name for him than Maury was.

How come it is, Dilsey said.

Mother says it is, Caddy said.

Huh, Dilsey said. Name aint going to help him. Hurt him, neither. Folks dont have no luck, changing names. My name been Dilsey since fore I could remember and it be Dilsey when they's long forgot me.

How will they know it's Dilsey, when it's long forgot, Dilsey, Caddy said.

It'll be in the Book, honey, Dilsey said. Writ out.

Can you read it, Caddy said.

Wont have to, Dilsey said. They'll read it for me. All I got to do is say Ise here.

The long wire came across my shoulder, and the fire went away. I began to cry.

Dilsey and Luster fought.

"I seen you." Dilsey said. "Oho, I seen you." She dragged Luster out of the corner, shaking him. "Wasn't nothing bothering him, was they. You just wait till your pappy come home. I wish I was young like I use to be, I'd tear them years right off your head. I good mind to lock you up in that cellar and not let you go to that show tonight, I sho is."

"Ow, mammy." Luster said. "Ow, mammy."

I put my hand out to where the fire had been.

"Catch him." Dilsey said. "Catch him back."

My hand jerked back and I put it in my mouth and Dilsey caught me. I could still hear the clock between my voice. Dilsey reached back and hit Luster on the head. My voice was going loud every time.

"Get that soda." Dilsey said. She took my hand out of my mouth. My voice went louder then and my hand tried to go back to my mouth, but Dilsey held it. My voice went loud. She sprinkled soda on my hand.

"Look in the pantry and tear a piece off of that rag hanging on the nail." she said. "Hush, now. You dont want to make your ma sick again, does you. Here, look at the fire. Dilsey make your hand stop hurting in just a minute. Look at the fire." She opened the fire door. I looked at the fire, but my hand didn't stop and I didn't stop. My hand was trying to go to my mouth but Dilsey held it.

She wrapped the cloth around it. Mother said,

"What is it now. Cant I even be sick in peace. Do I have to get up out of bed to come down to him, with two grown negroes to take care of him."

"He all right now." Dilsey said. "He going to quit. He just burnt his hand a little."

"With two grown negroes, you must bring him into the house, bawling." Mother said. "You got him started on purpose, because you know I'm sick." She came and stood by me. "Hush." she said. "Right this minute. Did you give him this cake."

"I bought it." Dilsey said. "It never come out of Jason's pantry. I fixed him some birthday."

"Do you want to poison him with that cheap store cake." Mother said. "Is that what you are trying to do. Am I never to have one minute's peace."

"You go on back up stairs and lay down." Dilsey said. "It'll quit smarting him in a minute now, and he'll hush. Come on, now."

"And leave him down here for you all to do something else to." Mother said. "How can I lie there, with him bawling down here. Benjamin. Hush this minute."

"They aint nowhere else to take him." Dilsey said. "We aint got the room we use to have. He cant stay out in the yard, crying where all the neighbors can see him."

"I know, I know." Mother said. "It's all my fault. I'll be gone soon, and you and Jason will both get along better." She began to cry.

"You hush that, now." Dilsey said. "You'll get yourself down again. You come on back up stairs. Luster going to take him to the liberry and play with him till I get his supper done."

Dilsey and Mother went out.

"Hush up." Luster said. "You hush up. You want me to burn your other hand for you. You aint hurt. Hush up."

"Here." Dilsey said. "Stop crying, now." She gave me the slipper, and I hushed. "Take him to the liberry." she said. "And if I hear him again, I going to whip you myself."

We went to the library. Luster turned on the light. The windows went black, and the dark tall place on the wall came and I went and touched it. It was like a door, only it wasn't a door.

The fire came behind me and I went to the fire and sat on the floor, holding the slipper. The fire went higher. It went onto the cushion in Mother's chair.

"Hush up." Luster said. "Cant you never get done for a while. Here I done built you a fire, and you wont even look at it."

Your name is Benjy. Caddy said. Do you hear. Benjy. Benjy.

Dont tell him that, Mother said. Bring him here.

Caddy lifted me under the arms.

Get up, Mau—— I mean Benjy, she said.

Dont try to carry him, Mother said. Cant you lead him over here. Is that too much for you to think of.

I can carry him, Caddy said. "Let me carry him up, Dilsey."

"Go on, Minute." Dilsey said. "You aint big enough to tote a flea. You go on and be quiet, like Mr Jason said."

There was a light at the top of the stairs. Father was there, in his shirt sleeves. The way he looked said Hush. Caddy whispered,

"Is Mother sick."

Versh set me down and we went into Mother's room. There was a fire. It was rising and falling on the walls. There was another fire in the mirror. I could smell the sickness. It was a cloth folded on Mother's head. Her hair was on the pillow. The fire didn't reach it, but it shone on her hand, where her rings were jumping.

"Come and tell Mother goodnight." Caddy said. We went to the bed. The fire went out of the mirror. Father got up from the bed and lifted me up and Mother put her hand on my head.

"What time is it." Mother said. Her eyes were closed.

"Ten minutes to seven." Father said.

"It's too early for him to go to bed." Mother said. "He'll wake up at daybreak, and I simply cannot bear another day like today."

"There, there." Father said. He touched Mother's face.

"I know I'm nothing but a burden to you." Mother said. "But I'll be gone soon. Then you will be rid of my bothering."

"Hush." Father said. "I'll take him downstairs awhile." He took me up. "Come on, old fellow. Let's go downstairs awhile. We'll have to be quiet while Quentin is studying, now."

Caddy went and leaned her face over the bed and Mother's hand came into the firelight. Her rings jumped on Caddy's back.

Mother's sick, Father said. Dilsey will put you to bed. Where's Quentin.

Versh getting him, Dilsey said.

Father stood and watched us go past. We could hear Mother in her room. Caddy said "Hush." Jason was still climbing the stairs. He had his hands in his pockets.

"You all must be good tonight." Father said. "And be quiet, so you wont disturb Mother."

"We'll be quiet." Caddy said. "You must be quiet now, Jason." she said. We tiptoed.

We could hear the roof. I could see the fire in the mirror too. Caddy lifted me again.

"Come on, now." she said. "Then you can come back to the fire. Hush, now."

"Candace." Mother said.

"Hush, Benjy." Caddy said. "Mother wants you a minute. Like a good boy. Then you can come back Benjy."

Caddy let me down, and I hushed.

"Let him stay here, Mother. When he's through look-ing at the fire, then you can tell him."

"Candace." Mother said. Caddy stooped and lifted me. We staggered. "Candace." Mother said.

"Hush." Caddy said. "You can still see it. Hush.'

"Bring him here." Mother said. "He's too big for you to carry. You must stop trying. You'll injure your back. All of our women have prided themselves on their car-riage. Do you want to look like a washer-woman."

"He's not too heavy." Caddy said. "I can carry him."

"Well, I dont want him carried, then." Mother said. "A five year old child. No, no. Not in my lap. Let him stand up."

"If you'll hold him, he'll stop." Caddy said. "Hush." she said. "You can go right back. Here. Here's your cushion. See."

"Dont, Candace." Mother said.

"Let him look at it and he'll be quiet." Caddy said. "Hold up just a minute while I slip it out. There, Benjy. Look."

I looked at it and hushed.

"You humour him too much." Mother said. "You and your father both. You dont realise that I am the one who has to pay for it. Damuddy spoiled Jason that way and it took him two years to outgrow it, and I am not strong enough to go through the same thing with Benjamin."

"You dont need to bother with him." Caddy said. "I like to take care of him. Dont I, Benjy."

"Candace." Mother said. "I told you not to call him that. It was bad enough when your father insisted on calling you by that silly nickname, and I will not have him called by one. Nicknames are vulgar. Only common people use them. Benjamin." she said

"Look at me." Mother said.

"Benjamin." she said. She took my face in her hands and turned it to hers.

"Benjamin." she said. "Take that cushion away, Candace."

"He'll cry." Caddy said.

"Take that cushion away, like I told you." Mother said. "He must learn to mind."

The cushion went away.

"Hush, Benjy." Caddy said.

"You go over there and sit down." Mother said. "Benjamin." She held my face to hers.

"Stop that." she said. "Stop it."

But I didn't stop and Mother caught me in her arms and began to cry, and I cried. Then the cushion came back and Caddy held it above Mother's head. She drew Mother back in the chair and Mother lay crying against the red and yellow cushion.

"Hush, Mother." Caddy said. "You go upstairs and lay down, so you can be sick. I'll go get Dilsey." She led me to the fire and I looked at the bright, smooth shapes. I could hear the fire and the roof.

Father took me up. He smelled like rain.

"Well, Benjy." he said. "Have you been a good boy today."

Caddy and Jason were fighting in the mirror.

"You, Caddy." Father said.

They fought. Jason began to cry.

"Caddy." Father said. Jason was crying. He wasn't fighting any more, but we could see Caddy fighting in the mirror and Father put me down and went into the mirror and fought too. He lifted Caddy up. She fought. Jason lay on the floor, crying. He had the scissors in his hand. Father held Caddy.

"He cut up all Benjy's dolls." Caddy said. "I'll slit his gizzle."

"Candace." Father said.

"I will." Caddy said. "I will." She fought. Father held her. She kicked at Jason. He rolled into the corner, out of the mirror. Father brought Caddy to the fire. They were all out of the mirror. Only the fire was in it. Like the fire was in a door.

"Stop that." Father said. "Do you want to make Mother sick in her room."

Caddy stopped. "He cut up all the dolls Mau—Benjy and I made." Caddy said. "He did it just for meanness."

"I didn't." Jason said. He was sitting up, crying. "I didn't know they were his. I just thought they were some old papers."

"You couldn't help but know." Caddy said. "You did it just."

"Hush." Father said. "Jason." he said.

"I'll make you some more tomorrow." Caddy said. "We'll make a lot of them. Here, you can look at the cushion, too."

Jason came in.

I kept telling you to hush, Luster said.

What's the matter now, Jason said.

"He just trying hisself." Luster said. "That the way he been going on all day."

"Why dont you let him alone, then." Jason said. "If you cant keep him quiet, you'll have to take him out to the kitchen. The rest of us cant shut ourselves up in a room like Mother does."

"Mammy say keep him out the kitchen till she get supper." Luster said.

"Then play with him and keep him quiet." Jason said.

"Do I have to work all day and then come home to a mad house." He opened the paper and read it.

You can look at the fire and the mirror and the cushion too, Caddy said. You wont have to wait until supper to look at the cushion, now. We could hear the roof. We could hear Jason too, crying loud beyond the wall.

Dilsey said, "You come, Jason. You letting him alone, is you."

"Yessum." Luster said.

"Where Quentin." Dilsey said. "Supper near bout ready."

"I dont know'm." Luster said. "I aint seen her."

Dilsey went away. "Quentin." she said in the hall. "Quentin. Supper ready."

We could hear the roof. Quentin smelled like rain, too.

What did Jason do, he said.

He cut up all Benjy's dolls, Caddy said.

Mother said to not call him Benjy, Quentin said. He sat on the rug by us. I wish it wouldn't rain, he said. You cant do anything.

You've been in a fight, Caddy said. Haven't you.

It wasn't much, Quentin said.

You can tell it, Caddy said. Father'll see it.

I dont care, Quentin said. I wish it wouldn't rain.

Quentin said, "Didn't Dilsey say supper was ready."

"Yessum." Luster said. Jason looked at Quentin. Then he read the paper again. Quentin came in. "She say it bout ready." Luster said. Quentin jumped down in Mother's chair. Luster said,

"Mr Jason."

"What." Jason said.

"Let me have two bits." Luster said.

"What for." Jason said.

"To go to the show tonight." Luster said.

"I thought Dilsey was going to get a quarter from Frony for you." Jason said.

"She did." Luster said. "I lost it. Me and Benjy hunted all day for that quarter. You can ask him."

"Then borrow one from him." Jason said. "I have to work for mine." He read the paper. Quentin looked at the fire. The fire was in her eyes and on her mouth. Her mouth was red.

"I tried to keep him away from there." Luster said.

"Shut your mouth." Quentin said. Jason looked at her.

"What did I tell you I was going to do if I saw you with that show fellow again." he said. Quentin looked at the fire. "Did you hear me." Jason said.

"I heard you." Quentin said. "Why dont you do it, then."

"Dont you worry." Jason said.

"I'm not." Quentin said. Jason read the paper again.

I could hear the roof. Father leaned forward and looked at Quentin.

Hello, he said. Who won.

"Nobody." Quentin said. "They stopped us. Teachers."

"Who was it." Father said. "Will you tell."

"It was all right." Quentin said. "He was as big as me."

"That's good." Father said. "Can you tell what it was about."

"It wasn't anything." Quentin said. "He said he would put a frog in her desk and she wouldn't dare to whip him."

"Oh." Father said. "She. And then what."

"Yes, sir." Quentin said. "And then I kind of hit him."

We could hear the roof and the fire, and a snuffling outside the door.

"Where was he going to get a frog in November." Father said.

"I dont know, sir." Quentin said.

We could hear them.

"Jason." Father said. We could hear Jason.

"Jason." Father said. "Come in here and stop that."

We could hear the roof and the fire and Jason.

"Stop that, now." Father said. "Do you want me to whip you again." Father lifted Jason up into the chair by him. Jason snuffled. We could hear the fire and the roof. Jason snuffled a little louder.

"One more time." Father said. We could hear the fire and the roof.

Dilsey said, All right. You all can come on to supper.

Versh smelled like rain. He smelled like a dog, too. We could hear the fire and the roof.

We could hear Caddy walking fast. Father and Mother looked at the door. Caddy passed it, walking fast. She didn't look. She walked fast.

"Candace." Mother said. Caddy stopped walking.

"Yes, Mother." she said.

"Hush, Caroline." Father said.

"Come here." Mother said.

"Hush, Caroline." Father said. "Let her alone."

Caddy came to the door and stood there, looking at Father and Mother. Her eyes flew at me, and away. I began to cry. It went loud and I got up. Caddy came in and stood with her back to the wall, looking at me. I went toward her, crying, and she shrank against the wall and I saw her eyes and I cried louder and pulled at her dress. She put her hands out but I pulled at her dress. Her eyes ran.

Versh said, Your name Benjamin now. You know how

*come your name Benjamin now. They making a bluegum
out of you. Mammy say in old time your granpa changed
nigger's name, and he turn preacher, and when they look
at him, he bluegum too. Didn't use to be bluegum,
neither. And when family woman look him in the eye in
the full of the moon, chile born bluegum. And one evening, when they was about a dozen them bluegum chillen
running round the place, he never come home. Possum
hunters found him in the woods, et clean. And you
know who et him. Them bluegum chillen did.*

We were in the hall. Caddy was still looking at me.
Her hand was against her mouth and I saw her eyes
and I cried. We went up the stairs. She stopped again,
against the wall, looking at me and I cried and she
went on and I came on, crying, and she shrank against
the wall, looking at me. She opened the door to her
room, but I pulled at her dress and we went to the bathroom and she stood against the door, looking at me.
Then she put her arm across her face and I pushed at
her, crying.

*What are you doing to him, Jason said. Why cant you
let him alone.*

*I aint touching him, Luster said. He been doing this
way all day long. He needs whipping.*

*He needs to be sent to Jackson, Quentin said. How
can anybody live in a house like this.*

*If you dont like it, young lady, you'd better get out,
Jason said.*

I'm going to, Quentin said. Dont you worry.

Versh said, "You move back some, so I can dry my
legs off." He shoved me back a little. "Dont you start
bellering, now. You can still see it. That's all you have to
do. You aint had to be out in the rain like I is. You's born

lucky and dont know it." He lay on his back before the fire.

"You know how come your name Benjamin now." Versh said. "Your mamma too proud for you. What mammy say."

"You be still there and let me dry my legs off." Versh said. "Or you know what I'll do. I'll skin your rinktum."

We could hear the fire and the roof and Versh.

Versh got up quick and jerked his legs back. Father said, "All right, Versh."

"I'll feed him tonight." Caddy said. "Sometimes he cries when Versh feeds him."

"Take this tray up," Dilsey said. "And hurry back and feed Benjy."

"Dont you want Caddy to feed you." Caddy said.

Has he got to keep that old dirty slipper on the table, Quentin said. *Why dont you feed him in the kitchen. It's like eating with a pig.*

If you dont like the way we eat, you'd better not come to the table, Jason said.

Steam came off of Roskus. He was sitting in front of the stove. The oven door was open and Roskus had his feet in it. Steam came off the bowl. Caddy put the spoon into my mouth easy. There was a black spot on the inside of the bowl.

Now, now, Dilsey said. He aint going to bother you no more.

It got down below the mark. Then the bowl was empty. It went away. "He's hungry tonight." Caddy said. The bowl came back. I couldn't see the spot. Then I could. "He's starved, tonight." Caddy said. "Look how much he's eaten."

Yes he will, Quentin said. You all send him out to spy on me. I hate this house. I'm going to run away.

Roskus said, "It going to rain all night."

You've been running a long time, not to 've got any further off than mealtime, Jason said.

See if I dont, Quentin said.

"Then I dont know what I going to do." Dilsey said. "It caught me in the hip so bad now I cant scarcely move. Climbing them stairs all evening."

Oh, I wouldn't be surprised, Jason said. I wouldn't be surprised at anything you'd do.

Quentin threw her napkin on the table.

Hush your mouth, Jason, Dilsey said. She went and put her arm around Quentin. Sit down, honey, Dilsey said. He ought to be shamed of hisself, throwing what aint your fault up to you.

"She sulling again, is she." Roskus said.

"Hush your mouth." Dilsey said.

Quentin pushed Dilsey away. She looked at Jason. Her mouth was red. She picked up her glass of water and swung her arm back, looking at Jason. Dilsey caught her arm. They fought. The glass broke on the table, and the water ran into the table. Quentin was running.

"Mother's sick again." Caddy said.

"Sho she is." Dilsey said. "Weather like this make anybody sick. When you going to get done eating, boy."

Goddamn you, Quentin said. Goddamn you. We could hear her running on the stairs. We went to the library.

Caddy gave me the cushion, and I could look at the cushion and the mirror and the fire.

"We must be quiet while Quentin's studying." Father said. "What are you doing, Jason."

"Nothing." Jason said.

"Suppose you come over here to do it, then." Fathe said.

Jason came out of the corner.

"What are you chewing." Father said.

"Nothing." Jason said.

"He's chewing paper again." Caddy said.

"Come here, Jason." Father said.

Jason threw into the fire. It hissed, uncurled, turning black. Then it was gray. Then it was gone. Caddy and Father and Jason were in Mother's chair. Jason's eyes were puffed shut and his mouth moved, like tasting. Caddy's head was on Father's shoulder. Her hair was like fire, and little points of fire were in her eyes, and I went and Father lifted me into the chair too, and Caddy held me. She smelled like trees.

She smelled like trees. In the corner it was dark, but I could see the window. I squatted there, holding the slipper. I couldn't see it, but my hands saw it, and I could hear it getting night, and my hands saw the slipper but I couldn't see myself, but my hands could see the slipper, and I squatted there, hearing it getting dark.

Here you is, Luster said. Look what I got. He showed it to me. You know where I got it. Miss Quentin gave it to me. I knowed they couldn't keep me out. What you doing, off in here. I thought you done slipped back out doors. Aint you done enough moaning and slobbering today, without hiding off in this here empty room, mumbling and taking on. Come on here to bed, so I can get up there before it starts. I cant fool with you all night tonight. Just let them horns toot the first toot and I done gone.

We didn't go to our room.

"This is where we have the measles." Caddy said. "Why do we have to sleep in here tonight."

"What you care where you sleep." Dilsey said. She shut the door and sat down and began to undress me. Jason began to cry. "Hush." Dilsey said.

"I want to sleep with Damuddy." Jason said.

"She's sick." Caddy said. "You can sleep with her when she gets well. Cant he, Dilsey."

"Hush, now." Dilsey said. Jason hushed.

"Our nighties are here, and everything." Caddy said. "It's like moving."

"And you better get into them." Dilsey said. "You be unbuttoning Jason."

Caddy unbuttoned Jason. He began to cry.

"You want to get whipped." Dilsey said. Jason hushed.

Quentin, Mother said in the hall.

What, Quentin said beyond the wall. We heard Mother lock the door. She looked in our door and came in and stooped over the bed and kissed me on the forehead.

When you get him to bed, go and ask Dilsey if she objects to my having a hot water bottle, Mother said. Tell her that if she does, I'll try to get along without it. Tell her I just want to know.

Yessum, Luster said. Come on. Get your pants off.

Quentin and Versh came in. Quentin had his face turned away. "What are you crying for." Caddy said.

"Hush." Dilsey said. "You all get undressed, now. You can go on home, Versh."

I got undressed and I looked at myself, and I began to cry. Hush, Luster said. Looking for them aint going to do no good. They're gone. You keep on like this, and we aint going have you no more birthday. He put my gown on. I hushed, and then Luster stopped, his head toward the window. Then he went to the window and looked out. He came back and took my arm. Here she come, he said. Be quiet, now. We went to the window and looked out. It came out of Quentin's window and climbed across into the tree. We watched the tree shaking. The shaking went down the tree, then it came out and we watched it go away across the grass. Then we couldn't see it. Come on, Luster said. There now. Hear them horns. You get in that bed while my foots behaves.

There were two beds. Quentin got in the other one. He turned his face to the wall. Dilsey put Jason in with him. Caddy took her dress off.

"Just look at your drawers." Dilsey said. "You better be glad your ma aint seen you."

"I already told on her." Jason said.

"I bound you would." Dilsey said.

"And see what you got by it." Caddy said. "Tattletale."

"What did I get by it." Jason said.

"Whyn't you get your nightie on." Dilsey said. She went and helped Caddy take off her bodice and drawers. "Just look at you." Dilsey said. She wadded the drawers and scrubbed Caddy behind with them. "It done soaked clean through onto you." she said. "But you wont get no bath this night. Here." She put Caddy's nightie on her and Caddy climbed into the bed and Dilsey went to the door and stood with her hand on the light. "You all be quiet now, you hear." she said.

"All right." Caddy said. "Mother's not coming in to-night." she said. "So we still have to mind me."

"Yes." Dilsey said. "Go to sleep, now."

"Mother's sick." Caddy said. "She and Damuddy are both sick."

"Hush." Dilsey said. "You go to sleep."

The room went black, except the door. Then the door went black. Caddy said, "Hush, Maury," putting her hand on me. So I stayed hushed. We could hear us. We could hear the dark.

It went away, and Father looked at us. He looked at Quentin and Jason, then he came and kissed Caddy and put his hand on my head.

"Is Mother very sick." Caddy said.

"No." Father said. "Are you going to take good care of Maury."

"Yes." Caddy said.

Father went to the door and looked at us again. Then the dark came back, and he stood black in the door, and then the door turned black again. Caddy held me and I could hear us all, and the darkness, and something I could smell. And then I could see the windows, where the trees were buzzing. Then the dark began to go in smooth, bright shapes, like it always does, even when Caddy says that I have been asleep.

JUNE

2

1910

WHEN THE SHADOW OF THE SASH APPEARED ON THE curtains it was between seven and eight oclock and then I was in time again, hearing the watch. It was Grandfather's and when Father gave it to me he said, Quentin, I give you the mausoleum of all hope and desire; it's rather excrutiating-ly apt that you will use it to gain the reducto absurdum of all human experience which can fit your individual needs no better than it fitted his or his father's. I give it to you not that you may remember time, but that you might forget it now and then for a moment and not spend all your breath trying to conquer it. Because no battle is ever won he said. They are not even fought. The field only reveals to man his own folly and despair, and victory is an illusion of philosophers and fools.

It was propped against the collar box and I lay listening to it. Hearing it, that is. I dont suppose anybody ever deliberately listens to a watch or a clock. You dont have to. You can be oblivious to the sound for a long while, then in a second of ticking it can create in the mind unbroken the long diminishing parade of time you didn't hear. Like Father said down the long and lonely light-rays you might see Jesus walking, like. And the good Saint Francis that said Little Sister Death, that never had a sister.

Through the wall I heard Shreve's bed-springs and then his slippers on the floor hishing. I got up and went to the dresser and slid my hand along it and touched the watch and turned it face-down and went back to bed. But the shadow of the sash was still there and I had learned to tell almost to the minute, so I'd have to turn my back to it, feeling the eyes animals used to have in the back of their heads when it was on top, itching. It's always the idle habits you acquire which you will regret. Father said that. That Christ was not crucified: he was worn away by a minute clicking of little wheels. That had no sister.

And so as soon as I knew I couldn't see it, I began to wonder what time it was. Father said that constant speculation regarding the position of mechanical hands on an arbitrary dial which is a symptom of mind-function. Excrement Father said like sweating. And I saying All right. Wonder. Go on and wonder.

If it had been cloudy I could have looked at the window, thinking what he said about idle habits. Thinking it would be nice for them down at New London if the weather held up like this. Why shouldn't it? The month of brides, the voice that breathed *She ran right out of the mirror, out of the banked scent. Roses. Roses. Mr and Mrs Jason Richmond Compson announce the marriage of.* Roses. Not virgins like dogwood, milkweed. I said I have committed incest, Father I said. Roses. Cunning and serene. If you attend Harvard one year, but dont see the boat-race, there should be a refund. Let Jason have it. Give Jason a year at Harvard.

Shreve stood in the door, putting his collar on, his glasses glinting rosily, as though he had washed them with his face. "You taking a cut this morning?"

"Is it that late?"

He looked at his watch. "Bell in two minutes."

"I didn't know it was that late." He was still looking at the watch, his mouth shaping. "I'll have to hustle. I cant stand another cut. The dean told me last week—" He put the watch back into his pocket. Then I quit talking.

"You'd better slip on your pants and run," he said. He went out.

I got up and moved about, listening to him through the wall. He entered the sitting-room, toward the door.

"Aren't you ready yet?"

"Not yet. Run along. I'll make it."

He went out. The door closed. His feet went down the corridor. Then I could hear the watch again. I quit moving around and went to the window and drew the curtains aside and watched them running for chapel, the same ones fighting the same heaving coat-sleeves, the same books and flapping collars flushing past like debris on a flood, and Spoade. Calling Shreve my husband. Ah let him alone, Shreve said, if he's got better sense than to chase after the little dirty sluts, whose business. In the South you are ashamed of being a virgin. Boys. Men. They lie about it. Because it means less to women, Father said. He said it was men invented virginity not women. Father said it's like death: only a state in which the others are left and I said, But to believe it doesn't matter and he said, That's what's so sad about anything: not only virginity, and I said, Why couldn't it have been me and not her who is unvirgin and he said, That's why that's sad too; nothing is even worth the changing of it.

and Shreve said if he's got better sense than to chase after the little dirty sluts and I said Did you ever have a sister? Did you? Did you?

Spoade was in the middle of them like a terrapin in a street full of scuttering dead leaves, his collar about his ears, moving at his customary unhurried walk. He was from South Carolina, a senior. It was his club's boast that he never ran for chapel and had never got there on time and had never been absent in four years and had never made either chapel or first lecture with a shirt on his back and socks on his feet. About ten oclock he'd come in Thompson's, get two cups of coffee, sit down and take his socks out of his pocket and remove his shoes and put them on while the coffee cooled. About noon you'd see him with a shirt and collar on, like anybody else. The others passed him running, but he never increased his pace at all. After a while the quad was empty.

A sparrow slanted across the sunlight, onto the window ledge, and cocked his head at me. His eye was round and bright. First he'd watch me with one eye, then flick! and it would be the other one, his throat pumping faster than any pulse. The hour began to strike. The sparrow quit swapping eyes and watched me steadily with the same one until the chimes ceased, as if he were listening too. Then he flicked off the ledge and was gone.

It was a while before the last stroke ceased vibrating. It stayed in the air, more felt than heard, for a long time. Like all the bells that ever rang still ringing in the long dying light-rays and Jesus and Saint Francis talking about his sister. Because if it were just to hell; if that were all of it. Finished. If things just finished themselves. Nobody else there but her and me. If we could just have done something so dreadful that they would have fled hell except us. *I have committed incest I said Father it*

was I it was not Dalton Ames And when he put Dalton
Ames. Dalton Ames. Dalton Ames. When he put the
pistol in my hand I didn't. That's why I didn't. He would
be there and she would and I would. Dalton Ames. Dalton Ames. Dalton Ames. If we could have just done something so dreadful and Father said That's sad too, people
cannot do anything that dreadful they cannot do anything very dreadful at all they cannot even remember tomorrow what seemed dreadful today and I said, You can
shirk all things and he said, Ah can you. And I will look
down and see my murmuring bones and the deep water
like wind, like a roof of wind, and after a long time they
cannot distinguish even bones upon the lonely and invio-
late sand. Until on the Day when He says Rise only the
flatiron would come floating up. It's not when you realise
that nothing can help you—religion, pride, anything—
it's when you realise that you dont need any aid. Dalton
Ames. Dalton Ames. Dalton Ames. If I could have been
his mother lying with open body lifted laughing, holding
his father with my hand refraining, seeing, watching him
die before he lived. *One minute she was standing in the
door*

I went to the dresser and took up the watch, with the
face still down. I tapped the crystal on the corner of the
dresser and caught the fragments of glass in my hand
and put them into the ashtray and twisted the hands off
and put them in the tray. The watch ticked on. I turned
the face up, the blank dial with little wheels clicking and
clicking behind it, not knowing any better. Jesus walking
on Galilee and Washington not telling lies. Father
brought back a watch-charm from the Saint Louis Fair
to Jason: a tiny opera glass into which you squinted with
one eye and saw a skyscraper, a ferris wheel all spidery,
Niagara Falls on a pinhead. There was a red smear on

the dial. When I saw it my thumb began to smart. I put the watch down and went into Shreve's room and got the iodine and painted the cut. I cleaned the rest of the glass out of the rim with the towel.

I laid out two suits of underwear, with socks, shirts, collars and ties, and packed my trunk. I put in everything except my new suit and an old one and two pairs of shoes and two hats, and my books. I carried the books into the sitting-room and stacked them on the table, the ones I had brought from home and the ones *Father said it used to be a gentleman was known by his books; nowadays he is known by the ones he has not returned* and locked the trunk and addressed it. The quarter hour sounded. I stopped and listened to it until the chimes ceased.

I bathed and shaved. The water made my finger smart a little, so I painted it again. I put on my new suit and put my watch on and packed the other suit and the accessories and my razor and brushes in my hand bag, and wrapped the trunk key into a sheet of paper and put it in an envelope and addressed it to Father, and wrote the two notes and sealed them.

The shadow hadn't quite cleared the stoop. I stopped inside the door, watching the shadow move. It moved almost perceptibly, creeping back inside the door, driving the shadow back into the door. *Only she was running already when I heard it. In the mirror she was running before I knew what it was. That quick, her train caught up over her arm she ran out of the mirror like a cloud, her veil swirling in long glints her heels brittle and fast clutching her dress onto her shoulder with the other hand, running out of the mirror the smells roses roses the voice that breathed o'er Eden. Then she was across the porch I couldn't hear her heels then in the moonlight like a cloud, the floating shadow of the veil running across the grass, into the bellowing. She ran out of her dress, clutching her bridal, running into the bellowing where T. P. in the dew Whooey Sassprilluh Benjy under the box bellowing. Father had a V-shaped silver cuirass on his running chest*

Shreve said, "Well, you didn't. . . . Is it a wedding or a wake?"

"I couldn't make it," I said.

"Not with all that primping. What's the matter? You think this was Sunday?"

"I reckon the police wont get me for wearing my new suit one time," I said.

"I was thinking about the Square students. Have you got too proud to attend classes too?"

"I'm going to eat first." The shadow on the stoop was gone. I stepped into sunlight, finding my shadow again. I walked down the steps just ahead of it. The half hour went. Then the chimes ceased and died away.

Deacon wasn't at the postoffice either. I stamped the two envelopes and mailed the one to Father and put Shreve's in my inside pocket, and then I remembered where I had last seen the Deacon. It was on Decoration Day, in a G. A. R. uniform, in the middle of the parade. If you waited long enough on any corner you would see him in whatever parade came along. The one before was on Columbus' or Garibaldi's or somebody's birthday. He was in the Street Sweeper's section, in a stovepipe hat, carrying a two inch Italian flag, smoking a cigar among the brooms and scoops. But the last time was the G. A. R. one, because Shreve said:

"There now. Just look at what your grandpa did to that poor old nigger."

"Yes," I said, "Now he can spend day after day march-

ing in parades. If it hadn't been for my grandfather, he'd
have to work like whitefolks."

I didn't see him anywhere. But I never knew even a
working nigger that you could find when you wanted
him, let alone one that lived off the fat of the land. A car
came along. I went over to town and went to Parker's
and had a good breakfast. While I was eating I heard a
clock strike the hour. But then I suppose it takes at least
one hour to lose time in, who has been longer than his-
tory getting into the mechanical progression of it.

When I finished breakfast I bought a cigar. The girl
said a fifty cent one was the best, so I took one and lit it
and went out to the street. I stood there and took a couple of puffs, then I held it in my hand and went on toward the corner. I passed a jeweller's window, but I
looked away in time. At the corner two bootblacks
caught me, one on either side, shrill and raucous, like
blackbirds. I gave the cigar to one of them, and the other
one a nickel. Then they let me alone. The one with the
cigar was trying to sell it to the other for the nickel.

There was a clock, high up in the sun, and I thought
about how, when you dont want to do a thing, your
body will try to trick you into doing it, sort of unawares.
I could feel the muscles in the back of my neck, and
then I could hear my watch ticking away in my pocket
and after a while I had all the other sounds shut away,
leaving only the watch in my pocket. I turned back up
the street, to the window. He was working at the table
behind the window. He was going bald. There was a
glass in his eye—a metal tube screwed into his face. I
went in.

The place was full of ticking, like crickets in September
grass, and I could hear a big clock on the wall above his
head. He looked up, his eye big and blurred and rushing

beyond the glass. I took mine out and handed it to him.

"I broke my watch."

He flipped it over in his hand. "I should say you have. You must have stepped on it."

"Yes, sir. I knocked it off the dresser and stepped on it in the dark. It's still running though."

He pried the back open and squinted into it. "Seems to be all right. I cant tell until I go over it, though. I'll go into it this afternoon."

"I'll bring it back later," I said. "Would you mind telling me if any of those watches in the window are right?"

He held my watch on his palm and looked up at me with his blurred rushing eye.

"I made a bet with a fellow," I said, "And I forgot my glasses this morning."

"Why, all right," he said. He laid the watch down and half rose on his stool and looked over the barrier. Then he glanced up at the wall. "It's twen—"

"Dont tell me," I said, "please sir. Just tell me if any of them are right."

He looked at me again. He sat back on the stool and pushed the glass up onto his forehead. It left a red circle around his eye and when it was gone his whole face looked naked. "What're you celebrating today?" he said. "That boat race aint until next week, is it?"

"No, sir. This is just a private celebration. Birthday. Are any of them right?"

"No. But they haven't been regulated and set yet. If you're thinking of buying one of them—"

"No, sir. I dont need a watch. We have a clock in our sitting room. I'll have this one fixed when I do." I reached my hand.

"Better leave it now."

"I'll bring it back later." He gave me the watch. I put

it in my pocket. I couldn't hear it now, above all the others. "I'm much obliged to you. I hope I haven't taken up your time."

"That's all right. Bring it in when you are ready. And you better put off this celebration until after we win that boat race."

"Yes, sir. I reckon I had."

I went out, shutting the door upon the ticking. I looked back into the window. He was watching me across the barrier. There were about a dozen watches in the window, a dozen different hours and each with the same assertive and contradictory assurance that mine had, without any hands at all. Contradicting one another. I could hear mine, ticking away inside my pocket, even though nobody could see it, even though it could tell nothing if anyone could.

And so I told myself to take that one. Because Father said clocks slay time. He said time is dead as long as it is being clicked off by little wheels; only when the clock stops does time come to life. The hands were extended, slightly off the horizontal at a faint angle, like a gull tilting into the wind. Holding all I used to be sorry about like the new moon holding water, niggers say. The jeweller was working again, bent over his bench, the tube tunnelled into his face. His hair was parted in the center. The part ran up into the bald spot, like a drained marsh in December.

I saw the hardware store from across the street. I didn't know you bought flat-irons by the pound.

The clerk said, "These weigh ten pounds." Only they were bigger than I thought. So I got two six-pound little ones, because they would look like a pair of shoes wrapped up. They felt heavy enough together, but I

thought again how Father had said about the reducto absurdum of human experience, thinking how the only opportunity I seemed to have for the application of Harvard. Maybe by next year; thinking maybe it takes two
years in school to learn to do that properly.

But they felt heavy enough in the air. A street car
came. I got on. I didn't see the placard on the front. It
was full, mostly prosperous looking people reading newspapers. The only vacant seat was beside a nigger. He
wore a derby and shined shoes and he was holding a
dead cigar stub. I used to think that a Southerner had to
be always conscious of niggers. I thought that Northerners would expect him to. When I first came East I kept
thinking You've got to remember to think of them as coloured people not niggers, and if it hadn't happened
that I wasn't thrown with many of them, I'd have wasted
a lot of time and trouble before I learned that the best
way to take all people, black or white, is to take them for
what they think they are, then leave them alone. That
was when I realised that a nigger is not a person so much
as a form of behaviour; a sort of obverse reflection of the
white people he lives among. But I thought at first that
I ought to miss having a lot of them around me because
I thought that Northerners thought I did, but I didn't
know that I really had missed Roskus and Dilsey and
them until that morning in Virginia. The train was
stopped when I waked and I raised the shade and looked
out. The car was blocking a road crossing, where two
white fences came down a hill and then sprayed outward
and downward like part of the skeleton of a horn, and
there was a nigger on a mule in the middle of the stiff
ruts, waiting for the train to move. How long he had
been there I didn't know, but he sat straddle of the mule,

his head wrapped in a piece of blanket, as if they had been built there with the fence and the road, or with the hill, carved out of the hill itself, like a sign put there saying You are home again. He didn't have a saddle and his feet dangled almost to the ground. The mule looked like a rabbit. I raised the window.

"Hey, Uncle," I said, "Is this the way?"

"Suh?" He looked at me, then he loosened the blanket and lifted it away from his ear.

"Christmas gift!" I said.

"Sho comin, boss. You done caught me, aint you?"

"I'll let you off this time." I dragged my pants out of the little hammock and got a quarter out. "But look out next time. I'll be coming back through here two days after New Year, and look out then." I threw the quarter out the window. "Buy yourself some Santy Claus."

"Yes, suh," he said. He got down and picked up the quarter and rubbed it on his leg. "Thanky, young marster. Thanky." Then the train began to move. I leaned out the window, into the cold air, looking back. He stood there beside the gaunt rabbit of a mule, the two of them shabby and motionless and unimpatient. The train swung around the curve, the engine puffing with short, heavy blasts, and they passed smoothly from sight that way, with that quality about them of shabby and timeless patience, of static serenity: that blending of childlike and ready incompetence and paradoxical reliability that tends and protects them it loves out of all reason and robs them steadily and evades responsibility and obligations by means too barefaced to be called subterfuge even and is taken in theft or evasion with only that frank and spontaneous admiration for the victor which a gentleman feels for anyone who beats him in a fair contest, and withal a fond and unflagging tolerance for white-folks' vagaries like that of a grandparent for unpredictable and troublesome children, which I had forgotten. And all that day, while the train wound through rushing gaps and along ledges where movement was only a labouring sound of the exhaust and groaning wheels and the eternal mountains stood fading into the thick sky, I thought of home, of the bleak station and the mud and the niggers and country folks thronging slowly about the square, with toy monkeys and wagons and candy in sacks and roman candles sticking out, and my insides would move like they used to do in school when the bell rang.

I wouldn't begin counting until the clock struck three. Then I would begin, counting to sixty and folding down one finger and thinking of the other fourteen fingers waiting to be folded down, or thirteen or twelve or eight or seven, until all of a sudden I'd realise silence and the unwinking minds, and I'd say "Ma'am?" "Your name is Quentin, isn't it?" Miss Laura said. Then more silence and the cruel unwinking minds and hands jerking into the silence. "Tell Quentin who discovered the Mississippi River, Henry." "DeSoto." Then the minds would go away, and after a while I'd be afraid I had gotten behind and I'd count fast and fold down another finger, then I'd be afraid I was going too fast and I'd slow up, then I'd get afraid and count fast again. So I never could come out even with the bell, and the released surging of feet moving already, feeling earth in the scuffed floor, and the day like a pane of glass struck a light, sharp blow, and my insides would move, sitting still. *Moving sitting still. One minute she was standing in the door. Benjy. Bellowing. Benjamin the child of mine old age bellowing. Caddy! Caddy!*

I'm going to run away. He began to cry she went and touched him. Hush. I'm not going to. Hush. He hushed. Dilsey.

He smell what you tell him when he want to. Dont have to listen nor talk.

Can he smell that new name they give him? Can he smell bad luck?

What he want to worry about luck for? Luck cant do him no hurt.

What they change his name for then if aint trying to help his luck?

The street car stopped, started, stopped again. Below the window I watched the crowns of people's heads passing beneath new straw hats not yet unbleached. There were women in the car now, with market baskets, and men in work-clothes were beginning to outnumber the shined shoes and collars.

The nigger touched my knee. "Pardon me," he said. I swung my legs out and let him pass. We were going beside a blank wall, the sound clattering back into the car, at the women with market baskets on their knees and a man in a stained hat with a pipe stuck in the band. I could smell water, and in a break in the wall I saw a glint of water and two masts, and a gull motionless in midair, like on an invisible wire between the masts, and I raised my hand and through my coat touched the letters I had written. When the car stopped I got off.

The bridge was open to let a schooner through. She was in tow, the tug nudging along under her quarter, trailing smoke, but the ship herself was like she was moving without visible means. A man naked to the waist was coiling down a line on the fo'c's'le head. His body was burned the colour of leaf tobacco. Another man in a straw hat without any crown was at the wheel. The ship went through the bridge, moving under bare poles like a ghost in broad day, with three gulls hovering above the stern like toys on invisible wires.

When it closed I crossed to the other side and leaned on the rail above the boathouses. The float was empty and the doors were closed. The crew just pulled in the late afternoon now, resting up before. The shadow of the bridge, the tiers of railing, my shadow leaning flat upon the water, so easily had I tricked it that it would not quit me. At least fifty feet it was, and if I only had something to blot it into the water, holding it until it was drowned, the shadow of the package like two shoes wrapped up lying on the water. Niggers say a drowned man's shadow was watching for him in the water all the time. It twinkled and glinted, like breathing, the float slow like breathing too, and debris half submerged, healing out to the sea and the caverns and the grottoes of the sea. The displacement of water is equal to the something of something. Reducto absurdum of all human experience, and two six-pound flat-irons weigh more than one tailor's goose. What a sinful waste Dilsey would say. Benjy knew it when Damuddy died. He cried. *He smell hit. He smell hit.*

The tug came back downstream, the water shearing in long rolling cylinders, rocking the float at last with the echo of passage, the float lurching onto the rolling cylinder with a plopping sound and a long jarring noise as the door rolled back and two men emerged, carrying a shell. They set it in the water and a moment later Bland came out, with the sculls. He wore flannels, a grey jacket and a stiff straw hat. Either he or his mother had read somewhere that Oxford students pulled in flannels and stiff hats, so early one March they bought Gerald a one pair shell and in his flannels and stiff hat he went on the river.

The folks at the boathouses threatened to call a policeman, but he went anyway. His mother came down in a
hired auto, in a fur suit like an arctic explorer's, and saw
him off in a twenty-five mile wind and a steady drove of
ice floes like dirty sheep. Ever since then I have believed that God is not only a gentleman and a sport; He
is a Kentuckian too. When he sailed away she made a
detour and came down to the river again and drove
along parallel with him, the car in low gear. They said
you couldn't have told they'd ever seen one another before, like a King and Queen, not even looking at one another, just moving side by side across Massachusetts on
parallel courses like a couple of planets.

He got in and pulled away. He pulled pretty well now.
He ought to. They said his mother tried to make him
give rowing up and do something else the rest of his class
couldn't or wouldn't do, but for once he was stubborn.
If you could call it stubbornness, sitting in his attitudes
of princely boredom, with his curly yellow hair and his
violet eyes and his eyelashes and his New York clothes,
while his mamma was telling us about Gerald's horses
and Gerald's niggers and Gerald's women. Husbands and
fathers in Kentucky must have been awful glad when she
carried Gerald off to Cambridge. She had an apartment
over in town, and Gerald had one there too, besides his
rooms in college. She approved of Gerald associating
with me because I at least revealed a blundering sense of
noblesse oblige by getting myself born below Mason and
Dixon, and a few others whose geography met the re-
quirements (minimum) Forgave, at least. Or condoned.
But since she met Spoade coming out of chapel one He
said she couldn't be a lady no lady would be out at that
hour of the night she never had been able to forgive him
for having five names, including that of a present Eng-

ush ducal house. I'm sure she solaced herself by being convinced that some misfit Maingault or Mortemar had got mixed up with the lodge-keeper's daughter. Which was quite probable, whether she invented it or not. Spoade was the world's champion sitter-a-round, no holds barred and gouging discretionary.

The shell was a speck now, the oars catching the sun in spaced glints, as if the hull were winking itself along. *Did you ever have a sister? No but they're all bitches. Did you ever have a sister? One minute she was. Bitches. Not bitch one minute she stood in the door* Dalton Ames. Dalton Ames. Dalton Shirts. I thought all the time they were khaki, army issue khaki, until I saw they were of heavy Chinese silk or finest flannel because they made his face so brown his eyes so blue. Dalton Ames. It just missed gentility. Theatrical fixture. Just papier-mache, then touch. Oh. Asbestos. Not quite bronze. *But wont see him at the house.*

Caddy's a woman too, remember. She must do things for women's reasons, too.

Why wont you bring him to the house, Caddy? Why must you do like nigger women do in the pasture the ditches the dark woods hot hidden furious in the dark woods.

And after a while I had been hearing my watch for some time and I could feel the letters crackle through my coat, against the railing, and I leaned on the railing, watching my shadow, how I had tricked it. I moved along the rail, but my suit was dark too and I could wipe my hands, watching my shadow, how I had tricked it. I walked it into the shadow of the quai. Then I went east.

Harvard my Harvard boy Harvard harvard That pimple-faced infant she met at the field-meet with coloured

ribbons. Skulking along the fence trying to whistle her
out like a puppy. Because they couldn't cajole him into
the diningroom Mother believed he had some sort of spell
he was going to cast on her when he got her alone. Yet
any blackguard *He was lying beside the box under the
window bellowing* that could drive up in a limousine
with a flower in his buttonhole. *Harvard. Quentin this
is Herbert. My Harvard boy. Herbert will be a big
brother has already promised Jason a position in the
bank.*

Hearty, celluloid like a drummer. Face full of teeth
white but not smiling. *I've heard of him up there.* All
teeth but not smiling. *You going to drive?*

Get in Quentin.

You going to drive.

*It's her car aren't you proud of your little sister owns
first auto in town Herbert his present. Louis has been
giving her lessons every morning didn't you get my letter* Mr and Mrs Jason Richmond Compson announce the
marriage of their daughter Candace to Mr Sydney Herbert Head on the twenty-fifth of April one thousand nine
hundred and ten at Jefferson Mississippi. At home after
the first of August number Something Something Avenue
South Bend Indiana. Shreve said Aren't you even going
to open it? *Three days. Times. Mr and Mrs Jason Richmond Compson* Young Lochinvar rode out of the west a
little too soon, didn't he?

I'm from the south. You're funny, aren't you.

O yes I knew it was somewhere in the country.

You're funny, aren't you. You ought to join the circus.

I did. That's how I ruined my eyes watering the elephant's fleas. *Three times* These country girls. You cant
even tell about them, can you. Well, anyway Byron never

had his wish, thank God. *But not hit a man in glasses.*
Aren't you even going to open it? *It lay on the table a*
candle burning at each corner upon the envelope tied in
a soiled pink garter two artificial flowers. Not hit a man
in glasses.

Country people poor things they never saw an auto before lots of them honk the horn Candace so *She wouldn't*
look at me they'll get out of the way *wouldn't look at me*
your father wouldn't like it if you were to injure one of
them I'll declare your father will simply have to get an
auto now I'm almost sorry you brought it down Herbert
I've enjoyed it so much of course there's the carriage but
so often when I'd like to go out Mr Compson has the
darkies doing something it would be worth my head to
interrupt he insists that Roskus is at my call all the time
but I know what that means I know how often people
make promises just to satisfy their consciences are you
going to treat my little baby girl that way Herbert but I
know you wont Herbert has spoiled us all to death Quentin did I write you that he is going to take Jason into his
bank when Jason finishes high school Jason will make a
splendid banker he is the only one of my children with
any practical sense you can thank me for that he takes
after my people the others are all Compson *Jason fur-*
nished the flour. They made kites on the back porch and
sold them for a nickel a piece, he and the Patterson boy.
Jason was treasurer.

There was no nigger in this street car, and the hats
unbleached as yet flowing past under the window. Going
to Harvard. We have sold Benjy's *He lay on the ground*
under the window, bellowing. We have sold Benjy's pas-
ture so that Quentin may go to Harvard a brother to you.
Your little brother.

You should have a car it's done you no end of good
dont you think so Quentin I call him Quentin at once you
see I have heard so much about him from Candace.

Why shouldn't you I want my boys to be more than
friends yes Candace and Quentin more than friends
Father I have committed what a pity you had no brother
or sister *No sister no sister had no sister* Dont ask Quentin he and Mr Compson both feel a little insulted when
I am strong enough to come down to the table I am going
on nerve now I'll pay for it after it's all over and you
have taken my little daughter away from me *My little
sister had no. If I could say Mother. Mother*

Unless I do what I am tempted to and take you instead I dont think Mr Compson could overtake the car.

Ah Herbert Candace do you hear that *She wouldn't
look at me soft stubborn jaw-angle not back-looking*
You needn't be jealous though it's just an old woman he's
flattering a grown married daughter I cant believe it.

Nonsense you look like a girl you are lots younger than
Candace colour in your cheeks like a girl *A face reproach-
ful tearful an odour of camphor and of tears a voice
weeping steadily and softly beyond the twilit door the
twilight-coloured smell of honeysuckle. Bringing empty
trunks down the attic stairs they sounded like coffins
French Lick. Found not death at the salt lick*

Hats not unbleached and not hats. In three years I can
not wear a hat. I could not. Was. Will there be hats then
since I was not and not Harvard then. Where the best of
thought Father said clings like dead ivy vines upon old
dead brick. Not Harvard then. Not to me, anyway. Again.
Sadder than was. Again. Saddest of all. Again.

Spoade had a shirt on; then it must be. When I can see
my shadow again if not careful that I tricked into the
water shall tread again upon my impervious shadow. But

no sister. I wouldn't have done it. *I wont have my daughter spied on* I wouldn't have.

How can I control any of them when you have always taught them to have no respect for me and my wishes I know you look down on my people but is that any reason for teaching my children my own children I suffered for to have no respect Trampling my shadow's bones into the concrete with hard heels and then I was hearing the watch, and I touched the letters through my coat.

I will not have my daughter spied on by you or Quentin or anybody no matter what you think she has done

At least you agree there is reason for having her watched

I wouldn't have I wouldn't have. *I know you wouldn't I didn't mean to speak so sharply but women have no respect for each other for themselves*

But why did she The chimes began as I stepped on my shadow, but it was the quarter hour. The Deacon wasn't in sight anywhere. *think I would have could have*

She didn't mean that that's the way women do things its because she loves Caddy

The street lamps would go down the hill then rise toward town I walked upon the belly of my shadow. I could extend my hand beyond it. *feeling Father behind me beyond the rasping darkness of summer and August* the street lamps Father and I protect women from one another from themselves our women *Women are like that they dont acquire knowledge of people we are for that they are just born with a practical fertility of suspicion that makes a crop every so often and usually right they have an affinity for evil for supplying whatever the evil lacks in itself for drawing it about them instinctively as you do bedclothing in slumber fertilising the mind for it*

*until the evil has served its purpose whether it ever ex-
isted or no* He was coming along between a couple of
freshmen. He hadn't quite recovered from the parade, for
he gave me a salute, a very superior-officerish kind.

"I want to see you a minute," I said, stopping.

"See me? All right. See you again, fellows," he said,
stopping and turning back; "glad to have chatted with
you." That was the Deacon, all over. Talk about your natural psychologists. They said he hadn't missed a train at
the beginning of school in forty years, and that he could
pick out a Southerner with one glance. He never missed,
and once he had heard you speak, he could name your
state. He had a regular uniform he met trains in, a sort of
Uncle Tom's cabin outfit, patches and all.

"Yes, suh. Right dis way, young marster, hyer we is,"
taking your bags. "Hyer, boy, come hyer and git dese
grips." Whereupon a moving mountain of luggage would
edge up, revealing a white boy of about fifteen, and the
Deacon would hang another bag on him somehow and
drive him off. "Now, den, dont you drap hit. Yes, suh,
young marster, jes give de old nigger yo room number,
and hit'll be done got cold dar when you arrives."

From then on until he had you completely subjugated
he was always in or out of your room, ubiquitous and gar-
rulous, though his manner gradually moved northward
as his raiment improved, until at last when he had bled
you until you began to learn better he was calling you
Quentin or whatever, and when you saw him next he'd be
wearing a cast-off Brooks suit and a hat with a Princeton
club I forget which band that someone had given him
and which he was pleasantly and unshakably convinced
was a part of Abe Lincoln's military sash. Someone
spread the story years ago, when he first appeared around
college from wherever he came from, that he was a grad-

uate of the divinity school. And when he came to understand what it meant he was so taken with it that he began to retail the story himself, until at last he must come
to believe he really had. Anyway he related long point-
less anecdotes of his undergraduate days, speaking famil-
iarly of dead and departed professors by their first names,
usually incorrect ones. But he had been guide mentor
and friend to unnumbered crops of innocent and lonely
freshmen, and I suppose that with all his petty chicanery
and hypocrisy he stank no higher in heaven's nostrils than
any other.

"Haven't seen you in three-four days," he said, staring
at me from his still military aura. "You been sick?"

"No. I've been all right. Working, I reckon. I've seen
you, though."

"Yes?"

"In the parade the other day."

"Oh, that. Yes, I was there. I dont care nothing about
that sort of thing, you understand, but the boys likes to
have me with them, the vet'runs does. Ladies wants all
the old vet'runs to turn out, you know. So I has to oblige
them."

"And on that Wop holiday too," I said. "You were ob-
liging the W. C. T. U. then, I reckon."

"That? I was doing that for my son-in-law. He aims to
get a job on the city forces. Street cleaner. I tells him
all he wants is a broom to sleep on. You saw me, did
you?"

"Both times. Yes."

"I mean, in uniform. How'd I look?"

"You looked fine. You looked better than any of them.
They ought to make you a general, Deacon."

He touched my arm, lightly, his hand that worn, gentle
quality of niggers' hands. "Listen. This aint for outside

talking. I dont mind telling you because you and me's the same folks, come long and short." He leaned a little to me, speaking rapidly, his eyes not looking at me. "I've got strings out, right now. Wait till next year. Just wait. Then see where I'm marching. I wont need to tell you how I'm fixing it; I say, just wait and see, my boy." He looked at me now and clapped me lightly on the shoulder and rocked back on his heels, nodding at me. "Yes, sir. I didnt turn Democrat three years ago for nothing. My son-in-law on the city; me—Yes, sir. If just turning Democrat'll make that son of a bitch go to work. . . . And me: just you stand on that corner yonder a year from two days ago, and see."

"l hope so. You deserve it, Deacon. And while I think about it—" I took the letter from my pocket. "Take this around to my room tomorrow and give it to Shreve. He'll have something for you. But not till tomorrow, mind."

He took the letter and examined it. "It's sealed up."

"Yes. And it's written inside, Not good until tomorrow."

"H'm," he said. He looked at the envelope, his mouth pursed. "Something for me, you say?"

"Yes. A present I'm making you."

He was looking at me now, the envelope white in his black hand, in the sun. His eyes were soft and irisless and brown, and suddenly I saw Roskus watching me from behind all his whitefolks' claptrap of uniforms and politics and Harvard manner, diffident, secret, inarticulate and sad. "You aint playing a joke on the old nigger, is you?"

"You know I'm not. Did any Southerner ever play a joke on you?"

"You're right. They're fine folks. But you cant live with them."

"Did you ever try?" I said. But Roskus was gone. Once more he was that self he had long since taught himself to wear in the world's eye, pompous, spurious, not quite gross.

"I'll confer to your wishes, my boy."

"Not until tomorrow, remember."

"Sure," he said; "understood, my boy. Well—"

"I hope—" I said. He looked down at me, benignant, profound. Suddenly I held out my hand and we shook, he gravely, from the pompous height of his municipal and military dream. "You're a good fellow, Deacon. I hope. . . . You've helped a lot of young fellows, here and there."

"I've tried to treat all folks right," he said. "I draw no petty social lines. A man to me is a man, wherever I find him."

"I hope you'll always find as many friends as you've made."

"Young fellows. I get along with them. They dont forget me, neither," he said, waving the envelope. He put it into his pocket and buttoned his coat. "Yes, sir," he said, "I've had good friends."

The chimes began again, the half hour. I stood in the belly of my shadow and listened to the strokes spaced and tranquil along the sunlight, among the thin, still little leaves. Spaced and peaceful and serene, with that quality of autumn always in bells even in the month of brides. *Lying on the ground under the window bellowing* He took one look at her and knew. Out of the mouths of babes. *The street lamps* The chimes ceased. I went back to the postoffice, treading my shadow into pavement. *go down the hill then they rise toward town like lanterns hung one above another on a wall.* Father said because she loves Caddy she loves people through their shortcomings. Uncle Maury straddling his legs before the fire must remove one hand long enough to drink Christmas. Jason ran on, his hands in his pockets fell down and lay there like a trussed fowl until Versh set him up. *Whyn't you keep them hands outen your pockets when you running you could stand up then* Rolling his head in the cradle rolling it flat across the back. Caddy told Jason Versh said that the reason Uncle Maury didn't work was that he used to roll his head in the cradle when he was little.

Shreve was coming up the walk, shambling, fatly earnest, his glasses glinting beneath the running leaves like little pools.

"I gave Deacon a note for some things. I may not be in this afternoon, so dont you let him have anything until tomorrow, will you?"

"All right." He looked at me. "Say, what're you doing today, anyhow? All dressed up and mooning around like the prologue to a suttee. Did you go to Psychology this morning?"

"I'm not doing anything. Not until tomorrow, now."

"What's that you got there?"

"Nothing. Pair of shoes I had half-soled. Not until tomorrow, you hear?"

"Sure. All right. Oh, by the way, did you get a letter off the table this morning?"

"No."

"It's there. From Semiramis. Chauffeur brought it before ten o'clock."

"All right. I'll get it. Wonder what she wants now."

"Another band recital, I guess. Tumpty ta ta Gerald blah. 'A little louder on the drum, Quentin.' God, I'm glad I'm not a gentleman." He went on, nursing a book, a little shapeless, fatly intent. *The street lamps* do you think so because one of our forefathers was a governor and three were generals and Mother's weren't

any live man is better than any dead man but no live or dead man is very much better than any other live or dead man *Done in Mother's mind though. Finished. Finished. Then we were all poisoned* you are confusing sin and morality women dont do that your Mother is thinking of morality whether it be sin or not has not occurred to her

Jason I must go away you keep the others I'll take Jason and go where nobody knows us so he'll have a chance to grow up and forget all this the others dont love me they have never loved anything with that streak of Compson selfishness and false pride Jason was the only one my heart went out to without dread

nonsense Jason is all right I was thinking that as soon as you feel better you and Caddy might go up to French Lick

and leave Jason here with nobody but you and the darkies

she will forget him then all the talk will die away *found not death at the salt licks*

maybe I could find a husband for her *not death at the salt licks*

The car came up and stopped. The bells were still ringing the half hour. I got on and it went on again, blotting the half hour. No: the three quarters. Then it would be ten minutes anyway. To leave Harvard *your Mother's dream for sold Benjy's pasture for*

what have I done to have been given children like these Benjamin was punishment enough and now for her to have no more regard for me her own mother I've suffered for her dreamed and planned and sacrificed I went down into the valley yet never since she opened her eyes

has she given me one unselfish thought at times I look at
her I wonder if she can be my child except Jason he has
never given me one moment's sorrow since I first held
him in my arms I knew then that he was to be my joy
and my salvation I thought that Benjamin was punishment enough for any sins I have committed I thought he
was my punishment for putting aside my pride and mar-
rying a man who held himself above me I dont complain
I loved him above all of them because of it because my
duty though Jason pulling at my heart all the while but
I see now that I have not suffered enough I see now that
I must pay for your sins as well as mine what have you
done what sins have your high and mighty people visited
upon me but you'll take up for them you always have
found excuses for your own blood only Jason can do
wrong because he is more Bascomb than Compson while
your own daughter my little daughter my baby girl she
is she is no better than that when I was a girl I was unfortunate I was only a Bascomb I was taught that there
is no halfway ground that a woman is either a lady or
not but I never dreamed when I held her in my arms
that any daughter of mine could let herself dont you
know I can look at her eyes and tell you may think she'd
tell you but she doesn't tell things she is secretive you
dont know her I know things she's done that I'd die before I'd have you know that's it go on criticise Jason ac-
cuse me of setting him to watch her as if it were a crime
while your own daughter can I know you dont love him
that you wish to believe faults against him you never
have yes ridicule him as you always have Maury you
cannot hurt me any more than your children already
have and then I'll be gone and Jason with no one to love
him shield him from this I look at him every day dread-
ing to see this Compson blood beginning to show in him

at last with his sister slipping out to see what do you call it then have you ever laid eyes on him will you even let me try to find out who he is it's not for myself I couldn't bear to see him it's for your sake to protect you but who can fight against bad blood you wont let me try we are to sit back with our hands folded while she not only drags your name in the dirt but corrupts the very air your children breathe Jason you must let me go away I cannot stand it let me have Jason and you keep the others they're not my flesh and blood like he is strangers nothing of mine and I am afraid of them I can take Jason and go where we are not known I'll go down on my knees and pray for the absolution of my sins that he may escape this curse try to forget that the others ever were

If that was the three quarters, not over ten minutes now. One car had just left, and people were already waiting for the next one. I asked, but he didn't know whether another one would leave before noon or not because you'd think that interurbans. So the first one was another trolley. I got on. You can feel noon. I wonder if even miners in the bowels of the earth. That's why whistles: because people that sweat, and if just far enough from sweat you wont hear whistles and in eight minutes you should be that far from sweat in Boston. Father said a man is the sum of his misfortunes. One day you'd think misfortune would get tired, but then time is your misfortune Father said. A gull on an invisible wire attached through space dragged. You carry the symbol of your frustration into eternity. Then the wings are bigger Father said only who can play a harp.

I could hear my watch whenever the car stopped, but not often they were already eating *Who would play a* Eating the business of eating inside of you space to space and time confused Stomach saying noon brain saying eat oclock All right I wonder what time it is what of it. People were getting out. The trolley didn't stop so often now, emptied by eating.

Then it was past. I got off and stood in my shadow and after a while a car came along and I got on and went back to the interurban station. There was a car ready to leave, and I found a seat next the window and it started and I watched it sort of frazzle out into slack tide flats, and then trees. Now and then I saw the river and I thought how nice it would be for them down at New London if the weather and Gerald's shell going solemnly up the glinting forenoon and I wondered what the old woman would be wanting now, sending me a note before ten oclock in the morning. What picture of Gerald I to be one of the *Dalton Ames oh asbestos Quentin has shot* background. Something with girls in it. Women do have *always his voice above the gabble voice* that breathed an affinity for evil, for believing that no woman is to be trusted, but that some men are too innocent to protect themselves. Plain girls. Remote cousins and family friends whom mere acquaintanceship invested with a sort of blood obligation noblesse oblige. And she sitting there telling us before their faces what a shame it was that Gerald should have all the family looks because a man didn't need it, was better off without it but without it a girl was simply lost. Telling us about Gerald's women in a *Quentin has shot Herbert he shot his voice through the floor of Caddy's room* tone of smug approbation. "When he was seventeen I said to him one day 'What a shame that you should have a mouth like that it should be on a girls face' and can you imagine *the curtains leaning in on the twilight upon the odour of the apple tree her head against the twilight her arms behind her head kimono-winged the voice that breathed o'er*

eden clothes upon the bed by the nose seen above the
apple what he said? just seventeen, mind. 'Mother' he
said 'it often is.' " And him sitting there in attitudes regal
watching two or three of them through his eyelashes.
They gushed like swallows swooping his eyelashes.
Shreve said he always had *Are you going to look after*
Benjy and Father

The less you say about Benjy and Father the better
when have you ever considered them Caddy

Promise

You needn't worry about them you're getting out in
good shape

Promise I'm sick you'll have to promise wondered who
invented that joke but then he always had considered
Mrs Bland a remarkably preserved woman he said she
was grooming Gerald to seduce a duchess sometime. She
called Shreve that fat Canadian youth twice she arranged a new room-mate for me without consulting me
at all, once for me to move out, once for

He opened the door in the twilight. His face looked
like a pumpkin pie.

"Well, I'll say a fond farewell. Cruel fate may part us,
but I will never love another. Never."

"What are you talking about?"

"I'm talking about cruel fate in eight yards of apricot
silk and more metal pound for pound that a galley slave
and the sole owner and proprietor of the unchallenged
peripatetic john of the late Confederacy." Then he told
me how she had gone to the proctor to have him moved
out and how the proctor had revealed enough low stubbornness to insist on consulting Shreve first. Then she
suggested that he send for Shreve right off and do it, and
he wouldnt do that, so after that she was hardly civil to
Shreve. "I make it a point never to speak harshly of fe-

males," Shreve said, "but that woman has got more ways like a bitch than any lady in these sovereign states and dominions." and now Letter on the table by hand, command orchid scented coloured If she knew I had passed almost beneath the window knowing it there without My dear Madam I have not yet had an opportunity of receiving your communication but I beg in advance to be excused today or yesterday and tomorrow or when As I remember that the next one is to be how Gerald throws his nigger downstairs and how the nigger plead to be allowed to matriculate in the divinity school to be near marster marse gerald and How he ran all the way to the station beside the carriage with tears in his eyes when marse gerald rid away I will wait until the day for the one about the sawmill husband came to the kitchen door with a shotgun Gerald went down and bit the gun in two and handed it back and wiped his hands on a silk handkerchief threw the handkerchief in the stove I've only heard that one twice

shot him through the I saw you come in here so I watched my chance and came along thought we might get acquainted have a cigar

Thanks I dont smoke

No things must have changed up there since my day mind if I light up

Help yourself

Thanks I've heard a lot I guess your mother wont mind if I put the match behind the screen will she a lot about you Candace talked about you all the time up there at the Licks   I got pretty jealous I says to myself who is this Quentin anyway I must see what this animal looks like because I was hit pretty hard see soon as I saw the little girl I dont mind telling you it never occurred to me it was her brother she kept talking about she couldnt have talked about you any more if you'd been the only man in the world husband wouldnt have been in it you wont change your mind and have a smoke

I dont smoke

In that case I wont insist even though it is a pretty fair weed cost me twenty-five bucks a hundred wholesale friend in Havana yes I guess there are lots of changes up there I keep promising myself a visit but I never get around to it been hitting the ball now for ten years I cant get away from the bank during school fellow's habits change things that seem important to an undergraduate you know tell me about things up there

I'm not going to tell Father and Mother if that's what you are getting at

Not going to tell not going to oh that that's what you are talking about is it you understand that I dont give a damn whether you tell or not understand that a thing like that unfortunate but no police crime I wasn't the first or the last I was just unlucky you might have been luckier

You lie

Keep your shirt on I'm not trying to make you tell anything you dont want to meant no offense of course a young fellow like you would consider a thing of that sort a lot more serious than you will in five years

I dont know but one way to consider cheating I dont think I'm likely to learn different at Harvard

We're better than a play you must have made the Dramat well you're right no need to tell them we'll let bygones be bygones eh no reason why you and I should let a little thing like that come between us I like you Quentin I like your appearance you dont look like these other hicks I'm glad we're going to hit off like this I've promised your mother to do something for Jason but I

would like to give you a hand too Jason would be just as
well off here but there's no future in a hole like this for a
young fellow like you

Thanks you'd better stick to Jason he'd suit you better
than I would

I'm sorry about that business but a kid like I was then
I never had a mother like yours to teach me the finer
points it would just hurt her unnecessarily to know it yes
you're right no need to that includes Candace of course

I said Mother and Father

Look here take a look at me how long do you think
you'd last with me

I wont have to last long if you learned to fight up at
school too   try and see how long I would

You damned little   what do you think you're getting at
Try and see

My God the cigar what would your mother say if she
found a blister on her mantel just in time too look here
Quentin we're about to do something we'll both regret I
like you liked you as soon as I saw you I says he must be
a damned good fellow whoever he is or Candace wouldnt
be so keen on him listen I've been out in the world now
for ten years things dont matter so much then you'll find
that out let's you and I get together on this thing sons of
old Harvard and all I guess I wouldnt know the place
now best place for a young fellow in the world I'm going
to send my sons there give them a better chance than I
had wait dont go yet let's discuss this thing a young man
gets these ideas and I'm all for them does him good while
he's in school forms his character good for tradition the
school but when he gets out into the world he'll have to
get his the best way he can because he'll find that everybody else is doing the same thing and be damned to here

let's shake hands and let bygones be bygones for your
mother's sake remember her health come on give me your
hand here look at it it's just out of convent look not a
blemish not even been creased yet see here

To hell with your money

No no come on I belong to the family now see I know
how it is with a young fellow he has lots of private affairs it's always pretty hard to get the old man to stump
up for I know havent I been there and not so long ago
either but now I'm getting married and all specially up
there come on dont be a fool listen when we get a chance
for a real talk I want to tell you about a little widow
over in town

I've heard that too keep your damned money

Call it a loan then just shut your eyes a minute and
you'll be fifty

Keep your hands off of me you'd better get that cigar
off the mantel

Tell and be damned then see what it gets you if you
were not a damned fool you'd have seen that I've got
them too tight for any half-baked Galahad of a brother
your mother's told me about your sort with your head
swelled up come in oh come in dear Quentin and I were
just getting acquainted talking about Harvard did you
want me cant stay away from the old man can she

Go out a minute Herbert I want to talk to Quentin

Come in come in let's all have a gabfest and get acquainted I was just telling Quentin

Go on Herbert go out a while

Well all right then I suppose you and bubber do want
to see one another once more eh

You'd better take that cigar off the mantel

Right as usual my boy then I'll toddle along let them

order you around while they can Quentin after day after
tomorrow it'll be pretty please to the old man wont it
dear give us a kiss honey

Oh stop that save that for day after tomorrow

I'll want interest then dont let Quentin do anything he
cant finish oh by the way did I tell Quentin the story
about the man's parrot and what happened to it a sad
story remind me of that think of it yourself ta-ta see you
in the funnypaper

Well

Well

What are you up to now

Nothing

You're meddling in my business again didn't you get
enough of that last summer

Caddy you've got fever *You're sick how are you sick*

I'm just sick. I cant ask.

Shot his voice through the

Not that blackguard Caddy

Now and then the river glinted beyond things in sort
of swooping glints, across noon and after. Well after now,
though we had passed where he was still pulling upstream majestical in the face of god gods. Better. Gods,
God would be canaille too in Boston Massachusetts.
Or maybe just not a husband. The wet oars winking
him along in bright winks and female palms. Adulant.
Adulant if not a husband he'd ignore God. *That blackguard, Caddy* The river glinted away beyond a swooping curve.

I'm sick you'll have to promise

Sick how are you sick

I'm just sick I cant ask anybody yet promise you will

*If they need any looking after it's because of you how
are you sick* Under the window we could hear the car

leaving for the station, the 8:10 train. To bring back cousins. Heads. Increasing himself head by head but not barbers. Manicure girls. We had a blood horse once. In the stable yes, but under leather a cur. *Quentin has shot all of their voices through the floor of Caddy's room*

The car stopped. I got off, into the middle of my shadow. A road crossed the track. There was a wooden marquee with an old man eating something out of a paper bag, and then the car was out of hearing too. The road went into the trees, where it would be shady, but June foliage in New England not much thicker than April at home in Mississippi. I could see a smoke stack. I turned my back to it, tramping my shadow into the dust. *There was something terrible in me sometimes at night I could see it grinning at me I could see it through them grinning at me through their faces it's gone now and I'm sick*

Caddy

Dont touch me just promise

If you're sick you cant

Yes I can after that it'll be all right it wont matter dont let them send him to Jackson promise

I promise Caddy Caddy

Dont touch me dont touch me

What does it look like Caddy

What

That that grins at you that thing through them

I could still see the smoke stack. That's where the water would be, heading out to the sea and the peaceful grottoes. Tumbling peacefully they would, and when He said Rise only the flat irons. When Versh and I hunted all day we wouldn't take any lunch, and at twelve oclock I'd get hungry. I'd stay hungry until about one, then all of a sudden I'd even forget that I wasn't hungry anymore. *The street lamps go down the hill then heard the car go down the hill. The chair-arm flat cool smooth under my forehead shaping the chair the apple tree leaning on my hair above the eden clothes by the nose seen* You've got fever I felt it yesterday it's like being near a stove.

Dont touch me.

Caddy you cant do it if you are sick. That blackguard.

I've got to marry somebody. *Then they told me the bone would have to be broken again*

At last I couldn't see the smoke stack. The road went beside a wall. Trees leaned over the wall, sprayed with sunlight. The stone was cool. Walking near it you could feel the coolness. Only our country was not like this country. There was something about just walking through it. A kind of still and violent fecundity that satisfied ever bread-hunger like. Flowing around you, not brooding and nursing every niggard stone. Like it were put to makeshift for enough green to go around among the trees and even the blue of distance not that rich chimaera. *told me the bone would have to be broken again and inside me it began to say Ah Ah Ah and I began to sweat. What do I care I know what a broken leg is all it is it wont be anything I'll just have to stay in the house a little longer that's all and my jaw-muscles getting numb and my mouth saying Wait Wait just a minute through the sweat ah ah ah behind my teeth and Father damn that horse damn that horse. Wait it's my fault. He came along the fence every morning with a basket toward the kitchen dragging a stick along the fence every morning I dragged myself to the window cast and all and laid for him with a piece of coal Dilsey said you goin to ruin yoself aint you got no mo sense than that not fo days since you bruck hit. Wait I'll get used to it in a minute wait just a minute I'll get*

Even sound seemed to fail in this air, like the air was worn out with carrying sounds so long. A dog's voice carries further than a train, in the darkness anyway. And some people's. Niggers. Louis Hatcher never even used his horn carrying it and that old lantern. I said, "Louis, when was the last time you cleaned that lantern?"

"I cleant hit a little while back. You member when all dat flood-watter wash dem folks away up yonder? I cleant hit dat ve'y day. Old woman and me settin fore de fire dat night and she say 'Louis, whut you gwine do ef dat flood git out dis fur?' and I say 'Dat's a fack. I reckon I had better clean dat lantun up.' So I cleant hit dat night."

"That flood was way up in Pennsylvania," I said. "It couldn't even have got down this far."

"Dat's whut you says," Louis said. "Watter kin git des ez high en wet in Jefferson ez hit kin in Pennsylvaney, I reckon. Hit's de folks dat says de high watter cant git dis fur dat comes floatin out on de ridge-pole, too."

"Did you and Martha get out that night?"

"We done jest that. I cleant dat lantun and me and her sot de balance of de night on top o dat knoll back de graveyard. En ef I'd a knowed of aihy one higher, we'd a been on hit instead."

"And you haven't cleaned that lantern since then."

"Whut I want to clean hit when dey aint no need?"

"You mean, until another flood comes along?"

"Hit kep us outen dat un."

"Oh, come on, Uncle Louis," I said.

"Yes, suh. You do you way en I do mine. Ef all I got to do to keep outen de high watter is to clean dis yere lantun, I wont quoil wid no man."

"Unc' Louis wouldn't ketch nothin wid a light he could see by," Versh said.

"I wuz huntin possums in dis country when dey was still drowndin nits in yo pappy's head wid coal oil, boy," Louis said. "Ketchin um, too."

"Dat's de troof," Versh said. "I reckon Unc' Louis done caught mo possums than aihy man in dis country."

"Yes, suh," Louis said, "I got plenty light fer possums to see, all right. I aint heard non o dem complainin. Hush, now. Dar he. Whooey. Hum awn, dawg." And we'd sit in the dry leaves that whispered a little with the slow respiration of our waiting and with the slow breathing of the earth and the windless October, the rank smell of the lantern fouling the brittle air, listening to the dogs and to the echo of Louis' voice dying away. He never raised it, yet on a still night we have heard it from our front porch. When he called the dogs in he sounded just like the horn he carried slung on his shoulder and never used, but clearer, mellower, as though his voice were a part of darkness and silence, coiling out of it, coiling into it again. WhoOoooo. WhoOoooo. WhoOooooooooooo-ooooo. *Got to marry somebody*

Have there been very many Caddy

I dont know too many will you look after Benjy and Father

You dont know whose it is then does he know

Dont touch me will you look after Benjy and Father

I began to feel the water before I came to the bridge. The bridge was of grey stone, lichened, dappled with slow moisture where the fungus crept. Beneath it the water was clear and still in the shadow, whispering and clucking about the stone in fading swirls of spinning sky. *Caddy that*

I've got to marry somebody Versh told me about a man mutilated himself. He went into the woods and did it with a razor, sitting in a ditch. A broken razor, flinging them backward over his shoulder tne same motion complete the jerked skein of blood backward not looping. But that's not it. It's not not having them. It's never to have had them then I could say O That That's Chinese I dont know Chinese. And Father said it's because you are a virgin: dont you see? Women are never virgins. Purity is a negative state and therefore contrary to nature. It's nature is hurting you not Caddy and I said That's just words and he said So is virginity and I said you dont know. You cant know and he said Yes. On the instant when we come to realise that tragedy is second-hand.

Where the shadow of the bridge fell I could see down for a long way, but not as far as the bottom. When you leave a leaf in water a long time after awhile the tissue will be gone and the delicate fibers waving slow as the motion of sleep. They dont touch one another, no matter how knotted up they once were, no matter how close they lay once to the bones. And maybe when He says Rise the eyes will come floating up too, out of the deep quiet and the sleep, to look on glory. And after awhile the flat irons would come floating up. I hid them under the end of the bridge and went back and leaned on the rail.

I could not see the bottom, but I could see a long way into the motion of the water before the eye gave out, and then I saw a shadow hanging like a fat arrow stemming into the current. Mayflies skimmed in and out of the shadow of the bridge just above the surface. *If it could just be a hell beyond that: the clean flame the two of us more than dead. Then you will have only me then only me then the two of us amid the pointing and the horror beyond the clean flame* The arrow increased without motion, then in a quick swirl the trout lipped a fly beneath the surface with that sort of gigantic delicacy of an elephant picking up a peanut. The fading vortex drifted away down stream and then I saw the arrow again, nose into the current, wavering delicately to the motion of the water above which the Mayflies slanted and poised. *Only you and me then amid the pointing and the horror walled by the clean flame*

The trout hung, delicate and motionless among the wavering shadows. Three boys with fishing poles came onto the bridge and we leaned on the rail and looked down at the trout. They knew the fish. He was a neighbourhood character.

"They've been trying to catch that trout for twenty-five years. There's a store in Boston offers a twenty-five dollar fishing rod to anybody that can catch him."

"Why dont you all catch him, then? Wouldnt you like to have a twenty-five dollar fishing rod?"

"Yes," they said. They leaned on the rail, looking down at the trout. "I sure would," one said.

"I wouldnt take the rod," the second said. "I'd take the money instead."

"Maybe they wouldnt do that," the first said. "I bet he'd make you take the rod."

"Then I'd sell it."

"You couldnt get twenty-five dollars for it."

"I'd take what I could get, then. I can catch just as many fish with this pole as I could with a twenty-five dollar one." Then they talked about what they would do with twenty-five dollars. They all talked at once, their voices insistent and contradictory and impatient, making of unreality a possibility, then a probability, then an incontrovertible fact, as people will when their desires become words.

"I'd buy a horse and wagon," the second said.

"Yes you would," the others said.

"I would. I know where I can buy one for twenty-five dollars. I know the man."

"Who is it?"

"That's all right who it is. I can buy it for twenty-five dollars."

"Yah," the others said, "He dont know any such thing. He's just talking."

"Do you think so?" the boy said. They continued to jeer at him, but he said nothing more. He leaned on the rail, looking down at the trout which he had already spent, and suddenly the acrimony, the conflict, was gone from their voices, as if to them too it was as though he had captured the fish and bought his horse and wagon, they too partaking of that adult trait of being convinced of anything by an assumption of silent superiority. I suppose that people, using themselves and each other so much by words, are at least consistent in attributing wisdom to a still tongue, and for a while I could feel the other two seeking swiftly for some means by which to cope with him, to rob him of his horse and wagon.

"You couldnt get twenty-five dollars for that pole," the first said. "I bet anything you couldnt."

"He hasnt caught that trout yet," the third said suddenly, then they both cried:

"Yah, wha'd I tell you? What's the man's name? I dare you to tell. There aint any such man."

"Ah, shut up," the second said. "Look, Here he comes again." They leaned on the rail, motionless, identical, their poles slanting slenderly in the sunlight, also identical. The trout rose without haste, a shadow in faint wavering increase; again the little vortex faded slowly downstream. "Gee," the first one murmured.

"We dont try to catch him anymore," he said. "We just watch Boston folks that come out and try."

"Is he the only fish in this pool?"

"Yes. He ran all the others out. The best place to fish around here is down at the Eddy."

"No it aint," the second said. "It's better at Bigelow's Mill two to one." Then they argued for a while about which was the best fishing and then left off all of a sudden to watch the trout rise again and the broken swirl of water suck down a little of the sky. I asked how far it was to the nearest town. They told me.

"But the closest car line is that way," the second said, pointing back down the road. "Where are you going?"

"Nowhere. Just walking."

"You from the college?"

"Yes. Are there any factories in that town?"

"Factories?" They looked at me.

"No," the second said. "Not there." They looked at my clothes. "You looking for work?"

"How about Bigelow's Mill?" the third said. "That's a factory."

"Factory my eye. He means a sure enough factory."

"One with a whistle," I said. "I havent heard any one oclock whistles yet."

"Oh," the second said. "There's a clock in the Unitarian steeple. You can find out the time from that. Havent you got a watch on that chain?"

"I broke it this morning." I showed them my watch. They examined it gravely.

"It's still running," the second said. "What does a watch like that cost?"

"It was a present," I said. "My father gave it to me when I graduated from high school."

"Are you a Canadian?" the third said. He had red hair.

"Canadian?"

"He dont talk like them," the second said. "I've heard them talk. He talks like they do in minstrel shows."

"Say," the third said, "aint you afraid he'll hit you?"

"Hit me?"

"You said he talks like a coloured man."

"Ah, dry up," the second said. "You can see the steeple when you get over that hill there."

I thanked them. "I hope you have good luck. Only dont catch that old fellow down there. He deserves to be let alone."

"Cant anybody catch that fish," the first said. They leaned on the rail, looking down into the water, the three poles like three slanting threads of yellow fire in the sun. I walked upon my shadow, tramping it into the dappled shade of trees again. The road curved, mounting away from the water. It crossed the hill, then descended winding, carrying the eye, the mind on ahead beneath a still green tunnel, and the square cupola above the trees and the round eye of the clock but far enough. I sat down at the roadside. The grass was ankle deep, myriad. The shadows on the road were as still as if they had been put there with a stencil, with slanting pencils of sunlight. But it was only a train, and after a while it died away beyond the trees, the long sound, and then I could hear my watch and the train dying away, as though it were running through another month or another summer somewhere, rushing away under the poised gull and all things rushing. Except Gerald. He would be sort of grand too, pulling in lonely state across the noon, rowing himself right out of noon, up the long bright air like an apotheosis, mounting into a drowsing infinity where only he and the gull, the one terrifically motionless, the other in a steady and measured pull and recover that partook of inertia itself, the world punily beneath their shadows on the sun. Caddy that blackguard that blackguard Caddy

Their voices came over the hill, and the three slender poles like balanced threads of running fire. They looked at me passing, not slowing.

"Well," I said, "I dont see him."

"We didnt try to catch him," the first said. "You cant catch that fish."

"There's the clock," the second said, pointing. "You can tell the time when you get a little closer."

"Yes," I said, "All right." I got up. "You all going to town?"

"We're going to the Eddy for chub," the first said.

"You cant catch anything at the Eddy," the second said.

"I guess you want to go to the mill, with a lot of fellows splashing and scaring all the fish away."

"You cant catch any fish at the Eddy."

"We wont catch none nowhere if we dont go on," the third said.

"I dont see why you keep on talking about the Eddy," the second said. "You cant catch anything there."

"You dont have to go," the first said. "You're not tied to me."

"Let's go to the mill and go swimming," the third said.

"I'm going to the Eddy and fish," the first said. "You can do as you please."

"Say, how long has it been since you heard of anybody catching a fish at the Eddy?" the second said to the third.

"Let's go to the mill and go swimming," the third said. The cupola sank slowly beyond the trees, with the round face of the clock far enough yet. We went on in the dappled shade. We came to an orchard, pink and white. It was full of bees; already we could hear them.

"Let's go to the mill and go swimming," the third said. A lane turned off beside the orchard. The third boy slowed and halted. The first went on, flecks of sunlight slipping along the pole across his shoulder and down the back of his shirt. "Come on," the third said. The second boy stopped too. *Why must you marry somebody Caddy*

Do you want me to say it do you think that if I say it it wont be

"Let's go up to the mill," he said. "Come on."

The first boy went on. His bare feet made no sound, falling softer than leaves in the thin dust. In the orchard the bees sounded like a wind getting up, a sound caught by a spell just under crescendo and sustained. The lane went along the wall, arched over, shattered with bloom, dissolving into trees. Sunlight slanted into it, sparse and eager. Yellow butterflies flickered along the shade like flecks of sun.

"What do you want to go to the Eddy for?" the second boy said. "You can fish at the mill if you want to."

"Ah, let him go," the third said. They looked after the first boy. Sunlight slid patchily across his walking shoulders, glinting along the pole like yellow ants.

"Kenny," the second said. *Say it to Father will you I will am my fathers Progenitive I invented him created I him Say it to him it will not be for he will say I was not and then you and I since philoprogenitive*

"Ah, come on," the boy said, "They're already in." They looked after the first boy. "Yah," they said suddenly, "go on then, mamma's boy. If he goes swimming he'll get his head wet and then he'll get a licking." They turned into the lane and went on, the yellow butterflies slanting about them along the shade.

*it is because there is nothing else I believe there is
something else but there may not be and then I You will
find that even injustice is scarcely worthy of what you believe yourself to be* He paid me no attention, his jaw set
in profile, his face turned a little away beneath his broken
hat.

"Why dont you go swimming with them?" I said. *that
blackguard Caddy*

Were you trying to pick a fight with him were you

*A liar and a scoundrel Caddy was dropped from his
club for cheating at cards got sent to Coventry caught
cheating at midterm exams and expelled*

Well what about it I'm not going to play cards with

"Do you like fishing better than swimming?" I said.
The sound of the bees diminished, sustained yet, as
though instead of sinking into silence, silence merely increased between us, as water rises. The road curved again
and became a street between shady lawns with white
houses. *Caddy that blackguard can you think of Benjy
and Father and do it not of me*

*What else can I think about what else have I thought
about* The boy turned from the street. He climbed a
picket fence without looking back and crossed the lawn
to a tree and laid the pole down and climbed into the
fork of the tree and sat there, his back to the road and
the dappled sun motionless at last upon his white shirt.
*Else have I thought about I cant even cry I died last year
I told you I had but I didnt know then what I meant I
didnt know what I was saying* Some days in late August
at home are like this, the air thin and eager like this,
with something in it sad and nostalgic and familiar. Man
the sum of his climatic experiences Father said. Man the
sum of what have you. A problem in impure properties

carried tediously to an unvarying nil: stalemate of dust
and desire. *But now I know I'm dead I tell you*

*Then why must you listen we can go away you and
Benjy and me where nobody knows us where* The buggy
was drawn by a white horse, his feet clopping in the thin
dust; spidery wheels chattering thin and dry, moving uphill beneath a rippling shawl of leaves. Elm. No: ellum.
Ellum.

*On what on your school money the money they sold
the pasture for so you could go to Harvard dont you see
you've got to finish now if you dont finish he'll have nothing*

Sold the pasture His white shirt was motionless in the
fork, in the flickering shade. The wheels were spidery.
Beneath the sag of the buggy the hooves neatly rapid
like the motions of a lady doing embroidery, diminishing
without progress like a figure on a treadmill being drawn
rapidly offstage. The street turned again. I could see the
white cupola, the round stupid assertion of the clock.
Sold the pasture

*Father will be dead in a year they say if he doesnt stop
drinking and he wont stop he cant stop since I since last
summer and then they'll send Benjy to Jackson I cant cry
I cant even cry one minute she was standing in the door
the next minute he was pulling at her dress and bellowing
his voice hammered back and forth between the walls in
waves and she shrinking against the wall getting smaller
and smaller with her white face her eyes like thumbs dug
into it until he pushed her out of the room his voice hammering back and forth as though its own momentum
would not let it stop as though there were no place for it
in silence bellowing*

When you opened the door a bell tinkled, but just once,

high and clear and small in the neat obscurity above the door, as though it were gauged and tempered to make that single clear small sound so as not to wear the bell out nor to require the expenditure of too much silence in restoring it when the door opened upon the recent warm scent of baking; a little dirty child with eyes like a toy bear's and two patent-leather pig-tails.

"Hello, sister." Her face was like a cup of milk dashed with coffee in the sweet warm emptiness. "Anybody here?"

But she merely watched me until a door opened and the lady came. Above the counter where the ranks of crisp shapes behind the glass her neat grey face her hair tight and sparse from her neat grey skull, spectacles in neat grey rims riding approaching like something on a wire, like a cash box in a store. She looked like a librarian. Something among dusty shelves of ordered certitudes long divorced from reality, desiccating peacefully, as if a breath of that air which sees injustice done

"Two of these, please, ma'am."

From under the counter she produced a square cut from a newspaper and laid it on the counter and lifted the two buns out. The little girl watched them with still and unwinking eyes like two currants floating motionless in a cup of weak coffee Land of the kike home of the wop. Watching the bread, the neat grey hands, a broad gold band on the left forefinger, knuckled there by a blue knuckle.

"Do you do your own baking, ma'am?"

"Sir?" she said. Like that. Sir? Like on the stage Sir? "Five cents. Was there anything else?"

"No, ma'am. Not for me. This lady wants something." She was not tall enough to see over the case, so she went to the end of the counter and looked at the little girl

"Did you bring her in here?"

"No, ma'am. She was here when I came."

"You little wretch," she said. She came out around the counter, but she didnt touch the little girl. "Have you got anything in your pockets?"

"She hasnt got any pockets," I said. "She wasnt doing anything. She was standing here, waiting for you."

"Why didnt the bell ring, then?" She glared at me. She just needed a bunch of switches, a blackboard behind her 2 x 2 e 5. "She'll hide it under her dress and a body'd never know it. You, child. How'd you get in here?"

The little girl said nothing. She looked at the woman, then she gave me a flying black glance and looked at the woman again, "Them foreigners," the woman said. "How'd she get in without the bell ringing?"

"She came in when I opened the door," I said. "It rang once for both of us. She couldnt reach anything from here, anyway. Besides, I dont think she would. Would you, sister?" The little girl looked at me, secretive, contemplative. "What do you want? bread?"

She extended her fist. It uncurled upon a nickel, moist and dirty, moist dirt ridged into her flesh. The coin was damp and warm. I could smell it, faintly metallic.

"Have you got a five cent loaf, please, ma'am?"

From beneath the counter she produced a square cut from a newspaper sheet and laid it on the counter and wrapped a loaf into it. I laid the coin and another one on the counter. "And another one of those buns, please, ma'am."

She took another bun from the case. "Give me that parcel," she said. I gave it to her and she unwrapped it and put the third bun in and wrapped it and took the coins and found two coppers in her apron and gave them to me. I handed them to the little girl. Her fingers closed about them, damp and hot, like worms.

"You going to give her that bun?" the woman said.

"Yessum," I said. "I expect your cooking smells as good to her as it does to me."

I took up the two packages and gave the bread to the little girl, the woman all iron-grey behind the counter, watching us with cold certitude. "You wait a minute," she said. She went to the rear. The door opened again and closed. The little girl watched me, holding the bread against her dirty-dress.

"What's your name?" I said. She quit looking at me, but she was still motionless. She didnt even seem to breathe. The woman returned. She had a funny looking thing in her hand. She carried it sort of like it might have been a dead pet rat.

"Here," she said. The child looked at her. "Take it," the woman said, jabbing it at the little girl. "It just looks peculiar. I calculate you wont know the difference when you eat it. Here. I cant stand here all day." The child took it, still watching her. The woman rubbed her hands on her apron. "I got to have that bell fixed," she said. She went to the door and jerked it open. The little bell tinkled once, faint and clear and invisible. We moved toward the door and the woman's peering back.

"Thank you for the cake," I said.

"Them foreigners," she said, staring up into the obscurity where the bell tinkled. "Take my advice and stay clear of them, young man."

"Yessum," I said. "Come on, sister." We went out. "Thank you, ma'am."

She swung the door to, then jerked it open again, mak-

ing the bell give forth its single small note. "Foreigners,"
she said, peering up at the bell.

We went on. "Well," I said, "How about some ice
cream?" She was eating the gnarled cake. "Do you like
ice cream?" She gave me a black still look, chewing.
"Come on."

We came to the drugstore and had some ice cream.
She wouldn't put the loaf down. "Why not put it down
so you can eat better?" I said, offering to take it. But she
held to it, chewing the ice cream like it was taffy. The
bitten cake lay on the table. She ate the ice cream steadily, then she fell to on the cake again, looking about at
the showcases. I finished mine and we went out.

"Which way do you live?" I said.

A buggy, the one with the horse it was. Only Doc Peabody is fat. Three hundred pounds. You ride with him on
the uphill side, holding on. Children. Walking easier than
holding uphill. *Seen the doctor yet have you seen Caddy*

*I dont have to I cant ask now afterward it will be
all right it wont matter*

Because women so delicate so mysterious Father said.
Delicate equilibrium of periodical filth between two
moons balanced. Moons he said full and yellow as harvest moons her hips thighs. Outside outside of them always but. Yellow. Feetsoles with walking like. Then
know that some man that all those mysterious and im-
perious concealed. With all that inside of them shapes an
outward suavity waiting for a touch to. Liquid putrefaction like drowned things floating like pale rubber
flabbily filled getting the odour of honeysuckle all mixed
up.

"You'd better take your bread on home, hadnt you?"

She looked at me. She chewed quietly and steadily; at

regular intervals a small distension passed smoothly down her throat. I opened my package and gave her one of the buns. "Goodbye," I said.

I went on. Then I looked back. She was behind me. "Do you live down this way?" She said nothing. She walked beside me, under my elbow sort of, eating. We went on. It was quiet, hardly anyone about *getting the odour of honeysuckle all mixed She would have told me not to let me sit there on the steps hearing her door twilight slamming hearing Benjy still crying Supper she would have to come down then getting honeysuckle all mixed up in it* We reached the corner.

"Well, I've got to go down this way," I said, "Goodbye." She stopped too. She swallowed the last of the cake, then she began on the bun, watching me across it. "Goodbye," I said. I turned into the street and went on, but I went to the next corner before I stopped.

"Which way do you live?" I said. "This way?" I pointed down the street. She just looked at me. "Do you live over that way? I bet you live close to the station, where the trains are. Dont you?" She just looked at me, serene and secret and chewing. The street was empty both ways, with quiet lawns and houses neat among the trees, but no one at all except back there. We turned and went back. Two men sat in chairs in front of a store.

"Do you all know this little girl? She sort of took up with me and I cant find where she lives."

They quit looking at me and looked at her.

"Must be one of them new Italian families," one said. He wore a rusty frock coat. "I've seen her before. What's your name, little girl?" She looked at them blackly for awhile, her jaws moving steadily. She swallowed without ceasing to chew.

"Maybe she cant speak English," the other said.

"They sent her after bread," I said. "She must be able to speak something."

"What's your pa's name?" the first said. "Pete? Joe? name John huh?" She took another bite from the bun.

"What must I do with her?" I said. "She just follows me. I've got to get back to Boston."

"You from the college?"

"Yes, sir. And I've got to get on back."

"You might go up the street and turn her over to Anse. He'll be up at the livery stable. The marshall."

"I reckon that's what I'll have to do," I said. "I've got to do something with her. Much obliged. Come on, sister."

We went up the street, on the shady side, where the shadow of the broken facade blotted slowly across the road. We came to the livery stable. The marshall wasnt there. A man sitting in a chair tilted in the broad low door, where a dark cool breeze smelling of ammonia blew among the ranked stalls, said to look at the post-office. He didn't know her either.

"Them furriners. I cant tell one from another. You might take her across the tracks where they live, and maybe somebody'll claim her."

We went to the postoffice. It was back down the street. The man in the frock coat was opening a newspaper.

"Anse just drove out of town," he said. "I guess you'd better go down past the station and walk past them houses by the river. Somebody there'll know her."

"I guess I'll have to," I said. "Come on, sister." She pushed the last piece of the bun into her mouth and swallowed it. "Want another?" I said. She looked at me, chewing, her eyes black and unwinking and friendly. I took the other two buns out and gave her one and bit into the other. I asked a man where the station was and he showed me. "Come on, sister."

We reached the station and crossed the tracks, where the river was. A bridge crossed it, and a street of jumbled frame houses followed the river, backed onto it. A shabby street, but with an air heterogeneous and vivid too. In the center of an untrimmed plot enclosed by a fence of gaping and broken pickets stood an ancient lopsided surrey and a weathered house from an upper window of which hung a garment of vivid pink.

"Does that look like your house?" I said. She looked at me over the bun. "This one?" I said, pointing. She just chewed, but it seemed to me that I discerned something affirmative, acquiescent even if it wasn't eager, in her air. "This one?" I said. "Come on, then." I entered the broken gate. I looked back at her. "Here?" I said. "This look like your house?"

She nodded her head rapidly, looking at me, gnawing into the damp halfmoon of the bread. We went on. A walk of broken random flags, speared by fresh coarse blades of grass, led to the broken stoop. There was no movement about the house at all, and the pink garment hanging in no wind from the upper window. There was a bell pull with a porcelain knob, attached to about six feet of wire when I stopped pulling and knocked. The little girl had the crust edgeways in her chewing mouth.

A woman opened the door. She looked at me, then she spoke rapidly to the little girl in Italian, with a rising inflection, then a pause, interrogatory. She spoke to her again, the little girl looking at her across the end of the crust, pushing it into her mouth with a dirty hand.

"She says she lives here," I said. "I met her down town. Is this your bread?"

"No spika," the woman said. She spoke to the little girl again. The little girl just looked at her.

"No live here?" I said. I pointed to the girl, then at her, then at the door. The woman shook her head. She spoke rapidly. She came to the edge of the porch and pointed down the road, speaking.

I nodded violently too. "You come show?" I said. I took her arm, waving my other hand toward the road. She spoke swiftly, pointing. "You come show," I said, trying to lead her down the steps.

"Si, si," she said, holding back, showing me whatever it was. I nodded again.

"Thanks. Thanks. Thanks." I went down the steps and walked toward the gate, not running, but pretty fast. I reached the gate and stopped and looked at her for a while. The crust was gone now, and she looked at me with her black, friendly stare. The woman stood on the stoop, watching us.

"Come on, then," I said. "We'll have to find the right one sooner or later."

She moved along just under my elbow. We went on. The houses all seemed empty. Not a soul in sight. A sort of breathlessness that empty houses have. Yet they couldnt all be empty. All the different rooms, if you could just slice the walls away all of a sudden Madam, your daughter, if you please. No. Madam, for God's sake, your daughter. She moved along just under my elbow, her shiny tight pigtails, and then the last house played out and the road curved out of sight beyond a wall, following the river. The woman was emerging from the broken gate, with a shawl over her head and clutched under her chin. The road curved on, empty. I found a coin and gave it to the little girl. A quarter. "Goodbye, sister," I said. Then I ran.

I ran fast, not looking back. Just before the road curved

away I looked back. She stood in the road, a small figure clasping the loaf of bread to her filthy little dress, her eyes still and black and unwinking. I ran on.

A lane turned from the road. I entered it and after a while I slowed to a fast walk. The lane went between back premises—unpainted houses with more of those gay and startling coloured garments on lines, a barn broken-backed, decaying quietly among rank orchard trees, unpruned and weedchoked, pink and white and murmurous with sunlight and with bees. I looked back. The entrance to the lane was empty. I slowed still more, my shadow pacing me, dragging its head through the weeds that hid the fence.

The lane went back to a barred gate, became defunctive in grass, a mere path scarred quietly into new grass. I climbed the gate into a woodlot and crossed it and came to another wall and followed that one, my shadow behind me now. There were vines and creepers where at home would be honeysuckle. Coming and coming especially in the dusk when it rained, getting honeysuckle all mixed up in it as though it were not enough without that, not unbearable enough. *What did you let him for kiss kiss*

I didn't let him I made him watching me getting mad What do you think of that? Red print of my hand coming up through her face like turning a light on under your hand her eyes going bright

It's not for kissing I slapped you. Girl's elbows at fifteen Father said you swallow like you had a fishbone in your throat what's the matter with you and Caddy across the table not to look at me. It's for letting it be some darn town squirt I slapped you you will will you now I guess you say calf rope. My red hand coming up out of her face. What do you think of that scouring her head into

the. Grass sticks crisscrossed into the flesh tingling scour-
ing her head. Say calf rope say it

I didnt kiss a dirty girl like Natalie anyway The wall
went into shadow, and then my shadow, I had tricked it
again. I had forgot about the river curving along the
road. I climbed the wall. And then she watched me jump
down, holding the loaf against her dress.

I stood in the weeds and we looked at one another for
a while.

"Why didnt you tell me you lived out this way, sister?"
The loaf was wearing slowly out of the paper; already it
needed a new one. "Well, come on then and show me the
house." *not a dirty girl like Natalie. It was raining we*
could hear it on the roof, sighing through the high sweet
emptiness of the barn.

There? touching her

Not there

There? not raining hard but we couldnt hear anything
but the roof and as if it was my blood or her blood

She pushed me down the ladder and ran off and left
me Caddy did

Was it there it hurt you when Caddy did ran off was it
there

Oh She walked just under my elbow, the top of her
patent leather head, the loaf fraying out of the newspaper.

"If you dont get home pretty soon you're going to wear
that loaf out. And then what'll your mamma say?" *I bet*
I can lift you up

You cant I'm too heavy

Did Caddy go away did she go to the house you cant
see the barn from our house did you ever try to see the
barn from

It was her fault she pushed me she ran away

I can lift you up see how I can

oh her blood or my blood Oh We went on in the thin dust, our feet silent as rubber in the thin dust where pencils of sun slanted in the trees. And I could feel water again running swift and peaceful in the secret shade.

"You live a long way, dont you. You're mighty smart to go this far to town by yourself." *It's like dancing sitting down did you ever dance sitting down? We could hear the rain, a rat in the crib, the empty barn vacant with horses. How do you hold to dance do you hold like this*

Oh

I used to hold like this you thought I wasnt strong enough didn't you

Oh Oh Oh Oh

I hold to use like this I mean did you hear what I said

I said

oh oh oh oh

The road went on, still and empty, the sun slanting more and more. Her stiff little pigtails were bound at the tips with bits of crimson cloth. A corner of the wrapping flapped a little as she walked, the nose of the loaf naked. I stopped.

"Look here. Do you live down this road? We havent passed a house in a mile, almost."

She looked at me, black and secret and friendly.

"Where do you live, sister? Dont you live back there in town?"

There was a bird somewhere in the woods, beyond the broken and infrequent slanting of sunlight.

"Your papa's going to be worried about you. Dont you reckon you'll get a whipping for not coming straight home with that bread?"

The bird whistled again, invisible, a sound meaningless and profound, inflexionless, ceasing as though cut off with the blow of a knife, and again, and that sense of water swift and peaceful above secret places, felt, not seen not heard.

"Oh, hell, sister." About half the paper hung limp. "That's not doing any good now." I tore it off and dropped it beside the road. "Come on. We'll have to go back to town. We'll go back along the river."

We left the road. Among the moss little pale flowers grew, and the sense of water mute and unseen. *I hold to use like this I mean I use to hold She stood in the door looking at us her hands on her hips*

You pushed me it was your fault it hurt me too

We were dancing sitting down I bet Caddy cant dance sitting down

Stop that stop that

i was just brushing the trash off the back of your dress

You keep your nasty old hands off of me it was your fault you pushed me down I'm mad at you

I dont care she looked at us stay mad she went away We began to hear the shouts, the splashings; I saw a brown body gleam for an instant.

Stay mad. My shirt was getting wet and my hair. Across the roof hearing the roof loud now I could see Natalie going through the garden among the rain. Get wet I hope you catch pneumonia go on home Cowface. I jumped hard as I could into the hogwallow and mud yellowed up to my waist stinking I kept on plunging until I fell down and rolled over in it "Hear them in swimming, sister? I wouldn't mind doing that myself." If I had time. When I have time. I could hear my watch. *mud was warmer than the rain it smelled awful. She had her back turned I went around in front of her. You know what I was doing? She turned her back I went around in front of her the rain creeping into the mud flatting her bodice through her dress it smelled horrible. I was hugging her that's what I was doing. She turned her back I went around in front of her. I was hugging her I tell you.*

I dont give a damn what you were doing

You dont you dont I'll make you I'll make you give a damn. She hit my hands away I smeared mud on her with the other hand I couldn't feel the wet smacking of her hand I wiped mud from my legs smeared it on her wet hard turning body hearing her fingers going into my face but I couldn't feel it even when the rain began to taste sweet on my lips

They saw us from the water first, heads and shoulders. They yelled and one rose squatting and sprang among them. They looked like beavers, the water lipping about their chins, yelling.

"Take that girl away! What did you want to bring a girl here for? Go on away!"

"She wont hurt you. We just want to watch you for a while."

They squatted in the water. Their heads drew into a clump, watching us, then they broke and rushed toward us, hurling water with their hands. We moved quick.

"Look out, boys; she wont hurt you."

"Go on away, Harvard!" It was the second boy, the one that thought the horse and wagon back there at the bridge. "Splash them, fellows!"

"Let's get out and throw them in," another said. "I aint afraid of any girl."

"Splash them! Splash them!" They rushed toward us, hurling water. We moved back. "Go on away!" they yelled. "Go on away!"

We went away. They huddled just under the bank, their slick heads in a row against the bright water. We went on. "That's not for us, is it." The sun slanted through to the moss here and there, leveller. "Poor kid, you're just a girl." Little flowers grew among the moss, littler than I had ever seen. "You're just a girl. Poor kid." There was a path, curving along beside the water. Then the water was still again, dark and still and swift. "Nothing but a girl. Poor sister." *We lay in the wet grass panting the rain like cold shot on my back. Do you care now do you do you*

My Lord we sure are in a mess get up. Where the rain touched my forehead it began to smart my hand came red away streaking off pink in the rain. Does it hurt

Of course it does what do you reckon

I tried to scratch your eyes out my Lord we sure do stink we better try to wash it off in the branch "There's town again, sister. You'll have to go home now. I've got to get back to school. Look how late it's getting. You'll go home now, wont you?" But she just looked at me with her black, secret, friendly gaze, the half-naked loaf clutched to her breast. "It's wet. I thought we jumped back in time." I took my handkerchief and tried to wipe the loaf, but the crust began to come off, so I stopped. "We'll just have to let it dry itself. Hold it like this." She held it like that. It looked kind of like rats had been eating it now. *and the water building and building up the squatting back the sloughed mud stinking surfaceward pocking the pattering surface like grease on a hot stove. I told you I'd make you*

I dont give a goddam what you do

Then we heard the running and we stopped and looked back and saw him coming up the path running, the level shadows flicking upon his legs.

"He's in a hurry. We'd—" then I saw another man, an oldish man running heavily, clutching a stick, and a boy naked from the waist up, clutching his pants as he ran.

"There's Julio," the little girl said, and then I saw his

Italian face and his eyes as he sprang upon me. We went down. His hands were jabbing at my face and he was saying something and trying to bite me, I reckon, and then they hauled him off and held him heaving and thrashing and yelling and they held his arms and he tried to kick me until they dragged him back. The little girl was howling, holding the loaf in both arms. The half-naked boy was darting and jumping up and down, clutching his trousers and someone pulled me up in time to see another stark naked figure come around the tranquil bend in the path running and change direction in mid-stride and leap into the woods, a couple of garments rigid as boards behind it. Julio still struggled. The man who had pulled me up said, "Whoa, now. We got you." He wore a vest but no coat. Upon it was a metal shield. In his other hand he clutched a knotted, polished stick.

"You're Anse, aren't you?" I said. "I was looking for you. What's the matter?"

"I warn you that anything you say will be used against you," he said. "You're under arrest."

"I killa heem," Julio said. He struggled. Two men held him. The little girl howled steadily, holding the bread. "You steala my seester," Julio said. "Let go, meesters."

"Steal his sister?" I said. "Why, I've been—"

"Shet up," Anse said. "You can tell that to Squire."

"Steal his sister?" I said. Julio broke from the men and sprang at me again, but the marshall met him and they struggled until the other two pinioned his arms again. Anse released him, panting.

"You durn furriner," he said, "I've got a good mind to take you up too, for assault and battery." He turned to me again. "Will you come peaceable, or do I handcuff you?"

"I'll come peaceable," I said. "Anything, just so I can

THE SOUND AND THE FURY

find someone—do something with—Stole his sister," I said. "Stole his—"

"I've warned you," Anse said, "He aims to charge you with meditated criminal assault. Here, you, make that gal shut up that noise."

"Oh," I said. Then I began to laugh. Two more boys with plastered heads and round eyes came out of the bushes, buttoning shirts that had already dampened onto their shoulders and arms, and I tried to stop the laughter, but I couldnt.

"Watch him, Anse, he's crazy, I believe."

"I'll h-have to qu-quit," I said, "It'll stop in a mu-minute. The other time it said ah ah ah," I said, laughing. "Let me sit down a while." I sat down, they watching me, and the little girl with her streaked face and the gnawed looking loaf, and the water swift and peaceful below the path. After a while the laughter ran out. But my throat wouldnt quit trying to laugh, like retching after your stomach is empty.

"Whoa, now," Anse said. "Get a grip on yourself."

"Yes," I said, tightening my throat. There was another yellow butterfly, like one of the sunflecks had come loose. After a while I didnt have to hold my throat so tight. I got up. "I'm ready. Which way?"

We followed the path, the two others watching Julio and the little girl and the boys somewhere in the rear. The path went along the river to the bridge. We crossed it and the tracks, people coming to the doors to look at us and more boys materializing from somewhere until when we turned into the main street we had quite a procession. Before the drugstore stood an auto, a big one, but I didn't recognise them until Mrs Bland said,

"Why, Quentin! Quentin Compson!" Then I saw Ger-

ald, and Spoade in the back seat, sitting on the back of
his neck. And Shreve. I didnt know the two girls.

"Quentin Compson!" Mrs Bland said.

"Good afternoon," I said, raising my hat. "I'm under
arrest. I'm sorry I didnt get your note. Did Shreve tell
you?"

"Under arrest?" Shreve said. "Excuse me," he said. He
heaved himself up and climbed over their feet and got
out. He had on a pair of my flannel pants, like a glove. I
didnt remember forgetting them. I didnt remember how
many chins Mrs Bland had, either. The prettiest girl was
with Gerald in front, too. They watched me through
veils, with a kind of delicate horror. "Who's under arrest?"
Shreve said. "What's this, mister?"

"Gerald," Mrs Bland said, "Send these people away.
You get in this car, Quentin."

Gerald got out. Spoade hadnt moved.

"What's he done, Cap?" he said. "Robbed a hen house?"

"I warn you," Anse said. "Do you know the prisoner?"

"Know him," Shreve said. "Look here—"

"Then you can come along to the squire's. You're ob-
structing justice. Come along." He shook my arm.

"Well, good afternoon," I said. "I'm glad to have seen
you all. Sorry I couldnt be with you."

"You, Gerald," Mrs Bland said.

"Look here, constable," Gerald said.

"I warn you you're interfering with an officer of the
law," Anse said. "If you've anything to say, you can come
to the squire's and make cognizance of the prisoner." We
went on. Quite a procession now, Anse and I leading. I
could hear them telling them what it was, and Spoade
asking questions, and then Julio said something violently
in Italian and I looked back and saw the little girl stand-

ing at the curb looking at me with her friendly, inscrutable regard.

"Git on home," Julio shouted at her, "I beat hell outa
you."

We went down the street and turned into a bit of lawn
in which, set back from the street, stood a one storey
building of brick trimmed with white. We went up the
rock path to the door, where Anse halted everyone
except us and made them remain outside. We entered a
bare room smelling of stale tobacco. There was a sheet
iron stove in the center of a wooden frame filled with
sand, and a faded map on the wall and the dingy plat of
a township. Behind a scarred littered table a man with a
fierce roach of iron grey hair peered at us over steel spectacles.

"Got him, did ye, Anse?" he said.

"Got him, Squire."

He opened a huge dusty book and drew it to him and
dipped a foul pen into an inkwell filled with what looked
like coal dust.

"Look here, mister," Shreve said.

"The prisoner's name," the squire said. I told him. He
wrote it slowly into the book, the pen scratching with ex-
cruciating deliberation.

"Look here, mister," Shreve said, "We know this fellow.
We—"

"Order in the court," Anse said.

"Shut up, bud," Spoade said. "Let him do it his way.
He's going to anyhow."

"Age," the squire said. I told him. He wrote that, his
mouth moving as he wrote. "Occupation." I told him.
"Harvard student, hey?" he said. He looked up at me,
bowing his neck a little to see over the spectacles. His

eyes were clear and cold, like a goat's. "What are you up to, coming out here kidnapping children?"

"They're crazy, Squire," Shreve said. "Whoever says this boy's kidnapping—"

Julio moved violently. "Crazy?" he said. "Dont I catcha heem, eh? Dont I see weetha my own eyes—"

"You're a liar," Shreve said. "You never—"

"Order, order," Anse said, raising his voice.

"You fellers shet up," the squire said. "If they dont stay quiet, turn 'em out, Anse." They got quiet. The squire looked at Shreve, then at Spoade, then at Gerald. "You know this young man?" he said to Spoade.

"Yes, your honour," Spoade said. "He's just a country boy in school up there. He dont mean any harm. I think the marshall'll find it's a mistake. His father's a congregational minister."

"H'm," the squire said. "What was you doing, exactly?" I told him, he watching me with his cold, pale eyes. "How about it, Anse?"

"Might have been," Anse said. "Them durn furriners."

"I American," Julio said. "I gotta da pape'."

"Where's the gal?"

"He sent her home," Anse said.

"Was she scared or anything?"

"Not till Julio there jumped on the prisoner. They were just walking along the river path, towards town. Some boys swimming told us which way they went."

"It's a mistake, Squire," Spoade said. "Children and dogs are always taking up with him like that. He cant help it."

"H'm," the squire said. He looked out of the window for a while. We watched him. I could hear Julio scratching himself. The squire looked back.

"Air you satisfied the gal aint took any hurt, you, there?"

"No hurt now," Julio said sullenly.

"You quit work to hunt for her?"

"Sure I quit. I run. I run like hell. Looka here, looka there, then man tella me he seen him giva her she eat. She go weetha."

"H'm," the squire said. "Well, son, I calculate you owe Julio something for taking him away from his work."

"Yes, sir," I said. "How much?"

"Dollar, I calculate."

I gave Julio a dollar.

"Well," Spoade said, "If that's all—I reckon he's discharged, your honour?"

The squire didn't look at him. "How far'd you run him, Anse?"

"Two miles, at least. It was about two hours before we caught him."

"H'm," the squire said. He mused a while. We watched him, his stiff crest, the spectacles riding low on his nose. The yellow shape of the window grew slowly across the floor, reached the wall, climbing. Dust motes whirled and slanted. "Six dollars."

"Six dollars?" Shreve said. "What's that for?"

"Six dollars," the squire said. He looked at Shreve a moment, then at me again.

"Look here," Shreve said.

"Shut up," Spoade said. "Give it to him, bud, and let's get out of here. The ladies are waiting for us. You got six dollars?"

"Yes," I said. I gave him six dollars.

"Case dismissed," he said.

"You get a receipt," Shreve said. "You get a signed receipt for that money."

The squire looked at Shreve mildly. "Case dismissed," he said without raising his voice.

"I'll be damned—" Shreve said.

"Come on here," Spoade said, taking his arm. "Good afternoon, Judge. Much obliged." As we passed out the door Julio's voice rose again, violent, then ceased. Spoade was looking at me, his brown eyes quizzical, a little cold. "Well, bud, I reckon you'll do your girl chasing in Boston after this."

"You damned fool," Shreve said, "What the hell do you mean anyway, straggling off here, fooling with these damn wops?"

"Come on," Spoade said, "They must be getting impatient."

Mrs Bland was talking to them. They were Miss Holmes and Miss Daingerfield and they quit listening to her and looked at me again with that delicate and curious horror, their veils turned back upon their little white noses and their eyes fleeing and mysterious beneath the veils.

"Quentin Compson," Mrs Bland said, "What would your mother say? A young man naturally gets into scrapes, but to be arrested on foot by a country policeman. What did they think he'd done, Gerald?"

"Nothing," Gerald said.

"Nonsense. What was it, you, Spoade?"

"He was trying to kidnap that little dirty girl, but they caught him in time," Spoade said.

"Nonsense," Mrs Bland said, but her voice sort of died away and she stared at me for a moment, and the girls drew their breaths in with a soft concerted sound. "Fiddlesticks," Mrs Bland said briskly, "If that isn't just like these ignorant lowclass Yankees. Get in, Quentin."

Shreve and I sat on two small collapsible seats. Gerald cranked the car and got in and we started.

"Now, Quentin, you tell me what all this foolishness is about," Mrs Bland said. I told them, Shreve hunched and furious on his little seat and Spoade sitting again on the back of his neck beside Miss Daingerfield.

"And the joke is, all the time Quentin had us all fooled," Spoade said. "All the time we thought he was the model youth that anybody could trust a daughter with, until the police showed him up at his nefarious work."

"Hush up, Spoade," Mrs Bland said. We drove down the street and crossed the bridge and passed the house where the pink garment hung in the window. "That's what you get for not reading my note. Why didnt you come and get it? Mr MacKenzie says he told you it was there."

"Yessum. I intended to, but I never went back to the room."

"You'd have let us sit there waiting I dont know how long, if it hadnt been for Mr MacKenzie. When he said you hadnt come back, that left an extra place, so we asked him to come. We're very glad to have you anyway, Mr MacKenzie." Shreve said nothing. His arms were folded and he glared straight ahead past Gerald's cap. It was a cap for motoring in England. Mrs Bland said so. We passed that house, and three others, and another yard where the little girl stood by the gate. She didnt have the bread now, and her face looked like it had been streaked with coaldust. I waved my hand, but she made no reply, only her head turned slowly as the car passed, following us with her unwinking gaze. Then we ran beside the wall, our shadows running along the wall, and after a while we passed a piece of torn newspaper lying beside the road and I began to laugh again. I could feel it in my throat and I looked off into the trees where the afternoon slanted, thinking of afternoon and of the bird and the boys in swimming. But still I couldnt stop it and then I knew that if I tried too hard to stop it I'd be crying and I thought about how I'd thought about I could not be a virgin, with so many of them walking along in the shadows and whispering with their soft girlvoices lingering in the shadowy places and the words coming out and perfume and eyes you could *f*eel not see, but if it was that simple to do it wouldnt be anything and if it wasnt anything, what was I and then Mrs Bland said, "Quentin? Is he sick, Mr MacKenzie?" and then Shreve's fat hand touched my knee and Spoade began talking and I quit trying to stop it.

"If that hamper is in his way, Mr MacKenzie, move it over on your side. I brought a hamper of wine because I think young gentlemen should drink wine, although my father, Gerald's grandfather" *ever do that Have you ever done that In the grey darkness a little light her hands locked about*

"They do, when they can get it," Spoade said. "Hey, Shreve?" *her knees her face looking at the sky the smell of honeysuckle upon her face and throat*

"Beer, too," Shreve said. His hand touched my knee again. I moved my knee again. *like a thin wash of lilac coloured paint talking about him bringing*

"You're not a gentleman," Spoade said. *him between us until the shape of her blurred not with dark*

"No. I'm Canadian," Shreve said. *talking about him the oar blades winking him along winking the Cap made for motoring in England and all time rushing beneath and they two blurred within the other forever more he had been in the army had killed men*

"I adore Canada," Miss Daingerfield said. "I think it's marvellous."

"Did you ever drink perfume?" Spoade said. *with one hand he could lift her to his shoulder and run with her running Running*

"No," Shreve said. *running the beast with two backs and she blurred in the winking oars running the swine of Euboeleus running coupled within how many Caddy*

"Neither did I," Spoade said. *I dont know too many there was something terrible in me terrible in me Father I have committed Have you ever done that We didnt we didnt do that did we do that*

"and Gerald's grandfather always picked his own mint before breakfast, while the dew was still on it. He wouldnt even let old Wilkie touch it do you remember Gerald but always gathered it himself and made his own julep. He was as crochety about his julep as an old maid, measuring everything by a recipe in his head. There was only one man he ever gave that recipe to; that was" *we did how can you not know it if youll just wait I'll tell you how it was it was a crime we did a terrible crime it cannot be hid you think it can but wait Poor Quentin youve never done that have you and I'll tell you how it was I'll tell Father then itll have to be because you love Father then we'll have to go away amid the pointing and the horror the clean flame I'll make you say we did I'm stronger than you I'll make you know we did you thought it was them but it was me listen I fooled you all the time it was me you thought I was in the house where that damn honeysuckle trying not to think the swing the cedars the secret surges the breathing locked drinking the wild breath the yes Yes Yes yes* "never be got to drink wine himself, but he always said that a hamper what book did you read that in the one where Geralds rowing

suit of wine was a necessary part of any gentlemen's picnic basket" *did you love them Caddy did you love them*
When they touched me I died

one minute she was standing there the next he was yelling and pulling at her dress they went into the hall and
up the stairs yelling and shoving at her up the stairs to
the bathroom door and stopped her back against the door
and her arm across her face yelling and trying to shove
her into the bathroom when she came in to supper T. P.
was feeding him he started again just whimpering at
first until she touched him then he yelled she stood there
her eyes like cornered rats then I was running in the grey
darkness it smelled of rain and all flower scents the damp
warm air released and crickets sawing away in the grass
pacing me with a small travelling island of silence Fancy
watched me across the fence blotchy like a quilt on a
line I thought damn that nigger he forgot to feed her
again I ran down the hill in that vacuum of crickets like
a breath travelling across a mirror she was lying in the
water her head on the sand spit the water flowing about
her hips there was a little more light in the water her
skirt half saturated flopped along her flanks to the waters
motion in heavy ripples going nowhere renewed themselves of their own movement I stood on the bank I could
smell the honeysuckle on the water gap the air seemed to
drizzle with honeysuckle and with the rasping of crickets a substance you could feel on the flesh

is Benjy still crying

I dont know yes I dont know

poor Benjy

I sat down on the bank the grass was damp a little
then I found my shoes wet

get out of that water are you crazy

but she didnt move her face was a white blur framed
out of the blur of the sand by her hair
    get out now
    she sat up then she rose her skirt flopped against her
draining she climbed the bank her clothes flopping sat
down
    why dont you wring it out do you want to catch cold
    yes
    the water sucked and gurgled across the sand spit and
on in the dark among the willows across the shallow the
water rippled like a piece of cloth holding still a little
light as water does
    he's crossed all the oceans all around the world
    then she talked about him clasping her wet knees her
face tilted back in the grey light the smell of honeysuckle
there was a light in mothers room and in Benjys where
T. P. was putting him to bed
    do you love him
    her hand came out I didnt move it fumbled down my
arm and she held my hand flat against her chest her heart
thudding
    no no
    did he make you then he made you do it let him he
was stronger than you and he tomorrow Ill kill him I
swear I will father neednt know until afterward and
then you and I nobody need ever know we can take my
school money we can cancel my matriculation Caddy you
hate him dont you dont you
    she held my hand against her chest her heart thudding
I turned and caught her arm
    Caddy you hate him dont you
    she moved my hand up against her throat her heart
was hammering there

poor Quentin

her face looked at the sky it was low so low that all smells and sounds of night seemed to have been crowded down like under a slack tent especially the honeysuckle it had got into my breathing it was on her face and throat like paint her blood pounded against my hand I was leaning on my other arm it began to jerk and jump and I had to pant to get any air at all out of that thick grey honeysuckle

yes I hate him I would die for him I've already died for him I die for him over and over again everytime this goes

when I lifted my hand I could still feel crisscrossed twigs and grass burning into the palm

poor Quentin

she leaned back on her arms her hands locked about her knees

youve never done that have you

what done what

that what I have what I did

yes yes lots of times with lots of girls

then I was crying her hand touched me again and I was crying against her damp blouse then she lying on her back looking past my head into the sky I could see a rim of white under her irises I opened my knife

do you remember the day damuddy died when you sat down in the water in your drawers

yes

I held the point of the knife at her throat

it wont take but a second just a second then I can do mine I can do mine then

all right can you do yours by yourself

yes the blades long enough Benjys in bed by now

yes

it wont take but a second Ill try not to hurt
all right
will you close your eyes
no like this youll have to push it harder
touch your hand to it
but she didnt move her eyes were wide open looking
past my head at the sky
Caddy do you remember how Dilsey fussed at you because your drawers were muddy
dont cry
Im not crying Caddy
push it are you going to
do you want me to
yes push it
touch your hand to it
dont cry poor Quentin
but I couldnt stop she held my head against her damp
hard breast I could hear her heart going firm and slow
now not hammering and the water gurgling among the
willows in the dark and waves of honeysuckle coming up
the air my arm and shoulder were twisted under me
what is it what are you doing
her muscles gathered I sat up
its my knife I dropped it
she sat up
what time is it
I dont know
she rose to her feet I fumbled along the ground
Im going let it go
I could feel her standing there I could smell her damp
clothes feeling her there
its right here somewhere
let it go you can find it tomorrow come on
wait a minute I'll find it

are you afraid to

here it is it was right here all the time

was it come on

I got up and followed we went up the hill the crickets hushing before us

its funny how you can sit down and drop something and have to hunt all around for it

the grey it was grey with dew slanting up into the grey sky then the trees beyond

damn that honeysuckle I wish it would stop

you used to like it

we crossed the crest and went on toward the trees she walked into me she gave over a little the ditch was a black scar on the grey grass she walked into me again she looked at me and gave over we reached the ditch

lets go this way

what for

lets see if you can still see Nancys bones I havent thought to look in a long time have you

it was matted with vines and briers dark

they were right here you cant tell whether you see them or not can you

stop Quentin

come on

the ditch narrowed closed she turned toward the trees

stop Quentin

Caddy

I got in front of her again

Caddy

stop it

I held her

Im stronger than you

she was motionless hard unyielding but still

I wont fight stop youd better stop

Caddy dont Caddy

it wont do any good dont you know it wont let me go

the honeysuckle drizzled and drizzled I could hear the crickets watching us in a circle she moved back went around me on toward the trees

you go on back to the house you neednt come

I went on

why dont you go on back to the house

damn that honeysuckle

we reached the fence she crawled through I crawled through when I rose from stooping he was coming out of the trees into the grey toward us coming toward us tall and flat and still even moving like he was still she went to him

this is Quentin Im wet Im wet all over you dont have to if you dont want to

their shadows one shadow her head rose it was above his on the sky higher their two heads

you dont have to if you dont want to

then not two heads the darkness smelled of rain of damp grass and leaves the grey light drizzling like rain the honeysuckle coming up in damp waves I could see her face a blur against his shoulder he held her in one arm like she was no bigger than a child he extended his hand

glad to know you

we shook hands then we stood there her shadow high against his shadow one shadow

whatre you going to do Quentin

walk a while I think Ill go through the woods to the road and come back through town

I turned away going

goodnight

Quentin

I stopped

what do you want

in the woods the tree frogs were going smelling rain in the air they sounded like toy music boxes that were hard to turn and the honeysuckle

come here

what do you want

come here Quentin

I went back she touched my shoulder leaning down her shadow the blur of her face leaning down from his high shadow I drew back

look out

you go on home

Im not sleepy Im going to take a walk

wait for me at the branch

Im going for a walk

Ill be there soon wait for me you wait

no Im going through the woods

I didnt look back the tree frogs didnt pay me any mind the grey light like moss in the trees drizzling but still it wouldnt rain after a while I turned went back to the edge of the woods as soon as I got there I began to smell honeysuckle again I could see the lights on the courthouse clock and the glare of town the square on the sky and the dark willows along the branch and the light in mothers windows the light still on in Benjys room and I stooped through the fence and went across the pasture running I ran in the grey grass among the crickets the honeysuckle getting stronger and stronger and the smell of water then I could see the water the colour of grey honeysuckle I lay down on the bank with my face close to the ground so I couldnt smell the honeysuckle I couldnt smell it then and I lay there feeling the earth going through my clothes listening to the water and after a

while I wasnt breathing so hard and I lay there thinking
that if I didnt move my face I wouldnt have to breathe
hard and smell it and then I wasnt thinking about anything at all she came along the bank and stopped I didnt
move

its late you go on home

what

you go on home its late

all right

her clothes rustled I didnt move they stopped rustling

are you going in like I told you

I didnt hear anything

Caddy

yes I will if you want me to I will

I sat up she was sitting on the ground her hands
clasped about her knee

go on to the house like I told you

yes Ill do anything you want me to anything yes

she didnt even look at me I caught her shoulder and
shook her hard

you shut up

I shook her

you shut up you shut up

yes

she lifted her face then I saw she wasnt even looking
at me at all I could see that white rim

get up

I pulled her she was limp I lifted her to her feet

go on now

was Benjy still crying when you left

go on

we crossed the branch the roof came in sight then the
window upstairs

hes asleep now

I had to stop and fasten the gate she went on in the grey light the smell of rain and still it wouldnt rain and honeysuckle beginning to come from the garden fence beginning she went into the shadow I could hear her feet then

Caddy

I stopped at the steps I couldnt hear her feet

Caddy

I heard her feet then my hand touched her not warm not cool just still her clothes a little damp still

do you love him now

not breathing except slow like far away breathing

Caddy do you love him now

I dont know

outside the grey light the shadows of things like dead things in stagnant water

I wish you were dead

do you you coming in now

are you thinking about him now

I dont know

tell me what youre thinking about tell me

stop stop Quentin

you shut up you shut up you hear me you shut up are you going to shut up

all right I will stop we'll make too much noise

Ill kill you do you hear

lets go out to the swing theyll hear you here

Im not crying do you say Im crying

no hush now we'll wake Benjy up

you go on into the house go on now

I am dont cry Im bad anyway you cant help it

theres a curse on us its not our fault is it our fault

hush come on and go to bed now

you cant make me theres a curse on us

finally I saw him he was just going into the barbershop
he looked out I went on and waited

Ive been looking for you two or three days

you wanted to see me

Im going to see you

he rolled the cigarette quickly with about two motions
he struck the match with his thumb

we cant talk here suppose I meet you somewhere

Ill come to your room are you at the hotel

no thats not so good you know that bridge over the
creek in there back of

yes all right

at one oclock right

yes

I turned away

Im obliged to you

look

I stopped looked back

she all right

he looked like he was made out of bronze his khaki
shirt

she need me for anything now

I'll be there at one

she heard me tell T. P. to saddle Prince at one oclock
she kept watching me not eating much she came too

what are you going to do

nothing cant I go for a ride if I want to

youre going to do something what is it

none of your business whore whore

T. P. had Prince at the side door

I wont want him Im going to walk

I went down the drive and out the gate I turned into
the lane then I ran before I reached the bridge I saw him
leaning on the rail the horse was hitched in the woods he

looked over his shoulder then he turned his back he didnt
look up until I came onto the bridge and stopped he had
a piece of bark in his hands breaking pieces from it and
dropping them over the rail into the water

I came to tell you to leave town

he broke a piece of bark deliberately dropped it carefully into the water watched it float away

I said you must leave town

he looked at me

did she send you to me

I say you must go not my father not anybody I say it

listen save this for a while I want to know if shes all
right have they been bothering her up there

thats something you dont need to trouble yourself
about

then I heard myself saying Ill give you until sundown
to leave town

he broke a piece of bark and dropped it into the water
then he laid the bark on the rail and rolled a cigarette
with those two swift motions spun the match over the
rail

what will you do if I dont leave

Ill kill you dont think that just because I look like a
kid to you

the smoke flowed in two jets from his nostrils across his
face

how old are you

I began to shake my hands were on the rail I thought if
I hid them hed know why

Ill give you until tonight

listen buddy whats your name Benjys the natural isnt
he you are

Quentin

my mouth said it I didnt say it at all

Ill give you till sundown

Quentin

he raked the cigarette ash carefully off against the rail he did it slowly and carefully like sharpening a pencil my hands had quit shaking

listen no good taking it so hard its not your fault kid it would have been some other fellow

did you ever have a sister did you

no but theyre all bitches

I hit him my open hand beat the impulse to shut it to his face his hand moved as fast as mine the cigarette went over the rail I swung with the other hand he caught it too before the cigarette reached the water he held both my wrists in the same hand his other hand flicked to his arm-pit under his coat behind him the sun slanted and a bird singing somewhere beyond the sun we looked at one an-other while the bird singing he turned my hands loose

look here

he took the bark from the rail and dropped it into the water it bobbed up the current took it floated away his hand lay on the rail holding the pistol loosely we waited

you cant hit it now

no

it floated on it was quite still in the woods I heard the bird again and the water afterward the pistol came up he didnt aim at all the bark disappeared then pieces of it floated up spreading he hit two more of them pieces of bark no bigger than silver dollars

thats enough I guess

he swung the cylinder out and blew into the barrel a thin wisp of smoke dissolved he reloaded the three chambers shut the cylinder he handed it to me butt first

what for I wont try to beat that

youll need it from what you said Im giving you this
one because youve seen what itll do
to hell with your gun
I hit him I was still trying to hit him long after he was
holding my wrists but I still tried then it was like I was
looking at him through a piece of coloured glass I could
hear my blood and then I could see the sky again and
branches against it and the sun slanting through them
and he holding me on my feet
did you hit me
I couldnt hear
what
yes how do you feel
all right let go
he let me go I leaned against the rail
do you feel all right
let me alone Im all right
can you make it home all right
go on let me alone
youd better not try to walk take my horse
no you go on
you can hang the reins on the pommel and turn him
loose he'll go back to the stable
let me alone you go on and let me alone
I leaned on the rail looking at the water I heard him
untie the horse and ride off and after a while I couldnt
hear anything but the water and then the bird again I
left the bridge and sat down with my back against a tree
and leaned my head against the tree and shut my eyes a
patch of sun came through and fell across my eyes and I
moved a little further around the tree I heard the bird
again and the water and then everything sort of rolled
away and I didnt feel anything at all I felt almost good

after all those days and the nights with honeysuckle coming up out of the darkness into my room where I was trying to sleep even when after a while I knew that he hadnt hit me that he had lied about that for her sake too and that I had just passed out like a girl but even that didnt matter anymore and I sat there against the tree with little flecks of sunlight brushing across my face like yellow leaves on a twig listening to the water and not thinking about anything at all even when I heard the horse coming fast I sat there with my eyes closed and heard its feet bunch scuttering the hissing sand and feet running and her hard running hands

fool fool are you hurt

I opened my eyes her hands running on my face

I didnt know which way until I heard the pistol I didnt know where I didnt think he and you running off slipping I didnt think he would have

she held my face between her hands bumping my head against the tree

stop stop that

I caught her wrists

quit that quit it

I knew he wouldnt I knew he wouldnt

she tried to bump my head against the tree

I told him never to speak to me again I told him

she tried to break her wrists free

let me go

stop it I'm stronger than you stop it now

let me go Ive got to catch him and ask his let me go Quentin please let me go let me go

all at once she quit her wrists went lax

yes I can tell him I can make him believe anytime I can make him

Caddy

she hadnt hitched Prince he was liable to strike out for home if the notion took him

anytime he will believe me

do you love him Caddy

do I what

she looked at me then everything emptied out of her eyes and they looked like the eyes in the statues blank and unseeing and serene

put your hand against my throat

she took my hand and held it flat against her throat

now say his name

Dalton Ames

I felt the first surge of blood there it surged in strong accelerating beats

say it again

her face looked off into the trees where the sun slanted and where the bird

say it again

Dalton Ames

her blood surged steadily beating and beating against my hand

It kept on running for a long time, but my face felt cold and sort of dead, and my eye, and the cut place on my finger was smarting again. I could hear Shreve working the pump, then he came back with the basin and a round blob of twilight wobbling in it, with a yellow edge like a fading balloon, then my reflection. I tried to see my face in it.

"Has it stopped?" Shreve said. "Give me the rag." He tried to take it from my hand.

"Look out," I said, "I can do it. Yes, it's about stopped now." I dipped the rag again, breaking the balloon. The rag stained the water. "I wish I had a clean one."

"You need a piece of beefsteak for that eye," Shreve said. "Damn if you wont have a shiner tomorrow. The son of a bitch," he said.

"Did I hurt him any?" I wrung out the handkerchief and tried to clean the blood off of my vest.

"You cant get that off," Shreve said. "You'll have to send it to the cleaner's. Come on, hold it on your eye, why dont you."

"I can get some of it off," I said. But I wasn't doing much good. "What sort of shape is my collar in?"

"I dont know," Shreve said. "Hold it against your eye. Here."

"Look out," I said. "I can do it. Did I hurt him any?"

"You may have hit him. I may have looked away just then or blinked or something. He boxed the hell out of you. He boxed you all over the place. What did you want to fight him with your fists for? You goddamn fool. How do you feel?"

"I feel fine," I said. "I wonder if I can get something to clean my vest."

"Oh, forget your damn clothes. Does your eye hurt?"

"I feel fine," I said. Everything was sort of violet and still, the sky green paling into gold beyond the gable of the house and a plume of smoke rising from the chimney without any wind. I heard the pump again. A man was filling a pail, watching us across his pumping shoulder. A woman crossed the door, but she didnt look out. I could hear a cow lowing somewhere.

"Come on," Shreve said, "Let your clothes alone and put that rag on your eye. I'll send your suit out first thing tomorrow."

"All right. I'm sorry I didn't bleed on him a little, at least."

"Son of a bitch," Shreve said. Spoade came out of the

house, talking to the woman I reckon, and crossed the yard. He looked at me with his cold, quizzical eyes.

"Well, bud," he said, looking at me, "I'll be damned if you dont go to a lot of trouble to have your fun. Kidnapping, then fighting. What do you do on your holidays? burn houses?"

"I'm all right," I said. "What did Mrs Bland say?"

"She's giving Gerald hell for bloodying you up. She'll give you hell for letting him, when she sees you. She dont object to the fighting, it's the blood that annoys her. I think you lost caste with her a little by not holding your blood better. How do you feel?"

"Sure," Shreve said, "If you cant be a Bland, the next best thing is to commit adultery with one or get drunk and fight him, as the case may be."

"Quite right," Spoade said. "But I didnt know Quentin was drunk."

"He wasnt," Shreve said. "Do you have to be drunk to want to hit that son of a bitch?"

"Well, I think I'd have to be pretty drunk to try it, after seeing how Quentin came out. Where'd he learn to box?"

"He's been going to Mike's every day, over in town," I said.

"He has?" Spoade said. "Did you know that when you hit him?"

"I dont know," I said. "I guess so. Yes."

"Wet it again," Shreve said. "Want some fresh water?"

"This is all right," I said. I dipped the cloth again and held it to my eye. "Wish I had something to clean my vest." Spoade was still watching me.

"Say," he said, "What did you hit him for? What was it he said?"

"I dont know. I dont know why I did."

"The first I knew was when you jumped up all of a sudden and said, 'Did you ever have a sister? did you?' and when he said No, you hit him. I noticed you kept on looking at him, but you didnt seem to be paying any attention to what anybody was saying until you jumped up and asked him if he had any sisters."

"Ah, he was blowing off as usual," Shreve said, "about his women. You know: like he does, before girls, so they dont know exactly what he's saying. All his damn innuendo and lying and a lot of stuff that dont make sense even. Telling us about some wench that he made a date with to meet at a dance hall in Atlantic City and stood her up and went to the hotel and went to bed and how he lay there being sorry for her waiting on the pier for him, without him there to give her what she wanted. Talking about the body's beauty and the sorry ends thereof and how tough women have it, without anything else they can do except lie on their backs. Leda lurking in the bushes, whimpering and moaning for the swan, see. The son of a bitch. I'd hit him myself. Only I'd grabbed up her damn hamper of wine and done it if it had been me."

"Oh," Spoade said, "the champion of dames. Bud, you excite not only admiration, but horror." He looked at me, cold and quizzical. "Good God," he said.

"I'm sorry I hit him," I said. "Do I look too bad to go back and get it over with?"

"Apologies, hell," Shreve said, "Let them go to hell. We're going to town."

"He ought to go back so they'll know he fights like a gentleman," Spoade said. "Gets licked like one, I mean."

"Like this?" Shreve said, "With his clothes all over blood?"

"Why, all right," Spoade said, "You know best."

"He cant go around in his undershirt," Shreve said, "He's not a senior yet. Come on, let's go to town."

"You neednt come," I said. "You go on back to the picnic."

"Hell with them," Shreve said. "Come on here."

"What'll I tell them?" Spoade said. "Tell them you and Quentin had a fight too?"

"Tell them nothing," Shreve said. "Tell her her option expired at sunset. Come on, Quentin. I'll ask that woman where the nearest interurban—"

"No," I said, "I'm not going back to town."

Shreve stopped, looking at me. Turning, his glasses looked like small yellow moons.

"What are you going to do?"

"I'm not going back to town yet. You go on back to the picnic. Tell them I wouldnt come back because my clothes were spoiled."

"Look here," he said, "What are you up to?"

"Nothing. I'm all right. You and Spoade go on back. I'll see you tomorrow." I went on across the yard, toward the road.

"Do you know where the station is?" Shreve said.

"I'll find it. I'll see you all tomorrow. Tell Mrs Bland I'm sorry I spoiled her party." They stood watching me. I went around the house. A rock path went down to the road. Roses grew on both sides of the path. I went through the gate, onto the road. It dropped downhill, toward the woods, and I could make out the auto beside the road. I went up the hill. The light increased as I mounted, and before I reached the top I heard a car. It sounded far away across the twilight and I stopped and listened to it. I couldnt make out the auto any longer, but Shreve was standing in the road before the house, looking up the hill. Behind him the yellow light lay like

a wash of paint on the roof of the house. I lifted my
hand and went on over the hill, listening to the car. Then
the house was gone and I stopped in the green and yellow light and heard the car growing louder and louder,
until just as it began to die away it ceased all together. I
waited until I heard it start again. Then I went on.

As I descended the light dwindled slowly, yet at the
same time without altering its quality, as if I and not
light were changing, decreasing, though even when the
road ran into trees you could have read a newspaper.
Pretty soon I came to a lane. I turned into it. It was
closer and darker than the road, but when it came out at
the trolley stop—another wooden marquee—the light
was still unchanged. After the lane it seemed brighter, as
though I had walked through night in the lane and come
out into morning again. Pretty soon the car came. I got
on it, they turning to look at my eye, and found a seat on
the left side.

The lights were on in the car, so while we ran between
trees I couldnt see anything except my own face and a
woman across the aisle with a hat sitting right on top of
her head, with a broken feather in it, but when we ran
out of the trees I could see the twilight again, that quality of light as if time really had stopped for a while, with
the sun hanging just under the horizon, and then we
passed the marquee where the old man had been eating
out of the sack, and the road going on under the twilight,
into twilight and the sense of water peaceful and swift
beyond. Then the car went on, the draught building
steadily up in the open door until it was drawing steadily
through the car with the odour of summer and darkness
except honeysuckle. Honeysuckle was the saddest odour
of all, I think. I remember lots of them. Wistaria was one.
On the rainy days when Mother wasnt feeling quite bad

enough to stay away from the windows we used to play under it. When Mother stayed in bed Dilsey would put old clothes on us and let us go out in the rain because she said rain never hurt young folks. But if Mother was up we always began by playing on the porch until she said we were making too much noise, then we went out and played under the wistaria frame.

This was where I saw the river for the last time this morning, about here. I could feel water beyond the twilight, smell. When it bloomed in the spring and it rained the smell was everywhere you didnt notice it so much at other times but when it rained the smell began to come into the house at twilight either it would rain more at twilight or there was something in the light itself but it always smelled strongest then until I would lie in bed thinking when will it stop when will it stop. The draft in the door smelled of water, a damp steady breath. Sometimes I could put myself to sleep saying that over and over until after the honeysuckle got all mixed up in it the whole thing came to symbolise night and unrest I seemed to be lying neither asleep nor awake looking down a long corridor of grey halflight where all stable things had become shadowy paradoxical all I had done shadows all I had felt suffered taking visible form antic and perverse mocking without relevance inherent themselves with the denial of the significance they should have affirmed thinking I was I was not who was not was not who.

I could smell the curves of the river beyond the dusk and I saw the last light supine and tranquil upon tideflats like pieces of broken mirror, then beyond them lights began in the pale clear air, trembling a little like butterflies hovering a long way off. Benjamin the child of. How he used to sit before that mirror. Refuge unfailing in which conflict tempered silenced reconciled. Benjamin the child of mine old age held hostage into Egypt. O Benjamin. Dilsey said it was because Mother was too proud for him. They come into white people's lives like that in sudden sharp black trickles that isolate white facts for an instant in unarguable truth like under a microscope; the rest of the time just voices that laugh when you see nothing to laugh at, tears when no reason for tears. They will bet on the odd or even number of mourners at a funeral. A brothel full of them in Memphis went into a religious trance ran naked into the street. It took three policemen to subdue one of them. Yes Jesus O good man Jesus O that good man.

The car stopped. I got out, with them looking at my eye. When the trolley came it was full. I stopped on the back platform.

"Seats up front," the conductor said. I looked into the car. There were no seats on the left side.

"I'm not going far," I said. "I'll just stand here."

We crossed the river. The bridge, that is, arching slow and high into space, between silence and nothingness where lights—yellow and red and green—trembled in the clear air, repeating themselves.

"Better go up front and get a seat," the conductor said.

"I get off pretty soon," I said. "A couple of blocks."

I got off before we reached the postoffice. They'd all be sitting around somewhere by now though, and then I was hearing my watch and I began to listen for the chimes and I touched Shreve's letter through my coat, the bitten shadows of the elms flowing upon my hand. And then as I turned into the quad the chimes did begin and I went on while the notes came up like ripples on a pool and passed me and went on, saying Quarter to what? All right. Quarter to what.

Our windows were dark. The entrance was empty. I walked close to the left wall when I entered, but it was empty: just the stairs curving up into shadows echoes of feet in the sad generations like light dust upon the shadows, my feet waking them like dust, lightly to settle again.

I could see the letter before I turned the light on, propped against a book on the table so I would see it. Calling him my husband. And then Spoade said they were going somewhere, would not be back until late, and Mrs Bland would need another cavalier. But I would have seen him and he cannot get another car for an hour because after six oclock. I took out my watch and listened to it clicking away, not knowing it couldnt even lie. Then I laid it face up on the table and took Mrs Bland's letter and tore it across and dropped the pieces into the waste basket and took off my coat, vest, collar, tie and shirt. The tie was spoiled too, but then niggers. Maybe a pattern of blood he could call that the one Christ was wearing. I found the gasoline in Shreve's room and spread the vest on the table, where it would be flat, and opened the gasoline.

the first car in town a girl Girl that's what Jason couldn't bear smell of gasoline making him sick then got madder than ever because a girl Girl had no sister but Benjamin Benjamin the child of my sorrowful if I'd just had a mother so I could say Mother Mother It took a lot of gasoline, and then I couldnt tell if it was still the stain or just the gasoline. It had started the cut to smarting again so when I went to wash I hung the vest on a chair and lowered the light cord so that the bulb would be drying the splotch. I washed my face and hands, but even then I could smell it within the soap stinging, constricting the nostrils a little. Then I opened the bag and took the shirt and collar and tie out and put the bloody ones in and closed the bag, and dressed. While I was brushing my hair the half hour went. But there was until the three quarters anyway, except suppose *seeing on the rushing darkness only his own face no broken feather unless two of them but not two like that going to Boston the same night then my face his face for an instant across the crashing when out of darkness two lighted windows in rigid fleeing crash gone his face and mine just I see saw did I see not goodbye the marquee empty of eating the road empty in darkness in silence the bridge arching into silence darkness sleep the water peaceful and swift not goodbye*

I turned out the light and went into my bedroom, out of the gasoline but I could still smell it. I stood at the window the curtains moved slow out of the darkness touching my face like someone breathing asleep, breathing slow into the darkness again, leaving the touch. *After they had gone up stairs Mother lay back in her chair, the camphor handkerchief to her mouth. Father hadn't moved he still sat beside her holding her hand the bellowing hammering away like no place for it in silence* When I was little there was a picture in one of our books, a dark place into which a single weak ray of light came slanting upon two faces lifted out of the shadow. *You know what I'd do if I were King?* she never was a queen or a fairy she was always a king or a giant or a general *I'd break that place open and drag them out and I'd whip them good* It was torn out, jagged out. I was glad. I'd have to turn back to it until the dungeon was Mother herself she and Father upward into weak light holding hands and us lost somewhere below even them without even a ray of light. Then the honeysuckle got into it. As soon as I turned off the light and tried to go to

sleep it would begin to come into the room in waves
building and building up until I would have to pant to
get any air at all out of it until I would have to get up
and feel my way like when I was a little boy *hands can
see touching in the mind shaping unseen door Door now
nothing hands can see* My nose could see gasoline, the
vest on the table, the door. The corridor was still empty
of all the feet in sad generations seeking water. *yet the
eyes unseeing clenched like teeth not disbelieving doubt-
ing even the absence of pain shin ankle knee the long invisible flowing of the stair-railing where a misstep in the
darkness filled with sleeping Mother Father Caddy Jason
Maury door I am not afraid only Mother Father Caddy
Jason Maury getting so far ahead sleeping I will sleep
fast when I door Door door* It was empty too, the pipes,
the porcelain, the stained quiet walls, the throne of con-
templation. I had forgotten the glass, but I could *hands
can see cooling fingers invisible swan-throat where less
than Moses rod the glass touch tentative not to drumming lean cool throat drumming cooling the metal the
glass full overfull cooling the glass the fingers flushing
sleep leaving the taste of dampened sleep in the long silence of the throat* I returned up the corridor, waking the
lost feet in whispering battalions in the silence, into the
gasoline, the watch telling its furious lie on the dark
table. Then the curtains breathing out of the dark upon
my face, leaving the breathing upon my face. A quarter
hour yet. And then I'll not be. The peacefullest words.
Peacefullest words. *Non fui. Sum. Fui. Non sum.* Somewhere I heard bells once. Mississippi or Massachusetts. I
was. I am not. Massachusetts or Mississippi. Shreve has a
bottle in his trunk. *Aren't you even going to open it* Mr
and Mrs Jason Richmond Compson announce the *Three
times. Days. Aren't you even going to open it* marriage of

their daughter Candace *that liquor teaches you to con-fuse the means with the end.* I am. Drink. I was not. Let us sell Benjy's pasture so that Quentin may go to Harvard and I may knock my bones together and together. I will be dead in. Was it one year Caddy said. Shreve has a bottle in his trunk. Sir I will not need Shreve's I have sold Benjy's pasture and I can be dead in Harvard Caddy said in the caverns and the grottoes of the sea tumbling peacefully to the wavering tides because Harvard is such a fine sound forty acres is no high price for a fine sound. A fine dead sound we will swap Benjy's pasture for a fine dead sound. It will last him a long time because he cannot hear it unless he can smell it *as soon as she came in the door he began to cry* I thought all the time it was just one of those town squirts that Father was always teasing her about until. I didnt notice him any more than any other stranger drummer or what thought they were army shirts until all of a sudden I knew he wasn't thinking of me at all as a potential source of harm, but was thinking of her when he looked at me was looking at me through her like through a piece of coloured glass *why must you meddle with me dont you know it wont do any good I thought you'd have left that for Mother and Jason*

did Mother set Jason to spy on you I wouldnt have. Women only use other people's codes of honour it's because she loves Caddy staying downstairs even when she was sick so Father couldnt kid Uncle Maury before Jason Father said Uncle Maury was too poor a classicist to risk the blind immortal boy in person he should have chosen Jason because Jason would have made only the same kind of blunder Uncle Maury himself would have made not one to get him a black eye the Patterson boy was smaller than Jason too they sold the kites for a nickel apiece until the trouble over finances Jason got a new partner still smaller one small enough anyway because T. P. said Jason still treasurer but Father said why should Uncle Maury work if he father could support five or six niggers that did nothing at all but sit with their feet in the oven he certainly could board and lodge Uncle Maury now and then and lend him a little money who kept his Father's belief in the celestial derivation of his own species at such a fine heat then Mother would cry and say that Father believed his people were better than hers that he was ridiculing Uncle Maury to teach us the same thing she couldnt see that Father was teaching us that all men are just accumulations dolls stuffed with sawdust swept up from the trash heaps where all previous dolls had been thrown away the sawdust flowing from what wound in what side that not for me died not. It used to be I thought of death as a man something like Grandfather a friend of his a kind of private and particular friend like we used to think of Grandfather's desk not to touch it not even to talk loud in the room where it was I always thought of them as being together somewhere all the time waiting for old Colonel Sartoris to come down and sit with them waiting on a high place beyond cedar trees Colonel Sartoris was on a still higher place looking out across at something and they were waiting for him to get done looking at it and come down Grandfather wore his uniform and we could hear the murmur of their voices from beyond the cedars they were always talking and Grandfather was always right.

The three quarters began. The first note sounded, measured and tranquil, serenely peremptory, emptying the unhurried silence for the next one and that's it if people could only change one another forever that way merge like a flame swirling up for an instant then blown

cleanly out along the cool eternal dark instead of lying
there trying not to think of the swing until all cedars
came to have that vivid dead smell of perfume that
Benjy hated so. Just by imagining the clump it seemed to
me that I could hear whispers secret surges smell the
beating of hot blood under wild unsecret flesh watching
against red eyelids the swine untethered in pairs rushing
coupled into the sea and he we must just stay awake
and see evil done for a little while its not always and i it
doesnt have to be even that long for a man of courage
and he do you consider that courage and i yes sir dont
you and he every man is the arbiter of his own virtues
whether or not you consider it courageous is of more importance than the act itself than any act otherwise you
could not be in earnest and i you dont believe i am serious and he i think you are too serious to give me any
cause for alarm you wouldnt have felt driven to the ex-
pedient of telling me you have committed incest otherwise and i i wasnt lying i wasnt lying and he you wanted
to sublimate a piece of natural human folly into a horror
and then exorcise it with truth and i it was to isolate her
out of the loud world so that it would have to flee us of
necessity and then the sound of it would be as though it
had never been and he did you try to make her do it and
i i was afraid to i was afraid she might and then it
wouldnt have done any good but if i could tell you we
did it would have been so and then the others wouldnt
be so and then the world would roar away and he and
now this other you are not lying now either but you are
still blind to what is in yourself to that part of general
truth the sequence of natural events and their causes
which shadows every mans brow even benjys you are not
thinking of finitude you are contemplating an apotheosis
in which a temporary state of mind will become

symmetrical above the flesh and aware both of itself and
of the flesh it will not quite discard you will not even be
dead and i temporary and he you cannot bear to think
that someday it will no longer hurt you like this now
were getting at it you seem to regard it merely as an experience that will whiten your hair overnight so to speak
without altering your appearance at all you wont do it
under these conditions it will be a gamble and the
strange thing is that man who is conceived by accident
and whose every breath is a fresh cast with dice already
loaded against him will not face that final main which he
knows before hand he has assuredly to face without es-
saying expedients ranging all the way from violence to
petty chicanery that would not deceive a child until
someday in very disgust he risks everything on a single
blind turn of a card no man ever does that under the first
fury of despair or remorse or bereavement he does it
only when he has realised that even the despair or remorse or bereavement is not particularly important to the
dark diceman and i temporary and he it is hard believing
to think that a love or a sorrow is a bond purchased without design and which matures willynilly and is recalled
without warning to be replaced by whatever issue the
gods happen to be floating at the time no you will not
do that until you come to believe that even she was not
quite worth despair perhaps and i i will never do that
nobody knows what i know and he i think youd better
go on up to cambridge right away you might go up into
maine for a month you can afford it if you are careful it
might be a good thing watching pennies has healed more
scars than jesus and i suppose i realise what you believe i
will realise up there next week or next month and he
then you will remember that for you to go to harvard
has been your mothers dream since you were born and

no compson has ever disappointed a lady and i temporary it will be better for me for all of us and he every
man is the arbiter of his own virtues but let no man pre-
scribe for another mans wellbeing and i temporary and
he was the saddest word of all there is nothing else in the
world its not despair until time its not even time until
it was

The last note sounded. At last it stopped vibrating and
the darkness was still again. I entered the sitting room
and turned on the light. I put my vest on. The gasoline
was faint now, barely noticeable, and in the mirror the
stain didnt show. Not like my eye did, anyway. I put on
my coat. Shreve's letter crackled through the cloth and I
took it out and examined the address, and put it in my
side pocket. Then I carried the watch into Shreve's room
and put it in his drawer and went to my room and got
a fresh handkerchief and went to the door and put my
hand on the light switch. Then I remembered I hadnt
brushed my teeth, so I had to open the bag again. I
found my toothbrush and got some of Shreve's paste and
went out and brushed my teeth. I squeezed the brush as
dry as I could and put it back in the bag and shut it,
and went to the door again. Before I snapped the
light out I looked around to see if there was anything
else, then I saw that I had forgotten my hat. I'd have to
go by the postoffice and I'd be sure to meet some of them,
and they'd think I was a Harvard Square student making
like he was a senior. I had forgotten to brush it too, but
Shreve had a brush, so I didnt have to open the bag any
more.

APRIL

6

1928

ONCE A BITCH ALWAYS A BITCH, WHAT I SAY. I SAYS you're lucky if her playing out of school is all that worries you. I says she ought to be down there in that kitchen right now, instead of up there in her room, gobbing paint on her face and waiting for six niggers that cant even stand up out of a chair unless they've got a pan full of bread and meat to balance them, to fix breakfast for her. And Mother says,

"But to have the school authorities think that I have no control over her, that I cant—"

"Well," I says, "You cant, can you? You never have tried to do anything with her," I says, "How do you expect to begin this late, when she's seventeen years old?"

She thought about that for a while.

"But to have them think that . . . I didn't even know she had a report card. She told me last fall that they had quit using them this year. And now for Professor Junkin to call me on the telephone and tell me if she's absent one more time, she will have to leave school. How does she do it? Where does she go? You're down town all day; you ought to see her if she stays on the streets."

"Yes," I says, "If she stayed on the streets. I dont reckon she'd be playing out of school just to do something she could do in public," I says.

"What do you mean?" she says.

"I dont mean anything," I says. "I just answered your question." Then she begun to cry again, talking about how her own flesh and blood rose up to curse her

"You asked me," I says.

"I dont mean you," she says. "You are the only one of them that isn't a reproach to me."

"Sure," I says, "I never had time to be. I never had time to go to Harvard like Quentin or drink myself into the ground like Father. I had to work. But of course if you want me to follow her around and see what she does, I can quit the store and get a job where I can work at night. Then I can watch her during the day and you can use Ben for the night shift."

"I know I'm just a trouble and a burden to you," she says, crying on the pillow.

"I ought to know it," I says. "You've been telling me that for thirty years. Even Ben ought to know it now. Do you want me to say anything to her about it?"

"Do you think it will do any good?" she says.

"Not if you come down there interfering just when I get started," I says. "If you want me to control her, just say so and keep your hands off. Everytime I try to, you come butting in and then she gives both of us the laugh."

"Remember she's your own flesh and blood," she says.

"Sure," I says, "that's just what I'm thinking of—flesh. And a little blood too, if I had my way. When people act like niggers, no matter who they are the only thing to do is treat them like a nigger."

"I'm afraid you'll lose your temper with her," she says.

"Well," I says, "You haven't had much luck with your

system. You want me to do anything about it, or not? Say one way or the other; I've got to get on to work."

"I know you have to slave your life away for us," she says. "You know if I had my way, you'd have an office of your own to go to, and hours that became a Bascomb. Because you are a Bascomb, despite your name. I know that if your father could have foreseen—"

"Well," I says, "I reckon he's entitled to guess wrong now and then, like anybody else, even a Smith or a Jones." She begun to cry again.

"To hear you speak bitterly of your dead father," she says.

"All right," I says, "all right. Have it your way. But as I haven't got an office, I'll have to get on to what I have got. Do you want me to say anything to her?"

"I'm afraid you'll lose your temper with her," she says.

"All right," I says, "I wont say anything, then."

"But something must be done," she says. "To have people think I permit her to stay out of school and run about the streets, or that I cant prevent her doing it. . . . Jason, Jason," she says, "How could you. How could you leave me with these burdens."

"Now, now," I says, "You'll make yourself sick. Why dont you either lock her up all day too, or turn her over to me and quit worrying over her?"

"My own flesh and blood," she says, crying. So I says,

"All right. I'll tend to her. Quit crying, now."

"Dont lose your temper," she says. "She's just a child, remember."

"No," I says, "I wont." I went out, closing the door.

"Jason," she says. I didn't answer. I went down the hall. "Jason," she says beyond the door. I went on down stairs. There wasn't anybody in the diningroom, then I

heard her in the kitchen. She was trying to make Dilsey
let her have another cup of coffee. I went in.

"I reckon that's your school costume, is it?" I says. "Or
maybe today's a holiday?"

"Just a half a cup, Dilsey," she says. "Please."

"No, suh," Dilsey says, "I aint gwine do it. You aint got
no business wid mo'n one cup, a seventeen year old gal,
let lone whut Miss Cahline say. You go on and git
dressed for school, so you kin ride to town wid Jason.
You fixin to be late again."

"No she's not," I says. "We're going to fix that right
now." She looked at me, the cup in her hand. She
brushed her hair back from her face, her kimono slipping
off her shoulder. "You put that cup down and come in
here a minute," I says.

"What for?" she says.

"Come on," I says. "Put that cup in the sink and come
in here."

"What you up to now, Jason?" Dilsey says.

"You may think you can run over me like you do your
grandmother and everybody else," I says, "But you'll find
out different. I'll give you ten seconds to put that cup
down like I told you."

She quit looking at me. She looked at Dilsey. "What
time is it, Dilsey?" she says. "When it's ten seconds, you
whistle. Just a half a cup, Dilsey, pl—"

I grabbed her by the arm. She dropped the cup. It
broke on the floor and she jerked back, looking at me,
but I held her arm. Dilsey got up from her chair.

"You, Jason," she says.

"You turn me loose," Quentin says, "I'll slap you."

"You will, will you?" I says, "You will will you?" She
slapped at me. I caught that hand too and held her like

a wildcat. "You will, will you?" I says. "You think you will?"

"You, Jason!" Dilsey says. I dragged her into the diningroom. Her kimono came unfastened, flapping about her; damn near naked. Dilsey came hobbling along. I turned and kicked the door shut in her face.

"You keep out of here," I says.

Quentin was leaning against the table, fastening her kimono. I looked at her.

"Now," I says, "I want to know what you mean, playing out of school and telling your grandmother lies and forging her name on your report and worrying her sick. What do you mean by it?"

She didn't say anything. She was fastening her kimono up under her chin, pulling it tight around her, looking at me. She hadn't got around to painting herself yet and her face looked like she had polished it with a gun rag. I went and grabbed her wrist. "What do you mean?" I says.

"None of your damn business," she says. "You turn me loose."

Dilsey came in the door. "You, Jason," she says.

"You get out of here, like I told you," I says, not even looking back. "I want to know where you go when you play out of school," I says. "You keep off the streets, or I'd see you. Who do you play out with? Are you hiding out in the woods with one of those damn slick-headed jellybeans? Is that where you go?"

"You—you old goddamn!" she says. She fought, but I held her. "You damn old goddamn!" she says.

"I'll show you," I says. "You may can scare an old woman off, but I'll show you who's got hold of you now." I held her with one hand, then she quit fighting and watched me, her eyes getting wide and black.

"What are you going to do?" she says.

"You wait until I get this belt out and I'll show you," I says, pulling my belt out. Then Dilsey grabbed my arm.

"Jason," she says, "You, Jason! Aint you shamed of yourself."

"Dilsey," Quentin says, "Dilsey."

"I aint gwine let him," Dilsey says, "Dont you worry, honey." She held to my arm. Then the belt came out and I jerked loose and flung her away. She stumbled into the table. She was so old she couldn't do any more than move hardly. But that's all right: we need somebody in the kitchen to eat up the grub the young ones cant tote off. She came hobbling between us, trying to hold me again. "Hit me, den," she says, "ef nothin else but hittin somebody wont do you. Hit me," she says.

"You think I wont?" I says.

"I dont put no devilment beyond you," she says. Then I heard Mother on the stairs. I might have known she wasn't going to keep out of it. I let go. She stumbled back against the wall, holding her kimono shut.

"All right," I says, "We'll just put this off a while. But dont think you can run it over me. I'm not an old woman, nor an old half dead nigger, either. You damn little slut," I says.

"Dilsey," she says, "Dilsey, I want my mother."

Dilsey went to her. "Now, now," she says, "He aint gwine so much as lay his hand on you while Ise here." Mother came on down the stairs.

"Jason," she says, "Dilsey."

"Now, now," Dilsey says, "I aint gwine let him tech you." She put her hand on Quentin. She knocked it down.

"You damn old nigger," she says. She ran toward the door.

"Dilsey," Mother says on the stairs. Quentin ran up the stairs, passing her. "Quentin," Mother says, "You, Quentin." Quentin ran on. I could hear her when she reached the top, then in the hall. Then the door slammed.

Mother had stopped. Then she came on. "Dilsey," she says.

"All right," Dilsey says, "Ise comin. You go on and git dat car and wait now," she says, "so you kin cahy her to school."

"Dont you worry," I says. "I'll take her to school and I'm going to see that she stays there. I've started this thing, and I'm going through with it."

"Jason," Mother says on the stairs.

"Go on, now," Dilsey says, going toward the door. "You want to git her started too? Ise comin, Miss Cahline."

I went on out. I could hear them on the steps. "You go on back to bed now," Dilsey was saying, "Dont you know you aint feeling well enough to git up yet? Go on back, now. I'm gwine to see she gits to school in time."

I went on out the back to back the car out, then I had to go all the way round to the front before I found them.

"I thought I told you to put that tire on the back of the car," I says.

"I aint had time," Luster says. "Aint nobody to watch him till mammy git done in de kitchen."

"Yes," I says, "I feed a whole damn kitchen full of niggers to follow around after him, but if I want an automobile tire changed, I have to do it myself."

"I aint had nobody to leave him wid," he says. Then he begun moaning and slobbering.

"Take him on round to the back," I says. "What the hell makes you want to keep him around here where people can see him?" I made them go on, before he got started bellowing good. It's bad enough on Sundays, with that damn field full of people that haven't got a side show and six niggers to feed, knocking a damn oversize mothball around. He's going to keep on running up and down that fence and bellowing every time they come in sight until first thing I know they're going to begin charging me golf dues, then Mother and Dilsey'll have to get a couple of china door knobs and a walking stick and work it out, unless I play at night with a lantern. Then they'd send us all to Jackson, maybe. God knows, they'd hold Old Home week when that happened.

I went on back to the garage. There was the tire, leaning against the wall, but be damned if I was going to put it on. I backed out and turned around. She was standing by the drive. I says,

"I know you haven't got any books: I just want to ask you what you did with them, if it's any of my business. Of course I haven't got any right to ask," I says, "I'm just the one that paid $11.65 for them last September."

"Mother buys my books," she says. "There's not a cent of your money on me. I'd starve first."

"Yes?" I says. "You tell your grandmother that and see what she says. You dont look all the way naked," I says, "even if that stuff on your face does hide more of you than anything else you've got on."

"Do you think your money or hers either paid for a cent of this?" she says.

"Ask your grandmother," I says. "Ask her what became of those checks. You saw her burn one of them, as I remember." She wasn't even listening, with her face all gummed up with paint and her eyes hard as a fice dog's.

"Do you know what I'd do if I thought your money or hers either bought one cent of this?" she says, putting her hand on her dress.

"What would you do?" I says, "Wear a barrel?"

"I'd tear it right off and throw it into the street," she says. "Dont you believe me?"

"Sure you would," I says. "You do it every time."

"See if I wouldn't," She says. She grabbed the neck of her dress in both hands and made like she would tear it.

"You tear that dress," I says, "And I'll give you a whipping right here that you'll remember all your life."

"See if I dont," she says. Then I saw that she really was trying to tear it, to tear it right off of her. By the time I got the car stopped and grabbed her hands there was about a dozen people looking. It made me so mad for a minute it kind of blinded me.

"You do a thing like that again and I'll make you sorry you ever drew breath," I says.

"I'm sorry now," she says. She quit, then her eyes turned kind of funny and I says to myself if you cry here in this car, on the street, I'll whip you. I'll wear you out. Lucky for her she didn't, so I turned her wrists loose and drove on. Luckily we were near an alley, where I could turn into the back street and dodge the square. They were already putting the tent up in Beard's lot. Earl had already given me the two passes for our show windows. She sat there with her face turned away, chewing her lip. "I'm sorry now," she says. "I dont see why I was ever born."

"And I know of at least one other person that dont understand all he knows about that," I says. I stopped in front of the school house. The bell had rung, and the last of them were just going in. "You're on time for once, anyway," I says. "Are you going in there and stay there, or am I coming with you and make you?" She got out and banged the door. "Remember what I say," I says, "I mean it. Let me hear one more time that you are slipping up and down back alleys with one of those damn squirts."

She turned back at that. "I dont slip around," she says. "I dare anybody to know everything I do."

"And they all know it, too," I says. "Everybody in this town knows what you are. But I wont have it anymore, you hear? I dont care what you do, myself," I says, "But I've got a position in this town, and I'm not going to have any member of my family going on like a nigger wench. You hear me?"

"I dont care," she says, "I'm bad and I'm going to hell, and I dont care. I'd rather be in hell than anywhere where you are."

"If I hear one more time that you haven't been to school, you'll wish you were in hell," I says. She turned and ran on across the yard. "One more time, remember," I says. She didn't look back.

I went to the postoffice and got the mail and drove on to the store and parked. Earl looked at me when I came in. I gave him a chance to say something about my being late, but he just said,

"Those cultivators have come. You'd better help Uncle Job put them up."

I went on to the back, where old Job was uncrating them, at the rate of about three bolts to the hour.

"You ought to be working for me," I says. "Every other no-count nigger in town eats in my kitchen."

"I works to suit de man whut pays me Sat'dy night," he says. "When I does dat, it dont leave me a whole lot of time to please other folks." He screwed up a nut. "Aint nobody works much in dis country cep de boll-weevil, noways," he says.

"You'd better be glad you're not a boll-weevil waiting on those cultivators," I says. "You'd work yourself to death before they'd be ready to prevent you."

"Dat's de troof," he says, "Boll-weevil got tough time. Work ev'y day in de week out in de hot sun, rain er shine. Aint got no front porch to set on en watch de wattermilyuns growin and Sat'dy dont mean nothin a-tall to him."

"Saturday wouldn't mean nothing to you, either," I says, "if it depended on me to pay you wages. Get those things out of the crates now and drag them inside."

I opened her letter first and took the check out. Just like a woman. Six days late. Yet they try to make men believe that they're capable of conducting a business. How long would a man that thought the first of the month came on the sixth last in business. And like as not, when they sent the bank statement out, she would want to know why I never deposited my salary until the sixth. Things like that never occur to a woman.

"I had no answer to my letter about Quentin's easter dress. Did it arrive all right? I've had no answer to the last two letters I wrote her, though the check in the second one was cashed with the other check. Is she sick? Let me know at once or I'll come there and see for myself. You promised you would let me know when she needed things. I will expect to hear from you before the 10th. No you'd better wire me at once. You are opening my letters to her. I know that as well as if I were looking at you. You'd better wire me at once about her to this address."

About that time Earl started yelling at Job, so I put them away and went over to try to put some life into him. What this country needs is white labour. Let these damn trifling niggers starve for a couple of years, then they'd see what a soft thing they have.

Along toward ten oclock I went up front. There was a drummer there. It was a couple of minutes to ten, and I invited him up the street to get a coca-cola. We got to talking about crops.

"There's nothing to it," I says, "Cotton is a speculator's crop. They fill the farmer full of hot air and get him to raise a big crop for them to whipsaw on the market, to trim the suckers with. Do you think the farmer gets anything out of it except a red neck and a hump in his back? You think the man that sweats to put it into the ground gets a red cent more than a bare living," I says. "Let him make a big crop and it wont be worth picking; let him make a small crop and he wont have enough to gin. And what for? so a bunch of damn eastern jews, I'm not talking about men of the jewish religion," I says, "I've known some jews that were fine citizens. You might be one yourself," I says.

"No," he says, "I'm an American."

"No offense," I says. "I give every man his due, regardless of religion or anything else. I have nothing against jews as an individual," I says. "It's just the race. You'll admit that they produce nothing. They follow the pioneers into a new country and sell them clothes."

"You're thinking of Armenians," he says, "aren't you. A pioneer wouldn't have any use for new clothes."

"No offense," I says. "I dont hold a man's religion against him."

"Sure," he says, "I'm an American. My folks have some French blood, why I have a nose like this. I'm an American, all right."

"So am I," I says. "Not many of us left. What I'm talking about is the fellows that sit up there in New York and trim the sucker gamblers."

"That's right," he says. "Nothing to gambling, for a poor man. There ought to be a law against it."

"Don't you think I'm right?" I says.

"Yes," he says, "I guess you're right. The farmer catches it coming and going."

"I know I'm right," I says. "It's a sucker game, unless a man gets inside information from somebody that knows what's going on. I happen to be associated with some people who're right there on the ground. They have one of the biggest manipulators in New York for an adviser. Way I do it," I says, "I never risk much at a time. It's the fellow that thinks he knows it all and is trying to make a killing with three dollars that they're laying for. That's why they are in the business."

Then it struck ten. I went up to the telegraph office. It opened up a little, just like they said. I went into the corner and took out the telegram again, just to be sure. While I was looking at it a report came in. It was up two points. They were all buying. I could tell that from what they were saying. Getting aboard. Like they didn't know it could go but one way. Like there was a law or something against doing anything but buying. Well, I reckon those eastern jews have got to live too. But I'll be damned if it hasn't come to a pretty pass when any damn foreigner that cant make a living in the country where God put him, can come to this one and take money right out of an American's pockets. It was up two points more. Four points. But hell, they were right there and knew what was going on. And if I wasn't going to take the advice, what was i paying them ten dollars a month for. I went out, then I remembered and came back and sent the wire. "All well. Q writing today."

"Q?" the operator says.

"Yes," I says, "Q. Cant you spell Q?"

"I just asked to be sure," he says.

"You send it like I wrote it and I'll guarantee you to be sure," I says. "Send it collect."

"What you sending, Jason?" Doc Wright says, looking over my shoulder. "Is that a code message to buy?"

"That's all right about that," I says. "You boys use your own judgment. You know more about it than those New York folks do."

"Well, I ought to," Doc says, "I'd a saved money this year raising it at two cents a pound."

Another report came in. It was down a point.

"Jason's selling," Hopkins says. "Look at his face."

"That's all right about what I'm doing," I says. "You boys follow your own judgment. Those rich New York jews have got to live like everybody else," I says.

I went on back to the store. Earl was busy up front. I went on back to the desk and read Lorraine's letter. "Dear daddy wish you were here. No good parties when daddys out of town I miss my sweet daddy." I reckon she does. Last time I gave her forty dollars. Gave it to her. I never promise a woman anything nor let her know what I'm going to give her. That's the only way to manage them. Always keep them guessing. If you cant think of any other way to surprise them, give them a bust in the jaw.

I tore it up and burned it over the spittoon. I make it a rule never to keep a scrap of paper bearing a woman's hand, and I never write them at all. Lorraine is always after me to write to her but I says anything I forgot to tell you will save till I get to Memphis again but I says I dont mind you writing me now and then in a plain envelope, but if you ever try to call me up on the telephone, Memphis wont hold you I says. I says when I'm up there I'm one of the boys, but I'm not going to ha /e any woman calling me on the telephone. Here I says, giving her the forty dollars. If you ever get drunk and take a notion to call me on the phone, just remember this and count ten before you do it.

"When'll that be?" she says.

"What?" I says.

"When you're coming back," she says.

"I'll let you know," I says. Then she tried to buy a beer, but I wouldn't let her. "Keep your money," I says. "Buy yourself a dress with it." I gave the maid a five, too. After all, like I say money has no value; it's just the way you spend it. It dont belong to anybody, so why try to hoard it. It just belongs to the man that can get it and keep it. There's a man right here in Jefferson made a lot of money selling rotten goods to niggers, lived in a room over the store about the size of a pigpen, and did his own cooking. About four or five years ago he was taken sick. Scared the hell out of him so that when he was up again he joined the church and bought himself a Chinese missionary, five thousand dollars a year. I often think how mad he'll be if he was to die and find out there's not any heaven, when he thinks about that five thousand a year. Like I say, he'd better go on and die now and save money.

When it was burned good I was just about to shove the others into my coat when all of a sudden something told me to open Quentin's before I went home, but about that time Earl started yelling for me up front, so I put them away and went and waited on the damn redneck while he spent fifteen minutes deciding whether he wanted a twenty cent hame string or a thirty-five cent one.

"You'd better take that good one," I says. "How do you

fellows ever expect to get ahead, trying to work with cheap equipment?"

"If this one aint any good," he says, "why have you got it on sale?"

"I didn't say it wasn't any good," I says, "I said it's not as good as that other one."

"How do you know it's not," he says. "You ever use airy one of them?"

"Because they dont ask thirty-five cents for it," I says. "That's how I know it's not as good."

He held the twenty cent one in his hands, drawing it through his fingers. "I reckon I'll take this hyer one," he says. I offered to take it and wrap it, but he rolled it up and put it in his overalls. Then he took out a tobacco sack and finally got it untied and shook some coins out. He handed me a quarter. "That fifteen cents will buy me a snack of dinner," he says.

"All right," I says, "You're the doctor. But dont come complaining to me next year when you have to buy a new outfit."

"I aint makin next year's crop yit," he says. Finally I got rid of him, but every time I took that letter out something would come up. They were all in town for the show, coming in in droves to give their money to something that brought nothing to the town and wouldn't leave anything except what those grafters in the Mayor's office will split among themselves, and Earl chasing back and forth like a hen in a coop, saying "Yes, ma'am, Mr Compson will wait on you. Jason, show this lady a churn or a nickel's worth of screen hooks."

Well, Jason likes work. I says no I never had university advantages because at Harvard they teach you how to go for a swim at night without knowing how to swim and at Sewanee they dont even teach you what water is. I says you might send me to the state University; maybe I'll learn how to stop my clock with a nose spray and then you can send Ben to the Navy I says or to the cavalry anyway, they use geldings in the cavalry. Then when she sent Quentin home for me to feed too I says I guess that's right too, instead of me having to go way up north for a job they sent the job down here to me and then Mother begun to cry and I says it's not that I have any objection to having it here; if it's any satisfaction to you I'll quit work and nurse it myself and let you and Dilsey keep the flour barrel full, or Ben. Rent him out to a sideshow; there must be folks somewhere that would pay a dime to see him, then she cried more and kept saying my poor afflicted baby and I says yes he'll be quite a help to you when he gets his growth not being more than one and a half times as high as me now and she says she'd be dead soon and then we'd all be better off and so I says all right, all right, have it your way. It's your grandchild, which is more than any other grandparents it's got can say for certain. Only I says it's only a question of time. If you believe she'll do what she says and not try to see it, you fool yourself because the first time that was that Mother kept on saying thank God you are not a Compson except in name, because you are all I have left now, you and Maury, and I says well I could spare Uncle Maury myself and then they came and said they were ready to start. Mother stopped crying then. She pulled her veil down and we went down stairs. Uncle Maury was coming out of the diningroom, his handkerchief to his mouth. They kind of made a lane and we went out the door just in time to see Dilsey driving Ben and T. P. back around the corner. We went down the steps and got in. Uncle Maury kept saying Poor little sister, poor little sister, talking around his mouth and patting Mother's hand. Talking around whatever it was.

"Have you got your band on?" she says. "Why dont they go on, before Benjamin comes out and makes a spectacle. Poor little boy. He doesn't know. He cant even realise."

"There, there," Uncle Maury says, patting her hand, talking around his mouth. "It's better so. Let him be unaware of bereavement until he has to."

"Other women have their children to support them in times like this," Mother says.

"You have Jason and me," he says.

"It's so terrible to me," she says, "Having the two of them like this, in less than two years."

"There, there," he says. After a while he kind of sneaked his hand to his mouth and dropped them out the window. Then I knew what I had been smelling. Clove stems. I reckon he thought that the least he could do at Father's funeral or maybe the sideboard thought it was still Father and tripped him up when he passed. Like I say, if he had to sell something to send Quentin to Harvard we'd all been a damn sight better off if he'd sold that sideboard and bought himself a one-armed strait jacket with part of the money. I reckon the reason all the Compson gave out before it got to me like Mother says, is that he drank it up. At least I never heard of him offering to sell anything to send me to Harvard.

So he kept on patting her hand and saying "Poor little sister," patting her hand with one of the black gloves that we got the bill for four days later because it was the twenty-sixth because it was the same day one month that Father went up there and got it and brought it home and wouldn't tell anything about where she was or anything and Mother crying and saying "And you didn't even see him? You didn't even try to get him to make any provision for it?" and Father says "No she shall not touch his money not one cent of it" and Mother says "He can be forced to by law. He can prove nothing, unless—Jason Compson," she says, "Were you fool enough to tell—"

"Hush, Caroline," Father says, then he sent me to help Dilsey get that old cradle out of the attic and I says,

"Well, they brought my job home tonight" because all the time we kept hoping they'd get things straightened out and he'd keep her because Mother kept saying she would at least have enough regard for the family not to jeopardize my chance after she and Quentin had had theirs.

"And whar else do she belong?" Dilsey says, "Who else gwine raise her 'cep me? Aint I raised eve'y one of y'all?"

"And a damn fine job you made of it," I says. "Anyway it'll give her something to sure enough worry over now." So we carried the cradle down and Dilsey started to set it up in her old room. Then Mother started sure enough.

"Hush, Miss Cahline," Dilsey says, "You gwine wake her up."

"In there?" Mother says, "To be contaminated by that atmosphere? It'll be hard enough as it is, with the heritage she already has."

"Hush," Father says, "Dont be silly."

"Why aint she gwine sleep in here," Dilsey says, "In the same room whar I put her ma to bed ev'y night of her life since she was big enough to sleep by herself."

"You dont know," Mother says, "To have my own daughter cast off by her husband. Poor little innocent baby," she says, looking at Quentin. "You will never know the suffering you've caused."

"Hush. Caroline," Father says.

"What you want to go on like that fo Jason fer?" Dil. sey says.

"I've tried to protect him," Mother says. "I've always tried to protect him from it. At least I can do my best to shield her."

"How sleepin in dis room gwine hurt her, I like to know," Dilsey says.

"I cant help it," Mother says. "I know I'm just a troublesome old woman. But I know that people cannot flout God's laws with impunity."

"Nonsense," Father said. "Fix it in Miss Caroline's room then, Dilsey."

"You can say nonsense," Mother says. "But she must never know. She must never even learn that name. Dilsey, I forbid you ever to speak that name in her hearing. If she could grow up never to know that she had a mother, I would thank God."

"Dont be a fool," Father says.

"I have never interfered with the way you brought them up," Mother says, "But now I cannot stand anymore. We must decide this now, tonight. Either that name is never to be spoken in her hearing, or she must go, or I will go. Take your choice."

"Hush," Father says, "You're just upset. Fix it in here, Dilsey."

"En you's about sick too," Dilsey says. "You looks like a hant. You git in bed and I'll fix you a toddy and see kin you sleep. I bet you aint had a full night's sleep since you lef."

"No," Mother says, "Dont you know what the doctor says? Why must you encourage him to drink? That's what's the matter with him now. Look at me, I suffer too, but I'm not so weak that I must kill myself with whiskey."

"Fiddlesticks," Father says, "What do doctors know? They make their livings advising people to do whatever they are not doing at the time, which is the extent of anyone's knowledge of the degenerate ape. You'll have a minister in to hold my hand next." Then Mother cried, and he went out. Went down stairs, and then I heard the sideboard. I woke up and heard him going down again. Mother had gone to sleep or something, because the house was quiet at last. He was trying to be quiet too, because I couldn't hear him, only the bottom of his nightshirt and his bare legs in front of the sideboard.

Dilsey fixed the cradle and undressed her and put her in it. She never had waked up since he brought her in the house.

"She pretty near too big fer hit," Dilsey says. "Dar now. I gwine spread me a pallet right acrost de hall, so you wont need to git up in de night."

"I wont sleep," Mother says. "You go on home. I wont mind. I'll be happy to give the rest of my life to her, if I can just prevent—"

"Hush, now," Dilsey says. "We gwine take keer of her. En you go on to bed too," she says to me, "You got to go to school tomorrow."

So I went out, then Mother called me back and cried on me awhile.

"You are my only hope," she says. "Every night I thank God for you." While we were waiting there for them to start she says Thank God if he had to be taken too, it is you left me and not Quentin. Thank God you are not a Compson, because all I have left now is you and Maury and I says, Well I could spare Uncle Maury myself. Well, he kept on patting her hand with his black glove, talking away from her. He took them off when his turn with the shovel came. He got up near the first, where they were holding the umbrellas over them, stamping every now and then and trying to kick the mud off their feet and sticking to the shovels so they'd have to knock it off, making a hollow sound when it fell on it, and when I stepped back around the hack I could see him behind a tombstone, taking another one out of a bottle. I thought he never was going to stop because I had on my new suit too, but it happened that there wasn't much mud on the wheels yet, only Mother saw it and says I dont know when you'll ever have another one and Uncle Maury says, "Now, now. Dont you worry at all. You have me to depend on, always."

And we have. Always. The fourth letter was from him But there wasn't any need to open it. I could have written it myself, or recited it to her from memory, adding ten dollars just to be safe. But I had a hunch about that other letter. I just felt that it was about time she was up to some of her tricks again. She got pretty wise after that first time. She found out pretty quick that I was a different breed of cat from Father. When they begun to get it filled up toward the top Mother started crying sure enough, so Uncle Maury got in with her and drove off. He says You can come in with somebody; they'll be glad to give you a lift. I'll have to take your mother on and I thought about saying, Yes you ought to brought two bottles instead of just one only I thought about where we were, so I let them go on. Little they cared how wet I got, because then Mother could have a whale of a time being afraid I was taking pneumonia.

Well, I got to thinking about that and watching them throwing dirt into it, slapping it on anyway like they were making mortar or something or building a fence, and I began to feel sort of funny and so I decided to walk around a while. I thought that if I went toward town they'd catch up and be trying to make me get in one of them, so I went on back toward the nigger grave-yard. I got under some cedars, where the rain didn't come much, only dripping now and then, where I could see when they got through and went away. After a while they were all gone and I waited a minute and came out.

I had to follow the path to keep out of the wet grass so I didn't see her until I was pretty near there, standing there in a black cloak, looking at the flowers. I knew who it was right off, before she turned and looked at me and lifted up her veil.

"Hello, Jason," she says, holding out her hand. We shook hands.

"What are you doing here?" I says. "I thought you promised her you wouldn't come back here. I thought you had more sense than that."

"Yes?" she says. She looked at the flowers again. There must have been fifty dollars' worth. Somebody had put one bunch on Quentin's. "You did?" she says.

"I'm not surprised though," I says. "I wouldn't put any-thing past you. You dont mind anybody. You dont give a damn about anybody."

"Oh," she says, "that job." She looked at the grave. "I'm sorry about that, Jason."

"I bet you are," I says. "You'll talk mighty meek now. But you needn't have come back. There's not anything left. Ask Uncle Maury, if you dont believe me."

"I dont want anything," she says. She looked at the grave. "Why didn't they let me know?" she says. "I just happened to see it in the paper. On the back page. Just happened to."

I didn't say anything. We stood there, looking at the grave, and then I got to thinking about when we were little and one thing and another and I got to feeling funny again, kind of mad or something, thinking about now we'd have Uncle Maury around the house all the time, running things like the way he left me to come home in the rain by myself. I says,

"A fine lot you care, sneaking in here soon as he's dead. But it wont do you any good. Dont think that you can take advantage of this to come sneaking back. If you cant stay on the horse you've got, you'll have to walk," I says. "We dont even know your name at that house," I says. "Do you know that? We don't even know you with him and Quentin," I says. "Do you know that?"

"I know it," she says. "Jason," she says, looking at the grave, "if you'll fix it so I can see her a minute I'll give you fifty dollars."

"You haven't got fifty dollars," I says.

"Will you?" she says, not looking at me.

"Let's see it," I says. "I dont believe you've got fifty dollars."

I could see where her hands were moving under her cloak, then she held her hand out. Damn if it wasn't full of money. I could see two or three yellow ones.

"Does he still give you money?" I says. "How much does he send you?"

"I'll give you a hundred," she says. "Will you?"

"Just a minute," I says, "And just like I say. I wouldn't have her know it for a thousand dollars."

"Yes," she says. "Just like you say do it. Just so I see her a minute. I wont beg or do anything. I'll go right on away."

"Give me the money," I says.

"I'll give it to you afterward," she says.

"Dont you trust me?" I says.

"No," she says. "I know you. I grew up with you."

"You're a fine one to talk about trusting people," I says.

"Well," I says, "I got to get on out of the rain. Goodbye."
I made to go away.

"Jason," she says. I stopped.

"Yes?" I says. "Hurry up. I'm getting wet."

"All right," she says. "Here." There wasn't anybody in sight. I went back and took the money. She still held to it. "You'll do it?" she says, looking at me from under the veil, "You promise?"

"Let go," I says, "You want somebody to come along and see us?"

She let go. I put the money in my pocket. "You'll do it, Jason?" she says. "I wouldn't ask you, if there was any other way."

"You're damn right there's no other way," I says. "Sure I'll do it. I said I would, didn't I? Only you'll have to do just like I say, now."

"Yes," she says, "I will." So I told her where to be, and went to the livery stable. I hurried and got there just as they were unhitching the hack. I asked if they had paid for it yet and he said No and I said Mrs Compson forgot something and wanted it again, so they let me take it. Mink was driving. I bought him a cigar, so we drove around until it begun to get dark on the back streets where they wouldn't see him. Then Mink said he'd have to take the team on back and so I said I'd buy him another cigar and so we drove into the lane and I went across the yard to the house. I stopped in the hall until I could hear Mother and Uncle Maury upstairs, then I went on back to the kitchen. She and Ben were there with Dilsey. I said Mother wanted her and I took her into the house. I found Uncle Maury's raincoat and put it around her and picked her up and went back to the lane and got in the hack. I told Mink to drive to the depot. He was afraid to pass the stable, so we had to go the back way and I saw her standing on the corner under the light and I told Mink to drive close to the walk and when I said Go on, to give the team a bat. Then I took the raincoat off of her and held her to the window and Caddy saw her and sort of jumped forward.

"Hit 'em, Mink!" I says, and Mink gave them a cut and we went past her like a fire engine. "Now get on that train like you promised," I says. I could see her running after us through the back window. "Hit 'em again," I says, "Let's get on home." When we turned the corner she was still running.

And so I counted the money again that night and put it away, and I didn't feel so bad. I says I reckon that'll show you. I reckon you'll know now that you cant beat me out of a job and get away with it. It never occurred to me she wouldn't keep her promise and take that train. But I didn't know much about them then; I didn't have any more sense than to believe what they said, because the next morning damn if she didn't walk right into the store, only she had sense enough to wear the veil and not speak to anybody. It was Saturday morning, because I was at the store, and she came right on back to the desk where I was, walking fast.

"Liar," she says, "Liar."

"Are you crazy?" I says. "What do you mean? coming in here like this?" She started in, but I shut her off. I says, "You already cost me one job; do you want me to lose this one too? If you've got anything to say to me, I'll meet you somewhere after dark. What have you got to say to me?" I says, "Didn't I do everything I said? I said see her a minute, didn't I? Well, didn't you?" She just stood there looking at me, shaking like an ague-fit, her hands clenched and kind of jerking. "I did just what I said I would," I says, "You're the one that lied. You prom·

ised to take that train. Didn't you Didn't you promise?
If you think you can get that money back, just try it," I
says. "If it'd been a thousand dollars, you'd still owe me
after the risk I took. And if I see or hear you're still in
town after number 17 runs," I says, "I'll tell Mother and
Uncle Maury. Then hold your breath until you see her
again." She just stood there, looking at me, twisting her
hands together.

"Damn you," she says, "Damn you."

"Sure," I says, "That's all right too. Mind what I say,
now. After number 17, and I tell them."

After she was gone I felt better. I says I reckon you'll
think twice before you deprive me of a job that was
promised me. I was a kid then. I believed folks when
they said they'd do things. I've learned better since. Besides, like I say I guess I dont need any man's help to get
along I can stand on my own feet like I always have.
Then all of a sudden I thought of Dilsey and Uncle
Maury. I thought how she'd get around Dilsey and that
Uncle Maury would do anything for ten dollars. And
there I was, couldn't even get away from the store to protect my own Mother. Like she says, if one of you had to
be taken, thank God it was you left me I can depend on
you and I says well I dont reckon I'll ever get far enough
from the store to get out of your reach. Somebody's got
to hold on to what little we have left, I reckon.

So as soon as I got home I fixed Dilsey. I told Dilsey
she had leprosy and I got the bible and read where a
man's flesh rotted off and I told her that if she ever
looked at her or Ben or Quentin they'd catch it too. So I
thought I had everything all fixed until that day when I
came home and found Ben bellowing. Raising hell and
nobody could quiet him. Mother said, Well, get him the
slipper then. Dilsey made out she didn't hear. Mother

said it again and I says I'd go I couldn't stand that damn noise. Like I say I can stand lots of things I dont expect much from them but if I have to work all day long in a damn store damn if I dont think I deserve a little peace and quiet to eat dinner in. So I says I'd go and Dilsey says quick, "Jason!"

Well, like a flash I knew what was up, but just to make sure I went and got the slipper and brought it back, and just like I thought, when he saw it you'd thought we were killing him. So I made Dilsey own up, then I told Mother. We had to take her up to bed then, and after things got quieted down a little I put the fear of God into Dilsey. As much as you can into a nigger, that is. That's the trouble with nigger servants, when they've been with you for a long time they get so full of self importance that they're not worth a damn. Think they run the whole family.

"I like to know whut's de hurt in lettin dat po chile see her own baby," Dilsey says. "If Mr Jason was still here hit ud be different."

"Only Mr Jason's not here," I says. "I know you wont pay me any mind, but I reckon you'll do what Mother says. You keep on worrying her like this until you get her into the graveyard too, then you can fill the whole house full of ragtag and bobtail. But what did you want to let that damn idiot see her for?"

"You's a cold man, Jason, if man you is," she says. "I thank de Lawd I got mo heart dan dat, even ef hit is black."

"At least I'm man enough to keep that flour barrel full," I says. "And if you do that again, you wont be eating out of it either."

So the next time I told her that if she tried Dilsey again, Mother was going to fire Dilsey and send Ben to

Jackson and take Quentin and go away. She looked at me for a while. There wasn't any street light close and I couldn't see her face much. But I could feel her looking at me. When we were little when she'd get mad and couldn't do anything about it her upper lip would begin to jump. Everytime it jumped it would leave a little more of her teeth showing, and all the time she'd be as still as a post, not a muscle moving except her lip jerking higher and higher up her teeth. But she didn't say anything. She just said,

"All right. How much?"

"Well, if one look through a hack window was worth a hundred," I says. So after that she behaved pretty well, only one time she asked to see a statement of the bank account.

"I know they have Mother's indorsement on them," she says, "But I want to see the bank statement. I want to see myself where those checks go."

"That's in Mother's private business," I says. "If you think you have any right to pry into her private affairs I'll tell her you believe those checks are being misappropriated and you want an audit because you dont trust her."

She didn't say anything or move. I could hear her whispering Damn you oh damn you oh damn you.

"Say it out," I says, "I dont reckon it's any secret what you and I think of one another. Maybe you want the money back," I says.

"Listen, Jason," she says, "Dont lie to me now. About her. I wont ask to see anything. If that isn't enough, I'll send more each month. Just promise that she'll—that she—You can do that. Things for her. Be kind to her. Little things that I cant, they wont let. . . . But you wont. You never had a drop of warm blood in you. Listen," she says, "If you'll get Mother to let me have her back, I'll give you a thousand dollars."

"You haven't got a thousand dollars," I says, "I know you're lying now."

"Yes I have. I will have. I can get it."

"And I know how you'll get it," I says, "You'll get it the same way you got her. And when she gets big enough—" Then I thought she really was going to hit at me, and then I didn't know what she was going to do. She acted for a minute like some kind of a toy that's wound up too tight and about to burst all to pieces.

"Oh, I'm crazy," she says, "I'm insane. I can't take her. Keep her. What am I thinking of. Jason," she says, grabbing my arm. Her hands were hot as fever. "You'll have to promise to take care of her, to—She's kin to you; your own flesh and blood. Promise, Jason. You have Father's name: do you think I'd have to ask him twice? once, even?"

"That's so," I says, "He did leave me something. What do you want me to do," I says, "Buy an apron and a go-cart? I never got you into this," I says. "I run more risk than you do, because you haven't got anything at stake. So if you expect—"

"No," she says, then she begun to laugh and to try to hold it back all at the same time. "No. I have nothing at stake," she says, making that noise, putting her hands to her mouth, "Nuh-nuh-nothing," she says.

"Here," I says, "Stop that!"

"I'm trying to," she says, holding her hands over her mouth. "Oh God, oh God."

"I'm going away from here," I says, "I cant be seen here. You get on out of town now, you hear?"

"Wait," she says, catching my arm. "I've stopped. I wont again. You promise, Jason?" she says, and me feel-

ing her eyes almost like they were touching my face,
"You promise? Mother—that money—if sometimes she
needs things—If I send checks for her to you, other ones
besides those, you'll give them to her? You wont tell?
You'll see that she has things like other girls?"

"Sure," I says, "As long as you behave and do like I tell
you."

And so when Earl came up front with his hat on he
says, "I'm going to step up to Rogers' and get a snack.
We wont have time to go home to dinner, I reckon."

"What's the matter we wont have time?" I says.

"With this show in town and all," he says. "They're going to give an afternoon performance too, and they'll all
want to get done trading in time to go to it. So we'd
better just run up to Rogers'."

"All right," I says, "It's your stomach. If you want to
make a slave of yourself to your business, it's all right
with me."

"I reckon you'll never be a slave to any business," he
says.

"Not unless it's Jason Compson's business," I says.

So when I went back and opened it the only thing that
surprised me was it was a money order not a check. Yes,
sir. You cant trust a one of them. After all the risk I'd
taken, risking Mother finding out about her coming down
here once or twice a year sometimes, and me having to
tell Mother lies about it. That's gratitude for you. And I
wouldn't put it past her to try to notify the postoffice not
to let anyone except her cash it. Giving a kid like that
fifty dollars. Why I never saw fifty dollars until I was
twenty-one years old, with all the other boys with the
afternoon off and all day Saturday and me working in a
store. Like I say, how can they expect anybody to control
her, with her giving her money behind our backs. She

has the same home you had I says, and the same raising. I reckon Mother is a better judge of what she needs than you are, that haven't even got a home. "If you want to give her money," I says, "You send it to Mother, dont be giving it to her. If I've got to run this risk every few months, you'll have to do like I say, or it's out."

And just about the time I got ready to begin on it because if Earl thought I was going to dash up the street and gobble two bits worth of indigestion on his account he was bad fooled. I may not be sitting with my feet on a mahogany desk but I am being paid for what I do inside this building and if I can manage to live a civilised life outside of it I'll go where I can. I can stand on my own feet; I dont need any man's mahogany desk to prop me up. So just about the time I got ready to start I'd have to drop everything and run to sell some redneck a dime's worth of nails or something, and Earl up there gobbling a sandwich and half way back already, like as not, and then I found that all the blanks were gone. I remembered then that I had aimed to get some more, but it was too late now, and then I looked up and there Quentin came. In the back door. I heard her asking old Job if I was there. I just had time to stick them in the drawer and close it.

She came around to the desk. I looked at my watch.

"You been to dinner already?" I says. "It's just twelve; I just heard it strike. You must have flown home and back."

"I'm not going home to dinner," she says. "Did I get a letter today?"

"Were you expecting one?" I says. "Have you got a sweetie that can write?"

"From Mother," she says. "Did I get a letter from Mother?" she says, looking at me.

"Mother got one from her," I says. "I haven't opened it. You'll have to wait until she opens it. She'll let you see it, I imagine."

"Please, Jason," she says, not paying any attention, "Did I get one?"

"What's the matter?" I says. "I never knew you to be this anxious about anybody. You must expect some money from her."

"She said she—" she says. "Please, Jason," she says, "Did I?"

"You must have been to school today, after all," I says, "Somewhere where they taught you to say please. Wait a minute, while I wait on that customer."

I went and waited on him. When I turned to come back she was out of sight behind the desk. I ran. I ran around the desk and caught her as she jerked her hand out of the drawer. I took the letter away from her, beating her knuckles on the desk until she let go.

"You would, would you?" I says.

"Give it to me," she says, "You've already opened it. Give it to me. Please, Jason. It's mine. I saw the name."

"I'll take a hame string to you," I says. "That's what I'll give you. Going into my papers."

"Is there some money in it?" she says, reaching for it. "She said she would send me some money. She promised she would. Give it to me."

"What do you want with money?" I says.

"She said she would," she says, "Give it to me. Please, Jason. I wont ever ask you anything again, if you'll give it to me this time."

"I'm going to, if you'll give me time," I says. I took the letter and the money order out and gave her the letter. She reached for the money order, not hardly glancing at the letter. "You'll have to sign it first," I says.

"How much is it?" she says.

"Read the letter," I says. "I reckon it'll say."

She read it fast, in about two looks.

"It dont say," she says, looking up. She dropped the letter to the floor. "How much is it?"

"It's ten dollars," I says.

"Ten dollars?" she says, staring at me.

"And you ought to be damn glad to get that," I says, "A kid like you. What are you in such a rush for money all of a sudden for?"

"Ten dollars?" she says, like she was talking in her sleep, "Just ten dollars?" She made a grab at the money order. "You're lying," she says. "Thief!" she says, "Thief!"

"You would, would you?" I says, holding her off.

"Give it to me!" she says, "It's mine. She sent it to me. I will see it. I will."

"You will?" I says, holding her, "How're you going to do it?"

"Just let me see it, Jason," she says, "Please. I wont ask you for anything again."

"Think I'm lying, do you?" I says. "Just for that you wont see it."

"But just ten dollars," she says, "She told me she—she told me—Jason, please please please. I've got to have some money. I've just got to. Give it to me, Jason. I'll do anything if you will."

"Tell me what you've got to have money for," I says.

"I've got to have it," she says. She was looking at me. Then all of a sudden she quit looking at me without moving her eyes at all. I knew she was going to lie. "It's some money I owe," she says. "I've got to pay it. I've got to pay it today."

"Who to?" I says. Her hands were sort of twisting. I could watch her trying to think of a lie to tell. "Have you been charging things at stores again?" I says. "You needn't bother to tell me that. If you can find anybody in this town that'll charge anything to you after what I told them, I'll eat it."

"It's a girl," she says, "It's a girl. I borrowed some money from a girl. I've got to pay it back. Jason, give it to me. Please. I'll do anything. I've got to have it. Mother will pay you. I'll write to her to pay you and that I wont ever ask her for anything again. You can see the letter. Please, Jason. I've got to have it."

"Tell me what you want with it, and I'll see about it," I says. "Tell me." She just stood there, with her hands working against her dress. "All right," I says, "If ten dollars is too little for you, I'll just take it home to Mother, and you know what'll happen to it then. Of course, if you're so rich you dont need ten dollars—"

She stood there, looking at the floor, kind of mumbling to herself. "She said she would send me some money. She said she sends money here and you say she dont send any. She said she's sent a lot of money here. She says it's for me. That it's for me to have some of it. And you say we haven't got any money."

"You know as much about that as I do," I says. "You've seen what happens to those checks."

"Yes," she says, looking at the floor. "Ten dollars," she says, "Ten dollars."

"And you'd better thank your stars it's ten dollars," I says. "Here," I says. I put the money order face down on the desk, holding my hand on it, "Sign it."

"Will you let me see it?" she says. "I just want to look at it. Whatever it says, I wont ask for but ten dollars. You can have the rest. I just want to see it."

"Not after the way you've acted," I says. "You've got to learn one thing, and that is that when I tell you to do something, you've got it to do. You sign your name on that line."

She took the pen, but instead of signing it she just stood there with her head bent and the pen shaking in her hand. Just like her mother. "Oh, God," she says, "oh, God."

"Yes," I says, "That's one thing you'll have to learn if you never learn anything else. Sign it now, and get on out of here."

She signed it. "Where's the money?" she says. I took the order and blotted it and put it in my pocket. Then I gave her the ten dollars.

"Now you go on back to school this afternoon, you hear?" I says. She didn't answer. She crumpled the bill up in her hand like it was a rag or something and went on out the front door just as Earl came in. A customer came in with him and they stopped up front. I gathered up the things and put on my hat and went up front.

"Been much busy?" Earl says.

"Not much," I says. He looked out the door.

"That your car over yonder?" he says. "Better not try to go out home to dinner. We'll likely have another rush just before the show opens. Get you a lunch at Rogers' and put a ticket in the drawer."

"Much obliged," I says. "I can still manage to feed myself, I reckon."

And right there he'd stay, watching that door like a hawk until I came through it again. Well, he'd just have to watch it for a while; I was doing the best I could. The time before I says that's the last one now; you'll have to remember to get some more right away. But who can remember anything in all this hurrah. And now this damn show had to come here the one day I'd have to hunt all over town for a blank check, besides all the other things

I had to do to keep the house running, and Earl watching the door like a hawk.

I went to the printing shop and told him I wanted to play a joke on a fellow, but he didn't have anything. Then he told me to have a look in the old opera house, where somebody had stored a lot of papers and junk out of the old Merchants' and Farmers' Bank when it failed, so I dodged up a few more alleys so Earl couldn't see me and finally found old man Simmons and got the key from him and went up there and dug around. At last I found a pad on a Saint Louis bank. And of course she'd pick this one time to look at it close. Well, it would have to do. I couldn't waste any more time now.

I went back to the store. "Forgot some papers Mother wants to go to the bank," I says. I went back to the desk and fixed the check. Trying to hurry and all. I says to myself it's a good thing her eyes are giving out, with that little whore in the house, a Christian forbearing woman like Mother. I says you know just as well as I do what she's going to grow up into but I says that's your business, if you want to keep her and raise her in your house just because of Father. Then she would begin to cry and say it was her own flesh and blood so I just says All right. Have it your way. I can stand it if you can.

I fixed the letter up again and glued it back and went out.

"Try not to be gone any longer than you can help," Earl says.

"All right," I says. I went to the telegraph office. The smart boys were all there.

"Any of you boys made your million yet?" I says.

"Who can do anything, with a market like that?" Doc says.

"What's it doing?" I says. I went in and looked. It was

three points under the opening. "You boys are not going to let a little thing like the cotton market beat you, are you?" I says. "I thought you were too smart for that."

"Smart, hell," Doc says. "It was down twelve points at twelve o'clock. Cleaned me out."

"Twelve points?" I says. "Why the hell didn't somebody let me know? Why didn't you let me know?" I says to the operator.

"I take it as it comes in," he says. "I'm not running a bucket shop."

"You're smart, aren't you?" I says. "Seems to me, with the money I spend with you, you could take time to call me up. Or maybe your damn company's in a conspiracy with those damn eastern sharks."

He didn't say anything. He made like he was busy.

"You're getting a little too big for your pants," I says. "First thing you know you'll be working for a living."

"What's the matter with you?" Doc says. "You're still three points to the good."

"Yes," I says, "If I happened to be selling. I haven't mentioned that yet, I think. You boys all cleaned out?"

"I got caught twice," Doc says. "I switched just in time."

"Well," I. O. Snopes says, "I've picked hit; I reckon taint no more than fair fer hit to pick me once in a while."

So I left them buying and selling among themselves at a nickel a point. I found a nigger and sent him for my car and stood on the corner and waited. I couldn't see Earl looking up and down the street, with one eye on the clock, because I couldn't see the door from here. After about a week he got back with it.

"Where the hell have you been?" I says, "Riding around where the wenches could see you?"

"I come straight as I could," he says, "I had to drive clean around the square, wid all dem wagons."

I never found a nigger yet that didn't have an airtight alibi for whatever he did. But just turn one loose in a car and he's bound to show off. I got in and went on around the square. I caught a glimpse of Earl in the door across the square.

I went straight to the kitchen and told Dilsey to hurry up with dinner.

"Quentin aint come yit," she says.

"What of that?" I says. "You'll be telling me next that Luster's not quite ready to eat yet. Quentin knows when meals are served in this house. Hurry up with it, now."

Mother was in her room. I gave her the letter. She opened it and took the check out and sat holding it in her hand. I went and got the shovel from the corner and gave her a match. "Come on," I says, "Get it over with. You'll be crying in a minute."

She took the match, but she didn't strike it. She sat there, looking at the check. Just like I said it would be.

"I hate to do it," she says, "To increase your burden by adding Quentin. . . ."

"I guess we'll get along," I says. "Come on. Get it over with."

But she just sat there, holding the check.

"This one is on a different bank," she says. "They have been on an Indianapolis bank."

"Yes," I says. "Women are allowed to do that too."

"Do what?" she says.

"Keep money in two different banks," I says.

"Oh," she says. She looked at the check a while. "I'm glad to know she's so . . . she has so much . . . God sees that I am doing right," she says.

"Come on," I says, "Finish it. Get the fun over."

"Fun?" she says, "When I think—"

"I thought you were burning this two hundred dollars a month for fun," I says. "Come on, now. Want me to strike the match?"

"I could bring myself to accept them," she says, "For my children's sake. I have no pride."

"You'd never be satisfied," I says, "You know you wouldn't. You've settled that once, let it stay settled. We can get along."

"I leave everything to you," she says. "But sometimes I become afraid that in doing this I am depriving you all of what is rightfully yours. Perhaps I shall be punished for it. If you want me to, I will smother my pride and accept them."

"What would be the good in beginning now, when you've been destroying them for fifteen years?" I says. "If you keep on doing it, you have lost nothing, but if you'd begin to take them now, you'll have lost fifty thousand dollars. We've got along so far, haven't we?" I says. "I haven't seen you in the poorhouse yet."

"Yes," she says, "We Bascombs need nobody's charity. Certainly not that of a fallen woman."

She struck the match and lit the check and put it in the shovel, and then the envelope, and watched them burn.

"You dont know what it is," she says, "Thank God you will never know what a mother feels."

"There are lots of women in this world no better than her," I says.

"But they are not my daughters," she says. "It's not myself," she says, "I'd gladly take her back, sins and all, because she is my flesh and blood. It's for Quentin's sake."

Well, I could have said it wasn't much chance of anybody hurting Quentin much, but like I say I dont expect much but I do want to eat and sleep without a couple of women squabbling and crying in the house.

"And yours," she says. "I know how you feel toward her."

"Let her come back," I says, "far as I'm concerned."

"No," she says. "I owe that to your father's memory."

"When he was trying all the time to persuade you to let her come home when Herbert threw her out?" I says.

"You dont understand," she says. "I know you dont intend to make it more difficult for me. But it's my place to suffer for my children," she says. "I can bear it."

"Seems to me you go to a lot of unnecessary trouble doing it," I says. The paper burned out. I carried it to the grate and put it in. "It just seems a shame to me to burn up good money," I says.

"Let me never see the day when my children will have to accept that, the wages of sin," she says. "I'd rather see even you dead in your coffin first."

"Have it your way," I says. "Are we going to have dinner soon?" I says, "Because if we're not, I'll have to go on back. We're pretty busy today." She got up. "I've told her once," I says. "It seems she's waiting on Quentin or Luster or somebody. Here, I'll call her. Wait." But she went to the head of the stairs and called.

"Quentin aint come yit," Dilsey says.

"Well, I'll have to get on back," I says. "I can get a sandwich downtown. I dont want to interfere with Dilsey's arrangements," I says. Well, that got her started again, with Dilsey hobbling and mumbling back and forth, saying,

"All right, all right, Ise puttin hit on fast as I kin."

"I try to please you all," Mother says, "I try to make things as easy for you as I can."

"I'm not complaining, am I?" I says. "Have I said a word except I had to go back to work?"

"I know," she says, "I know you haven't had the chance the others had, that you've had to bury yourself in a little country store. I wanted you to get ahead. I knew your father would never realise that you were the only one who had any business sense, and then when everything else failed I believed that when she married, and Herbert . . . after his promise . . ."

"Well, he was probably lying too," I says. "He may not have even had a bank. And if he had, I dont reckon he'd have to come all the way to Mississippi to get a man for it."

We ate awhile. I could hear Ben in the kitchen, where Luster was feeding him. Like I say, if we've got to feed another mouth and she wont take that money, why not send him down to Jackson. He'll be happier there, with people like him. I says God knows there's little enough room for pride in this family, but it dont take much pride to not like to see a thirty year old man playing around the yard with a nigger boy, running up and down the fence and lowing like a cow whenever they play golf over there. I says if they'd sent him to Jackson at first we'd all be better off today. I says, you've done your duty by him; you've done all anybody can expect of you and more than most folks would do, so why not send him there and get that much benefit out of the taxes we pay. Then she says, "I'll be gone soon. I know I'm just a burden to you" and I says "You've been saying that so long that I'm beginning to believe you" only I says you'd better be sure and not let me know you're gone because I'll sure have him on number seventeen that night and I says I think I know a place where they'll take her too and the name of it's not Milk street and Honey avenue either. Then she begun to cry and I says All right all right I have as much pride about my kinfolks as anybody even if I dont always know where they come from.

We ate for awhile. Mother sent Dilsey to the front to look for Quentin again.

"I keep telling you she's not coming to dinner," I says.

"She knows better than that," Mother says, "She knows I dont permit her to run about the streets and not come home at meal time. Did you look good, Dilsey?"

"Dont let her, then," I says.

"What can I do," she says. "You have all of you flouted me. Always."

"If you wouldn't come interfering, I'd make her mind," I says. "It wouldn't take me but about one day to straighten her out."

"You'd be too brutal with her," she says. "You have your Uncle Maury's temper."

That reminded me of the letter. I took it out and handed it to her. "You wont have to open it," I says. "The bank will let you know how much it is this time."

"It's addressed to you," she says.

"Go on and open it," I says. She opened it and read it and handed it to me.

" 'My dear young nephew,' it says,

'You will be glad to learn that I am now in a position to avail myself of an opportunity regarding which, for reasons which I will make obvious to you, I shall not go into details until I have an opportunity to divulge it to you in a more secure manner. My business experience has taught me to be chary of committing anything of a confidential nature to any more concrete medium than speech, and my extreme precaution in this instance should give you some inkling of its value. Needless to say, I have just completed a most exhaustive examination of all its phases, and I feel no hesitancy in telling you that it is that sort of golden chance that comes but once in a lifetime, and I now see clearly before me that goal toward which I have long and unflaggingly striven: i.e., the ultimate solidification of my affairs by which I may restore to its rightful position that family of which I have the honour to be the sole remaining male descendant; that family in which I have ever included your lady mother and her children.

'As it so happens, I am not quite in a position to avail myself of this opportunity to the uttermost which it warrants, but rather than go out of the family to do so, I am today drawing upon your Mother's bank for the small sum necessary to complement my own initial investment, for which I herewith enclose, as a matter of formality, my note of hand at eight percent per annum. Needless to say, this is merely a formality, to secure your Mother in the event of that circumstance of which man is ever the plaything and sport. For naturally I shall employ this sum as though it were my own and so permit your Mother to avail herself of this opportunity which my exhaustive investigation has shown to be a bonanza—if you will permit the vulgarism—of the first water and purest ray serene.

'This is in confidence, you will understand, from one business man to another; we will harvest our own vineyards, eh? And knowing your Mother's delicate health and that timorousness which such delicately nurtured Southern ladies would naturally feel regarding matters of business, and their charming proneness to divulge unwittingly such matters in conversation, I would suggest that you do not mention it to her at all. On second thought, I

advise you not to do so. It might be better to simply restore this sum to the bank at some future date, say, in a
lump sum with the other small sums for which I am in-
debted to her, and say nothing about it at all. It is our
duty to shield her from the crass material world as much
as possible.

                    'Your affectionate Uncle,
                              'Maury L. Bascomb.' "

"What do you want to do about it?" I says, flipping it
across the table.

"I know you grudge what I give him," she says.

"It's your money," I says. "If you want to throw it to
the birds even, it's your business."

"He's my own brother," Mother says. "He's the last Bascomb. When we are gone there wont be any more of
them."

"That'll be hard on somebody, I guess," I says. "All
right, all right," I says, "It's your money. Do as you
please with it. You want me to tell the bank to pay it?"

"I know you begrudge him," she says. "I realise the
burden on your shoulders. When I'm gone it will be easier on you."

"I could make it easier right now," I says. "All right,
all right, I wont mention it again. Move all bedlam in
here if you want to."

"He's your own brother," she says, "Even if he is afflicted."

"I'll take your bank book," I says. "I'll draw my
check today."

"He kept you waiting six days," she says. "Are you
sure the business is sound? It seems strange to me that a
solvent business cannot pay its employees promptly."

"He's all right," I says, "Safe as a bank. I tell him not to bother about mine until we get done collecting every month. That's why it's late sometimes."

"I just couldn't bear to have you lose the little I had to invest for you," she says. "I've often thought that Earl is not a good business man. I know he doesn't take you into his confidence to the extent that your investment in the business should warrant. I'm going to speak to him."

"No, you let him alone," I says. "It's his business."

"You have a thousand dollars in it."

"You let him alone," I says, "I'm watching things. I have your power of attorney. It'll be all right."

"You dont know what a comfort you are to me," she says. "You have always been my pride and joy, but when you came to me of your own accord and insisted on banking your salary each month in my name, I thanked God it was you left me if they had to be taken."

"They were all right," I says. "They did the best they could, I reckon."

"When you talk that way I know you are thinking bitterly of your father's memory," she says. "You have a right to, I suppose. But it breaks my heart to hear you."

I got up. "If you've got any crying to do," I says, "you'll have to do it alone, because I've got to get on back. I'll get the bank book."

"I'll get it," she says.

"Keep still," I says, "I'll get it." I went upstairs and got the bank book out of her desk and went back to town. I went to the bank and deposited the check and the money order and the other ten, and stopped at the telegraph office. It was one point above the opening. I had already lost thirteen points, all because she had to come helling in there at twelve, worrying me about that letter.

"What time did that report come in?" I says.

"About an hour ago," he says.

"An hour ago?" I says. "What are we paying you for?" I says, "Weekly reports? How do you expect a man to do anything? The whole damn top could blow off and we'd not know it."

"I dont expect you to do anything," he says. "They changed that law making folks play the cotton market."

"They have," I says. "I hadn't heard. They must have sent the news out over the Western Union."

I went back to the store. Thirteen points. Damn if I believe anybody knows anything about the damn thing except the ones that sit back in those New York offices and watch the country suckers come up and beg them to take their money. Well, a man that just calls shows he has no faith in himself, and like I say if you aren't going to take the advice, what's the use in paying money for it. Besides, these people are right up there on the ground; they know everything that's going on. I could feel the telegram in my pocket. I'd just have to prove that they were using the telegraph company to defraud. That would constitute a bucket shop. And I wouldn't hesitate that long, either. Only be damned if it doesn't look like a company as big and rich as the Western Union could get a market report out on time. Half as quick as they'll get a wire to you saying Your account closed out. But what the hell do they care about the people. They're hand in glove with that New York crowd. Anybody could see that.

When I came in Earl looked at his watch. But he didn't say anything until the customer was gone. Then he says, "You go home to dinner?"

"I had to go to the dentist," I says because it's not any of his business where I eat but I've got to be in the store with him all the afternoon. And with his jaw running off

after all I've stood. You take a little two by four country
storekeeper like I say it takes a man with just five hundred dollars to worry about it fifty thousand dollars' worth.

"You might have told me," he says. "I expected you
back right away."

"I'll trade you this tooth and give you ten dollars to
boot, any time," I says. "Our agreement was an hour for
dinner," I says, "and if you dont like the way I do, you
know what you can do about it."

"I've known that some time," he says. "If it hadn't been
for your mother I'd have done it before now, too. She's a
lady I've got a lot of sympathy for, Jason. Too bad
some other folks I know cant say as much."

"Then you can keep it," I says. "When we need any
sympathy I'll let you know in plenty of time."

"I've protected you about that business a long time,
Jason," he says.

"Yes?" I says, letting him go on. Listening to what he
would say before I shut him up.

"I believe I know more about where that automobile
came from than she does."

"You think so, do you?" I says. "When are you going
to spread the news that I stole it from my mother?"

"I dont say anything," he says, "I know you have her
power of attorney. And I know she still believes that
thousand dollars is in this business."

"All right," I says, "Since you know so much, I'll tell
you a little more: go to the bank and ask them whose account I've been depositing a hundred and sixty dollars
on the first of every month for twelve years."

"I dont say anything," he says, "I just ask you to be a
little more careful after this."

I never said anything more. It doesn't do any good.

I've found that when a man gets into a rut the best thing you can do is let him stay there. And when a man gets it in his head that he's got to tell something on you for your own good, good-night. I'm glad I haven't got the sort of conscience I've got to nurse like a sick puppy all the time. If I'd ever be as careful over anything as he is to keep his little shirt tail full of business from making him more than eight percent. I reckon he thinks they'd get him on the usury law if he netted more than eight percent. What the hell chance has a man got, tied down in a town like this and to a business like this. Why I could take his business in one year and fix him so he'd never have to work again, only he'd give it all away to the church or something. If there's one thing gets under my skin, it's a damn hypocrite. A man that thinks anything he dont understand all about must be crooked and that first chance he gets he's morally bound to tell the third party what's none of his business to tell. Like I say if I thought every time a man did something I didn't know all about he was bound to be a crook, I reckon I wouldn't have any trouble finding something back there on those books that you wouldn't see any use for running and telling somebody I thought ought to know about it, when for all I knew they might know a damn sight more about it now than I did, and if they didn't it was damn little of my business anyway and he says, "My books are open to anybody. Anybody that has any claim or believes she has any claim on this business can go back there and welcome."

"Sure, you wont tell," I says, "You couldn't square your conscience with that. You'll just take her back there and let her find it. You wont tell, yourself."

"I'm not trying to meddle in your business," he says. "I know you missed out on some things like Quentin had.

But your mother has had a misfortunate life too, and if she was to come in here and ask me why you quit, I'd have to tell her. It aint that thousand dollars. You know that. It's because a man never gets anywhere if fact and his ledgers dont square. And I'm not going to lie to anybody, for myself or anybody else."

"Well, then," I says, "I reckon that conscience of yours is a more valuable clerk than I am; it dont have to go home at noon to eat. Only dont let it interfere with my appetite," I says, because how the hell can I do anything right, with that damn family and her not making any effort to control her nor any of them, like that time when she happened to see one of them kissing Caddy and all next day she went around the house in a black dress and a veil and even Father couldn't get her to say a word except crying and saying her little daughter was dead and Caddy about fifteen then only in three years she'd been wearing haircloth or probably sandpaper at that rate. Do you think I can afford to have her running about the streets with every drummer that comes to town, I says, and them telling the new ones up and down the road where to pick up a hot one when they made Jefferson. I haven't got much pride, I can't afford it with a kitchen full of niggers to feed and robbing the state asylum of its star freshman. Blood, I says, governors and generals. It's a damn good thing we never had any kings and presidents; we'd all be down there at Jackson chasing butterflies. I say it'd be bad enough if it was mine; I'd at least be sure it was a bastard to begin with, and now even the Lord doesn't know that for certain probably.

So after awhile I heard the band start up, and then they begun to clear out. Headed for the show, every one of them. Haggling over a twenty cent hame string to save fifteen cents, so they can give it to a bunch of Yankees

that come in and pay maybe ten dollars for the privilege.
I went on out to the back.

"Well," I says, "If you dont look out, that bolt will
grow into your hand. And then I'm going to take an axe
and chop it out. What do you reckon the boll-weevils'll
eat if you dont get those cultivators in shape to raise
them a crop?" I says, "sage grass?"

"Dem folks sho do play dem horns," he says. "Tell me
man in dat show kin play a tune on a handsaw. Pick hit
like a banjo."

"Listen," I says. "Do you know how much that show'll
spend in this town? About ten dollars," I says. "The ten
dollars Buck Turpin has in his pocket right now."

"Whut dey give Mr Buck ten dollars fer?" he says.

"For the privilege of showing here," I says. "You can
put the balance of what they'll spend in your eye."

"You mean dey pays ten dollars jest to give dey show
here?" he says.

"That's all," I says. "And how much do you
reckon . . ."

"Gret day," he says, "You mean to tell me dey chargin
um to let um show here? I'd pay ten dollars to see dat
man pick dat saw, ef I had to. I figures dat tomorrow
mawnin I be still owin um nine dollars and six bits at
dat rate."

And then a Yankee will talk your head off about niggers getting ahead. Get them ahead, what I say. Get them
so far ahead you cant find one south of Louisville with a
blood hound. Because when I told him about how they'd
pick up Saturday night and carry off at least a thousand
dollars out of the county, he says,

"I dont begrudge um. I kin sho afford my two bits."

"Two bits hell," I says. "That dont begin it. How about
the dime or fifteen cents you'll spend for a damn two cent

box of candy or something. How about the time you're wasting right now, listening to that band."

"Dat's de troof," he says. "Well, ef I lives twell night hit's gwine to be two bits mo dey takin out of town, dat's sho."

"Then you're a fool," I says.

"Well," he says, "I dont spute dat neither. Ef dat uz a crime, all chain-gangs wouldn't be black."

Well, just about that time I happened to look up the alley and saw her. When I stepped back and looked at my watch I didn't notice at the time who he was because I was looking at the watch. It was just two thirty, forty-five minutes before anybody but me expected her to be out. So when I looked around the door the first thing I saw was the red tie he had on and I was thinking what the hell kind of a man would wear a red tie. But she was sneaking along the alley, watching the door, so I wasn't thinking anything about him until they had gone past. I was wondering if she'd have so little respect for me that she'd not only play out of school when I told her not to, but would walk right past the store, daring me not to see her. Only she couldn't see into the door because the sun fell straight into it and it was like trying to see through an automobile searchlight, so I stood there and watched her go on past, with her face painted up like a damn clown's and her hair all gummed and twisted and a dress that if a woman had come out doors even on Gayoso or Beale street when I was a young fellow with no more than that to cover her legs and behind, she'd been thrown in jail. I'll be damned if they dont dress like they were trying to make every man they passed on the street want to reach out and clap his hand on it. And so I was thinking what kind of a damn man would wear a red tie when all of a sudden I knew he was one of those show

folks well as if she'd told me. Well, I can stand a lot; if
I couldn't, damn if I wouldn't be in a hell of a fix, so
when they turned the corner I jumped down and followed. Me, without any hat, in the middle of the afternoon, having to chase up and down back alleys because
of my mother's good name. Like I say you cant do anything with a woman like that, if she's got it in her. If it's
in her blood, you cant do anything with her. The only
thing you can do is to get rid of her, let her go on and
live with her own sort.

I went on to the street, but they were out of sight.
And there I was, without any hat, looking like I was
crazy too. Like a man would naturally think, one of
them is crazy and another one drowned himself and the
other one was turned out into the street by her husband,
what's the reason the rest of them are not crazy too. All
the time I could see them watching me like a hawk, waiting for a chance to say Well I'm not surprised I expected
it all the time the whole family's crazy. Selling land to
send him to Harvard and paying taxes to support a state
University all the time that I never saw except twice at a
baseball game and not letting her daughter's name be
spoken on the place until after a while Father wouldn't
even come down town anymore but just sat there all day
with the decanter I could see the bottom of his nightshirt and his bare legs and hear the decanter clinking until finally T. P. had to pour it for him and she says You
have no respect for your Father's memory and I says I
dont know why not it sure is preserved well enough to
last only if I'm crazy too God knows what I'll do
about it just to look at water makes me sick and I'd just
as soon swallow gasoline as a glass of whiskey and Lorraine telling them he may not drink but if you dont believe he's a man I can tell you how to find out she says If

I catch you fooling with any of these whores you know
what I'll do she says I'll whip her grabbing at her I'll
whip her as long as I can find her she says and I says if
I dont drink that's my business but have you ever found
me short I says I'll buy you enough beer to take a
bath in if you want it because I've got every respect for a
good honest whore because with Mother's health and the
position I try to uphold to have her with no more respect
for what I try to do for her than to make her name and
my name and my Mother's name a byword in the town.

She had dodged out of sight somewhere. Saw me coming and dodged into another alley, running up and down
the alleys with a damn show man in a red tie that everybody would look at and think what kind of a damn man
would wear a red tie. Well, the boy kept speaking to me
and so I took the telegram without knowing I had taken
it. I didn't realise what it was until I was signing for it,
and I tore it open without even caring much what it was.
I knew all the time what it would be, I reckon. That was
the only thing else that could happen, especially holding
it up until I had already had the check entered on the
pass book.

I don't see how a city no bigger than New York can
hold enough people to take the money away from us
country suckers. Work like hell all day every day, send
them your money and get a little piece of paper back,
Your account closed at 20.62. Teasing you along, letting
you pile up a little paper profit, then bang! Your account
closed at 20.62. And if that wasn't enough, paying ten
dollars a month to somebody to tell you how to lose it
fast, that either dont know anything about it or is in ca-
hoots with the telegraph company. Well, I'm done with
them. They've sucked me in for the last time. Any fool
except a fellow that hasn't got any more sense than to

take a jew's word for anything could tell the market was going up all the time, with the whole damn delta about to be flooded again and the cotton washed right out of the ground like it was last year. Let it wash a man's crop out of the ground year after year, and them up there in Washington spending fifty thousand dollars a day keeping an army in Nicaragua or some place. Of course it'll overflow again, and then cotton'll be worth thirty cents a pound. Well, I just want to hit them one time and get my money back. I don't want a killing; only these small town gamblers are out for that, I just want my money back that these damn jews have gotten with all their guaranteed inside dope. Then I'm through; they can kiss my foot for every other red cent of mine they get.

I went back to the store. It was half past three almost. Damn little time to do anything in, but then I am used to that. I never had to go to Harvard to learn that. The band had quit playing. Got them all inside now, and they wouldn't have to waste any more wind. Earl says,

"He found you, did he? He was in here with it a while ago. I thought you were out back somewhere."

"Yes," I says, "I got it. They couldn't keep it away from me all afternoon. The town's too small. I've got to go out home a minute," I says. "You can dock me if it'll make you feel any better."

"Go ahead," he says, "I can handle it now. No bad news, I hope."

"You'll have to go to the telegraph office and find that out," I says. "They'll have time to tell you. I haven't."

"I just asked," he says. "Your mother knows she can depend on me."

"She'll appreciate it," I says. "I wont be gone any longer than I have to."

"Take your time," he says. "I can handle it now. You go ahead."

I got the car and went home. Once this morning, twice at noon, and now again, with her and having to chase all over town and having to beg them to let me eat a little of the food I am paying for. Sometimes I think what's the use of anything. With the precedent I've been set I must be crazy to keep on. And now I reckon I'll get home just in time to take a nice long drive after a basket of tomatoes or something and then have to go back to town smelling like a camphor factory so my head wont explode right on my shoulders. I keep telling her there's not a damn thing in that aspirin except flour and water for imaginary invalids. I says you dont know what a head-ache is. I says you think I'd fool with that damn car at all if it depended on me. I says I can get along without one I've learned to get along without lots of things but if you want to risk yourself in that old wornout surrey with a halfgrown nigger boy all right because I says God looks after Ben's kind, God knows He ought to do something for him but if you think I'm going to trust a thousand dollars' worth of delicate machinery to a half-grown nigger or a grown one either, you'd better buy him one yourself because I says you like to ride in the car and you know you do.

Dilsey said Mother was in the house. I went on into the hall and listened, but I didn't hear anything. I went up stairs, but just as I passed her door she called me.

"I just wanted to know who it was," she says. "I'm here alone so much that I hear every sound."

"You dont have to stay here," I says. "You could spend the whole day visiting like other women, if you wanted to." She came to the door.

"I thought maybe you were sick," she says. "Having to hurry through your dinner like you did."

"Better luck next time," I says. "What do you want?"

"Is anything wrong?" she says.

"What could be?" I says. "Cant I come home in the middle of the afternoon without upsetting the whole house?"

"Have you seen Quentin?" she says.

"She's in school," I says.

"It's after three," she says. "I heard the clock strike at least a half an hour ago. She ought to be home by now."

"Ought she?" I says. "When have you ever seen her before dark?"

"She ought to be home," she says. "When I was a girl . . ."

"You had somebody to make you behave yourself," I says. "She hasn't."

"I can't do anything with her," she says. "I've tried and I've tried."

"And you wont let me, for some reason," I says, "So you ought to be satisfied." I went on to my room. I turned the key easy and stood there until the knob turned. Then she says,

"Jason."

"What," I says.

"I just thought something was wrong."

"Not in here," I says. "You've come to the wrong place."

"I dont mean to worry you," she says.

"I'm glad to hear that," I says. "I wasn't sure. I thought I might have been mistaken. Do you want anything?"

After awhile she says, "No. Not any thing." Then she went away. I took the box down and counted out the money and hid the box again and unlocked the door and went out. I thought about the camphor, but it would be too late now, anyway. And I'd just have one more round trip. She was at her door, waiting.

"You want anything from town?" I says.

"No," she says. "I dont mean to meddle in your affairs. But I dont know what I'd do if anything happened to you, Jason."

"I'm all right," I says. "Just a headache."

"I wish you'd take some aspirin," she says. "I know you're not going to stop using the car."

"What's the car got to do with it?" I says. "How can a car give a man a headache?"

"You know gasoline always made you sick," she says. "Ever since you were a child. I wish you'd take some aspirin."

"Keep on wishing it," I says. "It wont hurt you."

I got in the car and started back to town. I had just turned onto the street when I saw a ford coming helling toward me. All of a sudden it stopped. I could hear the wheels sliding and it slewed around and backed and whirled and just as I was thinking what the hell they were up to, I saw that red tie. Then I recognised her face looking back through the window. It whirled into the alley. I saw it turn again, but when I got to the back street it was just disappearing, running like hell.

I saw red. When I recognised that red tie, after all I had told her, I forgot about everything. I never thought about my head even until I came to the first forks and had to stop. Yet we spend money and spend money on roads and damn if it isn't like trying to drive over a sheet of corrugated iron roofing. I'd like to know how a man could be expected to keep up with even a wheel-barrow. I think too much of my car; I'm not going to hammer it to pieces like it was a ford. Chances were they had stolen it, anyway, so why should they give a damn

Like I say blood always tells. If you've got blood like
that in you, you'll do anything. I says whatever claim you
believe she has on you has already been discharged; I
says from now on you have only yourself to blame because you know what any sensible person would do. I
says if I've got to spend half my time being a damn de-
tective, at least I'll go where I can get paid for it.

So I had to stop there at the forks. Then I remembered
it. It felt like somebody was inside with a hammer, beating on it. I says I've tried to keep you from being worried by her; I says far as I'm concerned, let her go to hell
as fast as she pleases and the sooner the better. I says
what else do you expect except every drummer and
cheap show that comes to town because even these town
jellybeans give her the go-by now. You dont know what
goes on I says, you dont hear the talk that I hear and you
can just bet I shut them up too. I says my people owned
slaves here when you all were running little shirt tail
country stores and farming land no nigger would look at
on shares.

If they ever farmed it. It's a good thing the Lord did
something for this country; the folks that live on it never
have. Friday afternoon, and from right here I could see
three miles of land that hadn't even been broken, and
every able bodied man in the county in town at that
show. I might have been a stranger starving to death,
and there wasn't a soul in sight to ask which way to town
even. And she trying to get me to take aspirin. I says
when I eat bread I'll do it at the table. I says you always
talking about how much you give up for us when you
could buy ten new dresses a year on the money you
spend for those damn patent medicines. It's not something to cure it I need it's just an even break not to have
to have them but as long as I have to work ten hours a

day to support a kitchen full of niggers in the style they're accustomed to and send them to the show with every other nigger in the county, only he was late already. By the time he got there it would be over.

After awhile he got up to the car and when I finally got it through his head if two people in a ford had passed him, he said yes. So I went on, and when I came to where the wagon road turned off I could see the tire tracks. Ab Russell was in his lot, but I didn't bother to ask him and I hadn't got out of sight of his barn hardly when I saw the ford. They had tried to hide it. Done about as well at it as she did at everything else she did. Like I say it's not that I object to so much; maybe she cant help that, it's because she hasn't even got enough consideration for her own family to have any discretion. I'm afraid all the time I'll run into them right in the middle of the street or under a wagon on the square, like a couple of dogs.

I parked and got out. And now I'd have to go way around and cross a plowed field, the only one I had seen since I left town, with every step like somebody was walking along behind me, hitting me on the head with a club. I kept thinking that when I got across the field at least I'd have something level to walk on, that wouldn't jolt me every step, but when I got into the woods it was full of underbrush and I had to twist around through it, and then I came to a ditch full of briers. I went along it for awhile, but it got thicker and thicker, and all the time Earl probably telephoning home about where I was and getting Mother all upset again.

When I finally got through I had had to wind around so much that I had to stop and figure out just where the car would be. I knew they wouldn't be far from it, just under the closest bush, so I turned and worked back toward the road. Then I couldn't tell just how far I was, so

I'd have to stop and listen, and then with my legs not using so much blood, it all would go into my head like it
would explode any minute, and the sun getting down
just to where it could shine straight into my eyes and my
ears ringing so I couldn't hear anything. I went on, trying to move quiet, then I heard a dog or something and
I knew that when he scented me he'd have to come helling up, then it would be all off.

I had gotten beggar lice and twigs and stuff all over
me, inside my clothes and shoes and all, and then I happened to look around and I had my hand right on
a bunch of poison oak. The only thing I couldn't understand was why it was just poison oak and not a snake or
something. So I didn't even bother to move it. I just stood
there until the dog went away. Then I went on.

I didn't have any idea where the car was now. I
couldn't think about anything except my head, and I'd
just stand in one place and sort of wonder if I had really
seen a ford even, and I didn't even care much whether I
had or not. Like I say, let her lay out all day and all night
with everything in town that wears pants, what do I care.
I dont owe anything to anybody that has no more
consideration for me, that wouldn't be a damn bit above
planting that ford there and making me spend a whole
afternoon and Earl taking her back there and showing
her the books just because he's too damn virtuous for this
world. I says you'll have one hell of a time in heaven,
without anybody's business to meddle in only dont you
ever let me catch you at it I says, I close my eyes to it because of your grandmother, but just you let me catch you
doing it one time on this place, where my mother lives.
These damn little slick haired squirts, thinking they are
raising so much hell, I'll show them something about hell
I says, and you too. I'll make him think that damn red

tie is the latch string to hell, if he thinks he can run the woods with my niece.

With the sun and all in my eyes and my blood going so I kept thinking every time my head would go on and burst and get it over with, with briers and things grabbing at me, then I came onto the sand ditch where they had been and I recognised the tree where the car was, and just as I got out of the ditch and started running I heard the car start. It went off fast, blowing the horn. They kept on blowing it, like it was saying Yah. Yah. Yaaahhhhhhhh, going out of sight. I got to the road just in time to see it go out of sight.

By the time I got up to where my car was, they were clean out of sight, the horn still blowing. Well, I never thought anything about it except I was saying Run. Run back to town. Run home and try to convince Mother that I never saw you in that car. Try to make her believe that I dont know who he was. Try to make her believe that I didn't miss ten feet of catching you in that ditch. Try to make her believe you were standing up, too.

It kept on saying Yahhhhh, Yahhhhh, Yaaahhhhhhhhhh, getting fainter and fainter. Then it quit, and I could hear a cow lowing up at Russell's barn. And still I never thought. I went up to the door and opened it and raised my foot. I kind of thought then that the car was leaning a little more than the slant of the road would be, but I never found it out until I got in and started off.

Well, I just sat there. It was getting on toward sundown, and town was about five miles. They never even had guts enough to puncture it, to jab a hole in it. They just let the air out. I just stood there for a while, thinking about that kitchen full of niggers and not one of them had time to lift a tire onto the rack and screw up a couple of bolts. It was kind of funny because even she couldn't have seen far enough ahead to take the pump out on purpose, unless she thought about it while he was letting out the air maybe. But what it probably was, was somebody took it out and gave it to Ben to play with for a squirt gun because they'd take the whole car to pieces if he wanted it and Dilsey says, Aint nobody teched yo car. What we want to fool with hit fer? and I says You're a nigger. You're lucky, do you know it? I says I'll swap with you any day because it takes a white man not to have anymore sense than to worry about what a little slut of a girl does.

I walked up to Russell's. He had a pump. That was just an oversight on their part, I reckon. Only I still couldn't believe she'd have had the nerve to. I kept thinking that. I dont know why it is I cant seem to learn that a woman'll do anything. I kept thinking, Let's forget for awhile how I feel toward you and how you feel toward me: I just wouldn't do you this way. I wouldn't do you this way no matter what you had done to me. Because like I say blood is blood and you cant get around it. It's not playing a joke that any eight year old boy could have thought of, it's letting your own uncle be laughed at by a man that would wear a red tie. They come into town and call us all a bunch of hicks and think it's too small to hold them. Well he doesn't know just how right he is. And her too. If that's the way she feels about it, she'd better keep right on going and a damn good riddance.

I stopped and returned Russell's pump and drove on to town. I went to the drugstore and got a coca-cola and then 1 went to the telegraph office. It had closed at 12.21, forty points down. Forty times five dollars; buy something with that if you can, and she'll say, I've got to have it I've just got to and I'll say that's too bad you'll have to try somebody else, I haven't got any money; I've been too busy to make any.

I just looked at him.

"I'll tell you some news," I says, "You'll be astonished to learn that I am interested in the cotton market," I says. "That never occurred to you, did it?"

"I did my best to deliver it," he says. "I tried the store twice and called up your house, but they didn't know where you were," he says, digging in the drawer.

"Deliver what?" I says. He handed me a telegram. "What time did this come?" I says.

"About half past three," he says.

"And now it's ten minutes past five," I says.

"I tried to deliver it," he says. "I couldn't find you."

"That's not my fault, is it?" I says. I opened it, just to see what kind of a lie they'd tell me this time. They must be in one hell of a shape if they've got to come all the way to Mississippi to steal ten dollars a month. Sell, it says. The market will be unstable, with a general downward tendency. Do not be alarmed following government report.

"How much would a message like this cost?" I says. He told me.

"They paid it," he says.

"Then I owe them that much," I says. "I already knew this. Send this collect," I says, taking a blank. Buy, I wrote, Market just on point of blowing its head off. Occasional flurries for purpose of hooking a few more country suckers who haven't got in to the telegraph office yet. Do not be alarmed. "Send that collect," I says.

He looked at the message, then he looked at the clock. "Market closed an hour ago," he says.

"Well," I says, "That's not my fault either. I didn't invent it; I just bought a little of it while under the impression that the telegraph company would keep me informed as to what it was doing."

"A report is posted whenever it comes in," he says.

"Yes," I says, "And in Memphis they have it on a blackboard every ten seconds," I says. "I was within sixty-seven miles of there once this afternoon."

He looked at the message. "You want to send this?" he says.

"I still haven't changed my mind," I says. I wrote the other one out and counted the money. "And this one too, if you're sure you can spell b-u-y."

I went back to the store. I could hear the band from down the street. Prohibition's a fine thing. Used to be they'd come in Saturday with just one pair of shoes in the family and him wearing them, and they'd go down to the express office and get his package; now they all go to the show barefooted, with the merchants in the door like a row of tigers or something in a cage, watching them pass. Earl says,

"I hope it wasn't anything serious."

"What?" I says. He looked at his watch. Then he went to the door and looked at the courthouse clock. "You ought to have a dollar watch," I says. "It wont cost you so much to believe it's lying each time."

"What?" he says.

"Nothing," I says. "Hope I haven't inconvenienced you."

"We were not busy much," he says. "They all went to the show. It's all right."

"If it's not all right," I says, "You know what you can do about it."

"I said it was all right," he says.

"I heard you," I says. "And if it's not all right, you know what you can do about it."

"Do you want to quit?" he says.

"It's not my business," I says. "My wishes dont matter. But dont get the idea that you are protecting me by keeping me."

"You'd be a good business man if you'd let yourself, Jason," he says.

"At least I can tend to my own business and let other peoples' alone," I says.

"I dont know why you are trying to make me fire you," he says. "You know you could quit anytime and there wouldn't be any hard feelings between us."

"Maybe that's why I dont quit," I says. "As long as I tend to my job, that's what you are paying me for." I went on to the back and got a drink of water and went on out to the back door. Job had the cultivators all set up at last. It was quiet there, and pretty soon my head got a little easier. I could hear them singing now, and then the band played again. Well, let them get every quarter and dime in the county; it was no skin off my back. I've done what I could; a man that can live as long as I have and not know when to quit is a fool. Especially as it's no business of mine. If it was my own daughter now it would be different, because she wouldn't have time to; she'd have to work some to feed a few invalids and idiots and niggers, because how could I have the face to bring anybody there. I've too much respect for anybody to do that. I'm a man, I can stand it, it's my own flesh and blood and I'd like to see the colour of the man's eyes that would speak disrespectful of any woman that was my friend it's these damn good women that do it I'd like to see the good, church-going woman that's half as square as Lorraine, whore or no whore. Like I say if I was to get married you'd go up like a balloon and you know it and she says I want you to be happy to have a family of your own not to slave your life away for us. But I'll be gone soon and then you can take a wife but you'll never find a woman who is worthy of you and I says yes I could. You'd get right up out of your grave you know you would. I says no thank you I have all the women I can take care of now if I married a wife she'd probably turn out to be a hophead or something. That's all we lack in this family, I says.

The sun was down beyond the Methodist church now, and the pigeons were flying back and forth around the steeple, and when the band stopped I could hear them cooing. It hadn't been four months since Christmas, and yet they were almost as thick as ever. I reckon Parson Walthall was getting a belly full of them now. You'd have thought we were shooting people, with him making speeches and even holding onto a man's gun when they came over. Talking about peace on earth good will toward all and not a sparrow can fall to earth. But what does he care how thick they get, he hasn't got anything to do; what does he care what time it is. He pays no taxes, he doesn't have to see his money going every year to have the courthouse clock cleaned to where it'll run. They had to pay a man forty-five dollars to clean it. I counted over a hundred half-hatched pigeons on the ground. You'd think they'd have sense enough to leave town. It's a good thing I dont have any more ties than a pigeon, I'll say that.

The band was playing again, a loud fast tune, like they were breaking up. I reckon they'd be satisfied now. Maybe they'd have enough music to entertain them while they drove fourteen or fifteen miles home and unharnessed in the dark and fed the stock and milked. All they'd have to do would be to whistle the music and tell the jokes to the live stock in the barn, and then they could count up how much they'd made by not taking the stock to the show too. They could figure that if a man had five children and seven mules, he cleared a quarter by taking his family to the show. Just like that. Earl came back with a couple of packages.

"Here's some more stuff going out," he says. "Where's Uncle Job?"

"Gone to the show, I imagine," I says. "Unless you watched him."

"He doesn't slip off," he says. "I can depend on him."

"Meaning me by that," I says.

He went to the door and looked out, listening.

"That's a good band," he says. "It's about time they were breaking up, I'd say."

"Unless they're going to spend the night there," I says. The swallows had begun, and I could hear the sparrows beginning to swarm in the trees in the courthouse yard. Every once in a while a bunch of them would come swirling around in sight above the roof, then go away. They are as big a nuisance as the pigeons, to my notion. You cant even sit in the courthouse yard for them. First thing you know, bing. Right on your hat. But it would take a millionaire to afford to shoot them at five cents a shot. If they'd just put a little poison out there in the square, they'd get rid of them in a day, because if a merchant cant keep his stock from running around the square, he'd better try to deal in something besides chickens, something that dont eat, like plows or onions. And if a man dont keep his dogs up, he either dont want it or he hasn't any business with one. Like I say if all the businesses in a town are run like country businesses, you're going to have a country town.

"It wont do you any good if they have broke up," I says. "They'll have to hitch up and take out to get home by midnight as it is."

"Well," he says, "They enjoy it. Let them spend a little money on a show now and then. A hill farmer works pretty hard and gets mighty little for it."

"There's no law making them farm in the hills," I says, "Or anywhere else."

"Where would you and me be, if it wasn't for the farmers?" he says.

"I'd be home right now," I says, "Lying down, with an ice pack on my head."

"You have these headaches too often," he says. "Why dont you have your teeth examined good? Did he go over them all this morning?"

"Did who?" I says.

"You said you went to the dentist this morning."

"Do you object to my having the headache on your time?" I says. "Is that it?" They were crossing the alley now, coming up from the show.

"There they come," he says. "I reckon I better get up front." He went on. It's a curious thing how no matter what's wrong with you, a man'll tell you to have your teeth examined and a woman'll tell you to get married. It always takes a man that never made much at anything to tell you how to run your business, though. Like these college professors without a whole pair of socks to their name, telling you how to make a million in ten years, and a woman that couldn't even get a husband can always tell you how to raise a family.

Old man Job came up with the wagon. After a while he got through wrapping the lines around the whip socket.

"Well," I says, "Was it a good show?"

"I aint been yit," he says. "But I kin be arrested in dat tent tonight, dough."

"Like hell you haven't," I says. "You've been away from here since three oclock. Mr Earl was just back here looking for you."

"I been tendin to my business," he says. "Mr Earl knows whar I been."

"You may can fool him," I says. "I wont tell on you."

"Den he's de onliest man here I'd try to fool," he says. "Whut I want to waste my time foolin a man whut I dont keer whether I sees him Sat'dy night er not? I wont try to fool you," he says. "You too smart fer me. Yes, suh," he says, looking busy as hell, putting five or six little packages into the wagon, "You's too smart fer me. Aint a man in dis town kin keep up wid you fer smartness. You fools a man whut so smart he cant even keep up wid hisself," he says, getting in the wagon and unwrapping the reins.

"Who's that?" I says.

"Dat's Mr Jason Compson," he says. "Git up dar, Dan!"

One of the wheels was just about to come off. I watched to see if he'd get out of the alley before it did. Just turn any vehicle over to a nigger, though. I says that old rattletrap's just an eyesore, yet you'll keep it standing there in the carriage house a hundred years just so that boy can ride to the cemetery once a week. I says he's not the first fellow that'll have to do things he doesn't want to. I'd make him ride in that car like a civilised man or stay at home. What does he know about where he goes or what he goes in, and us keeping a carriage and a horse so he can take a ride on Sunday afternoon.

A lot Job cared whether the wheel came off or not, long as he wouldn't have too far to walk back. Like I say the only place for them is in the field, where they'd have to work from sunup to sundown. They cant stand prosper·

ity or an easy job. Let one stay around white people for a while and he's not worth killing. They get so they can outguess you about work before your very eyes, like Roskus the only mistake he ever made was he got careless one day and died. Shirking and stealing and giving you a little more lip and a little more lip until some day you have to lay them out with a scantling or something. Well, it's Earl's business. But I'd hate to have my business advertised over this town by an old doddering nigger and a wagon that you thought every time it turned a corner it would come all to pieces.

The sun was all high up in the air now, and inside it was beginning to get dark. I went up front. The square was empty. Earl was back closing the safe, and then the clock begun to strike.

"You lock the back door," he says. I went back and locked it and came back. "I suppose you're going to the show tonight," he says. "I gave you those passes yesterday, didn't I?"

"Yes," I said. "You want them back?"

"No, no," he says, "I just forgot whether I gave them to you or not. No sense in wasting them."

He locked the door and said Goodnight and went on. The sparrows were still rattling away in the trees, but the square was empty except for a few cars. There was a ford in front of the drugstore, but I didn't even look at it. I know when I've had enough of anything. I dont mind trying to help her, but I know when I've had enough. I guess I could teach Luster to drive it, then they could chase her all day long if they wanted to, and I could stay home and play with Ben.

I went in and got a couple of cigars. Then I thought I'd have another headache shot for luck, and I stood and talked with them awhile.

"Well," Mac says, "I reckon you've got your money on the Yankees this year."

"What for?" I says.

"The Pennant," he says. "Not anything in the League can beat them."

"Like hell there's not," I says. "They're shot," I says. "You think a team can be that lucky forever?"

"I dont call it luck," Mac says.

"I wouldn't bet on any team that fellow Ruth played on," I says. "Even if I knew it was going to win."

"Yes?" Mac says.

"I can name you a dozen men in either League who're more valuable than he is," I says.

"What have you got against Ruth?" Mac says.

"Nothing," I says. "I haven't got any thing against him. I dont even like to look at his picture." I went on out. The lights were coming on, and people going along the streets toward home. Sometimes the sparrows never got still until full dark. The night they turned on the new lights around the courthouse it waked them up and they were flying around and blundering into the lights all night long. They kept it up two or three nights, then one morning they were all gone. Then after about two months they all came back again.

I drove on home. There were no lights in the house yet, but they'd all be looking out the windows, and Dilsey jawing away in the kitchen like it was her own food she was having to keep hot until I got there. You'd think to hear her that there wasn't but one supper in the world, and that was the one she had to keep back a few minutes on my account. Well at least I could come home one time without finding Ben and that nigger hanging on the gate like a bear and a monkey in the same cage. Just let it come toward sundown and he'd head for the gate like a cow for the barn, hanging onto it and bobbing his head and sort of moaning to himself. That's a hog for punishment for you. If what had happened to him for fooling with open gates had happened to me, I never would want to see another one. I often wondered what he'd be thinking about, down there at the gate, watching the girls going home from school, trying to want something he couldn't even remember he didn't and couldn't want any longer. And what he'd think when they'd be undressing him and he'd happen to take a look at himself and begin to cry like he'd do. But like I say they never did enough of that. I says I know what you need, you need what they did to Ben then you'd behave. And if you dont know what that was I says, ask Dilsey to tell you.

There was a light in Mother's room. I put the car up and went on into the kitchen. Luster and Ben were there.

"Where's Dilsey?" I says. "Putting supper on?"

"She upstairs wid Miss Cahline," Luster says. "Dey been goin hit. Ever since Miss Quentin come home. Mammy up there keepin um fom fightin. Is dat show come, Mr Jason?"

"Yes," I says.

"I thought I heard de band," he says. "Wish I could go," he says. "I could ef I jes had a quarter."

Dilsey came in. "You come, is you?" she says. "Whut you been up to dis evenin? You knows how much work I got to do; whyn't you git here on time?"

"Maybe I went to the show," I says. "Is supper ready?"

"Wish I could go," Luster said. "I could ef I jes had a quarter."

"You aint got no business at no show," Dilsey says. "You go on in de house and set down," she says. "Dont you go up stairs and get um started again, now."

"What's the matter?" I says.

"Quentin come in a while ago and says you been follerin her around all evenin and den Miss Cahline jumped on her. Whyn't you let her alone? Cant you live in de same house wid you own blood niece widout quoilin?"

"I cant quarrel with her," I says, "because I haven't seen her since this morning. What does she say I've done now? made her go to school? That's pretty bad," I says.

"Well, you tend to yo business and let her alone," Dilsey says, "I'll take keer of her ef you'n Miss Cahline'll let me. Go on in dar now and behave yoself twell I git supper on."

"Ef I jes had a quarter," Luster says, "I could go to dat show."

"En ef you had wings you could fly to heaven," Dilsey says. "I dont want to hear another word about dat show."

"That reminds me," I says, "I've got a couple of tickets they gave me." I took them out of my coat.

"You fixin to use um?" Luster says.

"Not me," I says. "I wouldn't go to it for ten dollars."

"Gimme one of um, Mr Jason," he says.

"I'll sell you one," I says. "How about it?"

"I aint got no money," he says.

"That's too bad," I says. I made to go out.

"Gimme one of um, Mr Jason," he says. "You aint gwine need um bofe."

"Hush yo mouf," Dilsey says, "Dont you know he aint gwine give nothing away?"

"How much you want fer hit?" he says.

"Five cents," I says.

"I aint got dat much," he says.

"How much you got?" I says.

"I aint got nothing," he says.

"All right," I says. I went on.

"Mr Jason," he says.

"Whyn't you hush up?" Dilsey says. "He jes teasin you. He fixin to use dem tickets hisself. Go on, Jason, and let him lone."

"I dont want them," I says. I came back to the stove. "I came in here to burn them up. But if you want to buy one for a nickel?" I says, looking at him and opening the stove lid.

"I aint got dat much," he says.

"All right," I says. I dropped one of them in the stove.

"You, Jason," Dilsey says, "Aint you shamed?"

"Mr Jason," he says, "Please, suh. I'll fix dem tires ev'ry day fer a mont'."

"I need the cash," I says. "You can have it for a nickel."

"Hush, Luster," Dilsey says. She jerked him back. "Go on," she says, "Drop hit in. Go on. Git hit over with."

"You can have it for a nickel," I says.

"Go on," Dilsey says. "He aint got no nickel. Go on. Drop hit in."

"All right," I says. I dropped it in and Dilsey shut the stove.

"A big growed man like you," she says. "Git on outen my kitchen. Hush," she says to Luster. "Dont you git Benjy started. I'll git you a quarter from Frony tonight and you kin go tomorrow night. Hush up, now."

I went on into the living room. I couldn't hear anything from upstairs. I opened the paper. After awhile Ben and Luster came in. Ben went to the dark place on the wall where the mirror used to be, rubbing his hands on it and slobbering and moaning. Luster begun punching at the fire.

"What're you doing?" I says. "We dont need any fire tonight."

"I trying to keep him quiet," he says. "Hit always cold Easter," he says.

"Only this is not Easter," I says. "Let it alone."

He put the poker back and got the cushion out of Mother's chair and gave it to Ben, and he hunkered down in front of the fireplace and got quiet.

I read the paper. There hadn't been a sound from upstairs when Dilsey came in and sent Ben and Luster on to the kitchen and said supper was ready.

"All right," I says. She went out. I sat there, reading the paper. After a while I heard Dilsey looking in at the door.

"Whyn't you come on and eat?" she says.

"I'm waiting for supper," I says.

"Hit's on the table," she says. "I done told you."

"Is it?" I says. "Excuse me. I didn't hear anybody come down."

"They aint comin," she says. "You come on and eat, so I can take something up to them."

"Are they sick?" I says. "What did the doctor say it was? Not Smallpox, I hope."

"Come on here, Jason," she says, "So I kin git done."

"All right," I says, raising the paper again. "I'm waiting for supper now."

I could feel her watching me at the door. I read the paper.

"Whut you want to ask like this fer?" she says. "When you knows how much bother I has anyway."

"If Mother is any sicker than she was when she came down to dinner, all right," I says. "But as long as I am buying food for people younger than I am, they'll have to come down to the table to eat it. Let me know when supper's ready," I says, reading the paper again. I heard her climbing the stairs, dragging her feet and grunting and groaning like they were straight up and three feet apart. I heard her at Mother's door, then I heard her call-ing Quentin, like the door was locked, then she went back to Mother's room and then Mother went and talked to Quentin. Then they came down stairs. I read the paper.

Dilsey came back to the door. "Come on," she says, "fo you kin think up some mo devilment. You just tryin yo-self tonight."

I went to the diningroom. Quentin was sitting with her head bent. She had painted her face again. Her nose looked like a porcelain insulator.

"I'm glad you feel well enough to come down," I says to Mother.

"It's little enough I can do for you, to come to the table," she says. "No matter how I feel. I realise that when a man works all day he likes to be surrounded by his family at the supper table. I want to please you. I only wish you and Quentin got along better. It would be easier for me."

"We get along all right," I says. "I dont mind her stay-ing locked up in her room all day if she wants to. But I cant have all this whoop-de-do and sulking at mealtimes. I know that's a lot to ask her, but I'm that way in my own house. Your house, I meant to say."

"It's yours," Mother says, "You are the head of it now."

Quentin hadn't looked up. I helped the plates and she begun to eat.

"Did you get a good piece of meat?" I says. "If you didn't, I'll try to find you a better one."

She didn't say anything.

"I say, did you get a good piece of meat?" I says.

"What?" she says. "Yes. It's all right."

"Will you have some more rice?" I says.

"No," she says.

"Better let me give you some more," I says.

"I dont want any more," she says.

"Not at all," I says, "You're welcome."

"Is your headache gone?" Mother says.

"Headache?" I says.

"I was afraid you were developing one," she says. "When you came in this afternoon."

"Oh," I says. "No, it didn't show up. We stayed so busy this afternoon I forgot about it."

"Was that why you were late?" Mother says. I could see Quentin listening. I looked at her. Her knife and fork were still going, but I caught her looking at me, then she looked at her plate again. I says,

"No. I loaned my car to a fellow about three o'clock and I had to wait until he got back with it." I ate for a while.

"Who was it?" Mother says.

"It was one of those show men," I says. "It seems his sister's husband was out riding with some town woman, and he was chasing them."

Quentin sat perfectly still, chewing.

"You ought not to lend your car to people like that," Mother says. "You are too generous with it. That's why I never call on you for it if I can help it."

"I was beginning to think that myself, for awhile," I says. "But he got back, all right. He says he found what he was looking for."

"Who was the woman?" Mother says.

"I'll tell you later," I says. "I dont like to talk about such things before Quentin."

Quentin had quit eating. Every once in a while she'd take a drink of water, then she'd sit there crumbling a biscuit up, her face bent over her plate.

"Yes," Mother says, "I suppose women who stay shut up like I do have no idea what goes on in this town."

"Yes," I says, "They dont."

"My life has been so different from that," Mother says. "Thank God I dont know about such wickedness. I dont even want to know about it. I'm not like most people."

I didn't say any more. Quentin sat there, crumbling the biscuit until I quit eating, then she says,

"Can I go now?" without looking at anybody.

"What?" I says. "Sure, you can go. Were you waiting on us?"

She looked at me. She had crumbled all the biscuit, but her hands still went on like they were crumbling it yet and her eyes looked like they were cornered or something and then she started biting her mouth like it ought to have poisoned her, with all that red lead.

"Grandmother," she says, "Grandmother—"

"Did you want something else to eat?" I says.

"Why does he treat me like this, Grandmother?" she says. "I never hurt him."

"I want you all to get along with one another," Mother says, "You are all that's left now, and I do want you all to get along better."

"It's his fault," she says, "He wont let me alone, and I have to. If he doesn't want me here, why wont he let me go back to—"

"That's enough," I says, "Not another word."

"Then why wont he let me alone?" she says. "He—he just—"

"He is the nearest thing to a father you've ever had." Mother says. "It's his bread you and I eat. It's only right that he should expect obedience from you."

"It's his fault," she says. She jumped up. "He makes me do it. If he would just—" she looked at us, her eyes cornered, kind of jerking her arms against her sides.

"If I would just what?" I says.

"Whatever I do, it's your fault," she says. "If I'm bad, it's because I had to be. You made me. I wish I was dead. I wish we were all dead." Then she ran. We heard her run up the stairs. Then a door slammed.

"That's the first sensible thing she ever said," I says.

"She didn't go to school today," Mother says.

"How do you know?" I says. "Were you down town?"

"I just know," she says. "I wish you could be kinder to her."

"If I did that I'd have to arrange to see her more than once a day," I says. "You'll have to make her come to the table every meal. Then I could give her an extra piece of meat every time."

"There are little things you could do," she says.

"Like not paying any attention when you ask me to see that she goes to school?" I says.

"She didn't go to school today," she says. "I just know she didn't. She says she went for a car ride with one of the boys this afternoon and you followed her."

"How could I," I says, "When somebody had my car all afternoon? Whether or not she was in school today is already past," I says, "If you've got to worry about it, worry about next Monday."

"I wanted you and she to get along with one another," she says. "But she has inherited all of the headstrong traits. Quentin's too. I thought at the time, with the heritage she would already have, to give her that name, too. Sometimes I think she is the judgment of Caddy and Quentin upon me."

"Good Lord," I says, "You've got a fine mind. No wonder you kept yourself sick all the time."

"What?" she says. "I dont understand."

"I hope not," I says. "A good woman misses a lot she's better off without knowing."

"They were both that way," she says, "They would make interest with your father against me when I tried to correct them. He was always saying they didn't need controlling, that they already knew what cleanliness and honesty were, which was all that anyone could hope to be taught. And now I hope he's satisfied."

"You've got Ben to depend on," I says, "Cheer up."

"They deliberately shut me out of their lives," she says, "It was always her and Quentin. They were always conspiring against me. Against you too, though you were too young to realise it. They always looked on you and me as outsiders, like they did your Uncle Maury. I always told your father that they were allowed too much freedom, to be together too much. When Quentin started to school we had to let her go the next year, so she could be with him. She couldn't bear for any of you to do anything she couldn't. It was vanity in her, vanity and false pride. And then when her troubles began I knew that Quentin would feel that he had to do something just as bad. But I didn't believe that he would have been so selfish as to—I didn't dream that he—"

"Maybe he knew it was going to be a girl," I says, "And that one more of them would be more than he could stand."

"He could have controlled her," she says. "He seemed to be the only person she had any consideration for. But that is a part of the judgment too, I suppose."

"Yes," I says, "Too bad it wasn't me instead of him. You'd be a lot better off."

"You say things like that to hurt me," she says. "I deserve it though. When they began to sell the land to send Quentin to Harvard I told your father that he must make an equal provision for you. Then when Herbert offered to take you into the bank I said, Jason is provided for now, and when all the expense began to pile up and I was forced to sell our furniture and the rest of the pasture, I wrote her at once because I said she will realise that she and Quentin have had their share and part of Jason's too and that it depends on her now to compensate him. I said she will do that out of respect for her father. I believed that, then. But I'm just a poor old woman; I was raised to believe that people would deny themselves for their own flesh and blood. It's my fault. You were right to reproach me."

"Do you think I need any man's help to stand on my feet?" I says, "Let alone a woman that cant name the father of her own child."

"Jason," she says.

"All right," I says. "I didn't mean that. Of course not."

"If I believed that were possible, after all my suffering."

"Of course it's not," I says. "I didn't mean it."

"I hope that at least is spared me," she says.

"Sure it is," I says, "She's too much like both of them to doubt that."

"I couldn't bear that," she says.

"Then quit thinking about it," I says. "Has she been worrying you any more about getting out at night?"

"No. I made her realise that it was for her own good and that she'd thank me for it some day. She takes her books with her and studies after I lock the door. I see the light on as late as eleven oclock some nights."

"How do you know she's studying?" I says.

"I don't know what else she'd do in there alone," she says. "She never did read any."

"No," I says, "You wouldn't know. And you can thank your stars for that," I says. Only what would be the use in saying it aloud. It would just have her crying on me again.

I heard her go up stairs. Then she called Quentin and
Quentin says What? through the door. "Goodnight,"
Mother says. Then I heard the key in the lock, and
Mother went back to her room.

When I finished my cigar and went up, the light was
still on. I could see the empty keyhole, but I couldn't
hear a sound. She studied quiet. Maybe she learned that
in school. I told Mother goodnight and went on to my
room and got the box out and counted it again. I could
hear the Great American Gelding snoring away like a
planing mill. I read somewhere they'd fix men that way
to give them women's voices. But maybe he didn't know
what they'd done to him. I dont reckon he even knew
what he had been trying to do, or why Mr Burgess
knocked him out with the fence picket. And if they'd
just sent him on to Jackson while he was under the ether,
he'd never have known the difference. But that would
have been too simple for a Compson to think of. Not
half complex enough. Having to wait to do it at all
until he broke out and tried to run a little girl down on
the street with her own father looking at him. Well, like
I say they never started soon enough with their cutting,
and they quit too quick. I know at least two more that
needed something like that, and one of them not over a
mile away, either. But then I dont reckon even that
would do any good. Like I say once a bitch always a
bitch. And just let me have twenty-four hours without
any damn New York jew to advise me what it's going to
do. I dont want to make a killing; save that to suck in
the smart gamblers with. I just want an even chance to
get my money back. And once I've done that they can
bring all Beale Street and all bedlam in here and two of
them can sleep in my bed and another one can have my
place at the table too.

APRIL
8
1928

THE DAY DAWNED BLEAK AND CHILL. A MOVING WALL of grey light out of the northeast which, instead of dissolving into moisture, seemed to disintegrate into minute and venomous particles, like dust that, when Dilsey opened the door of the cabin and emerged, needled laterally into her flesh, precipitating not so much a moisture as a substance partaking of the quality of thin, not quite congealed oil. She wore a stiff black straw hat perched upon her turban, and a maroon velvet cape with a border of mangy and anonymous fur above a dress of purple silk, and she stood in the door for awhile with her myriad and sunken face lifted to the weather, and one gaunt hand flac-soled as the belly of a fish, then she moved the cape aside and examined the bosom of her gown.

The gown fell gauntly from her shoulders, across her fallen breasts, then tightened upon her paunch and fell again, ballooning a little above the nether garments which she would remove layer by layer as the spring accomplished and the warm days, in colour regal and moribund. She had been a big woman once but now her skeleton rose, draped loosely in unpadded skin that tightened again upon a paunch almost dropsical, as though muscle and tissue had been courage or fortitude which the days or the years had consumed until only the indomitable skeleton was left rising like a ruin or a landmark above the somnolent and impervious guts, and above that the collapsed face that gave the impression of the bones themselves being outside the flesh, lifted into the driving day with an expression at once fatalistic and of a child's astonished disappointment, until she turned and entered the house again and closed the door.

The earth immediately about the door was bare. It had a patina, as though from the soles of bare feet in generations, like old silver or the walls of Mexican houses which have been plastered by hand. Beside the house, shading it in summer, stood three mulberry trees, the fledged leaves that would later be broad and placid as the palms of hands streaming flatly undulant upon the driving air. A pair of jaybirds came up from nowhere, whirled up on the blast like gaudy scraps of cloth or paper and lodged in the mulberries, where they swung in raucous tilt and recover, screaming into the wind that ripped their harsh cries onward and away like scraps of paper or of cloth in turn. Then three more joined them and they swung and tilted in the wrung branches for a time, screaming. The door of the cabin opened and Dilsey emerged once more, this time in a man's felt hat and an army overcoat, beneath the frayed skirts of which her blue gingham dress fell in uneven balloonings, streaming too about her as she crossed the yard and mounted the steps to the kitchen door.

A moment later she emerged, carrying an open umbrella now, which she slanted ahead into the wind, and crossed to the woodpile and laid the umbrella down, still open. Immediately she caught at it and arrested it and held to it for a while, looking about her. Then she closed it and laid it down and stacked stovewood into her crooked arm, against her breast, and picked up the umbrella and got it open at last and returned to the steps and held the wood precariously balanced while she contrived to close the umbrella, which she propped in the corner just within the door. She dumped the wood into the box behind the stove. Then she removed the overcoat and hat and took a soiled apron down from the wall and put it on and built a fire in the stove. While she was doing so, rattling the grate bars and clattering the lids, Mrs Compson began to call her from the head of the stairs.

She wore a dressing gown of quilted black satin, holding it close under her chin. In the other hand she held a red rubber hot water bottle and she stood at the head of the back stairway, calling "Dilsey" at steady and inflectionless intervals into the quiet stairwell that descended into complete darkness, then opened again where a grey window fell across it. "Dilsey," she called, without inflection or emphasis or haste, as though she were not listening for a reply at all. "Dilsey."

Dilsey answered and ceased clattering the stove, but before she could cross the kitchen Mrs Compson called her again, and before she crossed the diningroom and brought her head into relief against the grey splash of the window, still again.

"All right," Dilsey said, "All right, here I is. I'll fill hit soon ez I git some hot water." She gathered up her skirts and mounted the stairs, wholly blotting the grey light. "Put hit down dar en g'awn back to bed."

"I couldn't understand what was the matter," Mrs

Compson said. "I've been lying awake for an hour at least, without hearing a sound from the kitchen."

"You put hit down and g'awn back to bed," Dilsey said. She toiled painfully up the steps, shapeless, breathing heavily. "I'll have de fire gwine in a minute, en de water hot in two mo."

"I've been lying there for an hour, at least," Mrs Compson said. "I thought maybe you were waiting for me to come down and start the fire."

Dilsey reached the top of the stairs and took the water bottle. "I'll fix hit in a minute," she said. "Luster overslep dis mawnin, up half de night at dat show. I gwine build de fire myself. Go on now, so you wont wake de others twell I ready."

"If you permit Luster to do things that interfere with his work, you'll have to suffer for it yourself," Mrs Compson said. "Jason wont like this if he hears about it. You know he wont."

"Twusn't none of Jason's money he went on," Dilsey said. "Dat's one thing sho." She went on down the stairs. Mrs Compson returned to her room. As she got into bed again she could hear Dilsey yet descending the stairs with a sort of painful and terrific slowness that would have become maddening had it not presently ceased beyond the flapping diminishment of the pantry door.

She entered the kitchen and built up the fire and began to prepare breakfast. In the midst of this she ceased and went to the window and looked out toward her cabin, then she went to the door and opened it and shouted into the driving weather.

"Luster!" she shouted, standing to listen, tilting her face from the wind, "You, Luster?" She listened, then as she prepared to shout again Luster appeared around the corner of the kitchen.

"Ma'am?" he said innocently, so innocently that Dilsey looked down at him, for a moment motionless with something more than mere surprise.

"Whar you at?" she said.

"Nowhere," he said. "Jes in de cellar."

"Whut you doin in de cellar?" she said. "Dont stand dar in de rain, fool," she said.

"Aint doin nothin," he said. He came up the steps.

"Dont you dare come in dis do widout a armful of wood," she said. "Here I done had to tote yo wood en build yo fire bofe. Didn't I tole you not to leave dis place last night befo dat woodbox wus full to de top?"

"I did," Luster said, "I filled hit."

"Whar hit gone to, den?"

"I dont know'm. I aint teched hit."

"Well, you git hit full up now," she said. "And git on up den en see bout Benjy."

She shut the door. Luster went to the woodpile. The five jaybirds whirled over the house, screaming, and into the mulberries again. He watched them. He picked up a rock and threw it. "Whoo," he said, "Git on back to hell, whar you belong at. 'Taint Monday yit."

He loaded himself mountainously with stove wood. He could not see over it, and he staggered to the steps and up them and blundered crashing against the door, shedding billets. Then Dilsey came and opened the door for him and he blundered across the kitchen. "You, Luster!" she shouted, but he had already hurled the wood into the box with a thunderous crash. "H'h!" he said.

"Is you tryin to wake up de whole house?" Dilsey said. She hit him on the back of his head with the flat of her hand. "Go on up dar and git Benjy dressed, now."

"Yessum," he said. He went toward the outer door.

"Whar you gwine?" Dilsey said.

"I thought I better go round de house en in by de front, so I wont wake up Miss Cahline en dem."

"You go on up dem backstairs like I tole you en git Benjy's clothes on him," Dilsey said. "Go on, now."

"Yessum," Luster said. He returned and left by the diningroom door. After awhile it ceased to flap. Dilsey prepared to make biscuit. As she ground the sifter steadily above the bread board, she sang, to herself at first, something without particular tune or words, repetitive, mournful and plaintive, austere, as she ground a faint, steady snowing of flour onto the breadboard. The stove had begun to heat the room and to fill it with murmurous minors of the fire, and presently she was singing louder, as if her voice too had been thawed out by the growing warmth, and then Mrs Compson called her name again from within the house. Dilsey raised her face as if her eyes could and did penetrate the walls and ceiling and saw the old woman in her quilted dressing gown at the head of the stairs, calling her name with machinelike regularity.

"Oh, Lawd," Dilsey said. She set the sifter down and swept up the hem of her apron and wiped her hands and caught up the bottle from the chair on which she had laid it and gathered her apron about the handle of the kettle which was now jetting faintly. "Jes a minute," she called, "De water jes dis minute got hot."

It was not the bottle which Mrs Compson wanted, however, and clutching it by the neck like a dead hen Dilsey went to the foot of the stairs and looked upward.

"Aint Luster up dar wid him?" she said.

"Luster hasn't been in the house. I've been lying here listening for him. I knew he would be late, but I did hope he'd come in time to keep Benjamin from disturbing Ja-

son on Jason's one day in the week to sleep in the morn·
ing."

"I dont see how you expect anybody to sleep, wid you
standin in de hall, holl'in at folks fum de crack of
dawn," Dilsey said. She began to mount the stairs, toiling
heavily. "I sont dat boy up dar half hour ago."

Mrs Compson watched her, holding the dressing gown
under her chin. "What are you going to do?" she said.

"Gwine git Benjy dressed en bring him down to de
kitchen, whar he wont wake Jason en Quentin," Dilsey
said.

"Haven't you started breakfast yet?"

"I'll tend to dat too," Dilsey said. "You better git back
in bed twell Luster make yo fire. Hit cold dis mawnin."

"I know it," Mrs Compson said. "My feet are like ice.
They were so cold they waked me up." She watched Dilsey mount the stairs. It took her a long while. "You know
how it frets Jason when breakfast is late," Mrs Compson
said.

"I cant do but one thing at a time," Dilsey said. "You
git on back to bed, fo I has you on my hands dis mawnin
too."

"If you're going to drop everything to dress Benjamin,
I'd better come down and get breakfast. You know as
well as I do how Jason acts when it's late."

"En who gwine eat yo messin?" Dilsey said. "Tell me
dat. Go on now," she said, toiling upward. Mrs Compson stood watching her as she mounted, steadying herself
against the wall with one hand, holding her skirts up
with the other.

"Are you going to wake him up just to dress him?" she
said.

Dilsey stopped. With her foot lifted to the next step

she stood there, her hand against the wall and the grey splash of the window behind her, motionless and shapeless she loomed.

"He aint awake den?" she said.

"He wasn't when I looked in," Mrs Compson said. "But it's past his time. He never does sleep after half past seven. You know he doesn't."

Dilsey said nothing. She made no further move, but though she could not see her save as a blobby shape without depth, Mrs Compson knew that she had lowered her face a little and that she stood now like a cow in the rain, as she held the empty water bottle by its neck.

"You're not the one who has to bear it," Mrs Compson said. "It's not your responsibility. You can go away. You dont have to bear the brunt of it day in and day out. You owe nothing to them, to Mr Compson's memory. I know you have never had any tenderness for Jason. You've never tried to conceal it."

Dilsey said nothing. She turned slowly and descended, lowering her body from step to step, as a small child does, her hand against the wall. "You go on and let him alone," she said. "Dont go in dar no mo, now. I'll send Luster up soon as I find him. Let him alone, now."

She returned to the kitchen. She looked into the stove, then she drew her apron over her head and donned the overcoat and opened the outer door and looked up and down the yard. The weather drove upon her flesh, harsh and minute, but the scene was empty of all else that moved. She descended the steps, gingerly, as if for silence, and went around the corner of the kitchen. As she did so Luster emerged quickly and innocently from the cellar door.

Dilsey stopped. "Whut you up to?" she said.

"Nothin," Luster said, "Mr Jason say fer me to find out what dat water leak in de cellar fum."

"En when wus hit he say fer you to do dat?" Dilsey said. "last New Year's day, wasn't hit?"

"I thought I jes be lookin whiles dey sleep," Luster said. Dilsey went to the cellar door. He stood aside and she peered down into the obscurity odorous of dank earth and mould and rubber.

"Huh," Dilsey said. She looked at Luster again. He met her gaze blandly, innocent and open. "I dont know whut you up to, but you aint got no business doin hit. You jes tryin me too dis mawnin cause de others is, aint you? You git on up dar en see to Benjy, you hear?"

"Yessum," Luster said. He went on toward the kitchen steps, swiftly.

"Here," Dilsey said, "You git me another armful of wood while I got you."

"Yessum," he said. He passed her on the steps and went to the woodpile. When he blundered again at the door a moment later, again invisible and blind within and beyond his wooden avatar, Dilsey opened the door and guided him across the kitchen with a firm hand.

"Jes thow hit at dat box again," she said, "Jes thow hit."

"I got to," Luster said, panting, "I cant put hit down no other way."

"Den you stand dar en hold hit a while," Dilsey said. She unloaded him a stick at a time. "Whut got into you dis mawnin? Here I sont you fer wood en you aint never brought mo'n six sticks at a time to save yo life twell to-day. Whut you fixin to ax me kin you do now? Aint dat show lef town yit?"

"Yessum. Hit done gone."

She put the last stick into the box. "Now you go on up dar wid Benjy, like I tole you befo," she said. "And I dont want nobody else yellin down dem stairs at me twell I rings de bell. You hear me."

"Yessum," Luster said. He vanished through the swing door. Dilsey put some more wood in the stove and returned to the bread board. Presently she began to sing again.

The room grew warmer. Soon Dilsey's skin had taken on a rich, lustrous quality as compared with that as of a faint dusting of wood ashes which both it and Luster's had worn, as she moved about the kitchen, gathering about her the raw materials of food, coordinating the meal. On the wall above a cupboard, invisible save at night, by lamp light and even then evincing an enigmatic profundity because it had but one hand, a cabinet clock ticked, then with a preliminary sound as if it had cleared its throat, struck five times.

"Eight oclock," Dilsey said. She ceased and tilted her head upward, listening. But there was no sound save the clock and the fire. She opened the oven and looked at the pan of bread, then stooping she paused while someone descended the stairs. She heard the feet cross the dining-room, then the swing door opened and Luster entered, followed by a big man who appeared to have been shaped of some substance whose particles would not or did not cohere to one another or to the frame which supported it. His skin was dead looking and hairless; dropsical too, he moved with a shambling gait like a trained bear. His hair was pale and fine. It had been brushed smoothly down upon his brow like that of children in daguerrotypes. His eyes were clear, of the pale sweet blue of cornflowers, his thick mouth hung open, drooling a little.

"Is he cold?" Dilsey said. She wiped her hands on her apron and touched his hand.

"Ef he aint, I is," Luster said. "Always cold Easter. Aint never seen hit fail. Miss Cahline say ef you aint got time to fix her hot water bottle to never mind about hit."

"Oh, 'lawd," Dilsey said. She drew a chair into the corner between the woodbox and the stove. The man went obediently and sat in it. "Look in de dinin room and see whar I laid dat bottle down," Dilsey said. Luster fetched the bottle from the diningroom and Dilsey filled it and gave it to him. "Hurry up, now," she said. "See ef Jason wake now. Tell em hit's all ready."

Luster went out. Ben sat beside the stove. He sat loosely, utterly motionless save for his head, which made a continual bobbing sort of movement as he watched Dilsey with his sweet vague gaze as she moved about. Luster returned.

"He up," he said, "Miss Cahline say put hit on de table." He came to the stove and spread his hands palm down above the firebox. "He up, too," He said, "Gwine hit wid bofe feet dis mawnin."

"Whut's de matter now?" Dilsey said. "Git away fum dar. How kin I do anything wid you standin over de stove?"

"I cold," Luster said.

"You ought to thought about dat whiles you wus down dar in dat cellar," Dilsey said. "Whut de matter wid Jason?"

"Sayin me en Benjy broke dat winder in his room."

"Is dey one broke?" Dilsey said.

"Dat's whut he sayin," Luster said. "Say I broke hit."

"How could you, when he keep hit locked all day en night?"

"Say I broke hit chunkin rocks at hit," Luster said.

"En did you?"

"Nome," Luster said.

"Dont lie to me, boy," Dilsey said.

"I never done hit," Luster said. "Ask Benjy ef I did. I aint stud'in dat winder."

"Who could a broke hit, den?" Dilsey said. "He jes tryin hisself, to wake Quentin up," she said, taking the pan of biscuits out of the stove.

"Reckin so," Luster said. "Dese is funny folks. Glad I aint none of em."

"Aint none of who?" Dilsey said. "Lemme tell you somethin, nigger boy, you got jes es much Compson devilment in you es any of em. Is you right sho you never broke dat window?"

"Whut I want to break hit fur?"

"Whut you do any of you devilment fur?" Dilsey said. "Watch him now, so he cant burn his hand again twell I git de table set."

She went to the diningroom, where they heard her moving about, then she returned and set a plate at the kitchen table and set food there. Ben watched her, slobbering, making a faint, eager sound.

"All right, honey," she said, "Here yo breakfast. Bring his chair, Luster." Luster moved the chair up and Ben sat down, whimpering and slobbering. Dilsey tied a cloth about his neck and wiped his mouth with the end of it. "And see kin you kep fum messin up his clothes one time," she said, handing Luster a spoon.

Ben ceased whimpering. He watched the spoon as it rose to his mouth. It was as if even eagerness were muscle-bound in him too, and hunger itself inarticulate, not knowing it is hunger. Luster fed him with skill and detachment. Now and then his attention would return long enough to enable him to feint the spoon and cause Ben to close his mouth upon the empty air, but it was apparent that Luster's mind was elsewhere. His other hand lay on the back of the chair and upon that dead surface it moved tentatively, delicately, as if he were picking an inaudible tune out of the dead void, and once he even forgot to tease Ben with the spoon while his fingers teased out of the slain wood a soundless and involved arpeggio until Ben recalled him by whimpering again.

In the diningroom Dilsey moved back and forth. Presently she rang a small clear bell, then in the kitchen Luster heard Mrs Compson and Jason descending, and Jason's voice, and he rolled his eyes whitely with listening.

"Sure, I know they didn't break it," Jason said. "Sure, I know that. Maybe the change of weather broke it."

"I dont see how it could have," Mrs Compson said. "Your room stays locked all day long, just as you leave it when you go to town. None of us ever go in there except Sunday, to clean it. I dont want you to think that I would go where I'm not wanted, or that I would permit anyone else to."

"I never said you broke it, did I?" Jason said.

"I dont want to go in your room," Mrs Compson said. "I respect anybody's private affairs. I wouldn't put my foot over the threshold, even if I had a key."

"Yes," Jason said, "I know your keys wont fit. That's why I had the lock changed. What I want to know is, how that window got broken."

"Luster say he didn't do hit," Dilsey said.

"I knew that without asking him," Jason said. "Where's Quentin?" he said.

"Where she is ev'y Sunday mawnin," Dilsey said. "Whut got into you de last few days, anyhow?"

"Well, we're going to change all that," Jason said. "Go up and tell her breakfast is ready."

"You leave her alone now, Jason," Dilsey said. "She gits up fer breakfast ev'y week mawnin, en Cahline lets her stay in bed ev'y Sunday. You knows dat."

"I cant keep a kitchen full of niggers to wait on her pleasure, much as I'd like to," Jason said. "Go and tell her to come down to breakfast."

"Aint nobody have to wait on her," Dilsey said. "I puts her breakfast in de warmer en she—"

"Did you hear me?" Jason said.

"I hears you," Dilsey said. "All I been hearin, when you in de house. Ef hit aint Quentin er yo maw, hit's Luster en Benjy. Whut you let him go on dat way fer, Miss Cahline?"

"You'd better do as he says," Mrs Compson said, "He's head of the house now. It's his right to require us to respect his wishes. I try to do it, and if I can, you can too."

"Taint no sense in him bein so bad tempered he got to make Quentin git up jes to suit him," Dilsey said. "Maybe you think she broke dat window."

"She would, if she happened to think of it," Jason said. "You go and do what I told you."

"En I wouldn't blame her none ef she did," Dilsey said, going toward the stairs. "Wid you naggin at her all de blessed time yo in de house."

"Hush, Dilsey," Mrs Compson said, "It's neither your place nor mine to tell Jason what to do. Sometimes I think he is wrong, but I try to obey his wishes for you alls' sakes. If I'm strong enough to come to the table, Quentin can too."

Dilsey went out. They heard her mounting the stairs. They heard her a long while on the stairs.

"You've got a prize set of servants," Jason said. He helped his mother and himself to food. "Did you ever have one that was worth killing? You must have had some before I was big enough to remember."

"I have to humour them," Mrs Compson said. "I have to depend on them so completely. It's not as if I were strong. I wish I were. I wish I could do all the house work myself. I could at least take that much off your shoulders."

"And a fine pigsty we'd live in, too," Jason said. "Hurry up, Dilsey," he shouted.

"I know you blame me," Mrs Compson said, "for letting them off to go to church today."

"Go where?" Jason said. "Hasn't that damn show left yet?"

"To church," Mrs Compson said. "The darkies are having a special Easter service. I promised Dilsey two weeks ago that they could get off."

"Which means we'll eat cold dinner," Jason said, "or none at all."

"I know it's my fault," Mrs Compson said. "I know you blame me."

"For what?" Jason said. "You never resurrected Christ, did you?"

They heard Dilsey mount the final stair, then her slow feet overhead.

"Quentin," she said. When she called the first time Jason laid his knife and fork down and he and his mother appeared to wait across the table from one another, in identical attitudes; the one cold and shrewd, with close-thatched brown hair curled into two stubborn hooks, one on either side of his forehead like a bartender in caricature, and hazel eyes with black-ringed irises like marbles, the other cold and querulous, with perfectly white hair and eyes pouched and baffled and so dark as to appear to be all pupil or all iris.

"Quentin," Dilsey said, "Git up, honey. Dey waitin breakfast on you."

"I cant understand how that window got broken," Mrs

Compson said. "Are you sure it was done yesterday? It could have been like that a long time, with the warm weather. The upper sash, behind the shade like that."

"I've told you for the last time that it happened yesterday," Jason said. "Dont you reckon I know the room I live in? Do you reckon I could have lived in it a week with a hole in the window you could stick your hand—" his voice ceased, ebbed, left him staring at his mother with eyes that for an instant were quite empty of anything. It was as though his eyes were holding their breath, while his mother looked at him, her face flaccid and querulous, interminable, clairvoyant yet obtuse. As they sat so Dilsey said,

"Quentin. Dont play wid me, honey. Come on to breakfast, honey. Dey waitin fer you."

"I cant understand it," Mrs Compson said, "It's just as if somebody had tried to break into the house—" Jason sprang up. His chair crashed over backward. "What—" Mrs Compson said, staring at him as he ran past her and went jumping up the stairs, where he met Dilsey. His face was now in shadow, and Dilsey said,

"She sullin. Yo ma aint unlocked—" But Jason ran on past her and along the corridor to a door. He didn't call. He grasped the knob and tried it, then he stood with the knob in his hand and his head bent a little, as if he were listening to something much further away than the dimensioned room beyond the door, and which he already heard. His attitude was that of one who goes through the motions of listening in order to deceive himself as to what he already hears. Behind him Mrs Compson mounted the stairs, calling his name. Then she saw Dilsey and she quit calling him and began to call Dilsey instead.

"I told you she aint unlocked dat do' yit," Dilsey said

When she spoke he turned and ran toward her, but his voice was quiet, matter of fact. "She carry the key with her?" he said. "Has she got it now, I mean, or will she have—"

"Dilsey," Mrs Compson said on the stairs.

"Is which?" Dilsey said. "Whyn't you let—"

"The key," Jason said, "To that room. Does she carry it with her all the time. Mother." Then he saw Mrs Compson and he went down the stairs and met her. "Give me the key," he said. He fell to pawing at the pockets of the rusty black dressing sacque she wore. She resisted.

"Jason," she said, "Jason! Are you and Dilsey trying to put me to bed again?" she said, trying to fend him off, "Cant you even let me have Sunday in peace?"

"The key," Jason said, pawing at her, "Give it here." He looked back at the door, as if he expected it to fly open before he could get back to it with the key he did not have.

"You, Dilsey!" Mrs Compson said, clutching her sacque about her.

"Give me the key, you old fool!" Jason cried suddenly. From her pocket he tugged a huge bunch of rusted keys on an iron ring like a mediaeval jailer's and ran back up the hall with the two women behind him.

"You, Jason!" Mrs Compson said. "He will never find the right one," she said, "You know I never let anyone take my keys, Dilsey," she said. She began to wail.

"Hush," Dilsey said, "He aint gwine do nothin to her. I aint gwine let him."

"But on Sunday morning, in my own house," Mrs Compson said, "When I've tried so hard to raise them Christians. Let me find the right key, Jason," she said. She put her hand on his arm. Then she began to struggle with him, but he flung her aside with a motion of his elbow and looked around at her for a moment, his eyes cold and harried, then he turned to the door again and the unwieldy keys.

"Hush," Dilsey said, "You, Jason!"

"Something terrible has happened," Mrs Compson said, wailing again, "I know it has. You, Jason," she said, grasping at him again. "He wont even let me find the key to a room in my own house!"

"Now, now," Dilsey said, "Whut kin happen? I right here. I aint gwine let him hurt her. Quentin," she said, raising her voice, "Dont you be skeered, honey, I'se right here."

The door opened, swung inward. He stood in it for a moment, hiding the room, then he stepped aside. "Go in," he said in a thick, light voice. They went in. It was not a girl's room. It was not anybody's room, and the faint scent of cheap cosmetics and the few feminine objects and other evidences of crude and hopeless efforts to feminize it but added to its anonymity, giving it that dead and stereotyped transience of rooms in assignation houses. The bed had not been disturbed. On the floor lay a soiled undergarment of cheap silk a little too pink; from a half open bureau drawer dangled a single stocking. The window was open. A pear tree grew there, close against the house. It was in bloom and the branches scraped and rasped against the house and the myriad air, driving in the window, brought into the room the forlorn scent of the blossoms.

"Dar now," Dilsey said, "Didn't I told you she all right?"

"All right?" Mrs Compson said. Dilsey followed her into the room and touched her.

"You come on and lay down, now," she said. "I find her in ten minutes."

Mrs Compson shook her off. "Find the note," she said. "Quentin left a note when he did it."

"All right," Dilsey said, "I'll find hit. You come on to yo room, now."

"I knew the minute they named her Quentin this would happen," Mrs Compson said. She went to the bureau and began to turn over the scattered objects there— scent bottles, a box of powder, a chewed pencil, a pair of scissors with one broken blade lying upon a darned scarf dusted with powder and stained with rouge. "Find the note," she said.

"I is," Dilsey said. "You come on, now. Me and Jason'll find hit. You come on to yo room."

"Jason," Mrs Compson said, "Where is he?" She went to the door. Dilsey followed her on down the hall, to another door. It was closed. "Jason," she called through the door. There was no answer. She tried the knob, then she called him again. But there was still no answer, for he was hurling things backward out of the closet: garments, shoes, a suitcase. Then he emerged carrying a sawn section of tongue-and-groove planking and laid it down and entered the closet again and emerged with a metal box. He set it on the bed and stood looking at the broken lock while he dug a key ring from his pocket and selected a key, and for a time longer he stood with the selected key in his hand, looking at the broken lock, then he put the keys back in his pocket and carefully tilted the contents of the box out upon the bed. Still carefully he sorted the papers, taking them up one at a time and shaking them. Then he upended the box and shook it too and slowly replaced the papers and stood again, looking at the broken lock, with the box in his hands and his head bent. Outside the window he heard some jaybirds swirl shrieking past, and away, their cries whipping away along the wind, and an automobile passed somewhere and died away also. His mother spoke his name again beyond the door, but he didn't move. He heard Dilsey lead her away up the hall, and then a door closed. Then he replaced the box in the closet and flung the garments back into it and went down stairs to the telephone. While he stood there with the receiver to his ear, waiting, Dilsey came down the stairs. She looked at him, without stopping, and went on.

The wire opened. "This is Jason Compson," he said, his voice so harsh and thick that he had to repeat himself. "Jason Compson," he said, controlling his voice. "Have a car ready, with a deputy, if you cant go, in ten minutes. I'll be there—What?—Robbery. My house. I know who it—Robbery, I say. Have a car ready—What? Aren't you a paid law enforcement—Yes, I'll be there in five minutes. Have that car ready to leave at once. If you dont, I'll report it to the governor."

He clapped the receiver back and crossed the dining-room, where the scarce-broken meal now lay cold on the table, and entered the kitchen. Dilsey was filling the hot water bottle. Ben sat, tranquil and empty. Beside him Luster looked like a fice dog, brightly watchful. He was eating something. Jason went on across the kitchen.

"Aint you going to eat no breakfast?" Dilsey said. He paid her no attention. "Go and eat yo breakfast, Jason." He went on. The outer door banged behind him. Luster rose and went to the window and looked out.

"Whoo," he said, "Whut happenin up dar? He been beatin' Miss Quentin?"

"You hush yo mouf," Dilsey said. "You git Benjy started now en I beat yo head off. You keep him quiet es you kin twell I get back, now." She screwed the cap on the bottle and went out. They heard her go up the stairs, then they heard Jason pass the house in his car. Then there was no sound in the kitchen save the simmering murmur of the kettle and the clock.

"You know whut I bet?" Luster said. "I bet he beat her. I bet he knock her in de head en now he gone fer de doctor. Dat's whut I bet." The clock tick-tocked, solemn and profound. It might have been the dry pulse of the decaying house itself; after a while it whirred and cleared its throat and struck six times. Ben looked up at it, then he looked at the bullet-like silhouette of Luster's head in the window and he begun to bob his head again, drooling. He whimpered.

"Hush up, loony," Luster said without turning. "Look like we aint gwine git to go to no church today." But Ben sat in the chair, his big soft hands dangling between his knees, moaning faintly. Suddenly he wept, a slow bellowing sound, meaningless and sustained. "Hush," Luster said. He turned and lifted his hand. "You want me to whup you?" But Ben looked at him, bellowing slowly with each expiration. Luster came and shook him. "You hush dis minute!" he shouted. "Here," he said. He hauled Ben out of the chair and dragged the chair around facing the stove and opened the door to the firebox and shoved Ben into the chair. They looked like a tug nudging at a clumsy tanker in a narrow dock. Ben sat down again facing the rosy door. He hushed. Then they heard the clock again, and Dilsey slow on the stairs. When she entered he began to whimper again. Then he lifted his voice.

"Whut you done to him?" Dilsey said. "Why cant you let him lone dis mawnin, of all times?"

"I aint doin nothin to him," Luster said. "Mr Jason skeered him, dat's whut hit is. He aint kilt Miss Quentin, is he?"

"Hush, Benjy," Dilsey said. He hushed. She went to the window and looked out. "Is it quit rainin?" she said.

"Yessum," Luster said. "Quit long time ago."

"Den ya'll go out do's a while," she said. "I jes got Miss Cahline quiet now."

"Is we gwine to church?" Luster said.

"I let you know bout dat when de time come. You keep him away fum de house twell I calls you."

"Kin we go to de pastuh?" Luster said.

"All right. Only you keep him away fum de house. I done stood all I kin."

"Yessum," Luster said. "Whar Mr Jason gone, mammy?"

"Dat's some mo of yo business, aint it?" Dilsey said. She began to clear the table. "Hush, Benjy. Luster gwine take you out to play."

"Whut he done to Miss Quentin, mammy?" Luster said.

"Aint done nothin to her. You all git on outen here."

"I bet she aint here," Luster said.

Dilsey looked at him. "How you know she aint here?"

"Me and Benjy seed her clamb out de window last night. Didn't us, Benjy?"

"You did?" Dilsey said, looking at him.

"We sees her doin hit ev'y night," Luster said, "Clamb right down dat pear tree."

"Dont you lie to me, nigger boy," Dilsey said.

"I aint lyin. Ask Benjy ef I is."

"Whyn't you say somethin about it, den?"

"'Twarn't none o my business," Luster said. "I aint gwine git mixed up in white folks' business. Come on here, Benjy, les go out do's."

They went out. Dilsey stood for awhile at the table, then she went and cleared the breakfast things from the diningroom and ate her breakfast and cleaned up the kitchen. Then she removed her apron and hung it up and went to the foot of the stairs and listened for a moment. There was no sound. She donned the overcoat and the hat and went across to her cabin.

The rain had stopped. The air now drove out of the southeast, broken overhead into blue patches. Upon the crest of a hill beyond the trees and roofs and spires of town sunlight lay like a pale scrap of cloth, was blotted away. Upon the air a bell came, then as if at a signal, other bells took up the sound and repeated it.

The cabin door opened and Dilsey emerged, again in the maroon cape and the purple gown, and wearing soiled white elbow-length gloves and minus her head-cloth now. She came into the yard and called Luster. She waited awhile, then she went to the house and around it to the cellar door, moving close to the wall, and looked into the door. Ben sat on the steps. Before him Luster squatted on the damp floor. He held a saw in his left hand, the blade sprung a little by pressure of his hand, and he was in the act of striking the blade with the worn wooden mallet with which she had been making beaten biscuit for more than thirty years. The saw gave forth a single sluggish twang that ceased with lifeless alacrity, leaving the blade in a thin clean curve between Luster's hand and the floor. Still, inscrutable, it bellied.

"Dat's de way he done hit," Luster said. "I jes aint foun de right thing to hit it wid."

"Dat's whut you doin, is it?" Dilsey said. "Bring me dat mallet," she said.

"I aint hurt hit," Luster said.

"Bring hit here," Dilsey said. "Put dat saw whar you got hit first."

He put the saw away and brought the mallet to her. Then Ben wailed again, hopeless and prolonged. It was nothing. Just sound. It might have been all time and in-

justice and sorrow become vocal for an instant by a con-
junction of planets.

"Listen at him," Luster said, "He been gwine on dat
way ev'y since you sont us outen de house. I dont know
whut got in to him dis mawnin."

"Bring him here," Dilsey said.

"Come on, Benjy," Luster said. He went back down
the steps and took Ben's arm. He came obediently, wailing, that slow hoarse sound that ships make, that seems
to begin before the sound itself has started, seems to
cease before the sound itself has stopped.

"Run and git his cap," Dilsey said. "Dont make no
noise Miss Cahline kin hear. Hurry, now. We already
late."

"She gwine hear him anyhow, ef you dont stop him,"
Luster said.

"He stop when we git off de place," Dilsey said. "He
smellin hit. Dat's whut hit is."

"Smell whut, mammy?" Luster said.

"You go git dat cap," Dilsey said. Luster went on. They
stood in the cellar door, Ben one step below her. The sky
was broken now into scudding patches that dragged their
swift shadows up out of the shabby garden, over the
broken fence and across the yard. Dilsey stroked Ben's
head, slowly and steadily, smoothing the bang upon his
brow. He wailed quietly, unhurriedly. "Hush," Dilsey
said, "Hush, now. We be gone in a minute. Hush, now."
He wailed quietly and steadily.

Luster returned, wearing a stiff new straw hat with a
coloured band and carrying a cloth cap. The hat seemed
to isolate Luster's skull, in the beholder's eye as a spot-
light would, in all its individual planes and angles. So
peculiarly individual was its shape that at first glance the

hat appeared to be on the head of someone standing immediately behind Luster. Dilsey looked at the hat.

"Whyn't you wear yo old hat?" she said.

"Couldn't find hit," Luster said.

"I bet you couldn't. I bet you fixed hit last night so you couldn't find hit. You fixin to ruin dat un."

"Aw, mammy," Luster said, "Hit aint gwine rain."

"How you know? You go git dat old hat en put dat new un away."

"Aw, mammy."

"Den you go git de umbreller."

"Aw, mammy."

"Take yo choice," Dilsey said. "Git yo old hat, er de umbreller. I dont keer which."

Luster went to the cabin. Ben wailed quietly.

"Come on," Dilsey said, "Dey kin ketch up wid us. We gwine to hear de singin." They went around the house, toward the gate. "Hush," Dilsey said from time to time as they went down the drive. They reached the gate. Dilsey opened it. Luster was coming down the drive behind them, carrying the umbrella. A woman was with him. "Here dey come," Dilsey said. They passed out the gate. "Now, den," she said. Ben ceased. Luster and his mother overtook them. Frony wore a dress of bright blue silk and a flowered hat. She was a thin woman, with a flat, pleasant face.

"You got six weeks' work right dar on yo back," Dilsey said. "Whut you gwine do ef hit rain?"

"Git wet, I reckon," Frony said. "I aint never stopped no rain yit."

"Mammy always talkin bout hit gwine rain," Luster said.

"Ef I dont worry bout y'all, I dont know who is," Dilsey said. "Come on, we already late."

"Rev'un Shegog gwine preach today," Frony said.

"Is?" Dilsey said. "Who him?"

"He fum Saint Looey," Frony said. "Dat big preacher."

"Huh," Dilsey said, "Whut dey needs is a man kin put de fear of God into dese here triflin young niggers."

"Rev'un Shegog gwine preach today," Frony said. "So dey tells."

They went on along the street. Along its quiet length white people in bright clumps moved churchward, under the windy bells, walking now and then in the random and tentative sun. The wind was gusty, out of the southeast, chill and raw after the warm days.

"I wish you wouldn't keep on bringin him to church, mammy," Frony said. "Folks talkin."

"Whut folks?" Dilsey said.

"I hears em," Frony said.

"And I knows whut kind of folks," Dilsey said, "Trash white folks. Dat's who it is. Thinks he aint good enough fer white church, but nigger church aint good enough fer him."

"Dey talks, jes de same," Frony said.

"Den you send um to me," Dilsey said. "Tell um de good Lawd dont keer whether he smart er not. Dont nobody but white trash keer dat."

A street turned off at right angles, descending, and became a dirt road. On either hand the land dropped more sharply; a broad flat dotted with small cabins whose weathered roofs were on a level with the crown of the road. They were set in small grassless plots littered with broken things, bricks, planks, crockery, things of a once utilitarian value. What growth there was consisted of rank weeds and the trees were mulberries and locusts and sycamores—trees that partook also of the foul desiccation which surrounded the houses; trees whose very burgeoning seemed to be the sad and stubborn remnant of September, as if even spring had passed them by, leaving them to feed upon the rich and unmistakable smell of negroes in which they grew.

From the doors negroes spoke to them as they passed, to Dilsey usually:

"Sis' Gibson! How you dis mawnin?"

"I'm well. Is you well?"

"I'm right well, I thank you."

They emerged from the cabins and struggled up the shading levee to the road—men in staid, hard brown or black, with gold watch chains and now and then a stick; young men in cheap violent blues or stripes and swaggering hats; women a little stiffly sibilant, and children in garments bought second hand of white people, who looked at Ben with the covertness of nocturnal animals:

"I bet you wont go up en tech him."

"How come I wont?"

"I bet you wont. I bet you skeered to."

"He wont hurt folks. He des a loony."

"How come a loony wont hurt folks?"

"Dat un wont. I teched him."

"I bet you wont now."

"Case Miss Dilsey lookin."

"You wont no ways."

"He dont hurt folks. He des a loony."

And steadily the older people speaking to Dilsey, though, unless they were quite old, Dilsey permitted Frony to respond.

"Mammy aint feelin well dis mawnin."

"Dat's too bad. But Rev'un Shegog'll cure dat. He'll give her de comfort en de unburdenin."

The road rose again, to a scene like a painted backdrop. Notched into a cut of red clay crowned with oaks the road appeared to stop short off, like a cut ribbon. Beside it a weathered church lifted its crazy steeple like a painted church, and the whole scene was as flat and without perspective as a painted cardboard set upon the ultimate edge of the flat earth, against the windy sunlight of space and April and a midmorning filled with bells. Toward the church they thronged with slow sabbath deliberation. The women and children went on in, the men stopped outside and talked in quiet groups until the bell ceased ringing. Then they too entered.

The church had been decorated, with sparse flowers from kitchen gardens and hedgerows, and with streamers of coloured crepe paper. Above the pulpit hung a battered Christmas bell, the accordion sort that collapses. The pulpit was empty, though the choir was already in place, fanning themselves although it was not warm.

Most of the women were gathered on one side of the room. They were talking. Then the bell struck one time and they dispersed to their seats and the congregation sat for an instant, expectant. The bell struck again one time. The choir rose and began to sing and the congregation turned its head as one, as six small children—four girls with tight pigtails bound with small scraps of cloth like butterflies, and two boys with close napped heads,—entered and marched up the aisle, strung together in a harness of white ribbons and flowers, and followed by two men in single file. The second man was huge, of a light coffee colour, imposing in a frock coat and white tie. His head was magisterial and profound, his neck rolled above his collar in rich folds. But he was familiar to them, and so the heads were still reverted when he had passed, and it was not until the choir ceased singing that they realised that the visiting clergyman had already entered,

and when they saw the man who had preceded their
minister enter the pulpit still ahead of him an indescrib-
able sound went up, a sigh, a sound of astonishment and
disappointment.

The visitor was undersized, in a shabby alpaca coat.
He had a wizened black face like a small, aged monkey.
And all the while that the choir sang again and while the
six children rose and sang in thin, frightened, tune-
less whispers, they watched the insignificant looking man
sitting dwarfed and countrified by the minister's imposing
bulk, with something like consternation. They were still
looking at him with consternation and unbelief when the
minister rose and introduced him in rich, rolling tones
whose very unction served to increase the visitor's insignificance.

"En dey brung dat all de way fum Saint Looey," Frony
whispered.

"I've knowed de Lawd to use cuiser tools dan dat,"
Dilsey said. "Hush, now," she said to Ben, "Dey fixin to
sing again in a minute."

When the visitor rose to speak he sounded like a white
man. His voice was level and cold. It sounded too big to
have come from him and they listened at first through
curiosity, as they would have to a monkey talking. They
began to watch him as they would a man on a tight rope.
They even forgot his insignificant appearance in the vir-
tuosity with which he ran and poised and swooped upon
the cold inflectionless wire of his voice, so that at last,
when with a sort of swooping glide he came to rest again
beside the reading desk with one arm resting upon it at
shoulder height and his monkey body as reft of all motion as a mummy or an emptied vessel, the congregation
sighed as if it waked from a collective dream and moved
a little in its seats. Behind the pulpit the choir fanned

steadily. Dilsey whispered, "Hush, now. Dey fixin to sing in a minute."

Then a voice said, "Brethren."

The preacher had not moved. His arm lay yet across the desk, and he still held that pose while the voice died in sonorous echoes between the walls. It was as different as day and dark from his former tone, with a sad, timbrous quality like an alto horn, sinking into their hearts and speaking there again when it had ceased in fading and cumulate echoes.

"Brethren and sisteren," it said again. The preacher removed his arm and he began to walk back and forth before the desk, his hands clasped behind him, a meagre figure, hunched over upon itself like that of one long immured in striving with the implacable earth, "I got the recollection and the blood of the Lamb!" He tramped steadily back and forth beneath the twisted paper and the Christmas bell, hunched, his hands clasped behind him. He was like a worn small rock whelmed by the successive waves of his voice. With his body he seemed to feed the voice that, succubus like, had fleshed its teeth in him. And the congregation seemed to watch with its own eyes while the voice consumed him, until he was nothing and they were nothing and there was not even a voice but instead their hearts were speaking to one another in chanting measures beyond the need for words, so that when he came to rest against the reading desk, his monkey face lifted and his whole attitude that of a serene, tortured crucifix that transcended its shabbiness and insignificance and made it of no moment, a long moaning expulsion of breath rose from them, and a woman's single soprano: "Yes, Jesus!"

As the scudding day passed overhead the dingy windows glowed and faded in ghostly retrograde. A car passed along the road outside, labouring in the sand, died away. Dilsey sat bolt upright, her hand on Ben's knee. Two tears slid down her fallen cheeks, in and out of the myriad coruscations of immolation and abnegation and time.

"Brethren," the minister said in a harsh whisper, without moving.

"Yes, Jesus!" The woman's voice said, hushed yet.

"Breddren en sistuhn!" His voice rang again, with the horns. He removed his arm and stood erect and raised his hands. "I got de ricklickshun en de blood of de Lamb!" They did not mark just when his intonation, his pronunciation, became negroid, they just sat swaying a little in their seats as the voice took them into itself.

"When de long, cold—Oh, I tells you, breddren, when de long, cold—I sees de light en I sees de word, po sinner! Dey passed away in Egypt, de swingin chariots; de generations passed away. Wus a rich man: whar he now, O breddren? Was a po man: whar he now, O sistuhn? Oh I tells you, ef you aint got de milk en de dew of de old salvation when de long, cold years rolls away!"

"Yes, Jesus!"

"I tells you, breddren, en I tells you, sistuhn, dey'll come a time. Po sinner saying Let me lay down wid de Lawd, lemme lay down my load. Den whut Jesus gwine say, O breddren? O sistuhn? Is you got de ricklickshun en de Blood of de Lamb? Case I aint gwine load down heaven!"

He fumbled in his coat and took out a handkerchief and mopped his face. A low concerted sound rose from the congregation: "Mmmmmmmmmmmmmm!" The woman's voice said, "Yes, Jesus! Jesus!"

"Breddren! Look at dem little chillen settin dar. Jesus wus like dat once. He mammy suffered de glory en de pangs. Sometime maybe she helt him at de nightfall, whilst de angels singin him to sleep; maybe she look out de do' en see de Roman po-lice passin." He tramped back and forth, mopping his face. "Listen, breddren! I sees de day. Ma'y settin in de do' wid Jesus on her lap, de little Jesus. Like dem chillen dar, de little Jesus. I hears de angels singin de peaceful songs en de glory; I sees de closin eyes; sees Mary jump up, sees de sojer face: We gwine to kill! We gwine to kill! We gwine to kill yo little Jesus! I hears de weepin en de lamentation of de po mammy widout de salvation en de word of God!"

"Mmmmmmmmmmmmmmmmm! Jesus! Little Jesus!" and another voice, rising:

"I sees, O Jesus! Oh I sees!" and still another, without words, like bubbles rising in water.

"I sees hit, breddren! I sees hit! Sees de blastin, blindin sight! I sees Calvary, wid de sacred trees, sees de thief en de murderer en de least of dese; I hears de boasting en de braggin: Ef you be Jesus, lif up yo tree en walk! I hears de wailin of women en de evenin lamentations; I hears de weepin en de cryin en de turnt-away face of God: dey done kilt Jesus; dey done kilt my Son!"

"Mmmmmmmmmmmmmm. Jesus! I sees, O Jesus!"

"O blind sinner! Breddren, I tells you; sistuhn, I says to you, when de Lawd did turn His mighty face, say, Aint gwine overload heaven! I can see de widowed God shet His do'; I sees de whelmin flood roll between; I sees de darkness en de death everlastin upon de generations. Den, lo! Breddren! Yes, breddren! Whut I see? Whut I see, O sinner? I sees de resurrection en de light; sees de meek Jesus sayin Dey kilt Me dat ye shall live again; I died dat dem whut sees en believes shall never die. Breddren, O breddren! I sees de doom crack en hears de golden horns shoutin down de glory, en de arisen dead whut got de blood en de ricklickshun of de Lamb!"

In the midst of the voices and the hands Ben sat, rapt in his sweet blue gaze. Dilsey sat bolt upright beside, crying rigidly and quietly in the annealment and the blood of the remembered Lamb.

As they walked through the bright noon, up the sandy road with the dispersing congregation talking easily again group to group, she continued to weep, unmindful of the talk.

"He sho a preacher, mon! He didn't look like much at first, but hush!"

"He seed de power en de glory."

"Yes, suh. He seed hit. Face to face he seed hit."

Dilsey made no sound, her face did not quiver as the tears took their sunken and devious courses, walking with her head up, making no effort to dry them away even.

"Whyn't you quit dat, mammy?" Frony said. "Wid all dese people lookin. We be passin white folks soon."

"I've seed de first en de last," Dilsey said. "Never you mind me."

"First en last whut?" Frony said.

"Never you mind," Dilsey said. "I seed de beginnin, en now I sees de endin."

Before they reached the street, though, she stopped and lifted her skirt and dried her eyes on the hem of her topmost underskirt. Then they went on. Ben shambled along beside Dilsey, watching Luster who anticked along ahead, the umbrella in his hand and his new straw hat slanted viciously in the sunlight, like a big foolish dog watching a small clever one. They reached the gate and entered. Immediately Ben began to whimper again, and for a while all of them looked up the drive at the square, paintless house with its rotting portico.

"Whut's gwine on up dar today?" Frony said. "Something is."

"Nothin," Dilsey said. "You tend to yo business en let de white folks tend to deir'n."

"Somethin is," Frony said. "I heard him first thing dis mawnin. 'Taint none of my business, dough."

"En I knows whut, too," Luster said.

"You knows mo dan you got any use fer," Dilsey said. "Aint you jes heard Frony say hit aint none of yo business? You take Benjy on to de back and keep him quiet twell I put dinner on."

"I knows whar Miss Quentin is," Luster said.

"Den jes keep hit," Dilsey said. "Soon es Quentin need any of yo egvice, I'll let you know. Y'all g'awn en play in de back, now."

"You know whut gwine happen soon es dey start playin dat ball over yonder," Luster said.

"Dey wont start fer awhile yit. By dat time T. P. be here to take him ridin. Here, you gimme dat new hat."

Luster gave her the hat and he and Ben went on across the back yard. Ben was still whimpering, though not loud. Dilsey and Frony went to the cabin. After a while Dilsey emerged, again in the faded calico dress, and went to the kitchen. The fire had died down. There was no sound in the house. She put on the apron and went up stairs. There was no sound anywhere. Quentin's room was as they had left it. She entered and picked up the undergarment and put the stocking back in the drawer and closed it. Mrs Compson's door was closed. Dilsey stood beside it for a moment, listening. Then she opened it and entered, entered a pervading reek of camphor. The shades were drawn, the room in halflight, and the bed, so that at first she thought Mrs Compson was asleep and was about to close the door when the other spoke.

"Well?" she said, "What is it?"

"Hit's me," Dilsey said. "You want anything?"

Mrs Compson didn't answer. After awhile, without moving her head at all, she said: "Where's Jason?"

"He aint come back yit," Dilsey said. "Whut you want?"

Mrs Compson said nothing. Like so many cold, weak people, when faced at last by the incontrovertible disaster she exhumed from somewhere a sort of fortitude, strength. In her case it was an unshakable conviction regarding the yet unplumbed event. "Well," she said presently, "Did you find it?"

"Find whut? Whut you talkin about?"

"The note. At least she would have enough consideration to leave a note. Even Quentin did that."

"Whut you talkin about?" Dilsey said, "Dont you know she all right? I bet she be walkin right in dis do' befo dark."

"Fiddlesticks," Mrs Compson said, "It's in the blood. Like uncle, like niece. Or mother. I dont know which would be worse. I dont seem to care."

"Whut you keep on talkin that way fur?" Dilsey said. "Whut she want to do anything like that fur?"

"I dont know. What reason did Quentin have? Under God's heaven what reason did he have? It cant be simply to flout and hurt me. Whoever God is, He would not permit that. I'm a lady. You might not believe that from my offspring, but I am."

"You des wait en see," Dilsey said. "She be here by night, right dar in her bed." Mrs Compson said nothing. The camphor-soaked cloth lay upon her brow. The black robe lay across the foot of the bed. Dilsey stood with her hand on the door knob.

"Well," Mrs Compson said. "What do you want? Are

you going to fix some dinner for Jason and Benjamin, or not?"

"Jason aint come yit," Dilsey said. "I gwine fix somethin. You sho you dont want nothin? Yo bottle still hot enough?"

"You might hand me my Bible."

"I give hit to you dis mawnin, befo I left."

"You laid it on the edge of the bed. How long did you expect it to stay there?"

Dilsey crossed to the bed and groped among the shadows beneath the edge of it and found the Bible, face down. She smoothed the bent pages and laid the book on the bed again. Mrs Compson didn't open her eyes. Her hair and the pillow were the same color, beneath the wimple of the medicated cloth she looked like an old nun praying. "Dont put it there again," she said, without opening her eyes. "That's where you put it before. Do you want me to have to get out of bed to pick it up?"

Dilsey reached the book across her and laid it on the broad side of the bed. "You cant see to read, noways," she said. "You want me to raise de shade a little?"

"No. Let them alone. Go on and fix Jason something to eat."

Dilsey went out. She closed the door and returned to the kitchen. The stove was almost cold. While she stood there the clock above the cupboard struck ten times. "One oclock," she said aloud, "Jason aint comin home. Ise seed de first en de last," she said, looking at the cold stove, "I seed de first en de last." She set out some cold food on a table. As she moved back and forth she sang a hymn. She sang the first two lines over and over to the complete tune. She arranged the meal and went to the door and called Luster, and after a time Luster and Ben

entered. Ben was still moaning a little, as to himself.
"He aint never quit," Luster said.

"Y'all come on en eat," Dilsey said. "Jason aint coming
to dinner." They sat down at the table. Ben could manage solid food pretty well for himself, though even now,
with cold food before him, Dilsey tied a cloth about his
neck. He and Luster ate. Dilsey moved about the kitchen,
singing the two lines of the hymn which she remembered.
"Y'all kin g'awn en eat," she said, "Jason aint comin
home."

He was twenty miles away at that time. When he left
the house he drove rapidly to town, overreaching the
slow sabbath groups and the peremptory bells along the
broken air. He crossed the empty square and turned into
a narrow street that was abruptly quieter even yet, and
stopped before a frame house and went up the flower-
bordered walk to the porch.

Beyond the screen door people were talking. As he
lifted his hand to knock he heard steps, so he withheld
his hand until a big man in black broadcloth trousers and
a stiff-bosomed white shirt without collar opened the
door. He had vigorous untidy iron-grey hair and his grey
eyes were round and shiny like a little boy's. He took
Jason's hand and drew him into the house, still shaking it.

"Come right in," he said, "Come right in."

"You ready to go now?" Jason said.

"Walk right in," the other said, propelling him by the
elbow into a room where a man and a woman sat. "You
know Myrtle's husband, don't you? Jason Compson,
Vernon."

"Yes," Jason said. He did not even look at the man,
and as the sheriff drew a chair across the room the man
said,

"We'll go out so you can talk. Come on, Myrtle."

"No, no," the sheriff said, "You folks keep your **seat.**
I reckon it aint that serious, Jason? Have a seat."

"I'll tell you as we go along," Jason said. "Get your **hat**
and coat."

"We'll go out," the man said, rising.

"Keep your seat," the sheriff said. "Me and Jason will
go out on the porch."

"You get your hat and coat," Jason said. "They've
already got a twelve hour start." The sheriff led the way
back to the porch. A man and a woman passing spoke to
him. He responded with a hearty florid gesture. Bells
were still ringing, from the direction of the section known
as Nigger Hollow. "Get your hat, Sheriff," Jason said.
The sheriff drew up two chairs.

"Have a seat and tell me what the trouble is."

"I told you over the phone," Jason said, standing. "I
did that to save time. Am I going to have to go to law to
compel you to do your sworn duty?"

"You sit down and tell me about it," the sheriff said.
"I'll take care of you all right."

"Care, hell," Jason said. "Is this what you call taking
care of me?"

"You're the one that's holding us up," the sheriff said.
"You sit down and tell me about it."

Jason told him, his sense of injury and impotence feeding upon its own sound, so that after a time he forgot his
haste in the violent cumulation of his self justification and
his outrage. The sheriff watched him steadily with his
cold shiny eyes.

"But you dont know they done it," he said. "You just
think so."

"Dont know?" Jason said. "When I spent two damn
days chasing her through alleys, trying to keep her away

from him, after I told her what I'd do to her if I ever caught her with him, and you say I dont know that that little b—"

"Now, then," the sheriff said, "That'll do. That's enough of that." He looked out across the street, his hands in his pockets.

"And when I come to you, a commissioned officer of the law," Jason said.

"That show's in Mottson this week," the sheriff said.

"Yes," Jason said, "And if I could find a law officer that gave a solitary damn about protecting the people that elected him to office, I'd be there too by now." He repeated his story, harshly recapitulant, seeming to get an actual pleasure out of his outrage and impotence. The sheriff did not appear to be listening at all.

"Jason," he said, "What were you doing with three thousand dollars hid in the house?"

"What?" Jason said. "That's my business where I keep my money. Your business is to help me get it back."

"Did your mother know you had that much on the place?"

"Look here," Jason said, "My house has been robbed. I know who did it and I know where they are. I come to you as the commissioned officer of the law, and I ask you once more, are you going to make any effort to recover my property, or not?"

"What do you aim to do with that girl, if you catch them?"

"Nothing," Jason said, "Not anything. I wouldn't lay my hand on her. The bitch that cost me a job, the one chance I ever had to get ahead, that killed my father and is shortening my mother's life every day and made my name a laughing stock in the town. I wont do anything to her," he said. "Not anything."

"You drove that girl into running off, Jason," the sheriff said.

"How I conduct my family is no business of yours," Jason said. "Are you going to help me or not?"

"You drove her away from home," the sheriff said. "And I have some suspicions about who that money belongs to that I dont reckon I'll ever know for certain."

Jason stood, slowly wringing the brim of his hat in his hands. He said quietly: "You're not going to make any effort to catch them for me?"

"That's not any of my business, Jason. If you had any actual proof, I'd have to act. But without that I dont figger it's any of my business."

"That's your answer, is it?" Jason said. "Think well, now."

"That's it, Jason."

"All right," Jason said. He put his hat on. "You'll regret this. I wont be helpless. This is not Russia, where just because he wears a little metal badge, a man is immune to law." He went down the steps and got in his car and started the engine. The sheriff watched him drive away, turn, and rush past the house toward town.

The bells were ringing again, high in the scudding sunlight in bright disorderly tatters of sound. He stopped at a filling station and had his tires examined and the tank filled.

"Gwine on a trip, is you?" the negro asked him. He didn't answer. "Look like hit gwine fair off, after all," the negro said.

"Fair off, hell," Jason said, "It'll be raining like hell by twelve oclock." He looked at the sky, thinking about rain, about the slick clay roads, himself stalled somewhere miles from town. He thought about it with a sort of triumph, of the fact that he was going to miss dinner, that by starting now and so serving his compulsion of haste, he would be at the greatest possible distance from both towns when noon came. It seemed to him that, in this, circumstance was giving him a break, so he said to the negro:

"What the hell are you doing? Has somebody paid you to keep this car standing here as long as you can?"

"Dis here ti' aint got no air a-tall in hit," the negro said.

"Then get the hell away from there and let me have that tube," Jason said.

"Hit up now," the negro said, rising. "You kin ride now."

Jason got in and started the engine and drove off. He went into second gear, the engine spluttering and gasping, and he raced the engine, jamming the throttle down and snapping the choker in and out savagely. "It's goin to rain," he said, "Get me half way there, and rain like hell." And he drove on out of the bells and out of town, thinking of himself slogging through the mud, hunting a team. "And every damn one of them will be at church." He thought how he'd find a church at last and take a team and of the owner coming out, shouting at him and of himself striking the man down. "I'm Jason Compson. See if you can stop me. See if you can elect a man to office that can stop me," he said, thinking of himself entering the courthouse with a file of soldiers and dragging the sheriff out. "Thinks he can sit with his hands folded and see me lose my job. I'll show him about jobs." Of his niece he did not think at all, nor the arbitrary valuation of the money. Neither of them had had entity or individuality for him for ten years; together they merely symbolized the job in the bank of which he had been deprived before he ever got it.

The air brightened, the running shadow patches were not the obverse, and it seemed to him that the fact that the day was clearing was another cunning stroke on the part of the foe, the fresh battle toward which he was carrying ancient wounds. From time to time he passed churches, unpainted frame buildings with sheet iron steeples, surrounded by tethered teams and shabby motorcars, and it seemed to him that each of them was a picket-post where the rear guards of Circumstance peeped fleetingly back at him. "And damn You, too," he said, "See if You can stop me," thinking of himself, his file of soldiers with the manacled sheriff in the rear, dragging Omnipotence down from His throne, if necessary; of the embattled legions of both hell and heaven through which he tore his way and put his hands at last on his fleeing niece.

The wind was out of the southeast. It blew steadily upon his cheek. It seemed that he could feel the prolonged blow of it sinking through his skull, and suddenly with an old premonition he clapped the brakes on and stopped and sat perfectly still. Then he lifted his hand to his neck and began to curse, and sat there, cursing in a harsh whisper. When it was necessary for him to drive for any length of time he fortified himself with a handkerchief soaked in camphor, which he would tie about his throat when clear of town, thus inhaling the fumes, and he got out and lifted the seat cushion on the chance that there might be a forgotten one there. He looked beneath both seats and stood again for a while, cursing, seeing himself mocked by his own triumphing. He closed his eyes, leaning on the door. He could return and get the forgotten camphor, or he could go on. In either case, his head would be splitting, but at home he could be sure of finding camphor on Sunday, while if he went on he could not be sure. But if he went back, he would be an hour and a half later in reaching Mottson. "Maybe I can drive slow," he sa'd. "Maybe I can drive slow, thinking of something else—"

He got in and started. "I'll think of something else," he said, so he thought about Lorraine. He imagined himself in bed with her, only he was just lying beside her, pleading with her to help him, then he thought of the money again, and that he had been outwitted by a woman, a girl. If he could just believe it was the man who had robbed him. But to have been robbed of that which was to have compensated him for the lost job, which he had acquired through so much effort and risk, by the very symbol of the lost job itself, and worst of all, by a bitch of a girl. He drove on, shielding his face from the steady wind with the corner of his coat.

He could see the opposed forces of his destiny and his will drawing swiftly together now, toward a junction that would be irrevocable; he became cunning. I cant make a blunder, he told himself. There would be just one right thing, without alternatives: he must do that. He believed that both of them would know him on sight, while he'd have to trust to seeing her first, unless the man still wore the red tie. And the fact that he must depend on that red tie seemed to be the sum of the impending disaster; he could almost smell it, feel it above the throbbing of his head.

He crested the final hill. Smoke lay in the valley, and roofs, a spire or two above trees. He drove down the hill and into the town, slowing, telling himself again of the need for caution, to find where the tent was located first. He could not see very well now, and he knew that it was the disaster which kept telling him to go directly and get something for his head. At a filling station they told him that the tent was not up yet, but that the show cars were on a siding at the station. He drove there.

Two gaudily painted pullman cars stood on the track. He reconnoitred them before he got out. He was trying to breathe shallowly, so that the blood would not beat so in his skull. He got out and went along the station wall, watching the cars. A few garments hung out of the windows, limp and crinkled, as though they had been recently laundered. On the earth beside the steps of one sat three canvas chairs. But he saw no sign of life at all until a man in a dirty apron came to the door and emptied a pan of dishwater with a broad gesture, the sunlight glinting on the metal belly of the pan, then entered the car again.

Now I'll have to take him by surprise, before he can warn them, he thought. It never occurred to him that they might not be there, in the car. That they should not be there, that the whole result should not hinge on whether he saw them first or they saw him first, would be opposed to all nature and contrary to the whole rhythm of events. And more than that: he must see them first, get the money back, then what they did would be of no importance to him, while otherwise the whole world would know that he, Jason Compson, had been robbed by Quentin, his niece, a bitch.

He reconnoitred again. Then he went to the car and mounted the steps, swiftly and quietly, and paused at the door. The galley was dark, rank with stale food. The man was a white blur, singing in a cracked, shaky tenor. An old man, he thought, and not as big as I am. He entered the car as the man looked up.

"Hey?" the man said, stopping his song.

"Where are they?" Jason said. "Quick, now. In the sleeping car?"

"Where's who?" the man said.

"Dont lie to me," Jason said. He blundered on in the cluttered obscurity.

"What's that?" the other said, "Who you calling a liar?" And when Jason grasped his shoulder he exclaimed, "Look out, fellow!"

"Dont lie," Jason said, "Where are they?"

"Why, you bastard," the man said. His arm was frail and thin in Jason's grasp. He tried to wrench free, then he turned and fell to scrabbling on the littered table behind him.

"Come on," Jason said, "Where are they?"

"I'll tell you where they are," the man shrieked, "Lemme find my butcher knife."

"Here," Jason said, trying to hold the other, "I'm just asking you a question."

"You bastard," the other shrieked, scrabbling at the table. Jason tried to grasp him in both arms, trying to prison the puny fury of him. The man's body felt so old, so frail, yet so fatally single-purposed that for the first time Jason saw clear and unshadowed the disaster toward which he rushed.

"Quit it!" he said, "Here! Here! I'll get out. Give me time, and I'll get out."

"Call me a liar," the other wailed, "Lemme go. Lemme go just one minute. I'll show you."

Jason glared wildly about, holding the other. Outside it was now bright and sunny, swift and bright and empty, and he thought of the people soon to be going quietly home to Sunday dinner, decorously festive, and of himself trying to hold the fatal, furious little old man whom he dared not release long enough to turn his back and run.

"Will you quit long enough for me to get out?" he

said, "Will you?" But the other still struggled, and Jason freed one hand and struck him on the head. A clumsy, hurried blow, and not hard, but the other slumped immediately and slid clattering among pans and buckets to the floor. Jason stood above him, panting, listening. Then he turned and ran from the car. At the door he restrained himself and descended more slowly and stood there again. His breath made a hah hah hah sound and he stood there trying to repress it, darting his gaze this way and that, when at a scuffling sound behind him he turned in time to see the little old man leaping awkwardly and furiously from the vestibule, a rusty hatchet high in his hand.

He grasped at the hatchet, feeling no shock but knowing that he was falling, thinking So this is how it'll end, and he believed that he was about to die and when something crashed against the back of his head he thought How did he hit me there? Only maybe he hit me a long time ago, he thought, And I just now felt it, and he thought Hurry. Hurry. Get it over with, and then a furious desire not to die seized him and he struggled, hearing the old man wailing and cursing in his cracked voice.

He still struggled when they hauled him to his feet, but they held him and he ceased.

"Am I bleeding much?" he said, "The back of my head. Am I bleeding?" He was still saying that while he felt himself being propelled rapidly away, heard the old man's thin furious voice dying away behind him. "Look at my head," he said, "Wait, I—"

"Wait, hell," the man who held him said, "That damn little wasp'll kill you. Keep going. You aint hurt."

"He hit me," Jason said. "Am I bleeding?"

"Keep going," the other said. He led Jason on around

the corner of the station, to the empty platform where an express truck stood, where grass grew rigidly in a plot bordered with rigid flowers and a sign in electric lights: Keep your eye on Mottson, the gap filled by an eye with an electric pupil. The man released him.

"Now," he said, "You get on out of here and stay out. What were you trying to do? Commit suicide?"

"I was looking for two people," Jason said. "I just asked him where they were."

"Who you looking for?"

"It's a girl," Jason said. "And a man. He had on a red tie in Jefferson yesterday. With this show. They robbed me."

"Oh," the man said. "You're the one, are you. Well, they aint here."

"I reckon so," Jason said. He leaned against the wall and put his hand to the back of his head and looked at his palm. "I thought I was bleeding," he said. "I thought he hit me with that hatchet."

"You hit your head on the rail," the man said. "You better go on. They aint here."

"Yes. He said they were not here. I thought he was lying."

"Do you think I'm lying?" the man said.

"No," Jason said. "I know they're not here."

"I told him to get the hell out of there, both of them," the man said. "I wont have nothing like that in my show. I run a respectable show, with a respectable troupe."

"Yes," Jason said. "You dont know where they went?"

"No. And I dont want to know. No member of my show can pull a stunt like that. You her—brother?"

"No," Jason said. "It dont matter. I just wanted to see them. You sure he didn't hit me? No blood, I mean."

"There would have been blood if I hadn't got there

when I did. You stay away from here, now. That little bastard'll kill you. That your car yonder?"

"Yes."

"Well, you get in it and go back to Jefferson. If you find them, it wont be in my show. I run a respectable show. You say they robbed you?"

"No," Jason said, "It dont make any difference." He went to the car and got in. What is it I must do? he thought. Then he remembered. He started the engine and drove slowly up the street until he found a drugstore. The door was locked. He stood for a while with his hand on the knob and his head bent a little. Then he turned away and when a man came along after a while he asked if there was a drugstore open anywhere, but there was not. Then he asked when the northbound train ran, and the man told him at two thirty. He crossed the pavement and got in the car again and sat there. After a while two negro lads passed. He called to them.

"Can either of you boys drive a car?"

"Yes, suh."

"What'll you charge to drive me to Jefferson right away?"

They looked at one another, murmuring.

"I'll pay a dollar," Jason said.

They murmured again. "Couldn't go fer dat," one said.

"What will you go for?"

"Kin you go?" one said.

"I cant git off," the other said. "Whyn't you drive him up dar? You aint got nothin to do."

"Yes I is."

"Whut you got to do?"

They murmured again, laughing.

"I'll give you two dollars," Jason said. "Either of you."

"I cant git away neither," the first said.

"All right," Jason said. "Go on."

He sat there for sometime. He heard a clock strike the half hour, then people began to pass, in Sunday and Easter clothes. Some looked at him as they passed, at the man sitting quietly behind the wheel of a small car, with his invisible life ravelled out about him like a worn-out sock. After a while a negro in overalls came up.

"Is you de one wants to go to Jefferson?" he said.

"Yes," Jason said. "What'll you charge me?"

"Fo dollars."

"Give you two."

"Cant go fer no less'n fo." The man in the car sat quietly. He wasn't even looking at him. The negro said, "You want me er not?"

"All right," Jason said, "Get in."

He moved over and the negro took the wheel. Jason closed his eyes. I can get something for it at Jefferson, he told himself, easing himself to the jolting, I can get something there. They drove on, along the streets where people were turning peacefully into houses and Sunday dinners, and on out of town. He thought that. He wasn't thinking of home, where Ben and Luster were eating cold dinner at the kitchen table. Something—the absence of disaster, threat, in any constant evil—permitted him to forget Jefferson as any place which he had ever seen before, where his life must resume itself.

When Ben and Luster were done Dilsey sent them outdoors. "And see kin you keep let him alone twell fo oclock. T. P. be here den."

"Yessum," Luster said. They went out. Dilsey ate her dinner and cleared up the kitchen. Then she went to the foot of the stairs and listened, but there was no sound. She returned through the kitchen and out the outer door and stopped on the steps. Ben and Luster were not in

sight, but while she stood there she heard another sluggish twang from the direction of the cellar door and she
went to the door and looked down upon a repetition of
the morning's scene.

"He done it jes dat way," Luster said. He contemplated
the motionless saw with a kind of hopeful dejection. "I
aint got de right thing to hit it wid yit," he said.

"En you aint gwine find hit down here, neither," Dilsey
said. "You take him on out in de sun. You bofe get
pneumonia down here on dis wet flo."

She waited and watched them cross the yard toward
a clump of cedar trees near the fence. Then she went on
to her cabin.

"Now, dont you git started," Luster said, "I had enough
trouble wid you today." There was a hammock made of
barrel staves slatted into woven wires. Luster lay down
in the swing, but Ben went on vaguely and purposelessly.
He began to whimper again. "Hush, now," Luster said,
"I fixin to whup you." He lay back in the swing. Ben had
stopped moving, but Luster could hear him whimpering.
"Is you gwine hush, er aint you?" Luster said. He got up
and followed and came upon Ben squatting before a
small mound of earth. At either end of it an empty bottle
of blue glass that once contained poison was fixed in the
ground. In one was a withered stalk of jimson weed. Ben
squatted before it, moaning, a slow, inarticulate sound.
Still moaning he sought vaguely about and found a twig
and put it in the other bottle. "Whyn't you hush?" Luster
said, "You want me to give you somethin' to sho nough
moan about? Sposin I does dis." He knelt and swept the
bottle suddenly up and behind him. Ben ceased moaning.
He squatted, looking at the small depression where the
bottle had sat, then as he drew his lungs full Luster
brought the bottle back into view. "Hush!" he hissed,

"Dont you dast to beller! Dont you. Dar hit is. See? Here. You fixin to start ef you stays here. Come on, les go see ef dey started knockin ball yit." He took Ben's arm and drew him up and they went to the fence and stood side by side there, peering between the matted honeysuckle not yet in bloom.

"Dar," Luster said, "Dar come some. See um?"

They watched the foursome play onto the green and out, and move to the tee and drive. Ben watched, whimpering, slobbering. When the foursome went on he followed along the fence, bobbing and moaning. One said.

"Here, caddie. Bring the bag."

"Hush, Benjy," Luster said, but Ben went on at his shambling trot, clinging to the fence, wailing in his hoarse, hopeless voice. The man played and went on, Ben keeping pace with him until the fence turned at right angles, and he clung to the fence, watching the people move on and away.

"Will you hush now?" Luster said, "Will you hush now?" He shook Ben's arm. Ben clung to the fence, wailing steadily and hoarsely. "Aint you gwine stop?" Luster said, "Or is you?" Ben gazed through the fence. "All right, den," Luster said, "You want somethin to beller about?" He looked over his shoulder, toward the house. Then he whispered: "Caddy! Beller now. Caddy! Caddy! Caddy!"

A moment later, in the slow intervals of Ben's voice, Luster heard Dilsey calling. He took Ben by the arm and they crossed the yard toward her.

"I tole you he warn't gwine stay quiet," Luster said.

"You vilyun!" Dilsey said, "Whut you dont to him?"

"I aint done nothin. I tole you when dem folks start playin, he git started up."

"You come on here," Dilsey said. "Hush, Benjy. Hush,

now." But he wouldn't hush. They crossed the yard quickly and went to the cabin and entered. "Run git dat shoe," Dilsey said. "Dont you sturb Miss Cahline, now. Ef she say anything, tell her I got him. Go on, now; you kin sho do dat right, I reckon." Luster went out. Dilsey led Ben to the bed and drew him down beside her and she held him, rocking back and forth, wiping his drooling mouth upon the hem of her skirt. "Hush, now," she said, stroking his head, "Hush. Dilsey got you." But he bellowed slowly, abjectly, without tears; the grave hopeless sound of all voiceless misery under the sun. Luster returned, carrying a white satin slipper. It was yellow now, and cracked and soiled, and when they placed it into Ben's hand he hushed for a while. But he still whimpered, and soon he lifted his voice again.

"You reckon you kin find T. P.?" Dilsey said.

"He say yistiddy he gwine out to St John's today. Say he be back at fo."

Dilsey rocked back and forth. stroking Ben's head.

"Dis long time, O Jesus," she said, "Dis long time."

"I kin drive dat surrey, mammy." Luster said.

"You kill bofe y'all," Dilsey said, "You do hit fer devilment. I knows you got plenty sense to. But I cant trust you. Hush, now," she said. "Hush. Hush."

"Nome I wont," Luster said. "I drives wid T. P." Dilsey rocked back and forth, holding Ben. "Miss Cahline say ef you cant quiet him, she gwine git up en come down en do hit."

"Hush, honey," Dilsey said, stroking Ben's head. "Luster, honey," she said, "Will you think about yo ole mammy en drive dat surrey right?"

"Yessum," Luster said. "I drive hit jes like T. P."

Dilsey stroked Ben's head, rocking back and forth. "I does de bes I kin," she said, "Lawd knows dat. Go 'git it, den," she said, rising. Luster scuttled out. Ben held the slipper, crying. "Hush, now. Luster gone to git de surrey en take you to de graveyard. We aint gwine risk gitting yo cap," she said. She went to a closet contrived of a calico curtain hung across a corner of the room and got the felt hat she had worn. "We's down to worse'n dis, ef folks jes knowed," she said. "You's de Lawd's chile, anyway. En I be His'n too, fo long, praise Jesus. Here." She put the hat on his head and buttoned his coat. He wailed steadily. She took the slipper from him and put it away and they went out. Luster came up, with an ancient white horse in a battered and lopsided surrey.

"You gwine be careful, Luster?" she said.

"Yessum," Luster said. She helped Ben into the back seat. He had ceased crying, but now he began to whimper again.

"Hit's his flower," Luster said. "Wait, I'll git him one."

"You set right dar," Dilsey said. She went and took the cheekstrap. "Now, hurry en git him one." Luster ran around the house, toward the garden. He came back with a single narcissus.

"Dat un broke," Dilsey said, "Whyn't you git him a good un?"

"Hit de onliest one I could find," Luster said. "Y'all took all of um Friday to dec'rate de church. Wait, I'll fix hit." So while Dilsey held the horse Luster put a splint on the flower stalk with a twig and two bits of string and gave it to Ben. Then he mounted and took the reins. Dilsey still held the bridle.

"You knows de way now?" she said, "Up de street, round de square, to de graveyard, den straight back home."

"Yessum," Luster said, "Hum up, Queenie."

"You gwine be careful, now?"

"Yessum." Dilsey released the bridle.

"Hum up, Queenie," Luster said.

"Here," Dilsey said, "You han me dat whup."

"Aw, mammy," Luster said.

"Give hit here," Dilsey said, approaching the wheel. Luster gave it to her reluctantly.

"I wont never git Queenie started now."

"Never you mind about dat," Dilsey said. "Queenie know mo bout whar she gwine dan you does. All you got to do is set dar en hold dem reins. You knows de way, now?"

"Yessum. Same way T. P. goes ev'y Sunday."

"Den you do de same thing dis Sunday."

"Cose I is. Aint I drove fer T. P. mo'n a hund'ed times?"

"Den do hit again," Dilsey said. "G'awn, now. En ef you hurts Benjy, nigger boy, I dont know whut I do. You bound fer de chain gang, but I'll send you dar fo even chain gang ready fer you."

"Yessum," Luster said. "Hum up, Queenie."

He flapped the lines on Queenie's broad back and the surrey lurched into motion.

"You, Luster!" Dilsey said.

"Hum up, dar!" Luster said. He flapped the lines again. With subterranean rumblings Queenie jogged slowly down the drive and turned into the street, where Luster exhorted her into a gait resembling a prolonged and suspended fall in a forward direction.

Ben quit whimpering. He sat in the middle of the seat, holding the repaired flower upright in his fist, his eyes serene and ineffable. Directly before him Luster's bullet head turned backward continually until the house passed from view, then he pulled to the side of the street and while Ben watched him he descended and broke a switch from a hedge. Queenie lowered her head and fell to cropping the grass until Luster mounted and hauled her head up and harried her into motion again, then he squared his elbows and with the switch and the reins held high he assumed a swaggering attitude out of all proportion to the sedate clopping of Queenie's hooves and the organlike basso of her internal accompaniment. Motors passed them, and pedestrians; once a group of half grown negroes:

"Dar Luster. Whar you gwine, Luster? To de bone yard?"

"Hi," Luster said, "Aint de same boneyard y'all headed fer. Hum up, elefump."

They approached the square, where the Confederate soldier gazed with empty eyes beneath his marble hand into wind and weather. Luster took still another notch in himself and gave the impervious Queenie a cut with the switch, casting his glance about the square. "Dar Mr Jason's car," he said then he spied another group of negroes. "Les show dem niggers how quality does, Benjy," he said, "Whut you say?" He looked back. Ben sat, holding the flower in his fist, his gaze empty and untroubled. Luster hit Queenie again and swung her to the left at the monument.

For an instant Ben sat in an utter hiatus. Then he bellowed. Bellow on bellow, his voice mounted, with scarce interval for breath. There was more than astonishment in it, it was horror; shock; agony eyeless, tongueless; just sound, and Luster's eyes back-rolling for a white instant. "Gret God," he said, "Hush! Hush! Gret God!" He whirled again and struck Queenie with the switch. It broke and he cast it away and with Ben's voice mounting toward its unbelievable crescendo Luster caught up the end of the reins and leaned forward as Jason came jumping across the square and onto the step.

With a backhanded blow he hurled Luster aside and caught the reins and sawed Queenie about and doubled the reins back and slashed her across the hips. He cut her again and again, into a plunging gallop, while Ben's hoarse agony roared about them, and swung her about to the right of the monument. They he struck Luster over the head with his fist.

"Dont you know any better than to take him to the left?" he said. He reached back and struck Ben, breaking the flower stalk again. "Shut up!" he said, "Shut up!" He jerked Queenie back and jumped down. "Get to hell on home with him. If you ever cross that gate with him again, I'll kill you!"

"Yes, suh!" Luster said. He took the reins and hit Queenie with the end of them. "Git up! Git up, dar! Benjy, fer God's sake!"

Ben's voice roared and roared. Queenie moved again, her feet began to clop-clop steadily again, and at once Ben hushed. Luster looked quickly back over his shoulder, then he drove on. The broken flower drooped over Ben's fist and his eyes were empty and blue and serene again as cornice and façade flowed smoothly once more from left to right; post and tree, window and doorway, and signboard, each in its ordered place.

As I Lay Dying

To Hal Smith

DARL

JEWEL AND I COME UP FROM THE FIELD, FOLLOWING THE
path in single file. Although I am fifteen feet ahead of
him, anyone watching us from the cotton-house can see
Jewel's frayed and broken straw hat a full head above
my own.

The path runs straight as a plumb-line, worn smooth
by feet and baked brick-hard by July, between the green
rows of laid-by cotton, to the cotton-house in the centre
of the field, where it turns and circles the cotton-house at
four soft right angles and goes on across the field again,
worn so by feet in fading precision.

The cotton-house is of rough logs, from between which
the chinking has long fallen. Square, with a broken roof
set at a single pitch, it leans in empty and shimmering
dilapidation in the sunlight, a single broad window in
two opposite walls giving on to the approaches of the
path. When we reach it I turn and follow the path which
circles the house. Jewel, fifteen feet behind me, looking
straight ahead, steps in a single stride through the window. Still staring straight ahead, his pale eyes like wood
set into his wooden face, he crosses the floor in four
strides with the rigid gravity of a cigar-store Indian
dressed in patched overalls and endued with life from
the hips down, and steps in a single stride through the
opposite window and into the path again just as I come
around the corner. In single file and five feet apart and
Jewel now in front, we go on up the path toward the
foot of the bluff.

Tull's wagon stands beside the spring, hitched to the rail, the reins wrapped about the seat stanchion. In the wagon-bed are two chairs. Jewel stops at the spring and takes the gourd from the willow branch and drinks. I pass him and mount the path, beginning to hear Cash's saw.

When I reach the top he has quit sawing. Standing in a litter of chips, he is fitting two of the boards together. Between the shadow spaces they are yellow as gold, like soft gold, bearing on their flanks in smooth undulations the marks of the adze blade: a good carpenter, Cash is. He holds the two planks on the trestle, fitted along the edges in a quarter of the finished box. He kneels and squints along the edge of them, then he lowers them and takes up the adze. A good carpenter. Addie Bundren could not want a better one, a better box to lie in. It will give her confidence and comfort. I go on to the house, followed by the

Chuck   Chuck   Chuck

of the adze.

CORA

SO I SAVED OUT THE EGGS AND BAKED YESTERDAY. THE cakes turned out right well. We depend a lot on our chickens. They are good layers, what few we have left after the possums and such. Snakes, too, in the summer. A snake will break up a hen-house quicker than anything. So after they were going to cost so much more than Mr. Tull thought, and after I promised that the difference in the number of eggs would make it up, I had to be more careful than ever because it was on my final say-so we took them. We could have stocked cheaper chickens, but I gave my promise as Miss Lawington said when she advised me to get a good breed, because Mr. Tull himself admits that a good breed of cows or hogs pays in the long run. So when we lost so many of them we couldn't afford to use the eggs ourselves, because I could not have had Mr. Tull chide me when it was on my say-so we took them. So when Miss Lawington told me about the cakes I thought that I could bake them and earn enough at one time to increase the net value of the flock the equivalent of two head. And that by saving the eggs out one at a time, even the eggs wouldn't be costing anything. And that week they laid so well that I not only saved out enough eggs above what we had engaged to sell, to bake the cakes with, I had saved enough so that the flour and the sugar and the stove wood would not be costing anything. So I baked yesterday, more careful than ever I baked in my life, and the cakes turned out right well. But when we got to town this morning Miss Lawington told me the lady had changed her mind and was not going to have the party after all.

"She ought to taken those cakes anyway," Kate says.

"Well," I say, "I reckon she never had no use for them now."

"She ought to taken them," Kate says. "But those rich town ladies can change their minds. Poor folks can't."

Riches is nothing in the face of the Lord, for He can see into the heart. "Maybe I can sell them at the bazaar Saturday," I say. They turned out real well.

"You can't get two dollars a piece for them," Kate says.

"Well, it isn't like they cost me anything," I say. I saved them out and swapped a dozen of them for the sugar and flour. It isn't like the cakes cost me anything, as Mr. Tull himself realizes that the eggs I saved were over and beyond what we had engaged to sell, so it was like we had found the eggs or they had been given to us.

"She ought to taken those cakes when she same as gave you her word," Kate says. The Lord can see into the heart. If it is His will that some folks has different ideas of honesty from other folks, it is not my place to question His decree.

"I reckon she never had any use for them," I say. They turned out real well, too.

The quilt is drawn up to her chin, hot as it is, with only her two hands and her face outside. She is propped on the pillow, with her head raised so she can see out the window, and we can hear him every time he takes up the adze or the saw. If we were deaf we could almost watch her face and hear him, see him. Her face is wasted away so that the bones draw just under the skin in white lines. Her eyes are like two candles when you watch them gutter down into the sockets of iron candle-sticks. But the eternal and the everlasting salvation and grace is not upon her.

"They turned out real nice," I say. "But not like the cakes Addie used to bake." You can see that girl's washing and ironing in the pillow-slip, if ironed it ever was. Maybe it will reveal her blindness to her, laying there at the mercy and the ministration of four men and a tomboy girl. "There's not a woman in this section could ever bake with Addie Bundren," I say. "First thing we know she'll be up and baking again, and then we won't have any sale for ours at all." Under the quilt she makes no more of a hump than a rail would, and the only way you can tell she is breathing is by the sound of the mattress shucks. Even the hair at her cheek does not move, even with that girl standing right over her, fanning her with the fan. While we watch she swaps the fan to the other hand without stopping it.

"Is she sleeping?" Kate whispers.

"She's just watching Cash yonder," the girl says. We can hear the saw in the board. It sounds like snoring. Eula turns on the trunk and looks out the window. Her necklace looks real nice with her red hat. You wouldn't think it only cost twenty-five cents.

"She ought to taken those cakes," Kate says.

I could have used the money real well. But it's not like they cost me anything except the baking. I can tell him that anybody is likely to make a miscue, but it's not all of them that can get out of it without loss, I can tell him. It's not everybody can eat their mistakes, I can tell him.

Someone comes through the hall. It is Darl. He does not look in as he passes the door. Eula watches him as he goes on and passes from sight again toward the back. Her hand rises and touches her beads lightly, and then her hair. When she finds me watching her, her eyes go blank.

DARL

PA AND VERNON ARE SITTING ON THE BACK PORCH. PA IS tilting snuff from the lid of his snuff-box into his lower lip, holding the lip outdrawn between thumb and finger. They look around as I cross the porch and dip the gourd into the water bucket and drink.

"Where's Jewel?" pa says. When I was a boy I first learned how much better water tastes when it has set a while in a cedar bucket. Warmish-cool, with a faint taste like the hot July wind in cedar trees smells. It has to set at least six hours, and be drunk from a gourd. Water should never be drunk from metal.

And at night it is better still. I used to lie on the pallet in the hall, waiting until I could hear them all asleep, so I could get up and go back to the bucket. It would be black, the shelf black, the still surface of the water a round orifice in nothingness, where before I stirred it awake with the dipper I could see maybe a star or two in the bucket, and maybe in the dipper a star or two before I drank. After that I was bigger, older. Then I would wait until they all went to sleep so I could lie with my shirt-tail up, hearing them asleep, feeling myself without touching myself, feeling the cool silence blowing upon my parts and wondering if Cash was yonder in the darkness doing it too, had been doing it perhaps for the last two years before I could have wanted to or could have.

Pa's feet are badly splayed, his toes cramped and bent and warped, with no toenail at all on his little toes, from working so hard in the wet in homemade shoes when he was a boy. Beside his chair his brogans sit. They look as though they had been hacked with a blunt axe out of pig-iron. Vernon has been to town. I have never seen him go to town in overalls. His wife, they say. She taught school too, once.

I fling the dipper dregs to the ground and wipe my mouth on my sleeve. It is going to rain before morning. Maybe before dark. "Down to the barn," I say. "Harness-ing the team."

Down there fooling with that horse. He will go on through the barn, into the pasture. The horse will not be in sight: he is up there among the pine seedlings, in the cool. Jewel whistles, once and shrill. The horse snorts, then Jewel sees him, glinting for a gaudy instant among the blue shadows. Jewel whistles again; the horse comes dropping down the slope, stiff-legged, his ears cocking and flicking, his mis-matched eyes rolling, and fetches up twenty feet away, broadside on, watching Jewel over his shoulder in an attitude kittenish and alert.

"Come here, sir," Jewel says. He moves. Moving that quick his coat, bunching, tongues swirling like so many flames. With tossing mane and tail and rolling eye the horse makes another short curveting rush and stops again, feet bunched, watching Jewel. Jewel walks steadily to-ward him, his hands at his sides. Save for Jewel's legs they are like two figures carved for a tableau savage in the sun.

When Jewel can almost touch him, the horse stands on his hind legs and slashes down at Jewel. Then Jewel is enclosed by a glittering maze of hooves as by an illusion of wings; among them, beneath the upreared chest, he moves with the flashing limberness of a snake. For an instant before the jerk comes on to his arms he sees his whole body earth-free, horizontal, whipping snake-limber, until he finds the horse's nostrils and touches earth again. Then they are rigid, motionless, terrific, the horse back-thrust on stiffened, quivering legs, with lowered head; Jewel with dug heels, shutting off the horse's wind with one hand, with the other patting the horse's neck in short strokes myriad and caressing, cursing the horse with obscene ferocity.

They stand in rigid terrific hiatus, the horse trembling and groaning. Then Jewel is on the horse's back. He flows upward in a stooping swirl like the lash of a whip, his body in mid-air shaped to the horse. For another moment the horse stands spraddled, with lowered head, before it bursts into motion. They descend the hill in a series of spine-jolting jumps, Jewel high, leech-like on the withers, to the fence where the horse bunches to a scuttering halt again.

"Well," Jewel says, "you can quit now, if you got a-plenty."

Inside the barn Jewel slides running to the ground before the horse stops. The horse enters the stall, Jewel following. Without looking back the horse kicks at him, slamming a single hoof into the wall with a pistol-like report. Jewel kicks him in the stomach; the horse arches his neck back, crop-toothed; Jewel strikes him across the face with his fist and slides on to the trough and mounts upon it. Clinging to the hay-rack he lowers his head and peers out across the stall tops and through the doorway. The path is empty; from here he cannot even hear Cash sawing. He reaches up and drags down hay in hurried armfuls and crams it into the rack.

"Eat," he says. "Get the goddamn stuff out of sight while you got a chance, you pussel-gutted bastard. You sweet son of a bitch," he says.

JEWEL

IT'S BECAUSE HE STAYS OUT THERE, RIGHT UNDER THE WIN-
dow, hammering and sawing on that goddamn box.
Where she's got to see him. Where every breath she
draws is full of his knocking and sawing where she can
see him saying See. See what a good one I am making for
you. I told him to go somewhere else. I said Good God
do you want to see her in it. It's like when he was a little
boy and she says if she had some fertilizer she would try
to raise some flowers and he taken the bread-pan and
brought it back from the barn full of dung.

And now them others sitting there, like buzzards.
Waiting, fanning themselves. Because I said If you
wouldn't keep on sawing and nailing at it until a man
can't sleep even and her hands laying on the quilt like
two of them roots dug up and tried to wash and you
couldn't get them clean. I can see the fan and Dewey
Dell's arm. I said if you'd just let her alone. Sawing and
knocking, and keeping the air always moving so fast on
her face that when you're tired you can't breathe it, and
that goddamn adze going One lick less. One lick less.
One lick less until everybody that passes in the road will
have to stop and see it and say what a fine carpenter he
is. If it had just been me when Cash fell off of that
church and if it had just been me when pa laid sick with
that load of wood fell on him, it would not be happening
with every bastard in the county coming in to stare at
her because if there is a God what the hell is He for. It
would just be me and her on a high hill and me rolling

347

the rocks down the hill at their faces, picking them up
and throwing them down the hill, faces and teeth and all
by God until she was quiet and not that goddamn adze
going One lick less. One lick less and we could be quiet.

DARL

WE WATCH HIM COME AROUND THE CORNER AND
mount the steps. He does not look at us. "You
ready?" he says.

"If you're hitched up," I say. I say "Wait." He stops,
looking at pa. Vernon spits, without moving. He spits
with decorous and deliberate precision into the pocked
dust below the porch. Pa rubs his hands slowly on his
knees. He is gazing out beyond the crest of the bluff, out
across the land. Jewel watches him a moment, then he
goes on to the pail and drinks again.

"I mislike undecision as much as ere a man," pa says.

"It means three dollars," I say. The shirt across pa's
hump is faded lighter than the rest of it. There is no
sweat stain on his shirt. I have never seen a sweat stain
on his shirt. He was sick once from working in the sun
when he was twenty-two years old, and he tells people
that if he ever sweats, he will die. I suppose he believes
it.

"But if she don't last until you get back," he says. "She
will be disappointed."

Vernon spits into the dust. But it will rain before morning.

"She's counted on it," pa says. "She'll want to start right away. I know her. I promised her I'd keep the team here and ready, and she's counting on it."

"We'll need that three dollars then, sure," I say. He gazes out over the land, rubbing his hands on his knees. Since he lost his teeth his mouth collapses in slow repetition when he dips. The stubble gives his lower face that appearance that old dogs have. "You'd better make up your mind soon, so we can get there and get a load on before dark," I say.

"Ma ain't that sick," Jewel says. "Shut up, Darl."

"That's right," Vernon says. "She seems more like herself today than she has in a week. Time you and Jewel get back, she'll be setting up."

"You ought to know," Jewel says. "You been here often enough looking at her. You or your folks." Vernon looks at him. Jewel's eyes look like pale wood in his high-blooded face. He is a head taller than any of the rest of us, always was. I told them that's why ma always whipped him and petted him more. Because he was peakling around the house more. That's why she named him Jewel I told them.

"Shut up, Jewel," pa says, but as though he is not listening much. He gazes out across the land, rubbing his knees.

"You could borrow the loan of Vernon's team and we could catch up with you," I say. "If she didn't wait for us."

"Ah, shut your goddamn mouth," Jewel says.

"She'll want to go in ourn," pa says. He rubs his knees. "Don't ere a man mislike it more."

"It's laying there, watching Cash whittle on that

damn . . ." Jewel says. He says it harshly, savagely, but he does not say the word. Like a little boy in the dark to flail his courage and suddenly aghast into silence by his own noise.

"She wanted that like she wants to go in our own wagon," pa says. "She'll rest easier for knowing it's a good one, and private. She was ever a private woman. You know it well."

"Then let it be private," Jewel says. "But how the hell can you expect it to be——" He looks at the back of pa's head, his eyes like pale wooden eyes.

"Sho," Vernon says, "she'll hold on till it's finished. She'll hold on till everything's ready, till her own good time. And with the roads like they are now, it won't take you no time to get her to town."

"It's fixing up to rain," pa says. "I am a luckless man. I have ever been." He rubs his hands on his knees. "It's that durn doctor, liable to come at any time. I couldn't get word to him till so late. If he was to come tomorrow and tell her the time was nigh, she wouldn't wait. I know her. Wagon or no wagon, she wouldn't wait. Then she'd be upset, and I wouldn't upset her for the living world. With that family burying-ground in Jefferson and them of her blood waiting for her there, she'll be impatient. I promised my word me and the boys would get her there quick as mules could walk it, so she could rest quiet." He rubs his hands on his knees. "No man ever misliked it more."

"If everybody wasn't burning hell to get her there," Jewel says in that harsh, savage voice. "With Cash all day long right under the window, hammering and sawing at that——"

"It was her wish," pa says. "You got no affection nor gentleness for her. You never had. We would be beholden to no man," he says, "me and her. We have never yet been, and she will rest quieter for knowing it and that it was her own blood sawed out the boards and drove the nails. She was ever one to clean up after herself."

"It means three dollars," I say. "Do you want us to go, or not?" Pa rubs his knees. "We'll be back by to-morrow sundown."

"Well . . ." pa says. He looks out over the land, awry-haired, mouthing the snuff slowly against his gums.

"Come on," Jewel says. He goes down the steps. Vernon spits neatly into the dust.

"By sundown, now," pa says. "I would not keep her waiting."

Jewel glances back, then he goes on around the house. I enter the hall, hearing the voices before I reach the door. Tilting a little down the hill, as our house does, a breeze draws through the hall all the time, upslanting. A feather dropped near the front door will rise and brush along the ceiling, slanting backward, until it reaches the down-turning current at the back door: so with voices. As you enter the hall, they sound as though they were speaking out of the air about your head.

CORA

IT WAS THE SWEETEST THING I EVER SAW. IT WAS LIKE HE knew he would never see her again, that Anse Bundren was driving him from his mother's death-bed, never to see her in this world again. I always said Darl was different from those others. I always said he was the only one of them that had his mother's nature, had any natural affection. Not that Jewel, the one she laboured so to bear and coddled and petted so and him flinging into tantrums or sulking spells, inventing devilment to devil her till I would have frailed him time and time. Not him to come and tell her good-bye. Not him to miss a chance to make that extra three dollars at the price of his mother's good-bye kiss. A Bundren through and through, loving nobody, caring for nothing except how to get something with the least amount of work. Mr. Tull says Darl asked them to wait. He said Darl almost begged them on his knees not to force him to leave her in her condition. But nothing would do but Anse and Jewel must make that three dollars. Nobody that knows Anse could have expected different, but to think of that boy, that Jewel, selling all those years of self-denial and down-right partiality—they couldn't fool me: Mr. Tull says Mrs. Bundren liked Jewel the least of all, but I knew better. I knew she was partial to him, to the same quality in him that let her put up with Anse Bundren when Mr. Tull said she ought to poisoned him—for three dollars, denying his dying mother the good-bye kiss.

Why, for the last three weeks I have been coming over every time I could, coming sometimes when I shouldn't have, neglecting my own family and duties so that somebody would be with her in her last moments and she would not have to face the Great Unknown without one familiar face to give her courage. Not that I deserve credit for it: I will expect the same for myself. But thank God it will be the faces of my loved kin, my blood and flesh, for in my husband and children I have been more blessed than most, trials though they have been at times.

She lived, a lonely woman, lonely with her pride, trying to make folks believe different, hiding the fact that they just suffered her, because she was not cold in the coffin before they were carting her forty miles away to bury her, flouting the will of God to do it. Refusing to let her lie in the same earth with those Bundrens.

"But she wanted to go," Mr. Tull said. "It was her own wish to lie among her own people."

"Then why didn't she go alive?" I said. "Not one of them would have stopped her, with even that little one almost old enough now to be selfish and stone-hearted like the rest of them."

"It was her own wish," Mr. Tull said. "I heard Anse say it was."

"And you would believe Anse, of course," I said. "A man like you would. Don't tell me."

"I'd believe him about something he couldn't expect to make anything off of me by not telling," Mr. Tull said.

"Don't tell me," I said. "A woman's place is with her husband and children, alive or dead. Would you expect me to want to go back to Alabama and leave you and the girls when my time comes, that I left of my own will to cast my lot with yours for better and worse, until death and after?"

"Well, folks are different," he said.

I should hope so. I have tried to live right in the sight of God and man, for the honour and comfort of my Christian husband and the love and respect of my Christian children. So that when I lay me down in the consciousness of my duty and reward I will be surrounded by loving faces, carrying the farewell kiss of each of my loved ones into my reward. Not like Addie Bundren dying alone, hiding her pride and her broken heart. Glad to go. Lying there with her head propped up so she could watch Cash building the coffin, having to watch him so he would not skimp on it, like as not, with those men not worrying about anything except if there was time to earn another three dollars before the rain came and the river got too high to get across it. Like as not, if they hadn't decided to make that last load, they would have loaded her into the wagon on a quilt and crossed the river first and then stopped and give her time to die what Christian death they would let her.

Except Darl. It was the sweetest thing I ever saw. Sometimes I lose faith in human nature for a time; I am assailed by doubt. But always the Lord restores my faith and reveals to me His bounteous love for His creatures. Not Jewel, the one she had always cherished, not him. He was after that three extra dollars. It was Darl, the one that folks say is queer, lazy, pottering about the place no better than Anse, with Cash a good carpenter and always more building than he can get around to, and Jewel always doing something that made him some money or got him talked about, and that near-naked girl always standing over Addie with a fan so that every time a body tried to talk to her and cheer her up, would answer for her right quick, like she was trying to keep anybody from coming near her at all.

It was Darl. He come to the door and stood there, looking at his dying mother. He just looked at her, and I felt the bounteous love of the Lord again and His mercy. I saw that with Jewel she had just been pretending, but that it was between her and Darl that the understanding and the true love was. He just looked at her, not even coming in where she could see him and get upset, knowing that Anse was driving him away and he would never see her again. He said nothing, just looking at her.

"What you want, Darl?" Dewey Dell said, not stopping the fan, speaking up quick, keeping even him from her. He didn't answer. He just stood and looked at his dying mother, his heart too full for words.

DEWEY DELL

THE FIRST TIME ME AND LAFE PICKED ON DOWN THE ROW. Pa dassent sweat because he will catch his death from the sickness so everybody that comes to help us. And Jewel don't care about anything he is not kin to us in caring, not care-kin. And Cash like sawing the long hot sad yellow days up into planks and nailing them to something. And pa thinks because neighbours will always treat one another that way because he has always been too busy letting neighbours do for him to find out. And I did not think that Darl would, that sits at the supper table with his eyes gone further than the food and the lamp, full of the land dug out of his skull and the holes filled with distance beyond the land.

We picked on down the row, the woods getting closer and closer and the secret shade, picking on into the secret shade with my sack and Lafe's sack. Because I said will I or won't I when the sack was half-full because I said if the sack is full when we get to the woods it won't be me. I said if it don't mean for me to do it the sack will not be full and I will turn up the next row but if the sack is full, I cannot help it. It will be that I had to do it all the time and I cannot help it. And we picked on toward the secret shade and our eyes would drown together touching on his hands and my hands and I didn't say anything. I said "What are you doing?" and he said "I am picking into your sack." And so it was full when we came to the end of the row and I could not help it.

And so it was because I could not help it. It was then, and then I saw Darl and he knew. He said he knew without the words like he told me that ma is going to die without words, and I knew he knew because if he had said he knew with the words I would not have believed that he had been there and saw us. But he said he did know and I said "Are you going to tell pa are you going to kill him?" without the words I said it and he said "Why?" without the words. And that's why I can talk to him with knowing with hating because he knows.

He stands in the door, looking at her.

"What you want, Darl?" I say.

"She is going to die," he says. And old turkey-buzzard Tull coming to watch her die but I can fool them.

"When is she going to die?" I say.

"Before we get back," he says.

"Then why are you taking Jewel?" I say.

"I want him to help me load," he says.

TULL

Anse keeps on rubbing his knees. His overalls are faded; on one knee a serge patch cut out of a pair of Sunday pants, wore iron-slick. "No man mislikes it more than me," he says.

"A fellow's got to guess ahead now and then," I say. "But, come long and short, it won't be no harm done neither way."

"She'll want to get started right off," he says. "It's far enough to Jefferson at best."

"But the roads is good now," I say. It's fixing to rain tonight, too. His folks buries at New Hope, too, not three miles away. But it's just like him to marry a woman born a day's hard ride away and have her die on him.

He looks out over the land, rubbing his knees. "No man so mislikes it," he says.

"They'll get back in plenty of time," I say. "I wouldn't worry none."

"It means three dollars," he says.

"Might be it won't be no need for them to rush back, noways," I say. "I hope it."

"She's a-going," he says. "Her mind is set on it." It's a hard life on women, for a fact. Some women. I mind my mammy lived to be seventy and more. Worked every day, rain or shine; never a sick day since her last chap was born until one day she kind of looked around her and then she went and taken that lace-trimmed night-gown she had had forty-five years and never wore out of the chest and put it on and laid down on the bed and pulled the covers up and shut her eyes. "You all will have to look out for pa the best you can," she said. "I'm tired."

Anse rubs his hands on his knees. "The Lord giveth," he says. We can hear Cash a-hammering and sawing beyond the corner.

It's true. Never a truer breath was ever breathed. "The Lord giveth," I say.

That boy comes up the hill. He is carrying a fish nigh long as he is. He slings it to the ground and grunts "Hah" and spits over his shoulder like a man. Durn nigh long as he is.

"What's that?" I say. "A hog? Where'd you get it?"

"Down to the bridge," he says. He turns it over, the under-side caked over with dust where it is wet, the eye coated over, humped under the dirt.

"Are you aiming to leave it laying there?" Anse says.

"I aim to show it to ma," Vardaman says. He looks toward the door. We can hear the talking, coming out on the draught. Cash, too, knocking and hammering at the boards. "There's company in there," he says.

"Just my folks," I say. "They'd enjoy to see it, too."

He says nothing, watching the door. Then he looks down at the fish laying in the dust. He turns it over with his foot and prods at the eye-bump with his toe, gouging at it. Anse is looking out over the land. Vardaman looks at Anse's face, then at the door. He turns, going toward the corner of the house, when Anse calls him without looking around.

"You clean that fish," Anse says.

Vardaman stops. "Why can't Dewey Dell clean it?" he says.

"You clean that fish," Anse says.

"Aw, pa," Vardaman says.

"You clean it," Anse says. He don't look around. Varda-

man comes back and picks up the fish. It slides out of
his hands, smearing wet dirt on to him, and flops down,
dirtying itself again, gap-mouthed, goggle-eyed, hiding
into the dust like it was ashamed of being dead, like it
was in a hurry to get back hid again. Vardaman cusses it.
He cusses it like a grown man, standing a-straddle of it.
Anse don't look around. Vardaman picks it up again. He
goes on around the house, toting it in both arms like an
armful of wood, it overlapping him on both ends, head
and tail. Durn nigh big as he is.

Anse's wrists dangle out of his sleeves: I never see him
with a shirt on that looked like it was his in all my life.
They all looked like Jewel might have give him his old
ones. Not Jewel, though. He's long-armed, even if he is
spindling. Except for the lack of sweat. You could tell
they ain't been nobody else's but Anse's that way without
no mistake. His eyes look like pieces of burnt-out cinder
fixed in his face, looking out over the land.

When the shadow touches the steps he says "It's five
o'clock."

Just as I get up Cora comes to the door and says it's
time to get on. Anse reaches for his shoes. "Now, Mr.
Bundren," Cora says, "don't you get up now." He puts his
shoes on, stomping into them, like he does everything
like he is hoping all the time he really can't do it and can
quit trying to. When we go up the hall we can hear
them clumping on the floor like they was iron shoes. He
comes toward the door where she is, blinking his eyes,
kind of looking ahead of hisself before he sees, like he is
hoping to find her setting up, in a chair maybe or maybe
sweeping, and looks into the door in that surprised way
like he looks in and finds her still in bed every time and
Dewey Dell still a-fanning her with the fan. He stands
there, like he don't aim to move again nor nothing else

"Well, I reckon we better get on," Cora says. "I got to feed the chickens." It's fixing to rain, too. Clouds like that don't lie, and the cotton making every day the Lord sends. That'll be something else for him. Cash is still trimming at the boards. "If there's ere a thing we can do," Cora says.

"Anse'll let us know," I say.

Anse don't look at us. He looks around, blinking, in that surprised way, like he had wore hisself down being surprised and was even surprised at that. If Cash just works that careful on my barn.

"I told Anse it likely won't be no need," I say. "I so hope it."

"Her mind is set on it," he says. "I reckon she's bound to go."

"It comes to all of us," Cora says. "Let the Lord comfort you."

"About that corn," I say. I tell him again I will help him out if he gets into a tight, with her sick and all. Like most folks around here, I done holp him so much already I can't quit now.

"I aimed to get to it today," he says. "Seems like I can't get my mind on nothing."

"Maybe she'll hold out till you are laid by," I say.

"If God wills it," he says.

"Let Him comfort you," Cora says.

If Cash just works that careful on my barn. He looks up when we pass. "Don't reckon I'll get to you this week," he says.

"'Tain't no rush," I say. "Whenever you get around to it."

We get into the wagon. Cora sets the cake-box on her lap. It's fixing to rain, sho.

"I don't know what he'll do," Cora says. "I just don't know."

"Poor Anse," I say. "She kept him at work for thirty-odd years. I reckon she is tired."

"And I reckon she'll be behind him for thirty years more," Kate says. "Or if it ain't her, he'll get another one before cotton-picking."

"I reckon Cash and Darl can get married now," Eula says.

"That poor boy," Cora says. "The poor little tyke."

"What about Jewel?" Kate says.

"He can, too," Eula says.

"Humph," Kate says. "I reckon he will. I reckon so. I reckon there's more gals than one around here that don't want to see Jewel tied down. Well, they needn't to worry."

"Why, Kate!" Cora says. The wagon begins to rattle. "The poor little tyke," Cora says.

It's fixing to rain this night. Yes, sir. A rattling wagon is mighty dry weather, for a Birdsell. But that'll be cured. It will for a fact.

"She ought to taken them cakes after she said she would," Kate says.

ANSE

Durn that road. And it fixing to rain, too. I can stand here and same as see it with second-sight, a-shutting down behind them like a wall, shutting down betwixt them and my given promise. I do the best I can, much as I can get my mind on anything, but durn them boys.

A-laying there, right up to my door, where every bad luck that comes and goes is bound to find it. I told Addie it wasn't any luck living on a road when it come by here, and she said, for the world like a woman, "Get up and move, then." But I told her it wasn't no luck in it, because the Lord put roads for travelling: why He laid them down flat on the earth. When He aims for something to be always a-moving, He makes it long ways, like a road or a horse or a wagon, but when He aims for something to stay put, He makes it up-and-down ways, like a tree or a man. And so he never aimed for folks to live on a road, because which gets there first, I says, the road or the house? Did you ever know Him to set a road down by a house? I says. No you never, I says, because it's always men can't rest till they gets the house set where everybody that passes in a wagon can spit in the doorway, keeping the folks restless and wanting to get up and go somewheres else when He aimed for them to stay put like a tree or a stand of corn. Because if He'd a aimed for man to be always a-moving and going somewheres else, wouldn't He a put him longways on his belly, like a snake? It stands to reason He would.

Putting it where every bad luck prowling can find it and come straight to my door, charging me taxes on top of it. Making me pay for Cash having to get them carpenter notions when if it hadn't been no road come there, he wouldn't a got them; falling off of churches and lifting no hand in six months and me and Addie slaving and a-slaving, when there's plenty of sawing on this place he could do if he's got to saw.

And Darl, too. Talking me out of him, durn them. It ain't that I am afraid of work; I always have fed me and mine and kept a roof above us: it's that they would shorthand me just because he tends to his own business, just because he's got his eyes full of the land all the time. I says to them, he was all right at first, with his eyes full of the land, because the land laid up-and-down ways then; it wasn't till that ere road come and switched the land around longways and his eyes still full of the land, that they begun to threaten me out of him, trying to shorthand me with the law.

Making me pay for it. She was well and hale as ere a woman ever were, except for that road. Just laying down, resting herself in her own bed, asking naught of none. "Are you sick, Addie?" I said.

"I am not sick," she said.

"You lay you down and rest you," I said. "I knowed you are not sick. You're just tired. You lay you down and rest."

"I am not sick," she said. "I will get up."

"Lay still and rest," I said. "You are just tired. You can get up tomorrow." And she was laying there, well and hale as ere a woman ever were, except for that road.

"I never sent for you," I said. "I take you to witness I never sent for you."

"I know you didn't," Peabody said. "I bound that. Where is she?"

"She's a-laying down," I said. "She's just a little tired, but she'll ——"

"Get outen here, Anse," he said. "Go set on the porch a while."

And now I got to pay for it, me without a tooth in my head, hoping to get ahead enough so I could get my mouth fixed where I could eat God's own victuals as a man should, and her hale and well as ere a woman in the land until that day. Got to pay for being put to the need of that three dollars. Got to pay for the way for them boys to have to go away to earn it. And now I can see same as second sight the rain shutting down betwixt us, a-coming up that road like a durn man, like it wasn't ere a other house to rain on in all the living land.

I have heard men cuss their luck, and right, for they were sinful men. But I do not say it's a curse on me, because I have done no wrong to be cussed by. I am not religious, I reckon. But peace is my heart: I know it is. I have done things but neither better nor worse than them that pretend otherlike, and I know that Old Marster will care for me as for ere a sparrow that falls. But it seems hard that a man in his need could be so flouted by a road.

Vardaman comes around the house, bloody as a hog to his knees, and that ere fish chopped up with the axe like as not, or maybe throwed away for him to lie about the dogs et it. Well, I reckon I ain't no call to expect no more of him than of his mangrowed brothers. He comes along, watching the house, quiet, and sits on the steps. "Whew," he says, "I'm pure tired."

"Go wash them hands," I say. But couldn't no woman strove harder than Addie to make them right, man and boy: I'll say that for her.

"It was full of blood and guts as a hog," he says. But I just can't seem to get no heart into anything, with this here weather sapping me, too. "Pa," he says, "is ma sick some more?"

"Go wash them hands," I say. But I just can't seem to get no heart into it.

DARL

HE HAS BEEN TO TOWN THIS WEEK: THE BACK OF HIS neck is trimmed close, with a white line between hair and sunburn like a joint of white bone. He has not once looked back.

"Jewel," I say. Back running, tunnelled between the two sets of bobbing mule ears, the road vanishes beneath the wagon as though it were a ribbon and the front axle were a spool. "Do you know she is going to die, Jewel?"

It takes two people to make you, and one people to die. That's how the world is going to end.

I said to Dewey Dell: "You want her to die so you can get to town: is that it?" She wouldn't say what we both knew. "The reason you will not say it is, when you say it, even to yourself, you will know it is true: is that it? But you know it is true now. I can almost tell you the day when you knew it is true. Why won't you say it, even to yourself?" She will not say it. She just keeps on saying Are you going to tell pa? Are you going to kill him? "You cannot believe it is true because you cannot believe that Dewey Dell, Dewey Dell Bundren, could have such bad luck: is that it?"

The sun, an hour above the horizon, is poised like a bloody egg upon a crest of thunderheads; the light has turned copper: in the eye portentous, in the nose sulphurous, smelling of lightning. When Peabody comes, they will have to use the rope. He has pussel-gutted himself eating cold greens. With the rope they will haul him up the path, balloon-like up the sulphurous air.

"Jewel," I say, "do you know that Addie Bundren is going to die? Addie Bundren is going to die?"

PEABODY

WHEN ANSE FINALLY SENT FOR ME OF HIS OWN AC-cord, I said "He has wore her out at last." And I said a damn good thing and at first I would not go because there might be something I could do and I would have to haul her back, by God. I thought maybe they have the same sort of fool ethics in heaven they have in the Medical College and that it was maybe Vernon Tull sending for me again, getting me there in the nick of time, as Vernon always does things, getting the most for Anse's money like he does for his own. But when it got far enough into the day for me to read weather sign I knew it couldn't have been anybody but Anse that sent. I knew that nobody but a luckless man could ever need a doctor in the face of a cyclone. And I knew that if it had finally occurred to Anse himself that he needed one, it was already too late.

When I reach the spring and get down and hitch the team, the sun has gone down behind a bank of black cloud like a top-heavy mountain range, like a load of cinders dumped over there, and there is no wind. I could hear Cash sawing for a mile before I got there. Anse is standing at the top of the bluff above the path.

"Where's the horse?" I say.

"Jewel's taken and gone," he says. "Can't nobody else ketch hit. You'll have to walk up, I reckon."

"Me, walk up, weighing two hundred and twenty-five pounds?" I say. "Walk up that durn wall?" He stands there beside a tree. Too bad the Lord made the mistake of giving trees roots and giving the Anse Bundrens He makes feet and legs. If He'd just swapped them, there wouldn't ever be a worry about this country being deforested some day. Or any other country. "What do you aim for me to do?" I say. "Stay here and get blowed clean out of the county when that cloud breaks?" Even with the horse it would take me fifteen minutes to ride up across the pasture to the top of the ridge and reach the house. The path looks like a crooked limb blown against the bluff. Anse has not been in town in twelve years. And how his mother ever got up there to bear him, he being his mother's son.

"Vardaman's gittin' the rope," he says.

After a while Vardaman appears with the ploughline. He gives the end of it to Anse and comes down the path, uncoiling it.

"You hold it tight," I say. "I done already wrote this visit on to my books, so I'm going to charge you just the same, whether I get there or not."

"I got hit," Anse says. "You kin come on up."

I'll be damned if I can see why I don't quit. A man seventy years old, weighing two hundred and odd pounds, being hauled up and down a damn mountain on a rope. I reckon it's because I must reach the fifty-thousand dollar mark of dead accounts on my books before I can quit. "What the hell does your wife mean," I say, "taking sick on top of a durn mountain?"

"I'm right sorry," he says. He let the rope go, just dropped it, and he has turned toward the house. There is a little daylight up here still, of the colour of sulphur matches. The boards look like strips of sulphur. Cash does not look back. Vernon Tull says he brings each board up to the window for her to see it and say it is all right. The boy overtakes us. Anse looks back at him. "Where's the rope?" he says.

"It's where you left it," I say. "But never you mind that rope. I got to get back down that bluff. I don't aim for that storm to catch me up here. I'd blow too durn far once I got started."

The girl is standing by the bed, fanning her. When we enter she turns her head and looks at us. She has been dead these ten days. I suppose it's having been a part of Anse for so long that she cannot even make that change, if change it be. I can remember how when I was young I believed death to be a phenomenon of the body; now I know it to be merely a function of the mind—and that of the minds of the ones who suffer the bereavement. The nihilists say it is the end; the fundamentalists, the beginning; when in reality it is no more than a single tenant or family moving out of a tenement or a town.

She looks at us. Only her eyes seem to move. It's like they touch us, not with sight or sense, but like the stream from a hose touches you, the stream at the instant of impact as dissociated from the nozzle as though it had never been there. She does not look at Anse at all. She looks at me, then at the boy. Beneath the quilt she is no more than a bundle of rotten sticks.

"Well, Miss Addie," I say. The girl does not stop the fan. "How are you, sister?" I say. Her head lies gaunt on the pillow, looking at the boy. "You picked out a fine time to get me out here and bring up a storm." Then I send Anse and the boy out. She watches the boy as he leaves the room. She has not moved save her eyes.

He and Anse are on the porch when I come out, the boy sitting on the steps, Anse standing by a post, not even leaning against it, his arms dangling, the hair pushed and matted up on his head like a dipped rooster. He turns his head, blinking at me.

"Why didn't you send for me sooner?" I say.

"Hit was jest one thing and then another," he says. "That ere corn me and the boys was aimin' to git up with, and Dewey Dell a-takin' good keer of her, and folks comin' in, a-offerin' to help and sich, till I jest thought . . ."

"Damn the money," I say. "Did you ever hear of me worrying a fellow before he was ready to pay?"

"Hit ain't begrudgin' the money," he says. "I jest kept a-thinkin'. . . . She's goin', is she?" The durn little tyke is sitting on the top step, looking smaller than ever in the sulphur-coloured light. That's the one trouble with this country: everything, weather, all, hangs on too long. Like our rivers, our land: opaque, slow, violent; shaping and creating the life of man in its implacable and brooding image. "I knowed hit," Anse says. "All the while I made sho. Her mind is sot on hit."

"And a damn good thing, too," I say. "With a trifling——" He sits on the top step, small, motionless in faded overalls. When I came out he looked up at me, then at Anse. But now he has stopped looking at us. He just sits there.

"Have you told her yit?" Anse says.

"What for?" I say. "What the devil for?"

"She'll know hit. I knowed that when she see you she would know hit, same as writing. You wouldn't need to tell her. Her mind——"

Behind us the girl says, "Paw." I look at her, at her face.

"You better go quick," I say.

When we enter the room she is watching the door. She looks at me. Her eyes look like lamps blaring up just before the oil is gone. "She wants you to go out," the girl says.

"Now, Addie," Anse says, "when he come all the way from Jefferson to git you well?" She watches me: I can feel her eyes. It's like she was shoving at me with them. I have seen it before in women. Seen them drive from the room them coming with sympathy and pity, with actual help, and clinging to some trifling animal to whom they never were more than pack-horses. That's what they mean by the love that passeth understanding: that pride, that furious desire to hide that abject nakedness which we bring here with us, carry with us into operating rooms, carry stubbornly and furiously with us into the earth again. I leave the room. Beyond the porch Cash's saw snores steadily into the board. A minute later she calls his name, her voice harsh and strong.

"Cash," she says; "you, Cash!"

DARL

PA STANDS BESIDE THE BED. FROM BEHIND HIS LEG
Vardaman peers, with his round head and his eyes
round and his mouth beginning to open. She looks at pa;
all her failing life appears to drain into her eyes, urgent,
irremediable. "It's Jewel she wants," Dewey Dell says.

"Why, Addie," pa says, "him and Darl went to make
one more load. They thought there was time. That you
would wait for them, and that three dollars and all . . ."
He stoops, laying his hand on hers. For a while yet she
looks at him, without reproach, without anything at all,
as if her eyes alone are listening to the irrevocable cessation of his voice. Then she raises herself, who has not
moved in ten days. Dewey Dell leans down, trying to
press her back.

"Ma," she says; "ma."

She is looking out the window, at Cash stooping
steadily at the board in the failing light, labouring on toward darkness and into it as though the stroking of the
saw illumined its own motion, board and saw engendered.

"You, Cash," she shouts, her voice harsh, strong, and
unimpaired. "You, Cash!"

He looks up at the gaunt face framed by the window
in the twilight. It is a composite picture of all time since
he was a child. He drops the saw and lifts the board for
her to see, watching the window in which the face has
not moved. He drags a second plank into position and
slants the two of them into their final juxtaposition, ges-

turing toward the ones yet on the ground, shaping with his empty hand in pantomime the finished box. For a while still she looks down at him from the composite picture, neither with censure nor approbation. Then the face disappears.

She lies back and turns her head without so much as glancing at pa. She looks at Vardaman; her eyes, the life in them, rushing suddenly upon them; the two flames glare up for a steady instant. Then they go out as though someone had leaned down and blown upon them.

"Ma," Dewey Dell says; "ma!" Leaning above the bed, her hands lifted a little, the fan still moving like it has for ten days, she begins to keen. Her voice is strong, young, tremulous and clear, rapt with its own timbre and volume, the fan still moving steadily up and down, whispering the useless air. Then she flings herself across Addie Bundren's knees, clutching her, shaking her with the furious strength of the young before sprawling suddenly across the handful of rotten bones that Addie Bundren left, jarring the whole bed into a chattering sibilance of mattress shucks, her arms outflung and the fan in one hand still beating with expiring breath into the quilt.

From behind pa's leg Vardaman peers, his mouth full open and all colour draining from his face into his mouth, as though he has by some means fleshed his own teeth in himself, sucking. He begins to move slowly backward from the bed, his eyes round, his pale face fading into the dusk like a piece of paper pasted on a failing wall, and so out of the door.

Pa leans above the bed in the twilight, his humped silhouette partaking of that owl-like quality of awry-feathered, disgruntled outrage within which lurks a wisdom too profound or too inert for even thought.

"Durn them boys," he says.

Jewel, I say. Overhead the day drives level and grey, hiding the sun by a flight of grey spears. In the rain the mules smoke a little, splashed yellow with mud, the off one clinging in sliding lunges to the side of the road above the ditch. The tilted lumber gleams dull yellow, water-soaked and heavy as lead, tilted at a steep angle into the ditch above the broken wheel; about the shattered spokes and about Jewel's ankles a runnel of yellow neither water nor earth swirls, curving with the yellow road neither of earth nor water, down the hill dissolving into a streaming mass of dark green neither of earth nor sky. Jewel, I say.

Cash comes to the door, carrying the saw. Pa stands beside the bed, humped, his arms dangling. He turns his head, his shabby profile, his chin collapsing slowly as he works the snuff against his gums.

"She's gone," Cash says.

"She taken and left us," pa says. Cash does not look at him. "How nigh are you done?" pa says. Cash does not answer. He enters, carrying the saw. "I reckon you better get at it," pa says. "You'll have to do the best you can, with them boys gone off that-a-way." Cash looks down at her face. He is not listening to pa at all. He does not approach the bed. He stops in the middle of the floor, the saw against his leg, his sweating arms powdered lightly with sawdust, his face composed. "If you get in a tight, maybe some of them'll get here tomorrow and help you," pa says. "Vernon could." Cash is not listening. He is looking down at her peaceful, rigid face fading into the dusk as though darkness were a precursor of the ultimate earth, until at last the face seems to float detached upon it, lightly as the reflection of a dead leaf. "There is Christians enough to help you," pa says. Cash is not listening. After a while he turns without looking at pa and leaves the room. Then the saw begins to snore again. "They will help us in our sorrow," pa says.

The sound of the saw is steady, competent, unhurried, stirring the dying light so that at each stroke her face seems to wake a little into an expression of listening and of waiting, as though she were counting the strokes. Pa looks down at the face, at the black sprawl of Dewey Dell's hair, the outflung arms, the clutched fan now motionless on the fading quilt. "I reckon you better get supper on," he says.

Dewey Dell does not move.

"Git up, now, and put supper on," pa says. "We got to keep our strength up. I reckon Doctor Peabody's right hungry, coming all this way. And Cash'll need to eat quick and get back to work so he can finish it in time."

Dewey Dell rises, heaving to her feet. She looks down at the face. It is like a casting of fading bronze upon the pillow, the hands alone still with any semblance of life: a curled, gnarled inertness; a spent yet alert quality from which weariness, exhaustion, travail has not yet departed, as though they doubted even yet the actuality of rest, guarding with horned and penurious alertness the cessation which they know cannot last.

Dewey Dell stoops and slides the quilt from beneath them and draws it up over them to the chin, smoothing it down, drawing it smooth. Then without looking at pa she goes around the bed and leaves the room.

She will go out where Peabody is, where she can stand in the twilight and look at his back with such an expression that, feeling her eyes and turning, he will say; I would not let it grieve me, now. She was old, and sick too. Suffering more than we knew. She couldn't have got well. Vardaman's getting big now, and with you to take good care of them all. I would try not to let it grieve

*me. I expect you'd better go and get some supper ready.
It don't have to be much. But they'll need to eat, and
she looking at him, saying You could do so much for me
if you just would. If you just knew. I am I and you are
you and I know it and you don't know it and you could
do so much for me if you just would and if you just
would then I could tell you and then nobody would
have to know it except you and me and Darl.*

Pa stands over the bed, dangle-armed, humped, motionless. He raises his hand to his head, scouring his hair,
listening to the saw. He comes nearer and rubs his hand,
palm and back, on his thigh and lays it on her face and
then on the hump of quilt where her hands are. He
touches the quilt as he saw Dewey Dell do, trying to
smooth it up to the chin, but disarranging it instead. He
tries to smooth it again, clumsily, his hand awkward as
a claw, smoothing at the wrinkles which he made and
which continue to emerge beneath his hand with perverse
ubiquity, so that at last he desists, his hand falling to his
side and stroking itself again, palm and back, on his
thigh. The sound of the saw snores steadily into the
room. Pa breathes with a quiet, rasping sound, mouthing the snuff against his gums. "God's will be done," he
says. "Now I can get them teeth."

*Jewel's hat droops limp about his neck, channelling
water on to the soaked tow-sack tied about his shoulders
as, ankle-deep in the running ditch, he pries with a slipping two-by-four, with a piece of rotting log for fulcrum,
at the axle. Jewel, I say, she is dead, Jewel. Addie Bundren is dead.*

VARDAMAN

THEN I BEGIN TO RUN. I RUN TOWARD THE BACK AND come to the edge of the porch and stop. Then I begin to cry. I can feel where the fish was in the dust. It is cut up into pieces of not-fish now, not-blood on my hands and overalls. Then it wasn't so. It hadn't happened then. And now she is getting so far ahead I cannot catch her.

The trees look like chickens when they ruffle out into the cool dust on the hot days. If I jump off the porch I will be where the fish was, and it all cut up into not-fish now. I can hear the bed and her face and them and I can feel the floor shake when he walks on it that came and did it. That came and did it when she was all right but he came and did it.

"The fat son of a bitch."

I jump from the porch, running. The top of the barn comes swooping up out of the twilight. If I jump I can go through it like the pink lady in the circus, into the warm smelling, without having to wait. My hands grab at the bushes; beneath my feet the rocks and dirt go rubbling down.

Then I can breathe again, in the warm smelling. I enter the stall, trying to touch him, and then I can cry then I vomit the crying. As soon as he gets through kicking I can and then I can cry, the crying can.

"He kilt her. He kilt her."

The life in him runs under the skin, under my hand, running through the splotches, smelling up into my nose where the sickness is beginning to cry, vomiting the crying, and then I can breathe, vomiting it. It makes a lot of noise. I can smell the life running up from under my hands, up my arms, and then I can leave the stall.

I cannot find it. In the dark, along the dust, the walls I cannot find it. The crying makes a lot of noise. I wish it wouldn't make so much noise. Then I find it in the wagon-shed, in the dust, and I run across the lot and into the road, the stick jouncing on my shoulder.

They watch me as I run up, beginning to jerk back, their eyes rolling, snorting, jerking back on the hitch rein. I strike. I can hear the stick striking; I can see it hitting their heads, the breast-yoke, missing altogether sometimes as they rear and plunge, but I am glad.

"You kilt my maw!"

The stick breaks, they rearing and snorting, their feet popping loud on the ground; loud because it is going to rain and the air is empty for the rain. But it is still long enough. I run this way and that as they rear and jerk at the hitch-rein, striking.

"You kilt her!"

I strike at them, striking, they wheeling in a long lunge, the buggy wheeling on to two wheels and motionless like it is nailed to the ground and the horses motionless like they are nailed by the hind feet to the centre of a whirling-plate.

I run in the dust. I cannot see, running in the sucking dust where the buggy vanishes tilted on two wheels. I strike, the stick hitting into the ground, bouncing, striking into the dust and then into the air again and the dust sucking on down the road faster than if a car was in it. And then I can cry, looking at the stick. It is broken down to my hand, not longer than stove wood that was a long stick. I throw it away and I can cry. It does not make so much noise now.

Th℮ cow is standing in the barn door, chewing. When she sees me come into the lot she lows, her mouth full of flopping green, her tongue flopping.

"I ain't a-goin' to milk you. I ain't a-goin' to do nothing for them."

I hear her turn when I pass. When I turn she is just behind me with her sweet, hot, hard breath.

"Didn't I tell you I wouldn't?"

She nudges me, snuffing. She moans deep inside, her mouth closed. I jerk my hand, cursing her like Jewel does.

"Git, now."

I stoop my hand to the ground and run at her. She jumps back and whirls away and stops, watching me. She moans. She goes on to the path and stands there, looking up the path.

It is dark in the barn, warm, smelling, silent. I can cry quietly, watching the top of the hill.

Cash comes to the hill, limping where he fell off of the church. He looks down at the spring, then up the road and back toward the barn. He comes down the path stiffly and looks at the broken hitch-rein and at the dust in the road and then up the road, where the dust is gone.

"I hope they've got clean past Tull's by now. I so hope hit."

Cash turns and limps up the path.

"Durn him. I showed him. Durn him."

I am not crying now. I am not anything. Dewey Dell comes to the hill and calls me. "Vardaman." I am not anything. I am quiet. "You, Vardaman." I can cry quiet now, feeling and hearing my tears.

"Then hit want. Hit hadn't happened then. Hit was a-layin' right there on the ground. And now she's gittin ready to cook hit."

It is dark. I can hear wood, silence: I know them. But

not living sounds, not even him. It is as though the dark were resolving him out of his integrity, into an unrelated scattering of components—snuffings and stampings; smells of cooling flesh and ammoniac hair; an illusion of a coordinated whole of splotched hide and strong bones within which, detached and secret and familiar, an *is* different from my *is*. I see him dissolve—legs, a rolling eye, a gaudy splotching like cold flames—and float upon the dark in fading solution; all one yet neither; all either yet none. I can see hearing coil toward him, caressing, shaping his hard shape—fetlock, hip, shoulder and head; smell and sound. I am not afraid.

"Cooked and et. Cooked and et."

DEWEY DELL

H E COULD DO SO MUCH FOR ME IF HE JUST WOULD. HE could do everything for me. It's like everything in the world for me is inside a tub full of guts, so that you wonder how there can be any room in it for anything else very important. He is a big tub of guts and I am a little tub of guts and if there is not any room for anything else important in a big tub of guts, how can it be room in a little tub of guts. But I know it is there because God gave women a sign when something has happened bad.

It's because I am alone. If I could just feel it, it would be different, because I would not be alone. But if I were not alone, everybody would know it. And he could do so much for me, and then I would not be alone. Then I could be all right alone.

I would let him come in between me and Lafe, like Darl came in between me and Lafe, and so Lafe is alone too. He is Lafe and I am Dewey Dell, and when mother died I had to go beyond and outside of me and Lafe and Darl to grieve because he could do so much for me and he don't know it. He don't even know it.

From the back porch I cannot see the barn. Then the sound of Cash's sawing comes in from that way. It is like a dog outside the house, going back and forth around the house to whatever door you come to, waiting to come in. He said I worry more than you do and I said You don't know what worry is so I can't worry. I try to but I can't think long enough to worry.

I light the kitchen lamp. The fish, cut into jagged pieces, bleeds quietly in the pan. I put it into the cupboard quick, listening into the hall, hearing. It took her ten days to die; maybe she don't know it is yet. Maybe she won't go until Cash. Or maybe until Jewel. I take the dish of greens from the cupboard and the bread-pan from the cold stove, and I stop, watching the door.

"Where's Vardaman?" Cash says. In the lamp his saw-dusted arms look like sand.

"I don't know. I ain't seen him."

"Peabody's team run away. See if you can find Vardaman. The horse will let him catch him."

"Well. Tell them to come to supper."

I cannot see the barn. I said, I don't know how to worry. I don't know how to cry. I tried, but I can't. After a while the sound of the saw comes around, coming dark along the ground in the dust-dark. Then I can see him, going up and down above the plank.

"You come in to supper," I say. "Tell him." He could

do everything for me. And he don't know it. He is his guts and I am my guts. And I am Lafe's guts. That's it. I don't see why he didn't stay in town. We are country people not as good as town people. I don't see why he didn't. Then I can see the top of the barn. The cow stands at the foot of the path, lowing. When I turn back, Cash is gone.

I carry the buttermilk in. Pa and Cash and he are at the table.

"Where's that big fish Bud caught, sister?" he says.

I set the milk on the table. "I never had no time to cook it."

"Plain turnip greens is mighty spindling eating for a man my size," he says. Cash is eating. About his head the print of his hat is sweated into his hair. His shirt is blotched with sweat. He has not washed his hands and arms.

"You ought to took time," pa says. "Where's Varda-man?"

I go toward the door. "I can't find him."

"Here, sister," he says; "never mind about the fish. It'll save, I reckon. Come on and sit down."

"I ain't minding it," I say. "I'm going to milk before it sets in to rain."

Pa helps himself and pushes the dish on. But he does not begin to eat. His hands are half-closed on either side of his plate, his head bowed a little, his awry hair standing into the lamplight. He looks like right after the maul hits the steer and it no longer alive and don't yet know that it is dead.

But Cash is eating, and he is too. "You better eat something," he says. He is looking at pa. "Like Cash and me. You'll need it."

"Ay," pa says. He rouses up, like a steer that's been

kneeling in a pond and you run at it. "She would not begrudge me it."

When I am out of sight of the house, I go fast. The cow lows at the foot of the bluff. She nuzzles at me, snuffing, blowing her breath in a sweet, hot blast, through my dress, against my hot nakedness, moaning. "You got to wait a little while. Then I'll tend to you." She follows me into the barn where I set the bucket down. She breathes into the bucket, moaning. "I told you. You just got to wait, now. I got more to do than I can tend to." The barn is dark. When I pass, he kicks the wall a single blow. I go on. The broken plank is like a pale plank standing on end. Then I can see the slope, feel the air moving on my face again, slow, pale, with lesser dark and with empty seeing, the pine clumps blotched up the tilted slope, secret and waiting.

The cow in silhouette against the door nuzzles at the silhouette of the bucket, moaning.

Then I pass the stall. I have almost passed it. I listen to it saying for a long time before it can say the word and the listening part is afraid that there may not be time to say it. I feel my body, my bones and flesh beginning to part and open upon the alone, and the process of coming unalone is terrible. Lafe. Lafe. "Lafe" Lafe. Lafe. I lean a little forward, one foot advanced with dead walking. I feel the darkness rushing past my breast, past the cow; I begin to rush upon the darkness but the cow stops me and the darkness rushes on upon the sweet blast of her moaning breath, filled with wood and with silence.

"Vardaman. You, Vardaman."

He comes out of the stall. "You durn little sneak! You durn little sneak!"

He does not resist; the last of rushing darkness flees whistling away. "What? I ain't done nothing."

"You durn little sneak!" My hands shake him, hard. Maybe I couldn't stop them. I didn't know they could shake so hard. They shake both of us, shaking.

"I never done it," he says. "I never touched them."

My hands stop shaking him, but I still hold him. "What are you doing here? Why didn't you answer when I called you?"

"I ain't doing nothing."

"You go on to the house and get your supper."

He draws back. I hold him. "You quit now. You leave me be."

"What were you doing down here? You didn't come down here to sneak after me?"

"I never. I never. You quit, now. I didn't even know you was down here. You leave me be."

I hold him, leaning down to see his face, feel it with my eyes. He is about to cry. "Go on, now. I done put supper on and I'll be there soon as I milk. You better go on before he eats everything up. I hope that team runs clean back to Jefferson."

"He kilt her," he says. He begins to cry.

"Hush."

"She never hurt him and he come and kilt her."

"Hush." He struggles. I hold him. "Hush."

"He kilt her." The cow comes up behind us, moaning. I shake him again.

"You stop it, now. Right this minute. You're fixing to make yourself sick and then you can't go to town. You go on to the house and eat your supper."

"I don't want no supper. I don't want to go to town."

"We'll leave you here, then. Lessen you behave, we will

leave you. Go on, now, before that old green-eating tub of guts eats everything up from you." He goes on, disappearing slowly into the hill. The crest, the trees, the roof of the house stand against the sky. The cow nuzzles at me, moaning. "You'll just have to wait. What you got in you ain't nothing to what I got in me, even if you are a woman too." She follows me, moaning. Then the dead, hot, pale air breathes on my face again. He could fix it all right, if he just would. And he don't even know it. He could do everything for me if he just knowed it. The cow breathes upon my hips and back, her breath warm, sweet, stertorous, moaning. The sky lies flat down the slope, upon the secret clumps. Beyond the hill sheet-lightning stains upward and fades. The dead air shapes the dead earth in the dead darkness, further away than seeing shapes the dead earth. It lies dead and warm upon me, touching me naked through my clothes. I said You don't know what worry is. I don't know what it is. I don't know whether I am worrying or not. Whether I can or not. I don't know whether I can cry or not. I don't know whether I have tried to or not. I feel like a wet seed wild in the hot blind earth.

VARDAMAN

WHEN THEY GET IT FINISHED THEY ARE GOING TO PUT her in it and then for a long time I couldn't say it. I saw the dark stand up and go whirling away and I said "Are you going to nail her up in it, Cash? Cash? Cash?" I got shut up in the crib the new door it was too heavy for me it went shut I couldn't breathe because the rat was breathing up all the air. I said "Are you going to nail it shut, Cash? Nail it? *Nail* it?"

Pa walks around. His shadow walks around, over Cash going up and down above the saw, at the bleeding plank.

Dewey Dell said we will get some bananas. The train is behind the glass, red on the track. When it runs the track shines on and off. Pa said flour and sugar and coffee costs so much. Because I am a country boy because boys in town. Bicycles. Why do flour and sugar and coffee cost so much when he is a country boy. "Wouldn't you ruther have some bananas instead?" Bananas are gone, eaten. Gone. When it runs on the track shines again. "Why ain't I a town boy, pa?" I said God made me. I did not said to God to made me in the country. If He can make the train, why can't He make them all in the town because flour and sugar and coffee. "Wouldn't you ruther have bananas?"

He walks around. His shadow walks around.

It was not her. I was there, looking. I saw. I thought it was her, but it was not. It was not my mother. She went away when the other one laid down in her bed and drew the quilt up. She went away. "Did she go as far as town?" "She went farther than town." "Did all those rabbits and possums go farther than town?" God made the rabbits and possums. He made the train. Why must He make a different place for them to go if she is just like the rabbit.

Pa walks around. His shadow does. The saw sounds like it is asleep.

And so if Cash nails the box up, she is not a rabbit. and so if she is not a rabbit I couldn't breathe in the crib and Cash is going to nail it up. And so if she lets him it is not her. I know. I was there. I saw when it did not be her. I saw. They think it is and Cash is going to nail it up.

It was not her because it was laying right yonder in the dirt. And now it's all chopped up. I chopped it up. It's laying in the kitchen in the bleeding pan, waiting to be cooked and et. Then it wasn't and she was, and now it is and she wasn't. And tomorrow it will be cooked and et and she will be him and pa and Cash and Dewey Dell and there won't be anything in the box and so she can breathe. It was laying right yonder on the ground. I can get Vernon. He was there and he seen it, and with both of us it will be and then it will not be.

TULL

IT WAS NIGH TO MIDNIGHT AND IT HAD SET IN TO RAIN when he woke us. It had been a misdoubtful night, with the storm making; a night when a fellow looks for most anything to happen before he can get the stock fed and himself to the house an supper et and in bed with the rain starting, and when Peabody's team come up, lathered, with the broke harness dragging and the neck-yoke betwixt the off critter's legs, Cora says "It's Addie Bundren. She's gone at last."

"Peabody mought have been to ere a one of a dozen houses hereabouts," I says. "Besides, how do you know it's Peabody's team?"

"Well, ain't it?" she says. "You hitch up, now."

"What for?" I says. "If she is gone, we can't do nothing till morning. And it fixing to storm too.

"It's my duty," she says. "You put the team in."

But I wouldn't do it. "It stands to reason they'd send for us if they needed us. You don't even know she's gone yet."

"Why, don't you know that's Peabody's team? Do you claim it ain't? Well, then." But I wouldn't go. When folks wants a fellow, it's best to wait till they sends for him, I've found. "It's my Christian duty," Cora says. "Will you stand between me and my Christian duty?"

"You can stay there all day tomorrow, if you want," I says.

So when Cora waked me it had set in to rain. Even while I was going to the door with the lamp and it shining on the glass so he could see I am coming, it kept on knocking. Not loud, but steady, like he might have gone to sleep thumping, but I never noticed how low down on the door the knocking was till I opened it and never seen nothing. I held the lamp up, with the rain sparkling across it and Cora back in the hall saying "Who is it, Vernon?" but I couldn't see nobody a-tall at first until I looked down and around the door, lowering the lamp.

He looked like a drowned puppy, in them overalls, without no hat, splashed up to his knees where he had walked them four miles in the mud. "Well, I'll be durned," I says.

"Who is it, Vernon?" Cora says.

He looked at me, his eyes round and black in the middle like when you throw a light in a owl's face. "You mind that ere fish," he says.

"Come in the house," I says. "What is it? Is your maw——"

"Vernon," Cora says.

He stood kind of around behind the door, in the dark. The rain was blowing on to the lamp, hissing on it so I am scared every minute it'll break. "You was there," he says. "You seen it."

Then Cora come to the door. "You come right in outen the rain," she says, pulling him in and him watching me. He looked just like a drowned puppy. "I told you," Cora says. "I told you it was a-happening. You go and hitch."

"But he ain't said——" I says.

He looked at me, dripping on to the floor. "He's a-ruining the rug," Cora says. "You go get the team while I take him to the kitchen."

But he hung back, dripping, watching me with them eyes. "You was there. You seen it laying there. Cash is fixing to nail her up, and it was a-laying right there on the ground. You seen it. You seen the mark in the dirt. The rain never come up till after I was a-coming here. So we can get back in time."

I be durn if it didn't give me the creeps, even when I didn't know yet. But Cora did. "You get that team quick as you can," she says. "He's outen his head with grief and worry."

I be durn if it didn't give me the creeps. Now and then a fellow gets to thinking. About all the sorrow and afflictions in this world; how it's liable to strike anywhere, like lightning. I reckon it does take a powerful trust in the Lord to guard a fellow, though sometimes I think that Cora's a mite over-cautious, like she was trying to crowd the other folks away and get in closer than anybody else. But then, when something like this happens, I reckon she is right and you got to keep after it and I reckon I am blessed in having a wife that ever strives for sanctity and well-doing like she says I am.

Now and then a fellow gets to thinking about it. Not often, though. Which is a good thing. For the Lord aimed for him to do and not to spend too much time thinking, because his brain it's like a piece of machinery: it won't stand a whole lot of racking. It's best when it all runs along the same, doing the day's work and not no one part used no more than needful. I have said and I say again, that's ever living thing the matter with Darl: he just thinks by himself too much. Cora's right when she says all he needs is a wife to straighten him out. And when I think about that, I think that if nothing but being married will help a man, he's durn nigh hopeless. But I reckon Cora's right when she says the reason the Lord had to create women is because man don't know his own good when he sees it.

When I come back to the house with the team, they was in the kitchen. She was dressed on top of her night-gown with a shawl over her head and her umbrella and her Bible wrapped up in the oilcloth, and him sitting on a up-turned bucket on the stove-zinc where she had put him, dripping on to the floor. "I can't get nothing outen him except about a fish," she says. "It's a judgment on them. I see the hand of the Lord upon this boy for Anse Bundren's judgment and warning."

"The rain never come up till after I left," he says. "I had done left. I was on the way. And so it was there in the dust. You seen it. Cash is fixing to nail her, but you seen it."

When we got there is was raining hard, and him sitting on the seat between us, wrapped up in Cora's shawl. He hadn't said nothing else, just sitting there with Cora holding the umbrella over him. Now and then Cora would stop singing long enough to say "It's a judgment on Anse Bundren. May it show him the path of sin he is a-trodding." Then she would sing again, and him sitting there between us, leaning forward a little like the mules couldn't go fast enough to suit him.

"It was laying right yonder," he says, "but the rain come up after I taken and left. So I can go and open the windows, because Cash ain't nailed her yet."

It was long a-past midnight when we drove the last nail, and almost dust-dawn when I got back home and taken the team out and got back in bed, with Cora's nightcap laying on the other pillow. And be durned if even then it wasn't like I could still hear Cora singing and feel that boy leaning forward between us like he was ahead of the mules, and still see Cash going up and down with that saw, and Anse standing there like a scarecrow, like he was a steer standing knee-deep in a pond and somebody come by and set the pond up on edge and he ain't missed it yet.

It was nigh toward daybreak when we drove the last nail and toted it into the house, where she was laying on the bed with the window open and the rain blowing on her again. Twice he did it, and him so dead for sleep that Cora says his face looked like one of these here Christmas masts that had done been buried a while and then dug up, until at last they put her into it and nailed it down so he couldn't open the window on her no more. And the next morning they found him in his shirt-tail laying asleep on the floor like a felled steer, and the top of the box bored clean full of holes and Cash's new auger broke off in the last one. When they taken the lid off her they found that two of them had bored on into her face.

If it's a judgment, it ain't right. Because the Lord's got more to do than that. He's bound to have. Because the only burden Anse Bundren's ever had is himself. And when folks talks him low, I think to myself he ain't that less of a man or he couldn't a bore himself this long.

It ain't right. I be durn if it is. Because He said Suffer little children to come unto Me don't make it right, neither. Cora said, "I have bore you what the Lord God sent me. I faced it without fear nor terror because my faith was strong in the Lord, a-bolstering and sustaining me. If you have no son, it's because the Lord has decreed otherwise in His wisdom. And my life is and has ever been a open book to ere a man or woman among His creatures because I trust in my God and my reward."

I reckon she's right. I reckon if there's ere a man or woman anywhere that He could turn it all over to and go away with His mind at rest, it would be Cora. And I reckon she would make a few changes, no matter how He was running it. And I reckon they would be for man's good. Leastways, we would have to like them. Leastways, we might as well go on and make like we did.

DARL

THE LANTERN SITS ON A STUMP. RUSTED, GREASE-FOULED, its cracked chimney smeared on one side with a soaring smudge of soot, it sheds a feeble and sultry glare upon the trestles and the boards and the adjacent earth. Upon the dark ground the chips look like random smears of soft pale paint on a black canvas. The boards look like long smooth tatters torn from the flat darkness and turned backside out.

Cash labours about the trestles, moving back and forth, lifting and placing the planks with long clattering reverberations in the dead air as though he were lifting and dropping them at the bottom of an invisible well, the sounds ceasing without departing, as if any movement might dislodge them from the immediate air in reverberant repetition. He saws again, his elbow flashing slowly, a thin thread of fire running along the edge of the saw, lost and recovered at the top and bottom of each stroke in unbroken elongation, so that the saw appears to be six feet long, into and out of pa's shabby and aimless silhouette. "Give me that plank," Cash says. "No; the other one." He puts the saw down and comes and picks up the plank he wants, sweeping pa away with the long swinging gleam of the balanced board.

The air smells like sulphur. Upon the impalpable plane of it their shadows form as upon a wall, as though like sound they had not gone very far away in falling but had merely congealed for a moment, immediate and musing. Cash works on, half turned into the feeble light, one thigh and one pole-thin arm braced, his face sloped into the light with a rapt, dynamic immobility above his tireless elbow. Below the sky sheet-lightning slumbers lightly; against it the trees, motionless, are ruffled out to the last twig, swollen, increased as though quick with young.

It begins to rain. The first harsh, sparse, swift drops rush through the leaves and across the ground in a long sigh, as though of relief from intolerable suspense. They are big as buckshot, warm as though fired from a gun; they sweep across the lantern in a vicious hissing. Pa lifts his face, slack-mouthed, the wet black rim of snuff plastered close along the base of his gums; from behind his slack-faced astonishment he muses as though from beyond time, upon the ultimate outrage. Cash looks once at the sky, then at the lantern. The saw has not faltered, the running gleam of its pistoning edge unbroken. "Get something to cover the lantern," he says.

Pa goes to the house. The rain rushes suddenly down, without thunder, without warning of any sort; he is swept on to the porch upon the edge of it and in an instant Cash is wet to the skin. Yet the motion of the saw has not faltered, as though it and the arm functioned in a tranquil conviction that rain was an illusion of the mind. Then he puts down the saw and goes and crouches above the lantern, shielding it with his body, his back shaped lean and scrawny by his wet shirt as though he had been abruptly turned wrong-side out, shirt and all.

Pa returns. He is wearing Jewel's raincoat and carrying Dewey Dell's. Squatting over the lantern, Cash reaches back and picks up four sticks and drives them into the earth and takes Dewey Dell's raincoat from pa and spreads it over the sticks, forming a roof above the lantern. Pa watches him. "I don't know what you'll do," he says. "Darl taken his coat with him."

"Get wet," Cash says. He takes up the saw again; again it moves up and down, in and out of that unhurried imperviousness as a piston moves in the oil; soaked, scrawny, tireless, with the lean light body of a boy or an old man. Pa watches him, blinking, his face streaming; again he looks up at the sky with that expression of dumb and brooding outrage and yet of vindication, as though he had expected no less; now and then he stirs, moves, gaunt and streaming, picking up a board or a tool and then laying it down. Vernon Tull is there now, and Cash is wearing Mrs. Tull's raincoat and he and Vernon are hunting the saw. After a while they find it in pa's hand.

"Why don't you go on to the house, out of the rain?" Cash says. Pa looks at him, his face streaming slowly. It is as though upon a face carved by a savage caricaturist a monstrous burlesque of all bereavement flowed. "You go on in," Cash says. "Me and Vernon can finish it."

Pa looks at them. The sleeves of Jewel's coat are too short for him. Upon his face the rain streams, slow as cold glycerine. "I don't begrudge her the wetting," he says. He moves again and falls to shifting the planks, picking them up, laying them down again carefully, as though they are glass. He goes to the lantern and pulls at the propped raincoat until he knocks it down and Cash comes and fixes it back.

"You get on to the house," Cash says. He leads pa to the house and returns with the raincoat and folds it and places it beneath the shelter where the lantern sits. Vernon has not stopped. He looks up, still sawing.

"You ought to done that at first," he says. "You knowed it was fixing to rain."

"It's his fever," Cash says. He looks at the board.

"Ay," Vernon says. "He'd a come, anyway."

Cash squints at the board. On the long flank of it the rain crashes steadily, myriad, fluctuant. "I'm going to bevel it," he says.

"It'll take more time," Vernon says. Cash sets the plank on edge; a moment longer Vernon watches him, then he hands him the plane.

Vernon holds the board steady while Cash bevels the edge of it with the tedious and minute care of a jeweller. Mrs. Tull comes to the edge of the porch and calls Vernon. "How near are you done?" she says.

Vernon does not look up. "Not long. Some, yet."

She watches Cash stooping at the plank, the turgid savage gleam of the lantern slicking on the raincoat as he moves. "You go down and get some planks off the barn and finish it and come in out of the rain," she says. "You'll both catch your death." Vernon does not move. "Vernon," she says.

"We won't be long," he says. "We'll be done after a spell." Mrs. Tull watches them a while. Then she re-enters the house.

"If we get in a tight, we could take some of them planks," Vernon says. "I'll help you put them back."

Cash ceases the plane and squints along the plank, wiping it with his palm. "Give me the next one," he says.

Some time toward dawn the rain ceases. But it is not yet day when Cash drives the last nail and stands stiffly up and looks down at the finished coffin, the others watching him. In the lantern-light his face is calm, musing; slowly he strokes his hands on his raincoat thighs in a gesture deliberate, final and composed. Then the four of them—Cash and pa and Vernon and Peabody —raise the coffin to their shoulders and turn toward the house. It is light, yet they move slowly; empty, yet they carry it carefully; lifeless, yet they move with hushed precautionary words to one another, speaking of it as though, complete, it now slumbered lightly alive, wait-ing to come awake. On the dark floor their feet clump awkwardly, as though for a long time they have not walked on floors.

They set it down by the bed. Peabody says quietly: "Let's eat a snack. It's almost daylight. Where's Cash?"

He has returned to the trestles, stooped again in the lantern's feeble glare as he gathers up his tools and wipes them on a cloth carefully and puts them into the box with its leather sling to go over the shoulder. Then he takes up box, lantern and raincoat and returns to the house, mounting the steps into faint silhouette against the paling east.

In a strange room you must empty yourself for sleep. And before you are emptied for sleep, what are you. And when you are emptied for sleep, you are not. And when you are filled with sleep, you never were. I don't know what I am. I don't know if I am or not. Jewel knows he is, because he does not know that he does not know whether he is or not. He cannot empty himself for sleep because he is not what he is and he is what he is not. Beyond the unlamped wall I can hear the rain shaping the wagon that is ours, the load that is no longer theirs that felled and sawed it nor yet theirs that bought it and which is not ours either, lie on our wagon though it does, since only the wind and the rain shape it only to Jewel and me, that are not asleep. And since sleep is is-not and rain and wind are *was*, it is not. Yet the wagon *is*, because when the wagon is *was*, Addie Bundren will not be. And Jewel *is*, so Addie Bundren must be. And then I must be, or I could not empty myself for sleep in a strange room. And so if I am not emptied yet, I am *is*.

How often have I lain beneath rain on a strange roof, thinking of home.

CASH

I MADE IT ON THE BEVEL.

1. There is more surface for the nails to grip.
2. There is twice the gripping-surface to each seam.
3. The water will have to seep into it on a slant. Water moves easiest up and down or straight across.
4. In a house people are upright two-thirds of the time. So the seams and joints are made up-and-down. Because the stress is up-and-down.
5. In a bed where people lie down all the time, the joints and seams are made sideways, because the stress is sideways.
6. Except.
7. A body is not square like a cross-tie.
8. Animal magnetism.
9. The animal magnetism of a dead body makes the stress come slanting, so the seams and joints of a coffin are made on the bevel.
10. You can see by an old grave that the earth sinks down on the bevel.
11. While in a natural hole it sinks by the centre, the stress being up-and-down.
12. So I made it on the bevel.
13. It makes a neater job.

VARDAMAN

MY MOTHER IS A FISH.

TULL

IT WAS TEN O'CLOCK WHEN I GOT BACK, WITH PEABODY'S team hitched on to the back of the wagon. They had already dragged the buckboard back from where Quick found it upside down straddle of the ditch about a mile from the spring. It was pulled out of the road at the spring, and about a dozen wagons was already there. It was Quick found it. He said the river was up and still rising. He said it had already covered the highest watermark on the bridge-piling he had ever seen. "That bridge won't stand a whole lot of water," I said. "Has somebody told Anse about it?"

"I told him," Quick said. "He says he reckons them boys has heard and unloaded and are on the way back by now. He says they can load up and get across."

"He better go on and bury her at New Hope," Armstid said. "That bridge is old. I wouldn't monkey with it."

"His mind is set on taking her to Jefferson," Quick said.

"Then he better get at it soon as he can," Armstid said.

Anse meets us at the door. He has shaved, but not good. There is a long cut on his jaw, and he is wearing his Sunday pants and a white shirt with the neckband buttoned. It is drawn smooth over his hump, making it look bigger than ever, like a white shirt will, and his face is different too. He looks folks in the eye now, dignified, his face tragic and composed, shaking us by the hand as we walk up on to the porch and scrape our shoes, a little stiff in our Sunday clothes, our Sunday clothes rustling, not looking full at him as he meets us.

"The Lord giveth," we say.

"The Lord giveth."

That boy is not there. Peabody told about how he come into the kitchen, hollering, swarming and clawing at Cora when he found her cooking that fish, and how Dewey Dell taken him down to the barn. "My team all right?" Peabody says.

"All right," I tell him. "I give them a bait this morning. Your buggy seems all right too. It ain't hurt."

"And no fault of somebody's," he says. "I'd give a nickel to know where that boy was when that team broke away."

"If it's broke anywhere, I'll fix it," I say.

The women folks go on into the house. We can hear them, talking and fanning. The fans go whish, whish, whish and them talking, the talking sounding kind of like bees murmuring in a water-bucket. The men stop on the porch, talking some, not looking at one another.

"Howdy, Vernon," they say. "Howdy, Tull."

"Looks like more rain."

"It does for a fact."

"Yes, sir. It will rain some more."

"It come up quick."

"And going away slow. It don't fail."

I go around to the back. Cash is filling up the holes
he bored in the top of it. He is trimming out plugs for
them, one at a time, the wood wet and hard to work.
He could cut up a tin can and hide the holes and nobody wouldn't know the difference. Wouldn't mind,
anyway. I have seen him spend a hour trimming out
a wedge like it was glass he was working, when he
could have reached around and picked up a dozen
sticks and drove them into the joint and made it do.

When we finished I go back to the front. The men
have gone a little piece from the house, sitting on the
ends of the boards and on the saw-horses where we
made it last night, some sitting and some squatting.
Whitfield ain't come yet.

They look up at me, their eyes asking.

"It's about," I say. "He's ready to nail."

While they are getting up Anse comes to the door
and looks at us and we return to the porch. We scrape
our shoes again, careful, waiting for one another to go
in first, milling a little at the door. Anse stands inside
the door, dignified, composed. He waves us in and leads
the way into the room.

They had laid her in it reversed. Cash made it clock-
shape, like this   with every joint and seam
bevelled and   scrubbed with the plane,
tight as a drum and neat as a sewing basket, and they
had laid her in it head to foot so it wouldn't crush her
dress. It was her wedding dress and it had a flare-out bottom, and they had laid her head to foot in it so the dress
could spread out, and they had made her a veil out of

a mosquito bar so the auger holes in her face wouldn't show.

When we are going out, Whitfield comes. He is wet and muddy to the waist, coming in. "The Lord comfort this house," he says. "I was late because the bridge has gone. I went down to the old ford and swum my horse over, the Lord protecting me. His grace be upon this house."

We go back to the trestles and plank-ends and sit or squat.

"I knowed it would go," Armstid says.

"It's been there a long time, that ere bridge," Quick says.

"The Lord has kept it there, you mean," Uncle Billy says. "I don't know ere a man that's touched hammer to it in twenty-five years."

"How long has it been there, Uncle Billy?" Quick says.

"It was built in . . . let me see . . . It was in the year 1888," Uncle Billy says. "I mind it because the first man to cross it was Peabody coming to my house when Jody was born."

"If I'd crossed it every time your wife littered since, it'd a been wore out long before this, Billy," Peabody says.

We laugh, suddenly loud, then suddenly quiet again. We look a little aside at one another.

"Lots of folks has crossed it that won't cross no more bridges," Houston says.

"It's a fact," Littlejohn says. "It's so."

"One more ain't, no ways," Armstid says. "It'd taken them two-three days to got her to town in the wagon. They'd be gone a week, getting her to Jefferson and back."

"What's Anse so itching to take her to Jefferson for, anyway?" Houston says.

"He promised her," I say. "She wanted it. She come from there. Her mind was set on it."

"And Anse is set on it, too," Quick says.

"Ay," Uncle Billy says. "It's like a man that's let everything slide all his life to get set on something that will make the most trouble for everybody he knows."

"Well, it'll take the Lord to get her over that river now," Peabody says. "Anse can't do it."

"And I reckon He will," Quick says. "He's took care of Anse a long time, now."

"It's a fact," Littlejohn says.

"Too long to quit now," Armstid says.

"I reckon He's like everybody else around here," Uncle Billy says. "He's done it so long now He can't quit."

Cash comes out. He has put on a clean shirt; his hair, wet, is combed smooth down on his brow, smooth and black as if he had painted it on to his head. He squats stiffly among us, we watching him.

"You feeling this weather, ain't you?" Armstid says.

Cash says nothing.

"A broke bone always feels it," Littlejohn says. "A fellow with a broke bone can tell it a-coming."

"Lucky Cash got off with just a broke leg," Armstid says. "He might have hurt himself bedrid. How far'd you fall, Cash?"

"Twenty-eight foot, four and a half inches, about," Cash says. I move over beside him.

"A fellow can sho slip quick on wet planks," Quick says.

"It's too bad," I say. "But you couldn't a holp it."

"It's them durn women," he says. "I made it to balance with her. I made it to her measure and weight."

*If it takes wet boards for folks to fall, it's fixing to be
lots of falling before this spell is done.*

"You couldn't have holp it," I say.

*I don't mind the folks falling. It's the cotton and corn I
mind.*

*Neither does Peabody mind the folks falling. How
'bout it, Doc?*

*It's a fact. Washed clean outen the ground it will be.
Seems like something is always happening to it.*

*'Course it does. That's why it's worth anything. If noth-
ing didn't happen and everybody made a big crop, do
you reckon it would be worth the raising?*

*Well, I be durn if I like to see my work washed outen
the ground, work I sweat over.*

*It's a fact. A fellow wouldn't mind seeing it washed
up if he could just turn on the rain himself.*

*Who is that man can do that? Where is the colour of
his eyes?*

*Ay. The Lord made it to grow. It's Hisn to wash up
if He sees it fitten so.*

"You couldn't have holp it," I say.

"It's them durn women," he says.

In the house the women begin to sing. We hear the
first line commence, beginning to swell as they take hold,
and we rise and move toward the door, taking off our
hats and throwing our chews away. We do not go in. We
stop at the steps, clumped, holding our hats between our
lax hands in front or behind, standing with one foot advanced and our heads lowered, looking aside, down at
our hats in our hands and at the earth or now and then
at the sky and at one another's grave, composed face.

The song ends; the voices quaver away with a rich and
dying fall. Whitfield begins. His voice is bigger than him.

It's like they are not the same. It's like he is one, and his voice is one, swimming on two horses side by side across the ford and coming into the house, the mud-splashed one and the one that never even got wet, triumphant and sad. Somebody in the house begins to cry. It sounds like her eyes and her voice were turned back inside her, listening; we move, shifting to the other leg, meeting one another's eye and making like they hadn't touched.

Whitfield stops at last. The women sing again. In the thick air it's like their voices come out of the air, flowing together and on in the sad, comforting tunes. When they cease it's like they hadn't gone away. It's like they had just disappeared into the air and when we moved we would loose them again out of the air around us, sad and comforting. Then they finish and we put on our hats, our movements stiff, like we hadn't never wore hats before.

On the way home Cora is still singing. "I am bounding toward my God and my reward," she sings, sitting on the wagon, the shawl around her shoulders and the umbrella open over her, though it is not raining.

"She has hern," I say. "Wherever she went, she has her reward in being free of Anse Bundren." *She laid there three days in that box, waiting for Darl and Jewel to come clean back home and get a new wheel and go back to where the wagon was in the ditch. Take my team, Anse, I said.*

We'll wait for ourn, he said. She'll want it so. She was ever a particular woman.

On the third day they got back and they loaded her into the wagon and started and it already too late. You'll have to go all the way round by Samson's bridge. It'll take you a day to get there. Then you'll be forty miles from Jefferson. Take my team, Anse.

We'll wait for ourn. She'll want it so.

It was about a mile from the house we saw him, sitting on the edge of the slough. It hadn't had a fish in it never that I knowed. He looked around at us, his eyes round and calm, his face dirty, the pole across his knees. Cora was still singing.

"This ain't no good day to fish," I said. "You come on home with us and me and you'll go down to the river first thing in the morning and catch some fish."

"It's one in here," he said. "Dewey Dell seen it."

"You come on with us. The river's the best place."

"It's in here," he said. "Dewey Dell seen it."

"I'm bounding toward my God and my reward," Cora sung.

DARL

"IT'S NOT YOUR HORSE THAT'S DEAD, JEWEL," I SAY. HE SITS erect on the seat, leaning a little forward, wooden-backed. The brim of his hat has soaked free of the crown in two places, drooping across his wooden face so that, head lowered, he looks through it like through the visor of a helmet, looking long across the valley to where the barn leans against the bluff, shaping the invisible horse. "See then?" I say. High above the house, against the quick thick sky, they hang in narrowing circles. From here they are no more than specks, implacable, patient, portentous. "But it's not your horse that's dead."

"Goddamn you," he says. "Goddamn you."

I cannot love my mother because I have no mother. Jewel's mother is a horse.

Motionless, the tall buzzards hang in soaring circles, the clouds giving them an illusion of retrograde.

Motionless, wooden-backed, wooden-faced, he shapes the horse in a rigid stoop like a hawk, hook-winged. They are waiting for us, ready for the moving of it, waiting for him. He enters the stall and waits until it kicks at him so that he can slip past and mount on to the trough and pause, peering out across the intervening stall-tops toward the empty path, before he reaches into the loft.

"Goddamn him. Goddamn him."

CASH

I T WON'T BALANCE. IF YOU WANT TO TOTE AND RIDE ON a balance, we will have——"

"Pick up. Goddamn you, pick up."

"I'm telling you it won't tote and it won't ride on a balance unless——"

"Pick up! Pick up, goddamn your thick-nosed soul to hell, pick up!"

It won't balance. If they want it to tote and ride on a balance, they will have——

DARL

HE STOOPS AMONG US ABOVE IT, TWO OF THE EIGHT hands. In his face the blood goes in waves. In between them his flesh is greenish looking, about that smooth, thick, pale green of cow's cud; his face suffocated, furious, his lip lifted upon his teeth. "Pick up!" he says. "Pick up, goddamn your thick-nosed soul!"

He heaves, lifting one whole side so suddenly that we all spring into the lift to catch and balance it before he hurls it completely over. For an instant it resists, as though volitional. as though within it her pole-thin body clings furiously, even though dead, to a sort of modesty, as she would have tried to conceal a soiled garment that she could not prevent her body soiling. Then it breaks free, rising suddenly as though the emaciation of her body had added buoyancy to the planks or as though, seeing that the garment was about to be torn from her, she rushes suddenly after it in a passionate reversal that flouts its own desire and need. Jewel's face goes completely green and I can hear teeth in his breath.

We carry it down the hall, our feet harsh and clumsy on the floor, moving with shuffling steps, and through the door.

"Steady it a minute, now," pa says, letting to. He turns back to shut and lock the door, but Jewel will no. wait.

"Come on," he says in that suffocating voice. "Come on."

We lower it carefully down the steps. We move, balancing it as though it were something infinitely precious, our faces averted, breathing through our teeth to keep our nostrils closed. We go down the path, toward the slope.

"We better wait," Cash says. "I tell you it ain't balanced now. We'll need another hand on that hill."

"Then turn loose," Jewel says. He will not stop. Cash begins to fall behind, hobbling to keep up, breathing harshly; then he is distanced and Jewel carries the entire front end alone, so that, tilting as the path begins to slant, it begins to rush away from me and slip down the air like a sled upon invisible snow, smoothly evacuating atmosphere in which the sense of it is still shaped.

"Wait, Jewel," I say. But he will not wait. He is almost running now and Cash is left behind. It seems to me that the end which I now carry alone has no weight, as though it coasts like a rushing straw upon the furious tide of Jewel's despair. I am not even touching it, when, turning, he lets it overshoot him, swinging, and stops it and sloughs it into the wagon-bed in the same motion and looks back at me, his face suffused with fury and despair.

"Goddamn you. Goddamn you."

VARDAMAN

WE ARE GOING TO TOWN. DEWEY DELL SAYS IT WON'T be sold because it belongs to Santa Claus and he has taken it back with him until next Christmas. Then it will be behind the glass again, shining with waiting.

Pa and Cash are coming down the hill, but Jewel is going to the barn. "Jewel," pa says. Jewel does not stop. "Where are you going?" pa says. But Jewel does not stop. "You leave that horse here," pa says. Jewel stops and looks at pa. Jewel's eyes look like marbles. "You leave that horse here," pa says. "We'll all go in the wagon with ma, like she wanted."

But my mother is a fish. Vernon seen it. He was there.

"Jewel's mother is a horse," Darl said.

"Then mine can be a fish, can't it, Darl?" I said.

Jewel is my brother.

"Then mine will have to be a horse, too," I said.

"Why?" Darl said. "If pa is your pa, why does your ma have to be a horse just because Jewel's is?"

"Why does it?" I said. "Why does it, Darl?"

Darl is my brother.

"Then what is your ma, Darl?" I said.

"I haven't got ere one," Darl said. "Because if I had one, it is *was*. And if it is was, it can't be *is*. Can it?"

"No," I said.

"Then I am not," Darl said. "Am I?"

"No," I said.

I am. Darl is my brother.

"But you *are*, Darl," I said.

"I know it," Darl said. "That's why I am not *is*. *Are* is too many for one woman to foal."

Cash is carrying his tool-box. Pa looks at him. "I'll stop at Tull's on the way back," Cash says. "Get on that barn roof."

"It ain't respectful," pa says. "It's a deliberate flouting of her and of me."

"Do you want him to come all the way back here and carry them up to Tull's afoot?" Darl says. Pa looks at

Darl, his mouth chewing. Pa shaves every day now because my mother is a fish.

"It ain't right," pa says.

Dewey Dell has the package in her hand. She has the
basket with our dinner too.

"What's that?" pa says.

"Mrs. Tull's cakes," Dewey Dell says, getting into the
wagon. "I'm taking them to town for her."

"It ain't right," pa says. "It's a flouting of the dead."

It'll be there. It'll be there come Christmas, she says,
shining on the track. She says he won't sell it to no town
boys.

DARL

H E GOES ON TOWARD THE BARN, ENTERING THE LOT,
wooden-backed.

Dewey Dell carries the basket on one arm, in the other
hand something wrapped square in a newspaper. Her
face is calm and sullen, her eyes brooding and alert;
within them I can see Peabody's back like two round
peas in two thimbles: perhaps in Peabody's back two of
those worms which work surreptitious and steady
through you and out the other side and you waking suddenly from sleep or from waking, with on your face an
expression sudden, intent, and concerned. She sets the
basket into the wagon and climbs in, her leg coming long
from beneath her tightening dress: that lever which

moves the world; one of that caliper which measures the length and breadth of life. She sits on the seat beside Vardaman and sets the parcel on her lap.

Then he enters the barn. He has not looked back.

"It ain't right," pa says. "It's little enough for him to do for her."

"Go on," Cash says. "Leave him stay if he wants. He'll be all right here. Maybe he'll go up to Tull's and stay."

"He'll catch us," I say. "He'll cut across and meet us at Tull's lane."

"He would have rid that horse, too," pa says, "if I hadn't a stopped him. A durn spotted critter wilder than a cattymount. A deliberate flouting of her and of me."

The wagon moves; the mules' ears begin to bob. Behind us, above the house, motionless in tall and soaring circles, they diminish and disappear.

ANSE

I TOLD HIM NOT TO BRING THAT HORSE OUT OF RESPECT for his dead ma, because it wouldn't look right, him prancing along on a durn circus animal and her wanting us all to be in the wagon with her that sprung from her flesh and blood, but we hadn't no more than passed Tull's lane when Darl begun to laugh. Setting back there on the plank seat with Cash, with his dead ma lying in her coffin at his feet, laughing. How many times I told him it's doing such things as that that makes folks talk about him,

I don't know. I says I got some regard for what folks say
about my flesh and blood even if you haven't, even if I
have raised such a durn passel of boys, and when you
fixes it so folks can say such about you, it's a reflection
on your ma, I says, not me: I am a man and I can stand
it; it's on your womenfolks, your ma and sister that you
should care for, and I turned and looked back at him setting there, laughing.

"I don't expect you to have no respect for me," I says.
"But with your own ma not cold in her coffin yet."

"Yonder," Cash says, jerking his head toward the lane.
The horse is still a right smart piece away, coming up at
a good pace, but I don't have to be told who it is. I just
looked back at Darl, setting there laughing.

"I done my best," I says. "I tried to do as she would
wish it. The Lord will pardon me and excuse the conduct of them He sent me." And Darl setting on the plank
seat right above her where she was laying, laughing.

DARL

HE COMES UP THE LANE FAST, YET WE ARE THREE HUN-
dred yards beyond the mouth of it when he turns
into the road, the mud flying beneath the flickering drive
of the hooves. Then he slows a little, light and erect in
the saddle, the horse mincing through the mud.

Tull is in his lot. He looks at us, lifts his hand. We go

on, the wagon creaking, the mud whispering on the wheels. Vernon still stands there. He watches Jewel as he passes, the horse moving with a light, high-kneed driving gait, three hundred yards back. We go on, with a motion so soporific, so dreamlike as to be uninferant of progress, as though time and not space were decreasing between us and it.

It turns off at right angles, the wheel-marks of last Sunday healed away now: a smooth, red scoriation curving away into the pines; a white signboard with faded lettering: New Hope Church. 3 mi. It wheels up like a motionless hand lifted above the profound desolation of the ocean; beyond it the red road lies like a spoke of which Addie Bundren is the rim. It wheels past, empty, unscarred, the white signboard turns away its fading and tranquil assertion. Cash looks up the road quietly, his head turning as we pass it like an owl's head, his face composed. Pa looks straight ahead, humped. Dewey Dell looks at the road too, then she looks back at me, her eyes watchful and repudiant, not like that question which was in those of Cash, for a smouldering while. The signboard passes; the unscarred road wheels on. Then Dewey Dell turns her head. The wagon creaks on.

Cash spits over the wheel. "In a couple of days now it'll be smelling," he says.

"You might tell Jewel that," I say.

He is motionless now, sitting the horse at the junction, upright, watching us, no less still than the signboard that lifts its fading capitulation opposite him.

"It ain't balanced right for no long ride," Cash says.

"Tell him that, too," I say. The wagon creaks on.

A mile farther along he passes us, the horse, archnecked, reined back to a swift single-foot. He sits lightly, poised, upright, wooden-faced in the saddle, the

broken hat raked at a swaggering angle. He passes us
swiftly, without looking at us, the horse driving, its
hooves hissing in the mud. A gout of mud, back-flung,
plops on to the box. Cash leans forward and takes a tool
from his box and removes it carefully. When the road
crosses Whiteleaf, the willows leaning near enough, he
breaks off a branch and scours at the stain with the wet
leaves.

ANSE

I₁'S A HARD COUNTRY ON MAN; IT'S HARD. EIGHT MILES OF
the sweat of his body washed up outen the Lord's
earth, where the Lord Himself told him to put it. Nowhere in this sinful world can a honest, hard-working
man profit. It takes them that runs the stores in the
towns, doing no sweating, living off of them that sweats.
It ain't the hard-working man, the farmer. Sometimes I
wonder why we keep at it. It's because there is a reward
for us above, where they can't take their motors and
such. Every man will be equal there and it will be taken
from them that have and give to them that have not by
the Lord.

But it's a long wait, seems like. It's bad that a fellow
must earn the reward of his right-doing by flouting hisself and his dead. We drove all the rest of the day and
got to Samson's at dust-dark and then that bridge was
gone, too. They hadn't never seen the river so high, and

it's not done raining yet. There was old men that hadn't never seen nor heard of it being so in the memory of man. I am chosen of the Lord, for who He loveth, so doeth He chastiseth. But I be durn if He don't take some curious ways to show it, seems like.

But now I can get them teeth. That will be a comfort It will.

SAMSON

IT WAS JUST BEFORE SUNDOWN. WE WERE SITTING ON THE porch when the wagon came up the road with the five of them in it and the other one on the horse behind. One of them raised his hand, but they was going on past the store without stopping.

"Who's that?" MacCallum says: I can't think of his name: Rafe's twin; that one it was.

"It's Bundren, from down beyond New Hope," Quick says. "There's one of them Snopes horses Jewel's riding."

"I didn't know there was ere a one of them horses left," MacCallum says. "I thought you folks down there finally contrived to give them all away."

"Try and get that one," Quick says. The wagon went on.

"I bet old man Lon never gave it to him," I says.

"No," Quick says. "He bought it from pappy." The wagon went on. "They must not a heard about the bridge," he says.

"What're they doing up here, anyway?" MacCallum says.

"Taking a holiday since he got his wife buried, I reckon," Quick says. "Heading for town, I reckon, with Tull's bridge gone too. I wonder if they ain't heard about the bridge."

"They'll have to fly, then," I says. "I don't reckon there's ere a bridge between here and Mouth of Ishatawa."

They had something in the wagon. But Quick had been to the funeral three days ago and we naturally never thought anything about it except that they were heading away from home mighty late and that they hadn't heard about the bridge. "You better holler at them," MacCallum says. Durn it, the name is right on the tip of my tongue. So Quick hollered and they stopped and he went to the wagon and told them.

He come back with them. "They're going to Jefferson," he says. "The bridge at Tull's is gone, too." Like we didn't know it, and his face looked funny, around the nostrils, but they just sat there, Bundren and the girl and the chap on the seat, and Cash and the second one, the one folks talks about, on a plank across the tail-gate, and the other one on that spotted horse. But I reckon they was used to it by then because when I said to Cash that they'd have to pass by New Hope again and what they'd better do, he just says,

"I reckon we can get there."

I ain't much for meddling. Let every man run his own business to suit himself, I say. But after I talked to Rachel about them not having a regular man to fix her and it being July and all, I went back down to the barn and tried to talk to Bundren about it.

"I give her my promise," he says. "Her mind was set on it."

I notice how it takes a lazy man, a man that hates moving, to get set on moving once he does get started off, the same as he was set on staying still, like it ain't the moving he hates so much as the starting and stopping. And like he would be kind of proud of whatever come up to make the moving or the setting still look hard. He set there on the wagon, hunched up, blinking, listening to us tell about how quick the bridge went and how high the water was, and I be durn if he didn't act like he was proud of it, like he had made the river rise himself.

"You say it's higher than you ever see it before?" he says. "God's will be done," he says. "I reckon it won't go down much by morning, neither," he says.

"You better stay here tonight," I says, "and get a early start for New Hope tomorrow morning." I was just sorry for them bone-gaunted mules. I told Rachel, I says, "Well, would you have had me turn them away at dark, eight miles from home? What else could I do," I says. "It won't be but one night, and they'll keep it in the barn, and they'll sholy get started by daylight." And so I says, "You stay here tonight and early tomorrow you can go back to New Hope. I got tools enough, and the boys can go on right after supper and have it dug and ready if they want," and then I found that girl watching me. If her eyes had a been pistols, I wouldn't be talking now. I be dog if they didn't blaze at me. And so when I went down to the barn I come on them, her talking so she never noticed when I come up.

"You promised her," she says. "She wouldn't go until you promised. She thought she could depend on you. If you don't do it, it will be a curse on you."

"Can't no man say I don't aim to keep my word," Bundren says. "My heart is open to ere a man."

"I don't care what your heart is," she says. She was

whispering, kind of, talking fast. "You promised her. You've got to. You——" Then she seen me and quit, standing there. If they'd been pistols, I wouldn't be talking now. So when I talked to him about it, he says,

"I give her my promise. Her mind is set on it."

"But seems to me she'd rather have her ma buried close by, so she could——"

"It's Addie I give the promise to," he says. "Her mind is set on it."

So I told them to drive it into the barn because it was threatening rain again, and that supper was about ready. Only they didn't want to come in.

"I thank you," Bundren says. "We wouldn't discommode you. We got a little something in the basket. We can make out."

"Well," I says, "since you are so particular about your womenfolks, I am too. And when folks stops with us at meal-time and won't come to the table, my wife takes it as a insult."

So the girl went on to the kitchen to help Rachel. And then Jewel come to me.

"Sho," I says. "Help yourself outen the loft. Feed him when you bait the mules."

"I rather pay you for him," he says.

"What for?" I says. "I wouldn't begrudge no man a bait for his horse."

"I rather pay you," he says; I thought he said extra.

"Extra for what?" I says. "Won't he eat hay and corn?"

"Extra feed," he says. "I feed him a little extra and I don't want him beholden to no man."

"You can't buy no feed from me, boy," I says. "And if he can eat that loft clean, I'll help you load the barn on to the wagon in the morning."

"He ain't never been beholden to no man," he says. "I rather pay you for it."

And if I had my rathers, you wouldn't be here a-tall, I wanted to say. But I just says, "Then it's high time he commenced. You can't buy no feed from me."

When Rachel put supper on, her and the girl went and fixed some beds. But wouldn't any of them come in. "She's been dead long enough to get over that sort of foolishness," I says. Because I got just as much respect for the dead as ere a man, but you've got to respect the dead themselves, and a woman that's been dead in a box four days, the best way to respect her is to get her into the ground as quick as you can. But they wouldn't do it.

"It wouldn't be right," Bundren says. "Course, if the boys wants to go to bed, I reckon I can set up with her. I don't begrudge her it."

So when I went back down there they were squatting on the ground around the wagon, all of them. "Let that chap come to the house and get some sleep, anyway," I says. "And you better come too," I says to the girl. I wasn't aiming to interfere with them. And I sholy hadn't done nothing to her that I knowed.

"He's done already asleep," Bundren says. They had done put him to bed in the trough in a empty stall.

"Well, you come on, then," I says to her. But still she never said nothing. They just squatted there. You couldn't hardly see them. "How about you boys?" I says. "You got a full day tomorrow." After a while Cash says,

"I thank you. We can make out."

"We wouldn't be beholden," Bundren says. "I thank you kindly."

So I left them squatting there. I reckon after four days they was used to it. But Rachel wasn't.

"It's an outrage," she says. "An outrage."

"What could he 'a' done?" I says. "He give her his promised word."

"Who's talking about him?" she says. "Who cares about him?" she says, crying. "I just wish that you and him and all the men in the world that torture us alive and flout us dead, dragging us up and down the country——"

"Now, now," I says. "You're upset."

"Don't you touch me!" she says. "Don't you touch me!"

A man can't tell nothing about them. I lived with the same one fifteen years and I be durn if I can. And I imagined a lot of things coming up between us, but I be durn if I ever thought it would be a body four days dead and that a woman. But they make life hard on them not taking it as it comes up, like a man does.

So I laid there, hearing it commence to rain, thinking about them down there, squatting around the wagon and the rain on the roof, and thinking about Rachel crying there until after a while it was like I could still hear her crying even after she was asleep, and smelling it even when I knowed I couldn't. I couldn't decide even then whether I could or not, or if it wasn't just knowing it was what it was.

So next morning I never went down there. I heard them hitching up and then when I knowed they must be about ready to take out, I went out the front and went down the road toward the bridge until I heard the wagon come out of the lot and go back toward New Hope. And then when I come back to the house, Rachel jumped on me because I wasn't there to make them come in to breakfast. You can't tell about them. Just about when you decide they mean one thing, I be durn if you not only haven't got to change your mind, like as not you got to take a raw-hiding for thinking they meant it.

But it was still like I could smell it. And so I decided then that it wasn't smelling it, but it was just knowing it was there, like you will get fooled now and then. But when I went to the barn I knew different. When I walked into the hallway I saw something. It kind of hunkered up when I come in and I thought at first it was one of them got left, then I saw what it was. It was a buzzard. It looked around and saw me and went on down the hall, spraddle-legged, with its wings kind of hunkered out, watching me first over one shoulder and then over the other, like a old bald-headed man. When it got outdoors it begun to fly. It had to fly a long time before it ever got up into the air, with it thick and heavy and full of rain like it was.

If they was bent on going to Jefferson, I reckon they could have gone around up by Mount Vernon, like Mac-Callum did. He'll get home about day after tomorrow, horse-back. Then they'd be just eighteen miles from town. But maybe this bridge being gone too has learned him the Lord's sense and judgment.

That MacCallum. He's been trading with me off and on for twelve years. I have known him from a boy up; know his name as well as I do my own. But be durn if I can say it.

DEWEY DELL

THE SIGNBOARD COMES IN SIGHT. IT IS LOOKING OUT AT the road now, because it can wait. New Hope. 3 mi. it will say. New Hope. 3 mi. New Hope. 3 mi. And then the road will begin, curving away into the trees, empty with waiting, saying New Hope three miles.

I heard that my mother is dead. I wish I had time to let her die. I wish I had time to wish I had. It is because in the wild and outraged earth too soon too soon too soon. It's not that I wouldn't and will not it's that it is too soon too soon too soon.

Now it begins to say it. New Hope three miles. New Hope three miles. *That's what they mean by the womb of time: the agony and the despair of spreading bones, the hard girdle in which lie the outraged entrails of events.* Cash's head turns slowly as we approach, his pale, empty, sad, composed and questioning face following the red and empty curve; beside the back wheel Jewel sits the horse, gazing straight ahead.

The land runs out of Darl's eyes; they swim to pinpoints. They begin at my feet and rise along my body to my face, and then my dress is gone: I sit naked on the seat above the unhurrying mules, above the travail. *Suppose I tell him to turn. He will do what I say. Don't you know he will do what I say?* Once I waked with a black void rushing under me. I could not see. I saw Vardaman rise and go to the window and strike the knife into the fish, the blood gushing, hissing like steam but I could not see. *He'll do as I say. He always does. I can persuade him to anything. You know I can. Suppose I say Turn here.* That was when I died that time. *Suppose I do. We'll go to New Hope. We won't have to go to town.* I rose and took the knife from the streaming fish still hissing and I killed Darl.

When I used to sleep with Vardaman I had a nightmare once I thought I was awake but I couldn't see and couldn't feel the bed under me and I couldn't think what I was I couldn't think of my name I couldn't even think I am a girl I couldn't even think I nor even think I want to wake up nor remember what was opposite to awake so I could do that I knew that something was passing but I couldn't even think of time then all of a sudden I knew that something was it was wind blowing over me it was like the wind came and blew me back from where it was I was not blowing the room and Vardaman asleep and all of them back under me again and going on like a piece of cool silk dragging across my naked legs.

It blows cool out of the pines, a sad steady sound. New Hope. Was 3 mi. Was 3 mi. I believe in God I believe in God.

"Why didn't we go to New Hope, pa?" Vardaman says. "Mr. Samson said we was, but we done passed the road."

Darl says, "Look, Jewel." But he is not looking at me. He is looking at the sky. The buzzard is as still as if he were nailed to it.

We turn into Tull's lane. We pass the barn and go on, the wheels whispering in the mud, passing the green rows of cotton in the wild earth, and Vernon little across the field behind the plough. He lifts his hand as we pass and stands there looking after us for a long while.

"Look, Jewel," Darl says. Jewel sits on his horse like

they were both made out of wood, looking straight ahead.

I believe in God, God. God, I believe in God.

TULL

AFTER THEY PASSED I TAKEN THE MULE OUT AND LOOPED up the trace chains and followed. They were setting in the wagon at the end of the levee. Anse was setting there, looking at the bridge where it was swagged down into the river with just the two ends in sight. He was looking at it like he had believed all the time that folks had been lying to him about it being gone, but like he was hoping all the time it really was. Kind of pleased astonishment he looked, setting on the wagon in his Sunday pants, mumbling his mouth. Looking like a uncurried horse dressed up: I don't know.

The boy was watching the bridge where it was midsunk and logs and such drifted up over it and it swagging and shivering like the whole thing would go any minute, big-eyed he was watching it, like he was to a circus. And the gal, too. When I come up she looked around at me, her eyes kind of blaring up and going hard like I had made to touch her. Then she looked at Anse again and then back at the water again.

It was nigh up to the levee on both sides, the earth hid except for the tongue of it we was on going out to the bridge and then down into the water, and except for knowing how the road and the bridge used to look, a fellow couldn't tell where was the river and where the land. It was just a tangle of yellow and the levee not less wider than a knife-back kind of, with us setting in the wagon and on the horse and the mule.

Darl was looking at me, and then Cash turned and looked at me with that look in his eyes like when he was figuring on whether the planks would fit her that night, like he was measuring them inside of him and not asking you to say what you thought and not even letting on he was listening if you did say it, but listening all right. Jewel hadn't moved. He sat there on the horse, leaning a little forward, with that same look on his face when him and Darl passed the house yesterday, coming back to get her.

"If it was just up, we could drive across," Anse says. "We could drive right on across it."

Sometimes a log would get shoved over the jam and float on, rolling and turning, and we could watch it go on to where the ford used to be. It would slow up and whirl crossways and hang out of water for a minute, and you could tell by that that the ford used to be there.

"But that don't show nothing," I say. "It could be a bar of quicksand built up there." We watch the log. Then the gal is looking at me again.

"Mr. Whitfield crossed it," she says.

"He was a horse-back," I say. "And three days ago. It's riz five foot since."

"If the bridge was just up," Anse says.

The log bobs up and goes on again. There is a lot of trash and foam, and you can hear the water.

"But it's down," Anse says.

Cash says, "A careful fellow could walk across yonder on the planks and logs."

"But you couldn't tote nothing," I say. "Likely time you set foot on that mess, it'll all go, too. What you think, Darl?"

He is looking at me. He don't say nothing; just looks at me with them queer eyes of hisn that makes folks talk. I always say it ain't never been what he done so much or said or anything so much as how he looks at you. It's like he had got into the inside of you, someway. Like somehow you was looking at yourself and your doings outen his eyes. Then I can feel that gal watching me like I had made to touch her. She says something to Anse. ". . . Mr. Whitfield . . ." she says.

"I give her my promised word in the presence of the Lord," Anse says. "I reckon it ain't no need to worry."

But still he does not start the mules. We set there above the water. Another log bobs up over the jam and goes on; we watch it check up and swing slow for a minute where the ford used to be. Then it goes on.

"It might start falling tonight," I say. "You could lay over one more day."

Then Jewel turns sideways on the horse. He has not moved until then, and he turns and looks at me. His face is kind of green, then it would go red and then green again. "Get to hell on back to your damn ploughing," he says. "Who the hell asked you to follow us here?"

"I never meant no harm," I say.

"Shut up, Jewel," Cash says. Jewel looks back at the water, his face gritted, going red and green and then red. "Well," Cash says after a while, "what you want to do?"

Anse don't say nothing. He sets humped up, mumbling his mouth. "If it was just up, we could drive across it," he says.

"Come on," Jewel says, moving the horse.

"Wait," Cash says. He looks at the bridge. We look at

him, except Anse and the gal. They are looking at the water. "Dewey Dell and Vardaman and pa better walk across on the bridge," Cash says.

"Vernon can help them," Jewel says. "And we can hitch his mule ahead of ourn."

"You ain't going to take my mule into that water," I say.

Jewel looks at me. His eyes look like pieces of a broken plate. "I'll pay for your damn mule. I'll buy it from you right now."

"My mule ain't going into that water," I say.

"Jewel's going to use his horse," Darl says. "Why won't you risk your mule, Vernon?"

"Shut up, Darl," Cash says. "You and Jewel both."

"My mule ain't going into that water," I say.

DARL

HE SITS THE HORSE, GLARING AT VERNON, HIS LEAN FACE suffused up to and beyond the pale rigidity of his eyes. The summer when he was fifteen, he took a spell of sleeping. One morning when I went to feed the mules the cows were still in the tie-up and then I heard pa go back to the house and call him. When we came on back to the house for breakfast he passed us, carrying the milk buck-ets, stumbling along like he was drunk, and he was milk-ing when we put the mules in and went on to the field without him. We had been there an hour and still he never showed up. When Dewey Dell came with our lunch, pa sent her back to find Jewel. They found him in the tie-up, sitting on the stool, asleep.

After that, every morning pa would go in and wake him. He would go to sleep at the supper-table and soon as supper was finished he would go to bed, and when I came in to bed he would be lying there like a dead man. Yet still pa would have to wake him in the morning. He would get up, but he wouldn't hardly have half sense: he would stand for pa's jawing and complaining without a word and take the milk buckets and go to the barn, and once I found him asleep at the cow, the bucket in place and half-full and his hands up to the wrists in the milk and his head against the cow's flank.

After that Dewey Dell had to do the milking. He still got up when pa waked him, going about what we told him to do in that dazed way. It was like he was trying hard to do them; that he was as puzzled as anyone else.

"Are you sick?" ma said. "Don't you feel all right?"

"Yes," Jewel said. "I feel all right."

"He's just lazy, trying me," pa said, and Jewel standing there, asleep on his feet like as not. "Ain't you?" he said, waking Jewel up again to answer.

"No," Jewel said.

"You take off and stay in the house today," ma said.

"With that whole bottom piece to be busted out?" pa said. "If you ain't sick, what's the matter with you?"

"Nothing," Jewel said. "I'm all right."

"All right?" pa said. "You're asleep on your feet this minute."

"No," Jewel said. "I'm all right."

"I want him to stay at home today," ma said.

"I'll need him," pa said. "It's tight enough, with all of us to do it."

"You'll just have to do the best you can with Cash and Darl," ma said. "I want him to stay in today."

But he wouldn't do it. "I'm all right," he said, going on. But he wasn't all right. Anybody could see it. He was losing flesh, and I have seen him go to sleep chopping; watched the hoe going slower and slower up and down, with less and less of an arc, until it stopped and he leaning on it motionless in the hot shimmer of the sun.

Ma wanted to get the doctor, but pa didn't want to spend the money without it was needful, and Jewel did seem all right except for his thinness and his way of dropping off to sleep at any moment. He ate hearty enough, except for his way of going to sleep in his plate, with a piece of bread half-way to his mouth and his jaws still chewing. But he swore he was all right.

It was ma that got Dewey Dell to do his milking, paid her somehow, and the other jobs around the house that Jewel had been doing before supper she found some way for Dewey Dell and Vardaman to do them. And doing them herself when pa wasn't there. She would fix him special things to eat and hide them for him. And that may have been when I first found it out, that Addie Bundren should be hiding anything she did, who had tried to teach us that deceit was such that, in a world where it was, nothing else could be very bad or very important, not even poverty. And at times when I went in to go to bed she would be sitting in the dark by Jewel where he was asleep. And I knew that she was hating herself for that deceit and hating Jewel because she had to love him so that she had to act the deceit.

One night she was taken sick and when I went to the barn to put the team in and drive to Tull's, I couldn't find the lantern. I remembered noticing it on the nail the

night before, but it wasn't there now at midnight. So I
hitched in the dark and went on and came back with
Mrs. Tull just after daylight. And there the lantern was,
hanging on the nail where I remembered it and couldn't
find it before. And then one morning while Dewey Dell
was milking just before sun-up, Jewel came into the barn
from the back, through the hole in the back wall, with
the lantern in his hand.

I told Cash, and Cash and I looked at one another.

"Rutting," Cash said.

"Yes," I said. "But why the lantern? And every night,
too. No wonder he's losing flesh. Are you going to say
anything to him?"

"Won't do any good," Cash said.

"What he's doing now won't do any good, either."

"I know. But he'll have to learn that himself. Give him
time to realize that it'll save, that there'll be just as much
more tomorrow, and he'll be all right. I wouldn't tell anybody, I reckon."

"No," I said. "I told Dewey Dell not to. Not ma, anyway."

"No. Not ma."

After that I thought it was right comical: he acting so
bewildered and willing and dead for sleep and gaunt as
a bean-pole, and thinking he was so smart with it. And I
wondered who the girl was. I thought of all I knew that
it might be, but I couldn't say for sure.

" 'Taint any girl," Cash said. "It's a married woman
somewhere. Ain't any young girl got that much daring
and staying power. That's what I don't like about it."

"Why?" I said. "She'll be safer for him than a girl
would. More judgment."

He looked at me, his eyes fumbling, the words fumbling at what he was trying to say. "It ain't always the safe things in this world that a fellow . . ."

"You mean, the safe things are not always the best things?"

"Ay; best," he said, fumbling again. "It ain't the best things, the things that are good for him. . . . A young boy. A fellow kind of hates to see . . . wallowing in somebody else's mire . . ." That's what he was trying to say. When something is new and hard and bright, there ought to be something a little better for it than just being safe, since the safe things are just the things that folks have been doing so long they have woin the edges off and there's nothing to the doing of them that leaves a man to say, That was not done before and it cannot be done again.

So we didn't tell, not even when after a while he'd appear suddenly in the field beside us and go to work, without having had time to get home and make out he had been in bed all night. He would tell ma that he hadn't been hungry at breakfast or that he had eaten a piece of bread while he was hitching up the team. But Cash and I knew that he hadn't been home at all on those nights and he had come up out of the woods when we got to the field. But we didn't tell. Summer was almost over then; we knew that when the nights began to get cool, she would be done if he wasn't.

But when fall came and the nights began to get longer, the only difference was that he would always be in bed for pa to wake him, getting him up at last in that first state of semi-idiocy like when it first started, worse than when he had stayed out all night.

"She's sure a stayer," I told Cash. "I used to admire her, but I downright respect her now."

"It ain't a woman," he said.

"You know," I said. But he was watching me. "What is it then?"

"That's what I aim to find out," he said.

"You can trail him through the woods all night if you want to," I said. "I'm not."

"I ain't trailing him," he said.

"What do you call it, then?"

"I ain't trailing him," he said. "I don't mean it that way."

And so a few nights later I heard Jewel get up and climb out the window, and then I heard Cash get up and follow him. The next morning when I went to the barn, Cash was already there, the mules fed, and he was helping Dewey Dell milk. And when I saw him I knew that he knew what it was. Now and then I would catch him watching Jewel with a queer look, like having found out where Jewel went and what he was doing had given him something to really think about at last. But it was not a worried look; it was the kind of look I would see on him when I would find him doing some of Jewel's work around the house, work that pa still thought Jewel was doing and that ma thought Dewey Dell was doing. So I said nothing to him, believing that when he got done digesting it in his mind, he would tell me. But he never did.

One morning—it was November then, five months since it started—Jewel was not in bed and he didn't join us in the field. That was the first time ma learned anything about what had been going on. She sent Vardaman down to find where Jewel was, and after a while she came down too. It was as though, so long as the deceit ran along quiet and monotonous, all of us let ourselves be deceived, abetting it unawares or maybe through cowardice, since all people are cowards and naturally prefer any kind of treachery because it has a bland outside. But now it was like we had all—and by a kind of telepathic agreement of admitted fear—flung the whole thing back like covers on the bed and we all sitting bolt upright in our nakedness, staring at one another and saying "Now is the truth. He hasn't come home. Something has happened to him. We let something happen to him."

Then we saw him. He came up along the ditch and then turned straight across the field, riding the horse. Its mane and tail were going, as though in motion they were carrying out the splotchy pattern of its coat: he looked like he was riding on a big pinwheel, barebacked, with a rope bridle, and no hat on his head. It was a descendant of those Texas ponies Flem Snopes brought here twenty-five years ago and auctioned off for two dollars a head and nobody but old Lon Quick ever caught his and still owned some of the blood because he could never give it away.

He galloped up and stopped, his heels in the horse's ribs and it dancing and swirling like the shape of its mane and tail and the splotches of its coat had nothing whatever to do with the flesh-and-bone horse inside them, and he sat there, looking at us.

"Where did you get that horse?" pa said.

"Bought it," Jewel said. "From Mr. Quick."

"Bought it?" pa said. "With what? Did you buy that thing on my word?"

"It was my money," Jewel said. "I earned it. You won't need to worry about it."

"Jewel," ma said; "Jewel."

"It's all right," Cash said. "He earned the money. He cleaned up that forty acres of new ground Quick laid out last spring. He did it single-handed, working at night by

lantern. I saw him. So I don't reckon that horse cost anybody anything except Jewel. I don't reckon we need
worry."

"Jewel," ma said. "Jewel——" Then she said: "You
come right to the house and go to bed."

"Not yet," Jewel said. "I ain't got time. I got to get me a
saddle and bridle. Mr. Quick says he——"

"Jewel," ma said, looking at him. "I'll give—I'll give—
give——" Then she began to cry. She cried hard, not hiding her face, standing there in her faded wrapper, looking at him and him on the horse, looking down at her,
his face growing cold and a little sick looking until he
looked away quick and Cash came and touched her.

"You go on to the house," Cash said. "This here ground
is too wet for you. You go on, now." She put her hands to
her face then and after a while she went on, stumbling a
little on the ploughmarks. But pretty soon she straightened up and went on. She didn't look back. When she
reached the ditch she stopped and called Vardaman. He
was looking at the horse, kind of dancing up and down
by it.

"Let me ride, Jewel," he said. "Let me ride, Jewel."

Jewel looked at him, then he looked away again, holding the horse reined back. Pa watched him, mumbling his
lip.

"So you bought a horse," he said. "You went behind my
back and bought a horse. You never consulted me; you
know how tight it is for us to make by, yet you bought
a horse for me to feed. Taken the work from your flesh
and blood and bought a horse with it."

Jewel looked at pa, his eyes paler than ever.

"He won't never eat a mouthful of yours," he said. "Not
a mouthful. I'll kill him first. Don't you never think it.
Don't you never."

"Let me ride, Jewel," Vardaman said. "Let me ride, Jewel." He sounded like a cricket in the grass, a little one. "Let me ride, Jewel."

That night I found ma sitting beside the bed where he was sleeping, in the dark. She cried hard, maybe because she had to cry so quiet; maybe because she felt the same way about tears she did about deceit, hating herself for doing it, hating him because she had to. And then I knew that I knew. I knew that as plain on that day as I knew about Dewey Dell on that day.

TULL

So THEY FINALLY GOT ANSE TO SAY WHAT HE WANTED TO do, and him and the gal and the boy got out of the wagon. But even when we were on the bridge Anse kept on looking back, like he thought maybe, once he was outen the wagon, the whole thing would kind of blow up and he would find himself back yonder in the field again and her laying up there in the house, waiting to die and it to do all over again.

"You ought to let them taken your mule," he says, and the bridge shaking and swaying under us, going down into the moiling water like it went clean through to the other side of the earth, and the other end coming up outen the water like it wasn't the same bridge a-tall and that them that would walk up outen the water on that side must come from the bottom of the earth. But it was still whole; you could tell that by the way when this end swagged, it didn't look like the other end swagged at all: just like the other trees and the bank yonder were swinging back and forth slow like on a big clock. And them logs scraping and bumping at the sunk part and tilting end-up and shooting clean outen the water and tumbling on toward the ford and the waiting, slick, whirling, and foamy.

"What good would that 'a' done?" I says. "If your team can't find the ford and haul it across, what good would three mules or even ten mules do?"

"I ain't asking it of you," he says. "I can always do for me and mine. I ain't asking you to risk your mule. It ain't your dead; I am not blaming you."

"They ought to went back and laid over until tomorrow," I says. The water was cold. It was thick, like slush ice. Only it kind of lived. One part of you knowed it was just water, the same thing that had been running under this same bridge for a long time, yet when them logs would come spewing up outen it, you were not surprised, like they was a part of water, of the waiting and the threat.

It was like when we was across, up out of the water again and the hard earth under us, that I was surprised. It was like we hadn't expected the bridge to end on the other bank, on something tame like the hard earth again that we had tromped on before this time and knowed well. Like it couldn't be me here, because I'd have had better sense than to done what I just done. And when I looked back and saw the other bank and saw my mule standing there where I used to be and knew that I'd have to get back there some way, I knew it couldn't be, because I just couldn't think of anything that could make me cross that bridge ever even once. Yet here I was, and the fellow that could make himself cross it twice, couldn't be me, not even if Cora told him to.

It was that boy. I said "Here; you better take a holt of my hand," and he waited and held to me. I be durn if it wasn't like he come back and got me; like he was saying They won't nothing hurt you. Like he was saying about a fine place he knowed where Christmas come twice with Thanksgiving and lasts on through the winter and the spring and the summer, and if I just stayed with him I'd be all right too.

When I looked back at my mule it was like he was one of these here spy-glasses and I could look at him standing there and see all the broad land and my house sweated outen it like it was the more the sweat, the broader the land; the more the sweat, the tighter the house because it would take a tight house for Cora, to hold Cora like a jar of milk in the spring: you've got to have a tight jar or you'll need a powerful spring, if you have a big spring, why then you have the incentive to have tight, well-made jars, because it is your milk, sour or not, because you would rather have milk that will sour than to have milk that won't, because you are a man.

And him holding to my hand, his hand that hot and confident, so that I was like to say: Look-a-here. Can't you see that mule yonder? He never had no business over here, so he never come, not being nothing but a mule. Because a fellow can see ever now and then that children have more sense than him. But he don't like to admit it to them until they have beards. After they have a beard, they are too busy because they don't know if they'll ever quite make it back to where they were in sense before they was haired, so you don't mind admitting then to folks that are worrying about the same thing that ain't worth the worry that you are yourself.

Then we was over and we stood there, looking at Cash turning the wagon around. We watched them drive back down the road to where the trail turned off into the bottom. After a while the wagon was out of sight.

"We better get on down to the ford and git ready to help," I said.

"I give her my word," Anse says. "It is sacred on me. I know you begrudge it, but she will bless you in heaven."

"Well, they got to finish circumventing the land before they can dare the water," I said. "Come on."

"It's the turning back," he said. "It ain't no luck in turning back."

He was standing there, humped, mournful, looking at the empty road beyond the swagging and swaying bridge. And that gal, too, with the lunch-basket on one arm and that package under the other. Just going to town. Bent on it. They would risk the fire and the earth and the water and all just to eat a sack of bananas. "You ought to laid over a day," I said. "It would 'a' fell some by morning. It mought not 'a' rained tonight. And it can't get no higher."

"I give my promise," he says. "She is counting on it."

DARL

BEFORE US THE THICK DARK CURRENT RUNS. IT TALKS UP to us in a murmur become ceaseless and myriad, the yellow surface dimpled monstrously into fading swirls travelling along the surface for an instant, silent, imper-

manent and profoundly significant, as though just beneath the surface something huge and alive waked for a
moment of lazy alertness out of and into light slumber
again.

It clucks and murmurs among the spokes and about
the mules' knees, yellow, scummed with flotsam and
with thick soiled gouts of foam as though it had sweat,
lathering, like a driven horse. Through the undergrowth
it goes with a plaintive sound, a musing sound; in it the
unwinded cane and saplings lean as before a little gale,
swaying without reflections as though suspended on invisible wires from the branches overhead. Above the
ceaseless surface they stand—trees, cane, vines—rootless,
severed from the earth, spectral above a scene of immense yet circumscribed desolation filled with the voice
of the waste and mournful water.

Cash and I sit in the wagon; Jewel sits the horse at
the off rear-wheel. The horse is trembling, its eye rolling
wild and baby-blue in its long pink face, its breathing
stertorous like groaning. He sits erect, poised, looking
quietly and steadily and quickly this way and that, his
face calm, a little pale, alert. Cash's face is also gravely
composed; he and I look at one another with long prob-
ing looks, looks that plunge unimpeded through one another's eyes and into the ultimate secret place where for
an instant Cash and Darl crouch flagrant and unabashed
in all the old terror and the old foreboding, alert and
secret and without shame. When we speak our voices are
quiet, detached.

"I reckon we're still in the road, all right."

"Tull taken and cut them two big whiteoaks. I heard
tell how at high water in the old days they used to line
up the ford by them trees."

"I reckon he did that two years ago when he was log

ging down here. I reckon he never thought that anybody would ever use this ford again."

"I reckon not. Yes, it must have been then. He cut a sight of timber outen here then. Payed off that mortgage with it, I hear tell."

"Yes. Yes, I reckon so. I reckon Vernon could have done that."

"That's a fact. Most folks that logs in this here country, they need a durn good farm to support the sawmill. Or maybe a store. But I reckon Vernon could."

"I reckon so. He's a sight."

"Ay. Vernon is. Yes, it must still be here. He never would have got that timber out of here if he hadn't cleaned out that old road. I reckon we are still on it." He looks about quietly, at the position of the trees, leaning this way and that, looking back along the floorless road shaped vaguely high in air by the position of the lopped and felled trees, as if the road too had been soaked free of earth and floated upward, to leave in its spectral tracing a monument to a still more profound desolation than this above which we now sit, talking quietly of old security and old trivial things. Jewel looks at him, then at me, then his face turns in in that quiet, constant, questing about the scene, the horse trembling quietly and steadily between his knees.

"He could go on ahead slow and sort of feel it out," I say.

"Yes," Cash says, not looking at me. His face is in profile as he looks forward where Jewel has moved on ahead.

"He can't miss the river," I say. "He couldn't miss seeing it fifty yards ahead."

Cash does not look at me, his face in profile. "If I'd

just suspicioned it, I could 'a' come down last week and taken a sight on it."

"The bridge was up then," I say. He does not look at me. "Whitfield crossed it a-horse-back."

Jewel looks at us again, his expression sober and alert and subdued. His voice is quiet. "What you want me to do?"

"I ought to come down last week and taken a sight on it," Cash says.

"We couldn't have known," I say. "There wasn't any way for us to know."

"I'll ride on ahead," Jewel says. "You can follow where I am." He lifts the horse. It shrinks, bowed; he leans to it, speaking to it, lifting it forward almost bodily, it setting its feet down with gingerly splashings, trembling, breathing harshly. He speaks to it, murmurs to it. "Go on," he says. "I ain't going to let nothing hurt you. Go on, now."

"Jewel," Cash says. Jewel does not look back. He lifts the horse on.

"He can swim," I say. "If he'll just give the horse time, anyhow . . ." When he was born, he had a bad time of it. Ma would sit in the lamplight, holding him on a pillow on her lap. We would wake and find her so. There would be no sound from them.

"That pillow was longer than him," Cash says. He is leaning a little forward. "I ought to come down last week and sighted. I ought to done it."

"That's right," I say. "Neither his feet nor his head would reach the end of it. You couldn't have known," I say.

"I ought to done it," he says. He lifts the reins. The mules move, into the traces; the wheels murmur alive in the water. He looks back and down at Addie. "It ain't on a balance," he says.

At last the trees open; against the open river Jewel sits the horse, half turned, it belly deep now. Across the river we can see Vernon and pa and Vardaman and Dewey Dell. Vernon is waving at us, waving us further downstream.

"We are too high up," Cash says. Vernon is shouting too, but we cannot make out what he says for the noise of the water. It runs steady and deep now, unbroken, without sense of motion until a log comes along, turning slowly. "Watch it," Cash says. We watch it and see it falter and hang for a moment, the current building up behind it in a thick wave, submerging it for an instant before it shoots up and tumbles on.

"There it is," I say.

"Ay," Cash says. "It's there." We look at Vernon again. He is now flapping his arms up and down. We move on downstream, slowly and carefully, watching Vernon. He drops his hands. "This is the place," Cash says.

"Well, goddamn it, lets get across, then," Jewel says. He moves the horse on.

"You wait," Cash says. Jewel stops again.

"Well, by God——" he says. Cash looks at the water, then he looks back at Addie. "It ain't on a balance," he says.

"Then go on back to the goddamn bridge and walk across," Jewel says. "You and Darl both. Let me on that wagon."

Cash does not pay him any attention. "It ain't on a balance," he says. "Yes, sir. We got to watch it."

"Watch it, hell," Jewel says. "You get out of that wagon and let me have it. By God, if you're afraid to drive it over . . ." His eyes are pale as two bleached chips in his face. Cash is looking at him.

"We'll get it over," he says. "I tell you what you do. You ride on back and walk across the bridge and come down the other bank and meet us with the rope. Vernon'll take your horse home with him and keep it till we get back."

"You go to hell," Jewel says.

"You take the rope and come down the bank and be ready with it," Cash says. "Three can't do no more than two can—one to drive and one to steady it."

"Goddamn you," Jewel says.

"Let Jewel take the end of the rope and cross upstream of us and brace it," I say. "Will you do that, Jewel?"

Jewel watches me, hard. He looks quick at Cash, then back at me, his eyes alert and hard. "I don't give a damn. Just so we do something. Setting here, not lifting a god' damn hand . . ."

"Let's do that, Cash," I say.

"I reckon we'll have to," Cash says.

The river itself is not a hundred yards across, and pa and Vernon and Vardaman and Dewey Dell are the only things in sight not of that single monotony of desolation leaning with that terrific quality a little from right to left, as though we had reached the place where the motion of the wasted world accelerates just before the final precipice. Yet they appear dwarfed. It is as though the space between us were time: an irrevocable quality. It is as though time, no longer running straight before us in a diminishing line, now runs parallel between us like a looping string, the distance being the doubling accretion of the thread and not the interval between. The mules stand, their forequarters already sloped a little, their rumps high. They too are breathing now with a deep groaning sound; looking back once, their gaze sweeps across us with in their eyes a wild, sad, profound

and despairing quality as though they had already seen
in the thick water the shape of the disaster which they
could not speak and we could not see.

Cash turns back into the wagon. He lays his hands flat
on Addie, rocking her a little. His face is calm, down-
sloped, calculant, concerned. He lifts his box of tools
and wedges it forward under the seat; together we shove
Addie forward, wedging her between the tools and the
wagon-bed. Then he looks at me.

"No," I say. "I reckon I'll stay. Might take both of us."

From the tool-box he takes his coiled rope and carries
the end twice around the seat stanchion and passes the
end to me without tying it. The other end he pays out to
Jewel, who takes a turn about his saddle-horn.

He must force the horse down into the current. It
moves, high-kneed, arch-necked, boring and chafing.
Jewel sits lightly forward, his knees lifted a little; again his
swift alert calm gaze sweeps upon us and on. He lowers
the horse into the stream, speaking to it in a soothing
murmur. The horse slips, goes under to the saddle, surges
to its feet again, the current building up against Jewel's
thighs.

"Watch yourself," Cash says.

"I'm on it now," Jewel says. "You can come ahead
now."

Cash takes the reins and lowers the team carefully and
skilfully into the stream.

*I felt the current take us and I knew we were on the
ford by that reason, since it was only by means of that
slipping contact that we could tell that we were in motion at all. What had once been a flat surface was now a
succession of troughs and hillocks lifting and falling
about us, shoving at us, teasing at us with light lazy*

touches in the vain instants of solidity underfoot. Cash
looked back at me, and then I knew that we were gone.
But I did not realize the reason for the rope until I saw
the log. It surged up out of the water and stood for an
instant upright upon that surging and heaving desolation
like Christ. Get out and let the current take you down to
the bend, Cash said. You can make it all right. No, I
said, I'd get just as wet that way as this.

The log appears suddenly between two hills, as if it
had rocketed suddenly from the bottom of the river.
Upon the end of it a long gout of foam hangs like the
beard of an old man or a goat. When Cash speaks to me
I know that he has been watching it all the time, watching it and watching Jewel ten feet ahead of us. "Let the
rope go," he says. With his other hand he reaches down
and reeves the two turns from the stanchion. "Ride on,
Jewel," he says; "see if you can pull us ahead of the log."

Jewel shouts at the horse; again he appears to lift it
bodily between his knees. He is just above the top of the
ford and the horse has a purchase of some sort for it
surges forward, shining wetly half out of water, crashing
on in a succession of lunges. It moves unbelievably fast;
by that token Jewel realizes at last that the rope is free,
for I can see him sawing back on the reins, his head
turned, as the log rears in a long sluggish lunge between
us, bearing down upon the team. They see it too; for a
moment they also shine black out of water. Then the
downstream one vanishes, dragging the other with him;
the wagon sheers crosswise, poised on the crest of the
ford as the log strikes it, tilting it up and on. Cash is half
turned, the reins running taut from his hand and disappearing into the water, the other hand reached back
upon Addie, holding her jammed over against the high

side of the wagon. "Jump clear," he says quietly. "Stay away from the team and don't try to fight it. It'll swing you into the bend all right."

"You come too," I say. Vernon and Vardaman are running along the bank, pa and Dewey Dell stand watching us, Dewey Dell with the basket and the package in her arms. Jewel is trying to fight the horse back. The head of one mule appears, its eyes wide; it looks back at us for an instant, making a sound almost human. The head vanishes again.

"Back, Jewel," Cash shouts. "Back, Jewel." For another instant I see him leaning to the tilting wagon, his arm braced back against Addie and his tools; I see the bearded head of the rearing log strike up again, and beyond it Jewel holding the horse upreared, its head wrenched around, hammering its head with his fist. I jump from the wagon on the downstream side. Between two hills I see the mules once more. They roll up out of the water in succession, turning completely over, their legs stiffly extended as when they had lost contact with the earth.

VARDAMAN

CASH TRIED BUT SHE FELL OFF AND DARL JUMPED GO• ing under he went under and Cash hollering to catch her and I hollering running and hollering and Dewey Dell hollering at me Vardaman you vardaman you varda•

man and Vernon passed me because he was seeing her
come up and she jumped into the water again and
Darl hadn't caught her yet

He came up to see and I hollering catch her Darl catch
her and he didn't come back because she was too heavy
he had to go on catching at her and I hollering catch her
darl catch her darl because in the water she could go
faster than a man and Darl had to grabble for her so I
knew he could catch her because he is the best grabbler
even with the mules in the way again they dived up rolling their feet stiff rolling down again and their backs up
now and Darl had to again because in the water she
could go faster than a man or a woman and I passed Vernon and he wouldn't get in the water and help Darl he
would grabble for her with Darl he knew but he
wouldn't help

The mules dived up again diving their legs stiff their
stiff legs rolling slow and then Darl again and I hollering
catch her darl catch her head her into the bank darl
and Vernon wouldn't help and then Darl dodged past the
mules where he could he had her under the water coming
in to the bank coming in slow because in the water she
fought to stay under the water but Darl is strong and he
was coming in slow and so I knew he had her because he
came slow and I ran down into the water to help and I
couldn't stop hollering because Darl was strong and
steady holding her under the water even if she did fight
he would not let her go he was seeing me and he would
hold her and it was all right now it was all right now it
was all right

*Then he comes up out of the water. He comes a long
way up slow before his hands do but he's got to have
her got to so I can bear it. Then his hands come up and
all of him above the water. I can't stop. I have not got*

time to try. I will try to when I can but his hands came
empty out of the water emptying the water emptying
away

"Where is ma, Darl?" I said. "You never got her. You
knew she is a fish but you let her get away. You never
got her. Darl. Darl. Darl." I began to run along the bank,
watching the mules dive up slow again and then down
again.

TULL

WHEN I TOLD CORA HOW DARL JUMPED OUT OF THE
wagon and left Cash sitting there trying to save it
and the wagon turning over, and Jewel that was almost
to the bank fighting that horse back where it had more
sense than to go, she says "And you're one of the folks
that says Darl is the queer one, the one that ain't bright,
and him the only one of them that had sense enough to
get off that wagon. I notice Anse was too smart to been
on it a-tall."

"He couldn't 'a' done no good, if he'd been there," I
said. "They was going about it right and they would
have made it if it hadn't a-been for that log."

"Log, fiddlesticks," Cora said. "It was the hand of
God."

"Then how can you say it was foolish?" I said. "Nobody
can't guard against the hand of God. It would be sacrilege to try to."

"Then why dare it?" Cora says. "Tell me that."

"Anse didn't," I said. "That's just what you faulted him for."

"His place was there," Cora said. "If he had been a man, he would 'a' been there instead of making his sons do what he dursn't."

"I don't know what you want, then," I said. "One breath you say they was daring the hand of God to try it, and the next breath you jump on Anse because he wasn't with them." Then she begun to sing again, working at the wash-tub, with that singing look in her face like she had done give up folks and all their foolishness and had done went on ahead of them, marching up the sky, singing.

The wagon hung for a long time while the current built up under it, shoving it off the ford, and Cash leaning more and more, trying to keep the coffin braced so it wouldn't slip down and finish tilting the wagon over. Soon as the wagon got tilted good, to where the current could finish it, the log went on. It headed around the wagon and went on good as a swimming man could have done. It was like it had been sent there to do a job and done it and went on.

When the mules finally kicked loose, it looked for a minute like maybe Cash would get the wagon back. It looked like him and the wagon wasn't moving at all, and just Jewel fighting that horse back to the wagon. Then that boy passed me, running and hollering at Darl and the gal trying to catch him, and then I see the mules come rolling slow up out of the water, their legs spraddled stiff like they had balked upside down, and roll on into the water again.

Then the wagon tilted over and then it and Jewel and the horse was all mixed up together. Cash went outen

sight, still holding the coffin braced, and then I couldn't
tell anything for the horse lunging and splashing. I
thought that Cash had give up then and was swimming
for it and I was yelling at Jewel to come on back and then
all of a sudden him and the horse went under too and I
thought they was all going. I knew that the horse had got
dragged off the ford too, and with that wild drowning
horse and that wagon and that loose box, it was going to
be pretty bad, and there I was, standing knee deep in
the water, yelling at Anse behind me: "See what you
done now. See what you done now?"

The horse come up again. It was headed for the bank
now, throwing its head up, and then I saw one of them
holding to the saddle on the downstream side, so I started
running along the bank, trying to catch sight of Cash because he couldn't swim, yelling at Jewel where Cash was
like a durn fool, bad as that boy that was on down the
bank still hollering at Darl.

So I went down into the water so I could still keep
some kind of a grip in the mud, when I saw Jewel. He
was middle deep, so I knew he was on the ford, anyway,
leaning hard upstream, and then I see the rope and then
I see the water building up where he was holding the
wagon snubbed just below the ford.

So it was Cash holding to the horse when it come
splashing and scrambling up the bank, moaning and
groaning like a natural man. When I come to it it was
just kicking Cash loose from his holt on the saddle. His
face turned up a second when he was sliding back into
the water. It was grey, with his eyes closed and a long
swipe of mud across his face. Then he let go and turned
over in the water. He looked just like an old bundle of
clothes kind of washing up and down against the bank.
He looked like he was laying there in the water on his

face, rocking up and down a little, looking at something on the bottom.

We could watch the rope cutting down into the water, and we could feel the weight of the wagon kind of blump and lunge lazy like, like it just as soon as not, and that rope cutting down into the water hard as a iron bar. We could hear the water hissing on it like it was red hot. Like it was a straight iron bar stuck into the bottom and us holding the end of it, and the wagon lazing up and down, kind of pushing and prodding at us like it had come around and got behind us, lazy like, like it just as soon as not when it made up its mind. There was a shoat come by, blowed up like a balloon: one of them spotted shoats of Lon Quick's. It bumped against the rope like it was a iron bar and bumped off and went on, and us watching that rope slanting down into the water. We watched it.

DARL

Cash lies on his back on the earth, his head raised on a rolled garment. His eyes are closed, his face is grey, his hair plastered in a smooth smear across his forehead as though done with a paint-brush. His face appears sunken a little, sagging from the bony ridges of eye-sockets, nose, gums, as though the wetting had slacked the firmness which had held the skin full; his teeth, set in pale gums, are parted a little as if he had been laughing quietly. He lies pole-thin in his wet clothes, a little pool of vomit at his head and a thread of it running from the corner of his mouth and down his cheek where he couldn't turn his head quick or far enough, until Dewey Dell stoops and wipes it away with the hem of her dress.

Jewel approaches. He has the plane. "Vernon just found the square," he says. He looks down at Cash, dripping too. "Ain't he talked none yet?"

"He had his saw and hammer and chalk-line and rule," I say. "I know that."

Jewel lays the square down. Pa watches him. "They can't be far away," pa says. "It all went together. Was there ere a such misfortunate man."

Jewel does not look at pa. "You better call Vardaman back here," he says. He looks at Cash. Then he turns and goes away. "Get him to talk soon as he can," he says, "so he can tell us what else there was."

We return to the river. The wagon is hauled clear, the wheels chocked (carefully: we all helped; it is as though upon the shabby, familiar, inert shape of the wagon there lingered somehow, latent yet still immediate, that violence which had slain the mules that drew it not an hour since) above the edge of the flood. In the wagon bed it lies profoundly, the long pale planks hushed a little with wetting yet still yellow, like gold seen through water, save for two long muddy smears. We pass it and go on to the bank.

One end of the rope is made fast to a tree. At the edge of the stream, knee-deep, Vardaman stands, bent forward a little, watching Vernon with rapt absorption. He has stopped yelling and he is wet to the armpits. Vernon is at the other end of the rope, shoulder-deep in the river, looking back at Vardaman. "Further back than that," he says. "You git back by the tree and hold the rope for me, so it can't slip."

Vardaman backs along the rope, to the tree, moving blindly, watching Vernon. When we come up he looks at us once, his eyes round and a little dazed. Then he looks at Vernon again in that posture of rapt alertness.

"I got the hammer too," Vernon says. "Looks like we ought to done already got that chalk-line. It ought to floated."

"Floated clean away," Jewel says. "We won't get it. We ought to find the saw, though."

"I reckon so," Vernon says. He looks at the water. "That chalk-line, too. What else did he have?"

"He ain't talked yet," Jewel says, entering the water. He looks back at me. "You go back and get him roused up to talk," he says.

"Pa's there," I say. I follow Jewel into the water, along the rope. It feels alive in my hand, bellied faintly in a prolonged and resonant arc. Vernon is watching me.

"You better go," he says. "You better be there."

"Let's see what else we can get before it washes on down," I say.

We hold to the rope, the current curling and dimpling about our shoulders. But beneath that false blandness the true force of it leans against us lazily. I had not thought that water in July could be so cold. It is like hands moulding and prodding at the very bones. Vernon is still looking back toward the bank.

"Reckon it'll hold us all?" he says. We too look back, following the rigid bar of the rope as it rises from the water to the tree and Vardaman crouched a little beside it, watching us. "Wish my mule wouldn't strike out for home," Vernon says.

"Come on," Jewel says. "Let's get outen here."

We submerge in turn, holding to the rope, being clutched by one another while the cold wall of the water sucks the slanting mud backward and upstream from beneath our feet and we are suspended so, groping along the cold bottom. Even the mud there is not still. It has a chill, scouring quality, as though the earth under us were in motion too. We touch and fumble at one another's extended arms, letting ourselves go cautiously against the rope; or, erect in turn, watch the water suck and boil where one of the other two gropes beneath the surface. Pa has come down to the shore, watching us.

Vernon comes up, streaming, his face sloped down into his pursed blowing mouth. His mouth is bluish, like a circle of weathered rubber. He has the rule.

"He'll be glad of that," I say. "It's right new. He bought it just last month out of the catalogue."

"If we just knowed for sho what else," Vernon says, looking over his shoulder and then turning to face where Jewel had disappeared. "Didn't he go down 'fore me?" Vernon says.

"I don't know," I say. "I think so. Yes. Yes, he did."

We watch the thick curling surface, streaming away from us in slow whorls.

"Give him a pull on the rope," Vernon says.

"He's on your end of it," I say.

"Ain't nobody on my end of it," he says.

"Pull it in," I say. But he has already done that, holding the end above the water; and then we see Jewel. He is ten yards away; he comes up, blowing, and looks at us, tossing his long hair back with a jerk of his head, then he looks toward the bank; we can see him filling his lungs.

"Jewel," Vernon says, not loud, but his voice going full

and clear along the water, peremptory yet tactful. "It'll be back here. Better come back."

Jewel dives again. We stand there, leaning back against the current, watching the water where he disappeared, holding the dead rope between us like two men holding the nozzle of a fire-hose, waiting for the water. Suddenly Dewey Dell is behind us in the water. "You make him come back," she says. "Jewel!" she says. He comes up again, tossing his hair back from his eyes. He is swimming now, toward the bank, the current sweeping him downstream quartering. "You, Jewel!" Dewey Dell says. We stand holding the rope and see him gain the bank and climb out. As he rises from the water, he stoops and picks up something. He comes back along the bank. He has found the chalk-line. He comes opposite us and stands there, looking about as if he were seeking something. Pa goes on down the bank. He is going back to look at the mules again where their round bodies float and rub quietly together in the slack water within the bend.

"What did you do with the hammer, Vernon?" Jewel says.

"I give it to him," Vernon says, jerking his head at Vardaman. Vardaman is looking after pa. Then he looks at Jewel. "With the square." Vernon is watching Jewel. He moves toward the bank, passing Dewey Dell and me.

"You get on out of here," I say. She says nothing, looking at Jewel and Vernon.

"Where's the hammer?" Jewel says. Vardaman scuttles up the bank and fetches it.

"It's heavier than the saw," Vernon says. Jewel is tying the end of the chalk-line about the hammer shaft.

"Hammer's got the most wood in it," Jewel says. He and Vernon face one another, watching Jewel's hands.

"And flatter, too," Vernon says. "It'd float three to one, almost. Try the plane."

Jewel looks at Vernon. Vernon is tall, too; long and lean, eye to eye they stand in their close wet clothes. Lon Quick could look even at a cloudy sky and tell the time to ten minutes. Big Lon I mean, not little Lon.

"Why don't you get out of the water?" I say.

"It won't float like a saw," Jewel says.

"It'll float nigher to a saw than a hammer will," Vernon says.

"Bet you," Jewel says.

"I won't bet," Vernon says.

They stand there, watching Jewel's still hands.

"Hell," Jewel says. "Get the plane, then."

So they get the plane and tie it to the chalk-line and enter the water again. Pa comes back along the bank. He stops for a while and looks at us, hunched, mournful, like a failing steer or an old tall bird.

Vernon and Jewel return, leaning against the current. "Get out of the way," Jewel says to Dewey Dell. "Get out of the water."

She crowds against me a little so they can pass, Jewel holding the plane high as though it were perishable, the blue string trailing back over his shoulder. They pass us and stop; they fall to arguing quietly about just where the wagon went over.

"Darl ought to know," Vernon says. They look at me.

"I don't know," I says. "I wasn't there that long."

"Hell," Jewel says. They move on, gingerly, leaning against the current, reading the ford with their feet.

"Have you got a holt of the rope?" Vernon says. Jewel does not answer. He glances back at the shore, calculant, then at the water. He flings the plane outward, letting the string run through his fingers, his fingers turning blue where it runs over them. When the line stops, he hands it back to Vernon.

"Better let me go this time," Vernon says. Again Jewel does not answer; we watch him duck beneath the surface.

"Jewel," Dewey Dell whimpers.

"It ain't so deep there," Vernon says. He does not look back. He is watching the water where Jewel went under. When Jewel comes up he has the saw.

When we pass the wagon pa is standing beside it, scrubbing at the two mud smears with a handful of leaves. Against the jungle Jewel's horse looks like a patchwork quilt hung on a line.

Cash has not moved. We stand above him, holding the plane, the saw, the hammer, the square, the rule, the chalk-line, while Dewey Dell squats and lifts Cash's head. "Cash," she says; "Cash."

He opens his eyes, staring profoundly up at our inverted faces.

"If ever was such a misfortunate man," pa says.

"Look, Cash," we say, holding the tools up so he can see; "what else did you have?"

He tries to speak, rolling his head, shutting his eyes.

"Cash," we say; "Cash."

It is to vomit he is turning his head. Dewey Dell wipes his mouth on the wet hem of her dress; then he can speak.

"It's his saw-set," Jewel says. "The new one he bought when he bought the rule." He moves, turning away. Vernon looks up after him, still squatting. Then he rises and follows Jewel down to the water.

"If ever was such a misfortunate man," pa says. He looms tall above us as we squat; he looks like a figure carved clumsily from tough wood by a drunken caricaturist. "It's a trial," he says. "But I don't begrudge her it. No man can say I begrudge her it." Dewey Dell has laid Cash's head back on the folded coat, twisting his head a little to avoid the vomit. Beside him his tools lie. "A fellow might call it lucky it was the same leg he broke when he fell offen that church," pa says. "But I don't begrudge her it."

Jewel and Vernon are in the river again. From here they do not appear to violate the surface at all; it is as though it had severed them both at a single blow, the two torsos moving with infinitesimal and ludicrous care upon the surface. It looks peaceful, like machinery does after you have watched it and listened to it for a long time. As though the clotting which is you had dissolved into the myriad original motion, and seeing and hearing in themselves blind and deaf; fury in itself quiet with stagnation. Squatting, Dewey Dell's wet dress shapes for the dead eyes of three blind men those mammalian ludicrosities which are the horizons and the valleys of the earth.

CASH

IT WASN'T ON A BALANCE. I TOLD THEM THAT IF THEY wanted it to tote and ride on a balance, they would have to——

CORA

ONE DAY WE WERE TALKING. SHE HAD NEVER BEEN PURE
religious, not even after that summer at the camp
meeting when Brother Whitfield wrestled with her spirit,
singled her out and strove with the vanity in her mortal
heart, and I said to her many a time, "God gave you
children to comfort your hard human lot and for a token
of His own suffering and love, for in love you conceived
and bore them." I said that because she took God's love
and her duty to Him too much as a matter of course,
and such conduct is not pleasing to Him. I said, "He gave
us the gift to raise our voices in His undying praise" because I said there is more rejoicing in heaven over one
sinner than over a hundred that never sinned. And she
said "My daily life is an acknowledgment and expiation
of my sin" and I said "Who are you, to say what is sin
and what is not sin? It is the Lord's part to judge; ours to
praise His mercy and His holy name in the hearing of
our fellow mortals" because He alone can see into the
heart, and just because a woman's life is right in the sight
of man, she can't know if there is no sin in her heart without she opens her heart to the Lord and receives His
grace. I said, "Just because you have been a faithful wife
is no sign that there is no sin in your heart, and just because your life is hard is no sign that the Lord's grace
is absolving you." And she said, "I know my own sin. I
know that I deserve my punishment. I do not begrudge
it." And I said, "It is out of your vanity that you would
judge sin and salvation in the Lord's place. It is our mor-

tal lot to suffer and to raise our voices in praise of Him who judges the sin and offers the salvation through our trials and tribulations time out of mind amen. Not even after Brother Whitfield, a godly man if ever one breathed God's breath, prayed for you and strove as never a man could except him," I said.

Because it is not us that can judge our sins or know what is sin in the Lord's eyes. She has had a hard life, but so does every woman. But you'd think from the way she talked that she knew more about sin and salvation than the Lord God Himself, than them who have strove and laboured with the sin in this human world. When the only sin she ever committed was being partial to Jewel that never loved her and was its own punishment, in preference to Darl that was touched by God Himself and considered queer by us mortals and that did love her. I said, "There is your sin. And your punishment too. Jewel is your punishment. But where is your salvation? And life is short enough," I said, "to win eternal grace in. And God is a jealous God. It is His to judge and to mete; not yours."

"I know," she said. "I——" Then she stopped, and I said,

"Know what?"

"Nothing," she said. "He is my cross and he will be my salvation. He will save me from the water and from the fire. Even though I have laid down my life, he will save me."

"How do you know, without you open your heart to Him and lift your voice in His praise?" I said. Then I realized that she did not mean God. I realized that out of the vanity of her heart she had spoken sacrilege. And I went down on my knees right there. I begged her to kneel and open her heart and cast from it the devil of vanity and cast herself upon the mercy of the Lord. But she wouldn't. She just sat there, lost in her vanity and her pride, that had closed her heart to God and set that selfish mortal boy in His place. Kneeling there I prayed for her. I prayed for that poor blind woman as I had never prayed for me and mine.

ADDIE

I N THE AFTERNOON WHEN SCHOOL WAS OUT AND THE last one had left with his little dirty snuffling nose, instead of going home I would go down the hill to the spring where I could be quiet and hate them. It would be quiet there then, with the water bubbling up and away and the sun slanting quiet in the trees and the quiet smelling of damp and rotting leaves and new earth; especially in the early spring, for it was worst then.

I could just remember how my father used to say that the reason for living was to get ready to stay dead a long time. And when I would have to look at them day after day, each with his and her secret and selfish thought, and blood strange to each other blood and strange to mine, and think that this seemed to be the only way I could get ready to stay dead, I would hate my father for having ever planted me. I would look forward to the times when they faulted, so I could whip them. When the switch fell I could feel it upon my flesh; when it welted and ridged it was my blood that ran, and I would think with each blow of the switch: Now you are aware of me! Now I am something in your secret and selfish life, who have marked your blood with my own for ever and ever.

And so I took Anse. I saw him pass the school-house three or four times before I learned that he was driving four miles out of his way to do it. I noticed then how he was beginning to hump—a tall man and young—so that he looked already like a tall bird hunched in the cold weather, on the wagon-seat. He would pass the school-house, the wagon creaking slow, his head turning slow to watch the door of the school-house as the wagon passed, until he went on around the curve and out of sight. One day I went to the door and stood there when he passed. When he saw me he looked quickly away and did not look back again.

In the early spring it was worst. Sometimes I thought that I could not bear it, lying in bed at night, with the wild geese going north and their honking coming faint and high and wild out of the wild darkness, and during the day it would seem as though I couldn't wait for the last one to go so I could go down to the spring. And so when I looked up that day and saw Anse standing there in his Sunday clothes, turning his hat round and round in his hands, I said:

"If you've got any womenfolks, why in the world don't they make you get your hair cut?"

"I ain't got none," he said. Then he said suddenly, driving his eyes at me like two hounds in a strange yard: "That's what I come to see you about."

"And make you hold your shoulders up," I said. "You haven't got any? But you've got a house. They tell me you've got a house and a good farm. And you live there alone, doing for yourself, do you?" He just looked at me, turning the hat in his hands. "A new house," I said. "Are you going to get married?"

And he said again, holding his eyes to mine: "That's what I come to see you about."

Later he told me, "I ain't got no people. So that won't be no worry to you. I don't reckon you can say the same."

"No. I have people. In Jefferson."

His face fell a little. "Well, I got a little property. I'm forehanded; I got a good honest name. I know how town folks are, but maybe when they talk to me . . ."

"They might listen," I said. "But they'll be hard to talk to." He was watching my face. "They're in the cemetery."

"But your living kin," he said. "They'll be different."

"Will they?" I said. "I don't know. I never had any other kind."

So I took Anse. And when I knew that I had Cash, I knew that living was terrible and that this was the answer to it. That was when I learned that words are no good; that words don't ever fit even what they are trying to say at. When he was born I knew that motherhood was invented by someone who had to have a word for it because the ones that had the children didn't care whether there was a word for it or not. I knew that fear was invented by someone that had never had the fear; pride, who never had the pride. I knew that it had been, not that they had dirty noses, but that we had had to use one another by words like spiders dangling by their mouths from a beam, swinging and twisting and never touching, and that only through the blows of the switch could my blood and their blood flow as one stream. I knew that it had been, not that my aloneness had to be violated over and over each day, but that it had never been violated until Cash came. Not even by Anse in the nights.

He had a word, too. Love, he called it. But I had been used to words for a long time. I knew that that word was like the others: just a shape to fill a lack; that when the right time came, you wouldn't need a word for that any more than for pride or fear. Cash did not need to say it to me nor I to him, and I would say, Let Anse use it, if he wants to. So that it was Anse or love; love or Anse: it didn't matter.

I would think that even while I lay with him in the dark and Cash asleep in the cradle within the swing of my hand. I would think that if he were to wake and cry, I would suckle him, too. Anse or love: it didn't matter. My aloneness had been violated and then made whole again by the violation: time, Anse, love, what you will, outside the circle.

Then I found that I had Darl. At first I would not believe it. Then I believed that I would kill Anse. It was as though he had tricked me, hidden within a word like within a paper screen and struck me in the back through it. But then I realized that I had been tricked by words older than Anse or love, and that the same word had tricked Anse too, and that my revenge would be that he would never know I was taking revenge. And when Darl was born I asked Anse to promise to take me back to Jefferson when I died, because I knew that father had been right, even when he couldn't have known he was right any more than I could have known I was wrong.

"Nonsense," Anse said; "you and me ain't nigh done chapping yet, with just two."

He did not know that he was dead, then. Sometimes I

would lie by him in the dark, hearing the land that was now of my blood and flesh, and I would think: Anse. Why Anse. Why are you Anse. I would think about his name until after a while I could see the word as a shape, a vessel, and I would watch him liquefy and flow into it like cold molasses flowing out of the darkness into the vessel, until the jar stood full and motionless: a significant shape profoundly without life like an empty door frame; and then I would find that I had forgotten the name of the jar. I would think: The shape of my body where I used to be a virgin is in the shape of a and I couldn't think Anse, couldn't remember Anse. It was not that I could think of myself as no longer unvirgin, because I was three now. And when I would think Cash and Darl that way until their names would die and solidify into a shape and then fade away, I would say, All right. It doesn't matter. It doesn't matter what they call them.

And so when Cora Tull would tell me I was not a true mother, I would think how words go straight up in a thin line, quick and harmless, and how terribly doing goes along the earth, clinging to it, so that after a while the two lines are too far apart for the same person to straddle from one to the other; and that sin and love and fear are just sounds that people who never sinned nor loved nor feared have for what they never had and cannot have until they forget the words. Like Cora, who could never even cook.

She would tell me what I owed to my children and to Anse and to God. I gave Anse the children. I did not ask for them. I did not even ask him for what he could have given me: not-Anse. That was my duty to him, to not ask that, and that duty I fulfilled. I would be I; I would let him be the shape and echo of his word. That was more than he asked, because he could not have asked for that and been Anse, using himself so with a word.

And then he died. He did not know he was dead. I would lie by him in the dark, hearing the dark land talking of God's love and His beauty and His sin; hearing the dark voicelessness in which the words are the deeds, and the other words that are not deeds, that are just the gaps in peoples' lacks, coming down like the cries of the geese out of the wild darkness in the old terrible nights, fumbling at the deeds like orphans to whom are pointed out in a crowd two faces and told, That is your father, your mother.

I believed that I had found it. I believed that the reason was the duty to the alive, to the terrible blood, the red bitter flood boiling through the land. I would think of sin as I would think of the clothes we both wore in the world's face, of the circumspection necessary because he was he and I was I; the sin the more utter and terrible since he was the instrument ordained by God who created the sin, to sanctify that sin He had created. While I waited for him in the woods, waiting for him before he saw me, I would think of him as dressed in sin. I would think of him as thinking of me as dressed also in sin, he the more beautiful since the garment which he had exchanged for sin was sanctified. I would think of the sin as garments which we would remove in order to shape and coerce the terrible blood to the forlorn echo of the dead word high in the air. Then I would lay with Anse again—I did not lie to him: I just refused, just as I refused my breast to Cash and Darl after their time was up—hearing the dark land talking the voiceless speech.

I hid nothing. I tried to deceive no one. I would not have cared. I merely took the precautions that he thought necessary for his sake, not for my safety, but just as I wore clothes in the world's face. And I would think then when Cora talked to me, of how the high dead words in time seemed to lose even the significance of their dead sound.

Then it was over. Over in the sense that he was gone and I knew that, see him again though I would, I would never again see him coming swift and secret to me in the woods dressed in sin like a gallant garment already blowing aside with the speed of his secret coming.

But for me it was not over. I mean, over in the sense of beginning and ending, because to me there was no beginning nor ending to anything then. I even held Anse refraining still, not that I was holding him recessional, but as though nothing else had ever been. My children were of me alone, of the wild blood boiling along the earth, of me and of all that lived; of none and of all. Then I found that I had Jewel. When I waked to remember to discover it, he was two months gone.

My father said that the reason for living is getting ready to stay dead. I knew at last what he meant and that he could not have known what he meant himself, because a man cannot know anything about cleaning up the house afterward. And so I have cleaned my house. With Jewel—I lay by the lamp, holding up my own head, watching him cap and suture it before he breathed —the wild blood boiled away and the sound of it ceased. Then there was only the milk, warm and calm, and I lying calm in the slow silence, getting ready to clean my house.

I gave Anse Dewey Dell to negative Jewel. Then I gave him Vardaman to replace the child I had robbed him of. And now he has three children that are his and not mine. And then I could get ready to die.

One day I was talking to Cora. She prayed for me because she believed I was blind to sin, wanting me to kneel and pray too, because people to whom sin is just a matter of words, to them salvation is just words too.

WHITFIELD

WHEN THEY TOLD ME SHE WAS DYING, ALL THAT NIGHT I wrestled with Satan, and I emerged victorious. I woke to the enormity of my sin; I saw the true light at last, and I fell on my knees and confessed to God and asked his guidance and received it. "Rise," He said; "repair to that home in which you have put a living lie, among those people with whom you have outraged My Word; confess your sin aloud. It is for them, for that deceived husband, to forgive you: not I."

So I went. I heard that Tull's bridge was gone; I said "Thanks, O Lord, O Mighty Ruler of all"; for by those dangers and difficulties which I should have to surmount I saw that He had not abandoned me; that my reception again into His holy peace and love would be the sweeter for it. "Just let me not perish before I have begged the forgiveness of the man whom I betrayed," I prayed; "let me not be too late; let not the tale of mine and her transgression come from her lips instead of mine. She had sworn then that she would never tell it, but eternity is a fearsome thing to face: have I not wrestled thigh to thigh with Satan myself? let me not have also the sin of her

broken vow upon my soul. Let not the waters of Thy
mighty wrath encompass me until I have cleansed my
soul in the presence of them whom I injured."

It was His hand that bore me safely above the flood,
that fended from me the dangers of the waters. My horse
was frightened, and my own heart failed me as the logs
and the uprooted trees bore down upon my littleness. But
not my soul: time after time I saw them averted at destruction's final instant, and I lifted my voice above the
noise of the flood: "Praise to thee, O Mighty Lord and
King. By this token shall I cleanse my soul and gain
again into the fold of Thy undying love."

I knew then that forgiveness was mine. The flood, the
danger, behind, and as I rode on across the firm earth
again and the scene of my Gethsemane drew closer and
closer, I framed the words which I should use. I would
enter the house; I would stop her before she had spoken;
I would say to her husband: "Anse, I have sinned. Do
with me as you will."

It was already as though it were done. My soul felt
freer, quieter than it had in years; already I seemed to
dwell in abiding peace again as I rode on. To either side
I saw His hand; in my heart I could hear His voice:
"Courage. I am with thee."

Then I reached Tull's house. His youngest girl came
out and called to me as I was passing. She told me that
she was already dead.

I have sinned, O Lord. Thou knowest the extent of my
remorse and the will of my spirit. But He is merciful; He
will accept the will for the deed, Who knew that when I
framed the words of my confession it was to Anse I
spoke them, even though he was not there. It was He in
His infinite wisdom that restrained the tale from her dying lips as she lay surrounded by those who loved and

trusted her; mine the travail by water which I sustained by the strength of His hand. Praise to Thee in Thy bounteous and omnipotent love; O praise.

I entered the house of bereavement, the lowly dwelling where another erring mortal lay while her soul faced the awful and irrevocable judgment, peace to her ashes.

"God's grace upon this house," I said.

DARL

ON THE HORSE HE RODE UP TO ARMSTID'S AND CAME *back on the horse,* leading Armstid's team. We hitched up and laid Cash on top of Addie. When we laid him down he vomited again, but he got his head over the wagon bed in time.

"He taken a lick in the stomach too," Vernon said.

"The horse may have kicked him in the stomach too," I said. "Did he kick you in the stomach, Cash?"

He tried to say something. Dewey Dell wiped his mouth again.

"What's he say?" Vernon said.

"What is it, Cash?" Dewey Dell said. She leaned down. "His tools," she said. Vernon got them and put them into the wagon. Dewey Dell lifted Cash's head so he could see. We drove on, Dewey Dell and I sitting beside Cash to steady him *and he riding on ahead on the horse.* Vernon stood watching us for a while. Then he turned and went back toward the bridge. He walked gingerly, be-

ginning to flap the wet sleeves of his shirt as though he
had just got wet.

He was sitting the horse before the gate. Armstid was
waiting at the gate. We stopped *and he got down* and we
lifted Cash down and carried him into the house, where
Mrs. Armstid had the bed ready. We left her and Dewey
Dell undressing him.

We followed pa out to the wagon. He went back and
got into the wagon and drove on, we following on foot,
into the lot. The wetting had helped, because Armstid
said, "You welcome to the house. You can put it there."
*He followed, leading the horse, and stood beside the
wagon, the reins in his hand.*

"I thank you," pa said. "We'll use in the shed yonder.
I know it's a imposition on you."

"You're welcome to the house," Armstid said. *He had
that wooden look on his face again; that bold, surly, high-
coloured rigid look like his face and eyes were two col-
ours of wood, the wrong one pale and the wrong one
dark. His shirt was beginning to dry, but it still clung
close upon him when he moved.*

"She would appreciate it," pa said.

We took the team out and rolled the wagon back under the shed. One side of the shed was open.

"It won't rain under," Armstid said. "But if you'd
rather . . ."

Back of the barn was some rusted sheets of tin roofing.
We took two of them and propped them against the
open side.

"You're welcome to the house," Armstid said.

"I thank you," pa said. "I'd take it right kind if you'd
give them a little snack."

"Sho," Armstid said. "Lula'll have supper ready soon as
she gets Cash comfortable." *He had gone back to the*

horse and he was taking the saddle off, his damp shirt
lapping flat to him when he moved.

Pa wouldn't come in the house.

"Come in and eat," Armstid said. "It's nigh ready."

"I wouldn't crave nothing," pa said. "I thank you."

"You come in and dry and eat," Armstid said. "It'll be
all right here."

"It's for her," pa said. "It's for her sake I am taking the
food. I got no team, no nothing. But she will be grateful
to ere a one of you."

"Sho," Armstid said. "You folks come in and dry."

But after Armstid gave pa a drink, he felt better, and
when we went in to see about Cash *he hadn't come in
with us. When I looked back he was leading the horse
into the barn* he was already talking about getting another team, and by supper time he had good as bought
it. *He is down there in the barn, sliding fluidly past the
gaudy lunging swirl, into the stall with it. He climbs on
to the manger and drags the hay down and leaves the
stall and seeks and finds the curry-comb. Then he returns
and slips quickly past the single crashing thump and up
against the horse, where it cannot over-reach. He applies
the curry-comb, holding himself within the horse's striking radius with the agility of an acrobat, cursing the horse
in a whisper of obscene caress. Its head flashes back,
tooth-cropped; its eyes roll in the dusk like marbles on a
gaudy velvet cloth as he strikes it upon the face with the
back of the curry-comb.*

ARMSTID

B UT TIME I GIVE HIM ANOTHER SUP OF WHISKY AND supper was about ready, he had done already bought a team from somebody, on a credit. Picking and choosing he were by then, saying how he didn't like this span and wouldn't put his money in nothing so-and-so owned, not even a hen coop.

"You might try Snopes," I said. "He's got three-four span. Maybe one of them would suit you."

Then he begun to mumble his mouth, looking at me like it was me that owned the only span of mules in the country and wouldn't sell them to him, when I knew that like as not it would be my team that would ever get them out of the lot at all. Only I don't know what they would do with them, if they had a team. Littlejohn had told me that the levee through Haley bottom had done gone for two miles and that the only way to get to Jefferson would be to go around by Mottson. But that was Anse's business.

"He's a close man to trade with," he says, mumbling his mouth. But when I give him another sup after supper, he cheered up some. He was aiming to go back to the barn and set up with her. Maybe he thought that if he just stayed down there ready to take out, Santa Claus would maybe bring him a span of mules. "But I reckon I can talk him around," he says. "A man'll always help a fellow in a tight, if he's got ere a drop of Christian blood in him."

"Of course you're welcome to the use of mine," I said.

me knowing how much he believed that was the reason.

"I thank you," he said. "She'll want to go in ourn," and him knowing how much I believed that was the reason.

After supper Jewel rode over to the Bend to get Peabody. I heard he was to be there today at Varner's. Jewel come back about midnight. Peabody had gone down below Inverness somewhere, but Uncle Billy come back with him, with his satchel of horse-physic. Like he says, a man ain't so different from a horse or a mule, come long come short, except a mule or a horse has got a little more sense. "What you been into now, boy?" he says, looking at Cash. "Get me a mattress and a chair and a glass of whisky," he says.

He made Cash drink the whisky, then he run Anse out of the room. "Lucky it was the same leg he broke last summer," Anse says, mournful, mumbling and blinking. "That's something."

We folded the mattress across Cash's legs and set the chair on the mattress and me and Jewel set on the chair and the gal held the lamp and Uncle Billy taken a chew of tobacco and went to work. Cash fought pretty hard for a while, until he fainted. Then he laid still, with big balls of sweat standing on his face like they had started to roll down and then stopped to wait for him.

When he waked up, Uncle Billy had done packed up and left. He kept on trying to say something until the gal leaned down and wiped his mouth. "It's his tools," she said.

"I brought them in," Darl said. "I got them."

He tried to talk again; she leaned down. "He wants to see them," she said. So Darl brought them in where he could see them. They shoved them under the side of the bed, where he could reach his hand and touch them when he felt better. Next morning Anse taken that horse and rode over to the Bend to see Snopes. Him and Jewel stood in the lot talking a while, then Anse got on the horse and rode off. I reckon that was the first time Jewel ever let anybody ride that horse, and until Anse come back he hung around in that swole-up way, watching the road like he was half a mind to take out after Anse and get the horse back.

Along toward nine o'clock it begun to get hot. That was when I see the first buzzard. Because of the wetting, I reckon. Anyway it wasn't until well into the day that I see them. Lucky the breeze was setting away from the house, so it wasn't until well into the morning. But soon as I see them it was like I could smell it in the field a mile away from just watching them, and then circling and circling for everybody in the county to see what was in my barn.

I was still a good half a mile from the house when I heard that boy yelling. I thought maybe he might have fell into the well or something, so I whipped up and come into the lot on the lope.

There must have been a dozen of them setting along the ridge-pole of the barn, and that boy was chasing another one around the lot like it was a turkey and it just lifting enough to dodge him and go flopping back to the roof of the shed again where he had found it setting on the coffin. It had got hot then, right, and the breeze had dropped or changed or something, so I went and found Jewel, but Lula come out.

"You got to do something," she said. "It's a outrage."

"That's what I aim to do," I said.

"It's a outrage," she said. "He should be lawed for treat‐ing her so."

"He's getting her into the ground the best he can," I said. So I found Jewel and asked him if he didn't want to take one of the mules and go over to the Bend and see about Anse. He didn't say nothing. He just looked at me with his jaws going bone-white and them bone-white eyes of hisn, then he went and begun to call Darl.

"What you fixing to do?" I said.

He didn't answer. Darl come out. "Come on," Jewel said.

"What you aim to do?" Darl said.

"Going to move the wagon," Jewel said over his shoulder.

"Don't be a fool," I said. "I never meant nothing. You couldn't help it." And Darl hung back too, but nothing wouldn't suit Jewel.

"Shut your goddamn mouth," he says.

"It's got to be somewhere," Darl said. "We'll take out soon as pa gets back."

"You won't help me?" Jewel says, them white eyes of hisn kind of blaring and his face shaking like he had a aguer.

"No," Darl said. "I won't. Wait till pa gets back."

So I stood in the door and watched him push and haul at that wagon. It was on a downhill, and once I thought he was fixing to beat out the back end of the shed. Then the dinner-bell rung. I called him, but he didn't look around. "Come on to dinner," I said. "Tell that boy." But he didn't answer, so I went on to dinner. The gal went down to get that boy, but she come back without him. About half through dinner we heard him yelling again, running that buzzard out.

"It's a outrage," Lula said; "a outrage."

"He's doing the best he can," I said. "A fellow don't trade with Snopes in thirty minutes. They'll set in the shade all afternoon to dicker."

"Do?" she says. "Do? He's done too much, already."

And I reckon he had. Trouble is, his quitting was just about to start our doing. He couldn't buy no team from nobody, let alone Snopes, withouten he had something to mortgage he didn't know would mortgage yet. And so when I went back to the field I looked at my mules and same as told them good-bye for a spell. And when I come back that evening and the sun shining all day on that shed, I wasn't so sho I would regret it.

He come riding up just as I went out to the porch, where they all was. He looked kind of funny: kind of more hang-dog than common, and kind of proud too. Like he had done something he thought was cute but wasn't so sho now how other folks would take it.

"I got a team," he said.

"You bought a team from Snopes?" I said.

"I reckon Snopes ain't the only man in this country that can drive a trade," he said.

"Sho," I said. He was looking at Jewel, with that funny look, but Jewel had done got down from the porch and was going toward the horse. To see what Anse had done to it, I reckon.

"Jewel," Anse says. Jewel looked back. "Come here," Anse says. Jewel come back a little and stopped again.

"What you want?" he said.

"So you got a team from Snopes," I said. "He'll send them over tonight, I reckon? You'll want a early start to-morrow, long as you'll have to go by Mottson."

Then he quit looking like he had been for a while. He got that badgered look like he used to have, mumbling his mouth.

"I do the best I can," he said. " 'Fore God, if there were ere a man in the living world suffered the trials and floutings I have suffered."

"A fellow that just beat Snopes in a trade ought to

feel pretty good," I said. "What did you give him, Anse?"

He didn't look at me. "I give a chattel mortgage on my cultivator and seeder," he said.

"But they ain't worth forty dollars. How far do you aim to get with a forty-dollar team?"

They were all watching him now, quiet and steady. Jewel was stopped, half-way back, waiting to go on to the horse. "I give other things," Anse said. He begun to mumble his mouth again, standing there like he was waiting for somebody to hit him and him with his mind already made up not to do nothing about it.

"What other things?" Darl said.

"Hell," I said. "You take my team. You can bring them back. I'll get along some way."

"So that's what you were doing in Cash's clothes last night," Darl said. He said it just like he was reading it outen the paper. Like he never give a durn himself one way or the other. Jewel had come back now, standing there, looking at Anse with them marble eyes of hisn. "Cash aimed to buy that talking machine from Suratt with that money," Darl said.

Anse stood there, mumbling his mouth. Jewel watched him. He ain't never blinked yet.

"But that's just eight dollars more," Darl said, in that voice like he was just listening and never give a durn himself. "That still won't buy a team."

Anse looked at Jewel quick, kind of sliding his eyes that way, then he looked down again. "God knows, if there were ere a man," he says. Still they didn't say nothing. They just watched him, waiting, and him sliding his eyes toward their feet and up their legs but no higher. "And the horse," he says.

"What horse?" Jewel said. Anse just stood there. I be durn, if a man can't keep the upper hand of his sons, he ought to run them away from home, no matter how big they are. And if he can't do that, I be durn if he oughtn't to leave himself. I be durn if I wouldn't. "You mean, you tried to swap my horse?" Jewel says.

Anse stands there, dangle-armed. "For fifteen years I ain't had a tooth in my head," he says. "God knows it. He knows in fifteen years I ain't et the victuals He aimed for man to eat to keep his strength up, and me saving a nickel here and a nickel there so my family wouldn't suffer it, to buy them teeth so I could eat God's appointed food. I give that money. I thought that if I could do without eating, my sons could do without riding. God knows I did."

Jewel stands with his hands on his hips, looking at Anse. Then he looks away. He looked out across the field, his face still as a rock, like it was somebody else talking about somebody else's horse and him not even listening. Then he spit, slow, and said "Hell" and he turned and went on to the gate and unhitched the horse and got on it. It was moving when he come into the saddle and by the time he was on it they was tearing down the road like the Law might have been behind them. They went out of sight that way, the two of them looking like some kind of a spotted cyclone.

"Well," I says. "You take my team," I said. But he wouldn't do it. And they wouldn't even stay, and that boy chasing them buzzards all day in the hot sun until he was nigh as crazy as the rest of them. "Leave Cash here, anyway," I said. But they wouldn't do that. They made a pallet for him with quilts on top of the coffin and laid him on it and set his tools by him, and we put my team in and hauled the wagon about a mile down the road.

"If we'll bother you here," Anse says, "just say so."

"Sho," I said. "It'll be fine here. Safe, too. Now let's go back and eat supper."

"I thank you," Anse said. "We got a little something in the basket. We can make out."

"Where'd you get it?" I said.

"We brought it from home."

"But it'll be stale now," I said. "Come and get some hot victuals."

But they wouldn't come. "I reckon we can make out," Anse said. So I went home and et and taken a basket back to them and tried again to make them come back to the house.

"I thank you," he said. "I reckon we can make out." So I left them there, squatting around a little fire, waiting; God knows what for.

I come on home. I kept thinking about them there, and about that fellow tearing away on that horse. And that would be the last they would see of him. And I be durn if I could blame him. Not for wanting to not give up his horse, but for getting shut of such a durn fool as Anse.

Or that's what I thought then. Because be durn if there ain't something about a durn fellow like Anse that seems to make a man have to help him, even when he knows he'll be wanting to kick himself next minute. Because about a hour after breakfast next morning Eustace Grimm that works Snopes' place come up with a span of mules, hunting Anse.

"I thought him and Anse never traded," I said.

"Sho," Eustace said. "All they liked was the horse. Like I said to Mr. Snopes, he was letting this team go for fifty dollars, because if his uncle Flem had a just kept them Texas horses when he owned them, Anse wouldn't a-never——"

"The horse?" I said. "Anse's boy taken that horse and cleared out last night, probably half-way to Texas by now, and Anse——"

"I didn't know who brung it," Eustace said. "I never see them. I just found the horse in the barn this morning when I went to feed, and I told Mr. Snopes and he said to bring the team on over here."

Well, that'll be the last they'll ever see of him now, sho enough. Come Christmas time they'll maybe get a postal card from him in Texas, I reckon. And if it hadn't a been Jewel, I reckon it'd a been me; I owe him that much, my-self. I be durn if Anse don't conjure a man, some way. I be durn if he ain't a sight.

VARDAMAN

NOW THERE ARE SEVEN OF THEM, IN LITTLE TALL black circles.

"Look, Darl," I say; "see?"

He looks up. We watch them in little tall black circles of not-moving.

"Yesterday there were just four," I say.

There were more than four on the barn.

"Do you know what I would do if he tries to light on the wagon again?" I say.

"What would you do?" Darl says.

"I wouldn't let him light on her," I say. "I wouldn't let him light on Cash, either."

Cash is sick. He is sick on the box. But my mother is a fish.

"We got to get some medicine in Mottson," pa says. "I reckon we'll just have to."

"How do you feel, Cash?" Darl says.

"It don't bother none," Cash says.

"Do you want it propped a little higher?" Darl says.

Cash has a broken leg. He has had two broken legs. He lies on the box with a quilt rolled under his head and a piece of wood under his knee.

"I reckon we ought to left him at Armstid's," pa says.

I haven't got a broken leg and pa hasn't and Darl hasn't and "It's just the bumps," Cash says. "It kind of grinds together a little on a bump. I don't bother none." *Jewel has gone away. He and his horse went away one supper time.*

"It's because she wouldn't have us beholden," pa says. "'Fore God, I do the best that ere a man." *Is it because Jewel's mother is a horse, Darl? I said.*

"Maybe I can draw the ropes a little tighter," Darl says. *That's why Jewel and I were both in the shed and she was in the wagon because the horse lives in the barn and I had to keep on running the buzzard away from*

"If you just would," Cash says. And Dewey Dell hasn't got a broken leg and I haven't. Cash is my brother.

We stop. When Darl loosens the rope Cash begins to sweat again. His teeth look out.

"Hurt?" Darl says.

"I reckon you better put it back," Cash says.

Darl puts the rope back, pulling hard. Cash's teeth look out.

"Hurt?" Darl says.

"It don't bother none," Cash says.

"Do you want pa to drive slower?" Darl says.

"No," Cash says. "Ain't no time to hang back. It don't bother none."

"We'll have to get some medicine at Mottson," pa says. "I reckon we'll have to."

"Tell him to go on," Cash says. We go on. Dewey Dell leans back and wipes Cash's face. Cash is my brother. *But Jewel's mother is a horse. My mother is a fish. Darl says that when we come to the water again I might see her and Dewey Dell said, She's in the box; how could she have got out? She got out through the holes I bored, into the water I said, and when we come to the water again I am going to see her. My mother is not in the box. My mother does not smell like that. My mother is a fish.*

"Those cakes will be in fine shape by the time we get to Jefferson," Darl says.

Dewey Dell does not look around.

"You better try to sell them in Mottson," Darl says.

"When will we get to Mottson, Darl?" I say.

"Tomorrow," Darl says. "If this team don't rack to pieces. Snopes must have fed them on sawdust."

"Why did he feed them on sawdust, Darl?" I say.

"Look," Darl says. "See?"

"Now there are nine of them, tall in little tall black circles.

When we come to the foot of the hill pa stops and Darl and Dewey Dell and I get out. Cash can't walk because he has a broken leg. "Come up, mules," pa says. The mules walk hard; the wagon creaks. Darl and Dewey Dell and I walk behind the wagon, up the hill. When we come to the top of the hill pa stops and we get back into the wagon.

Now there are ten of them, tall in little tall black circles on the sky.

"No," Cash says. "Ain't no time to hang back. It don't
bother none."
"You could have banked it at Mottson," pa says.
"I reckon so," Cash says.
"Tell him to go on," Cash says. We go on. Dewey Dell
leans back and wipes Cash's face. Cash is a by brother.

MOSELEY

⸻

I HAPPENED TO LOOK UP, AND SAW HER OUTSIDE THE WIN-
dow, looking in. Not close to the glass, and not looking at anything in particular; just standing there with her
head turned this way and her eyes full on me and kind
of blank too, like she was waiting for a sign. When I
looked up again she was moving toward the door.

She kind of bumbled at the screen door a minute, like
they do, and came in. She had on a stiff-brimmed straw
hat setting on the top of her head and she was carrying
a package wrapped in newspaper: I thought that she had
a quarter or a dollar at the most, and that after she stood
around awhile she would maybe buy a cheap comb or
a bottle of nigger toilet water, so I never disturbed her
for a minute or so except to notice that she was pretty
in a kind of sullen, awkward way, and that she looked a
sight better in her gingham dress and her own complexion
than she would after she bought whatever she would
finally decide on. Or tell that she wanted. I knew that
she had already decided before she came in. But you
have to let them take their time. So I went on with what
I was doing, figuring to let Albert wait on her when he
caught up at the fountain, when he came back to me.

"That woman," he said. "You better see what she
wants."

"What does she want?" I said.

"I don't know. I can't get anything out of her. You
better wait on her."

So I went around the counter. I saw that she was

barefooted, standing with her feet flat and easy on the floor, like she was used to it. She was looking at me, hard, holding the package; I saw she had about as black a pair of eyes as ever I saw, and she was a stranger. I never remembered seeing her in Mottson before. "What can I do for you?" I said.

Still she didn't say anything. She stared at me without winking. Then she looked back at the folks at the fountain. Then she looked past me, toward the back of the store.

"Do you want to look at some toilet things?" I said. "Or is it medicine you want?"

"That's it," she said. She looked quick back at the fountain again. So I thought maybe her ma or somebody had sent her in for some of this female dope and she was ashamed to ask for it. I knew she couldn't have a complexion like hers and use it herself, let alone not being much more than old enough to barely know what it was for. It's a shame, the way they poison themselves with it. But a man's got to stock it or go out of business in this country.

"Oh," I said. "What do you use? We have——" She looked at me again, almost like she had said hush, and looked toward the back of the store again.

"I'd liefer go back there," she said.

"All right," I said. You have to humour them. You save time by it. I followed her to the back. She put her hand on the gate. "There's nothing back there but the prescription case," I said. "What do you want?" She stopped and looked at me. It was like she had taken some kind of a lid off her face, her eyes. It was her eyes: kind of dumb and hopeful and sullenly willing to be disappointed all at the same time. But she was in trouble of some sort; I could see that. "What's your trouble?" I said. "Tell me what it is you want. I'm pretty busy." I wasn't meaning to hurry her, but a man just hasn't got the time they have out there.

"It's the female trouble," she said.

"Oh," I said. "Is that all?" I thought maybe she was younger than she looked, and her first one had scared her, or maybe one had been a little abnormal as it will in young women. "Where's your ma?" I said. "Haven't you got one?"

"She's out yonder in the wagon," she said.

"Why not talk to her about it before you take any medicine," I said. "Any woman would have told you about it." She looked at me, and I looked at her again and said, "How old are you?"

"Seventeen," she said.

"Oh," I said. "I thought maybe you were . . ." She was watching me. But then, in the eyes all of them look like they had no age and knew everything in the world, anyhow. "Are you too regular, or not regular enough?"

She quit looking at me but she didn't move. "Yes," she said. "I reckon so. Yes."

"Well, which?" I said. "Don't you know?" It's a crime and a shame; but after all, they'll buy it from somebody. She stood there, not looking at me. "You want something to stop it?" I said. "Is that it?"

"No," she said. "That's it. It's already stopped."

"Well, what——" Her face was lowered a little, still, like they do in all their dealings with a man so he don't ever know just where the lightning will strike next. "You are not married, are you?" I said.

"No."

"Oh," I said. "And how long has it been since it stopped? about five months maybe?"

"It ain't been but two," she said.

"Well, I haven't got anything in my store you want to buy," I said, "unless it's a nipple. And I'd advise you to buy that and go back home and tell your pa, if you have one, and let him make somebody buy you a wedding li- cence. Was that all you wanted?"

But she just stood there, not looking at me.

"I got the money to pay you," she said.

"Is it your own, or did he act enough of a man to give you the money?"

"He give it to me. Ten dollars. He said that would be enough."

"A thousand dollars wouldn't be enough in my store and ten cents wouldn't be enough," I said. "You take my advice and go home and tell you pa or your brothers if you have any or the first man you come to in the road."

But she didn't move. "Lafe said I could get it at the drug-store. He said to tell you me and him wouldn't never tell nobody you sold it to us."

"And I just wish your precious Lafe had come for it himself; that's what I wish. I don't know: I'd have had a little respect for him then. And you can go back and tell him I said so—if he ain't half-way to Texas by now, which I don't doubt. Me, a respectable druggist, that's kept store and raised a family and been a church-member for fifty-six years in this town. I'm a good mind to tell your folks myself, if I can just find who they are."

She looked at me now, her eyes and face kind of blank again like when I first saw her through the window. "I didn't know," she said. "He told me I could get some- thing at the drug-store. He said they might not want to sell it to me, but if I had ten dollars and told them I wouldn't never tell nobody . . ."

"He never said this drug-store," I said. "If he did or mentioned my name, I defy him to prove it. I defy him to repeat it or I'll prosecute him to the full extent of the law, and you can tell him so."

"But maybe another drug-store would," she said.

"Then I don't want to know it. Me, that's——" Then I looked at her. But it's a hard life they have; sometimes a man . . . if there can ever be any excuse for sin, which it can't be. And then, life wasn't made to be easy on folks: they wouldn't ever had any reason to be good and die. "Look here," I said. "You get that notion out of your head. The Lord gave you what you have, even if He did use the devil to do it; you let Him take it away from you if it's His will to do so. You go on back to Lafe and you and him take that ten dollars and get married with it."

"Lafe said I could get something at the drug-store," she said.

"Then go and get it," I said. "You won't get it here."

She went out, carrying the package, her feet making a little hissing on the floor. She bumbled again at the door and went out. I could see her through the glass going on down the street.

It was Albert told me about the rest of it. He said the wagon was stopped in front of Grummet's hardware store, with the ladies all scattering up and down the street with handkerchief to their noses, and a crowd of hard-nosed men and boys standing around the wagon, listening to the marshal arguing with the man. He was a kind of tall, gaunted man sitting on the wagon, saying it was a public street and he reckoned he had as much right there as anybody, and the marshal telling him he would have to move on; folks couldn't stand it. It had been dead eight days, Albert said. They came from some place out in Yoknapatawpha county, trying to get to Jefferson with it. It must have been like a piece of rotten cheese coming into

an ant-hill, in that ramshackle wagon that Albert said
folks were scared would fall all to pieces before they
could get it out of town, with that home-made box and
another fellow with a broken leg lying on a quilt on top
of it, and the father and a little boy sitting on the seat
and the marshal trying to make them get out of town.

"It's a public street," the man says. "I reckon we can
stop to buy something same as airy other man. We got
the money to pay for hit, and hit ain't airy law that says
a man can't spend his money where he wants."

They had stopped to buy some cement. The other
son was in Grummet's, trying to make Grummet break
a sack and let him have ten cents' worth, and finally
Grummet broke the sack to get him out. They wanted
the cement to fix the fellow's broken leg, someway.

"Why, you'll kill him," the marshal said. "You'll cause
him to lose his leg. You take him on to a doctor, and you
get this thing buried soon as you can. Don't you know
you're liable to jail for endangering the public health?"

"We're doing the best we can," the father said. Then
he told a long tale about how they had to wait for the
wagon to come back and how the bridge was washed
away and how they went eight miles to another bridge
and it was gone too so they came back and swum the
ford and the mules got drowned and how they got another team and found that the road was washed out and
they had to come clean around by Mottson, and then
the one with the cement came back and told him to shut
up.

"We'll be gone in a minute," he told the marshal.

"We never aimed to bother nobody," the father said.

"You take that fellow to a doctor," the marshal told
the one with the cement.

"I reckon he's all right," he said.

"It ain't that we're hard-hearted," the marshal said "But I reckon you can tell yourself how it is."

"Sho," the other said. "We'll take out soon as Dewey Dell comes back. She went to deliver a package."

So they stood there with the folks backed off with handkerchiefs to their faces, until in a minute the girl came up with that newspaper package.

"Come on," the one with the cement said, "we've lost too much time." So they got in the wagon and went on. And when I went to supper it still seemed like I could smell it. And the next day I met the marshal and I began to sniff and said,

"Smell anything?"

"I reckon they're in Jefferson by now," he said.

"Or in jail. Well, thank the Lord it's not our jail."

"That's a fact," he said.

DARL

"**H**ERE'S A PLACE," PA SAYS. HE PULLS THE TEAM UP and sits looking at the house. "We could get some water over yonder."

"All right," I say. "You'll have to borrow a bucket from them, Dewey Dell."

"God knows," pa says. "I wouldn't be beholden, God knows."

"If you see a good-sized can, you might bring it," I say. Dewey Dell gets down from the wagon, carrying the package. "You had more trouble than you expected, selling those cakes in Mottson," I say. How do our lives ravel out into the no-wind, no-sound, the weary gestures wearily recapitulant: echoes of old compulsions with no-hand on no-strings: in sunset we fall into furious attitudes, dead gestures of dolls. Cash broke his leg and now the sawdust is running out. He is bleeding to death is Cash.

"I wouldn't be beholden," pa says. "God knows."

"Then make some water yourself," I say. "We can use Cash's hat."

When Dewey Dell comes back the man comes with her. Then he stops and she comes on and he stands there and after a while he goes back to the house and stands on the porch, watching us.

"We better not try to lift him down," pa says. "We can fix it here."

"Do you want to be lifted down, Cash?" I say.

"Won't we get to Jefferson tomorrow?" he says. He is watching us, his eyes interrogatory, intent, and sad. "I can last it out."

"It'll be easier on you," pa says. "It'll keep it from rubbing together."

"I can last it," Cash says. "We'll lose time stopping."

"We done bought the cement, now," pa says.

"I could last it," Cash says. "It ain't but one more day. It don't bother to speak of." He looks at us, his eyes wide in his thin grey face, questioning. "It sets up so," he says.

"We done bought it now," pa says.

I mix the cement in the can, stirring the slow water into the pale-green thick coils. I bring the can to the wagon where Cash can see. He lies on his back, his thin profile in silhouette, ascetic and profound against the sky. "Does that look about right?" I say.

"You don't want too much water, or it won't work right," he says.

"Is this too much?"

"Maybe if you could get a little sand," he says. "It ain't but one more day," he says. "It don't bother me none."

Vardaman goes back down the road to where we crossed the branch and returns with sand. He pours it slowly into the thick coiling in the can. I go to the wagon again.

"Does that look all right?"

"Yes," Cash says. "I could have lasted. It don't bother me none."

We loosen the splints and pour the cement over his leg, slow.

"Watch out for it," Cash says. "Don't get none on it if you can help."

"Yes," I say. Dewey Dell tears a piece of paper from the package and wipes the cement from the top of it as it drips from Cash's leg.

"How does that feel?"

"It feels fine," he says. "It's cold. It feels fine."

"If it'll just help you," pa says. "I asks your forgiveness. I never forseen it no more than you."

"It feels fine," Cash says.

If you could just ravel out into time. That would be nice. It would be nice if you could just ravel out into time.

We replace the splints, the cords, drawing them tight, the cement in thick pale green slow surges among the cords, Cash watching us quietly with that profound questioning look.

"That'll steady it," I say.

"Ay," Cash says. "I'm obliged."

Then we all turn on the wagon and watch him. He is

coming up the road behind us, wooden-backed, wooden-faced, moving only from his hips down. He comes up without a word, with his pale rigid eyes in his high sullen face, and gets into the wagon.

"Here's a hill," pa says. "I reckon you'll have to get out and walk."

VARDAMAN

DARL AND JEWEL AND DEWEY DELL AND I ARE WALKING up the hill behind the wagon. Jewel came back. He came up the road and got into the wagon. He was walking. Jewel hasn't got a horse any more. Jewel is my brother. Cash is my brother. Cash has a broken leg. We fixed Cash's leg so it doesn't hurt. Cash is my brother. Jewel is my brother too, but he hasn't got a broken leg.

Now there are five of them, tall in little tall black circles.

"Where do they stay at night, Darl?" I say. "When we stop at night in the barn, where do they stay?"

The hill goes off into the sky. Then the sun comes up from behind the hill and the mules and the wagon and pa walk on the sun. You cannot watch them, walking slow on the sun. In Jefferson it is red on the track behind the glass. The track goes shining round and round. Dewey Dell says so.

Tonight I am going to see where they stay while we are in the barn.

DARL

"Jewel," I say, "whose son are you?"
The breeze was setting up from the barn, so we
put her under the apple tree, where the moonlight can
dapple the apple tree upon the long slumbering flanks
within which now and then she talks in little trickling
bursts of secret and murmurous bubbling. I took Vardaman to listen. When we came up the cat leaped down
from it and flicked away with silver claw and silver eye
into the shadow.

"Your mother was a horse, but who was your father,
Jewel?"

"You goddamn lying son of a bitch."

"Don't call me that," I say.

"You goddamn lying son of a bitch."

"Don't you call me that, Jewel." In the tall moonlight
his eyes look like spots of white paper pasted on a high
small football.

After supper Cash began to sweat a little. "It's getting
a little hot," he said. "It was the sun shining on it all day,
I reckon."

"You want some water poured on it?" we say. "Maybe
that will ease it some."

"I'd be obliged," Cash said. "It was the sun shining on
it, I reckon. I ought to thought and kept it covered."

"We ought to thought," we said. "You couldn't have
suspicioned."

"I never noticed it getting hot," Cash said. "I ought to
minded it."

So we poured the water over it. His leg and foot below the cement look like they had been boiled. "Does that feel better?" we said.

"I'm obliged," Cash said. "It feels fine."

Dewey Dell wipes his face with the hem of her dress.

"See if you can get some sleep," we say.

"Sho," Cash says. "I'm right obliged. It feels fine now."

Jewel, I say, Who was your father, Jewel?

Goddamn you. Goddamn you.

VARDAMAN

SHE WAS UNDER THE APPLE TREE AND DARL AND I GO across the moon and the cat jumps down and runs and we can hear her inside the wood. "Hear?" Darl says. "Put your ear close."

I put my ear close and I can hear her. Only I can't tell what she is saying.

"What is she saying, Darl?" I say. "Who is she talking to?"

"She's talking to God," Darl says. "She is calling on Him to help her."

"What does she want Him to do?" I say.

"She wants Him to hide her away from the sight of man," Darl says.

"Why does she want to hide her away from the sight of man, Darl?"

"So she can lay down her life," Darl says.

"Why does she want to lay down her life, Darl?"

"Listen," Darl says. We hear her. We hear her turn over on her side. "Listen," Darl says.

"She's turned over," I say. "She's looking at me through the wood."

"Yes," Darl says.

"How can she see through the wood, Darl?"

"Come," Darl says. "We must let her be quiet. Come."

"She can't see out there, because the holes are in the top," I say. "How can she see, Darl?"

"Let's go see about Cash," Darl says.

And I saw something Dewey Dell told me not to tell nobody.

Cash is sick in his leg. We fixed his leg this afternoon, but he is sick in it again, lying on the bed. We pour water on his leg and then he feels fine.

"I feel fine," Cash says. "I'm obliged to you."

"Try to get some sleep," we say.

"I feel fine," Cash says. "I'm obliged to you."

And I saw something Dewey Dell told me not to tell nobody. It is not about pa and it is not about Cash and it is not about Jewel and it is not about Dewey Dell and it is not about me.

Dewey Dell and I are going to sleep on the pallet. It is on the back porch, where we can see the barn, and the moon shines on half of the pallet and we will lie half in the white and half in the black, with the moonlight on our legs. And then I am going to see where they stay at night while we are in the barn. We are not in the barn to-night but I can see the barn and so I am going to find where they stay at night.

We lie on the pallet, with our legs in the moon.

"Look," I say, "my legs look black. Your legs look black, too."

"Go to sleep," Dewey Dell says.

Jefferson is a far piece.

"Dewey Dell."

"If it's not Christmas now, how will it be there?"

It goes round and round on the shining track. Then the track goes shining round and round.

"Will what be there?"

"That train. In the window."

"You go to sleep. You can see tomorrow if it's there."

Maybe Santa Claus won't know they are town boys.

"Dewey Dell."

"You go to sleep. He ain't going to let none of them town boys have it."

It was behind the window, red on the track, and the track shining round and round. It made my heart hurt. And then it was pa and Jewel and Darl and Mr. Gillespie's boy. Mr. Gillespie's boy's legs come down under his nightshirt. When he goes into the moon, his legs fuzz. They go on around the house toward the apple tree.

"What are they going to do, Dewey Dell?"

They went around the house toward the apple tree.

"I can smell her," I say. "Can you smell her, too?"

"Hush," Dewey Dell says. "The wind's changed. Go to sleep."

And so I am going to know where they stay at night soon. They come around the house, going across the yard in the moon, carrying her on their shoulders. They carry her down to the barn, the moon shining flat and quiet on her. Then they come back and go into the house again. While they were in the moon, Mr. Gillespie's boy's legs fuzzed. And then I waited and I said Dewey Dell? and then I waited and then I went to find where they stay at night and I saw something that Dewey Dell told me not to tell nobody.

DARL

AGAINST THE DARK DOORWAY HE SEEMS TO MATERIALIZE
out of darkness, lean as a racehorse in his underclothes in the beginning of the glare. He leaps to the
ground with on his face an expression of furious unbelief.
He has seen me without even turning his head or his eyes
in which the glare swims like two small torches. "Come
on," he says, leaping down the slope toward the barn.

For an instant longer he runs silver in the moonlight,
then he springs out like a flat figure cut cleanly from tin
against an abrupt and soundless explosion as the whole
loft of the barn takes fire at once, as though it had been
stuffed with powder. The front, the conical façade with
the square orifice of doorway broken only by the square
squat shape of the coffin on the saw-horses like a cubistic
bug, comes into relief. Behind me pa and Gillespie and
Mack and Dewey Dell and Vardaman emerge from the
house.

He pauses at the coffin, stooping, looking at me, his
face furious. Overhead the flames sound like thunder;
across us rushes a cool draught: there is no heat in it at
all yet, and a handful of chaff lifts suddenly and sucks
swiftly along the stalls where a horse is screaming.
"Quick," I say; "the horses."

He glares a moment longer at me, then at the roof overhead, then he leaps toward the stall where the horse
screams. It plunges and kicks, the sound of the crashing
blows sucking up into the sound of the flames. They
sound like an interminable train crossing an endless tres-

tle. Gillespie and Mack pass me, in knee-length night-shirts, shouting, their voices thin and high and meaning-less and at the same time profoundly wild and sad: ". . . cow . . . stall . . ." Gillespie's nightshirt rushes ahead of him on the draft, ballooning about his hairy thighs.

The stall door has swung shut. Jewel thrusts it back with his buttocks and he appears, his back arched, the muscles ridged through his garments as he drags the horse out by its head. In the glare its eyes roll with soft, fleet, wild opaline fire; its muscles bunch and run as it flings its head about, lifting Jewel clear of the ground. He drags it on, slowly, terrifically; again he gives me across his shoulder a single glare furious and brief. Even when they are clear of the barn the horse continues to fight and lash backward toward the doorway until Gillespie passes me, stark naked, his nightshirt wrapped about the mule's head, and beats the maddened horse on out of the door.

Jewel returns, running; again he looks down at the cof-fin. But he comes on. "Where's cow?" he cries, passing me. I follow him. In the stall Mack is struggling with the other mule. When its head turns into the glare I can see the wild rolling of its eye too, but it makes no sound. It just stands there, watching Mack over its shoulder, swing-ing its hindquarters toward him whenever he approaches. He looks back at us, his eyes and mouth three round holes in his face on which the freckles look like English peas on a plate. His voice is thin, high, far away.

"I can't do nothing. . . ." It is as though the sound had been swept from his lips and up and away, speaking back to us from an immense distance of exhaustion. Jewel slides past us; the mule whirls and lashes out, but he has already gained its head. I lean to Mack's ear:

"Nightshirt. Around his head."

Mack stares at me. Then he rips the nightshirt off and flings it over the mule's head, and it becomes docile at once. Jewel is yelling at him: "Cow? Cow?"

"Back," Mack cries. "Last stall."

The cow watches us as we enter. She is backed into the corner, head lowered, still chewing though rapidly. But she makes no move. Jewel has paused, looking up, and suddenly we watch the entire floor to the loft dissolve. It just turns to fire; a faint litter of sparks rains down. He glances about. Back under the trough is a three-legged milking-stool. He catches it up and swings it into the planking of the rear wall. He splinters a plank, then another, a third; we tear the fragments away. While we are stooping at the opening something charges into us from behind. It is the cow; with a single whistling breath she rushes between us and through the gap and into the outer glare, her tail erect and rigid as a broom nailed upright to the end of her spine.

Jewel turns back into the barn. "Here," I say; "Jewel!" I grasp at him; he strikes my hand down. "You fool," I say, "don't you see you can't make it back yonder?" The hall-way looks like a searchlight turned into rain. "Come on," I say, "around this way."

When we are through the gap he begins to run. "Jewel," I say, running. He darts around the corner. When I reach it he has almost reached the next one, running against the glare like that figure cut from tin. Pa and Gillespie and Mack are some distance away, watching the barn, pink against the darkness where for the time the moonlight has been vanquished. "Catch him!" I cry; "stop him!"

When I reach the front, he is struggling with Gillespie; the one lean in underclothes, the other stark naked. They are like two figures in a Greek frieze, isolated out of all reality by the red glare. Before I can reach them he has

struck Gillespie to the ground and turned and run back
into the barn.

The sound of it has become quite peaceful now, like
the sound of the river did. We watch through the dissolving proscenium of the doorway as Jewel runs crouch-
ing to the far end of the coffin and stoops to it. For an
instant he looks up and out at us through the rain of
burning hay like a portière of flaming beads, and I can
see his mouth shape as he calls my name.

"Jewel!" Dewey Dell cries; "Jewel!" It seems to me that
I now hear the accumulation of her voice through the
last five minutes, and I hear her scuffling and struggling
as pa and Mack hold her, screaming, "Jewel! Jewel!" But
he is no longer looking at us. We see his shoulders strain
as he up-ends the coffin and slides it single-handed from
the saw-horses. It looms unbelievably tall, hiding him: I
would not have believed that Addie Bundren would have
needed that much room to lie comfortable in; for another
instant it stands upright while the sparks rain on it in
scattering bursts as though they engendered other sparks
from the contact. Then it topples forward, gaining momentum, revealing Jewel and the sparks raining on him
too in engendering gusts, so that he appears to be enclosed in a thin nimbus of fire. Without stopping it over-
ends and rears again, pauses, then crashes slowly forward
and through the curtain. This time Jewel is riding upon
it, clinging to it, until it crashes down and flings him forward and clear and Mack leaps forward into a thin smell
of scorching meat and slaps at the widening crimson-
edged holes that bloom like flowers in his undershirt.

VARDAMAN

WHEN I WENT TO FIND WHERE THEY STAY AT NIGHT, I *saw something*. They said, "Where is Darl? Where did Darl go?"

They carried her back under the apple tree.

The barn was still red, but it wasn't a barn now. It was sunk down, and the red went swirling up. The barn went swirling up in little red pieces, against the sky and the stars so that the stars moved backward.

And then Cash was still awake. He turned his head from side to side, with sweat on his face.

"Do you want some more water on it, Cash?" Dewey Dell said.

Cash's leg and foot turned black. We held the lamp and looked at Cash's foot and leg where it was black.

"Your foot looks like a nigger's foot, Cash," I said.

"I reckon we'll have to bust it off," pa said.

"What in the tarnation you put it on there for?" Mr. Gillespie said.

"I thought it would steady it some," pa said. "I just aimed to help him."

They got the flatiron and the hammer. Dewey Dell held the lamp. They had to hit it hard. And then Cash went to sleep.

"He's asleep now," I said. "It can't hurt him while he's asleep."

It just cracked. It wouldn't come off.

"It'll take the hide, too," Mr. Gillespie said. "Why in

the tarnation you put it on there? Didn't none of you think to grease his leg first?"

"I just aimed to help him," pa said. "It was Darl put it on."

"Where is Darl?" they said.

"Didn't none of you have more sense than that?" Mr. Gillespie said. "I'd 'a' thought he would, anyway."

Jewel was lying on his face. His back was red. Dewey Dell put the medicine on it. The medicine was made out of butter and soot, to draw out the fire. Then his back was black.

"Does it hurt, Jewel?" I said. "Your back looks like a nigger's, Jewel," I said. Cash's foot and leg looked like a nigger's. Then they broke it off. Cash's leg bled.

"You go on back and lay down," Dewey Dell said. "You ought to be asleep."

"Where is Darl?" they said.

He is out there under the apple tree with her, lying on her. He is there so the cat won't come back. I said, "Are you going to keep the cat away, Darl?"

The moonlight dappled on him too. On her it was still, but on Darl it dappled up and down.

"You needn't to cry," I said. "Jewel got her out. You needn't to cry, Darl."

The barn is still red. It used to be redder than this. Then it went swirling, making the stars run backward without falling. It hurt my heart like the train did.

When I went to find where they stay at night, I saw something that Dewey Dell says I mustn't never tell nobody.

DARL

W E HAVE BEEN PASSING THE SIGNS FOR SOME TIME
now: the drug-stores, the clothing stores, the patent
medicine and the garages and cafés, and the mile-boards
diminishing, becoming more starkly re-accruent: 3 mi. 2
mi. From the crest of a hill, as we get into the wagon
again, we can see the smoke low and flat, seemingly un-
moving in the unwinded afternoon.

"Is that it, Darl?" Vardaman says. "Is that Jefferson?"
He too has lost flesh; like ours, his face has an expression
strained, dreamy, and gaunt.

"Yes," I say. He lifts his head and looks at the sky. High
against it they hang in narrowing circles, like the smoke,
with an outward semblance of form and purpose, but
with no inference of motion, progress or retrograde. We
mount the wagon again where Cash lies on the box,
the jagged shards of cement cracked about his leg. The
shabby mules droop rattling and clanking down the hill.

"We'll have to take him to the doctor," pa says.
"I reckon it ain't no way around it." The back of Jewel's
shirt, where it touches him, stains slow and black with
grease. Life was created in the valleys. It blew up on to
the hills on the old terrors, the old lusts, the old despairs.
That's why you must walk up the hills so you can ride
down.

Dewey Dell sits on the seat, the newspaper package on
her lap. When we reach the foot of the hill where the
road flattens between close walls of trees, she begins to

look about quietly from one side of the road to the other. At last she says,

"I got to stop."

Pa looks at her, his shabby profile that of anticipant and disgruntled annoyance. He does not check the team.

"What for?"

"I got to go to the bushes," Dewey Dell says.

Pa does not check the team. "Can't you wait till we get to town? It ain't over a mile now."

"Stop," Dewey Dell says. "I got to go to the bushes."

Pa stops in the middle of the road and we watch Dewey Dell descend, carrying the package. She does not look back.

"Why not leave your cakes here?" I say. "We'll watch them."

She descends steadily, not looking at us.

"How would she know where to go to if she waited till we get to town?" Vardaman says. "Where would you go to do it in town, Dewey Dell?"

She lifts the package down and turns and disappears among the trees and undergrowth.

"Don't be no longer than you can help," pa says. "We ain't got no time to waste." She does not answer. After a while we cannot hear her even. "We ought to done like Armstid and Gillespie said and sent word to town and had it dug and ready," he said.

"Why didn't you?" I say. "You could have telephoned."

"What for?" Jewel says. "Who the hell can't dig a hole in the ground?"

A car comes over the hill. It begins to sound the horn, slowing. It runs along the roadside in low gear, the outside wheels in the ditch, and passes us and goes on. Vardaman watches it until it is out of sight.

"How far is it now, Darl?" he says.

"Not far," I say.

"We ought to done it," pa says. "I just never wanted to be beholden to none except her flesh and blood."

"Who the hell can't dig a damn hole in the ground?" Jewel says.

"It ain't respectful, talking that way about her grave," pa says. "You all don't know what it is. You never pure loved her, none of you." Jewel does not answer. He sits a little stiffly erect, his body arched away from his shirt. His high-coloured jaw juts.

Dewey Dell returns. We watch her emerge from the bushes, carrying the package, and climb into the wagon. She now wears her Sunday dress, her beads, her shoes and stockings.

"I thought I told you to leave them clothes to home," pa says. She does not answer, does not look at us. She sits the package in the wagon and gets in. The wagon moves on.

"How many more hills now, Darl?" Vardaman says.

"Just one," I say. "The next one goes right up into town."

This hill is red sand, bordered on either hand by negro cabins; against the sky ahead the massed telephone lines run, and the clock on the court-house lifts among the trees. In the sand the wheels whisper, as though the very earth would hush our entry. We descend as the hill commences to rise.

We follow the wagon, the whispering wheels, passing the cabins where faces come suddenly to the doors, white-eyed. We hear sudden voices, ejaculant. Jewel has been looking from side to side; now his head turns forward and I can see his ears taking on a still deeper tone of furious red. Three negroes walk beside the road ahead of us; ten feet ahead of them a white man walks. When we pass the negroes their heads turn suddenly with that expression of shock and instinctive outrage. "Great God," one says; "what they got in that wagon?"

Jewel whirls. "Son of a bitches," he says. As he does so he is abreast of the white man, who has paused. It is as though Jewel had gone blind for the moment, for it is the white man toward whom he whirls.

"Darl!" Cash says from the wagon. I grasp at Jewel. The white man has fallen back a pace, his face still slack-jawed; then his jaw tightens, claps to. Jewel leans above him, his jaw muscles gone white.

"What did you say?" he says.

"Here," I say. "He don't mean anything, mister. Jewel," I say. When I touch him he swings at the man. I grasp his arm; we struggle. Jewel has never looked at me. He is trying to free his arm. When I see the man again he has an open knife in his hand.

"Hold up, mister," I say; "I've got him. Jewel," I say.

"Thinks because he's a goddam town fellow," Jewel says, panting, wrenching at me. "Son of a bitch," he says.

The man moves. He begins to edge around me, watching Jewel, the knife low against his flank. "Can't no man call me that," he says. Pa has got down, and Dewey Dell is holding Jewel, pushing at him. I release him and face the man.

"Wait," I say. "He don't mean nothing. He's sick; got burned in a fire last night, and he ain't himself."

"Fire or no fire," the man says, "can't no man call me that."

"He thought you said something to him," I say.

"I never said nothing to him. I never see him before."

" 'Fore God," pa says; " 'fore God."

"I know," I say. "He never meant anything. He'll take it back."

"Let him take it back, then."

"Put up your knife, and he will."

The man looks at me. He looks at Jewel. Jewel is quiet now.

"Put up your knife," I say.

The man shuts the knife.

" 'Fore God," pa says. " 'Fore God."

"Tell him you didn't mean anything, Jewel," I say.

"I thought he said something," Jewel says. "Just because he's——"

"Hush," I say. "Tell him you didn't mean it."

"I didn't mean it," Jewel says.

"He better not," the man says. "Calling me a——"

"Do you think he's afraid to call you that?" I say.

The man looks at me. "I never said that," he said.

"Don't think it, neither," Jewel says.

"Shut up," I say. "Come on. Drive on, pa."

The wagon moves. The man stands watching us. Jewel does not look back. "Jewel would 'a' whipped him," Vardaman says.

We approach the crest, where the street runs, where cars go back and forth; the mules haul the wagon up and on to the crest and the street. Pa stops them. The street runs on ahead, where the square opens and the monument stands before the court-house. We mount again while the heads turn with that expression which we know; save Jewel. He does not get on, even though the wagon has started again. "Get in, Jewel," I say. "Come on. Let's get away from here." But he does not get in. Instead he sets his foot on the turning hub of the rear wheel, one hand grasping the stanchion, and with the hub turning

smoothly under his sole he lifts the other foot and squats there, staring straight ahead, motionless, lean, wooden-backed, as though carved squatting out of the lean wood.

CASH

IT WASN'T NOTHING ELSE TO DO. IT WAS EITHER SEND HIM to Jackson, or have Gillespie sue us, because he knowed some way that Darl set fire to it. I don't know how he knowed, but he did. Vardaman see him do it, but he swore he never told nobody but Dewey Dell and that she told him not to tell nobody. But Gillespie knowed it. But he would 'a' suspicioned it sooner or later. He could have done it that night just watching the way Darl acted.

And so pa said, "I reckon there ain't nothing else to do," and Jewel said,

"You want to fix him now?"

"Fix him?" pa said.

"Catch him and tie him up," Jewel said. "Goddam it, do you want to wait until he sets fire to the goddam team and wagon?"

But there wasn't no use in that. "There ain't no use in that," I said. "We can wait till she is underground." A fellow that's going to spend the rest of his life locked up, he ought to be let to have what pleasure he can have before he goes.

"I reckon he ought to be there," pa says. "God knows,

it's a trial on me. Seems like it ain't no end to bad luck when once it starts."

Sometimes I ain't so sho who's got ere a right to say when a man is crazy and when he ain't. Sometimes I think it ain't none of us pure crazy and ain't none of us pure sane until the balance of us talks him that-a-way. It's like it ain't so much what a fellow does, but it's the way the majority of folks is looking at him when he does it.

Because Jewel is too hard on him. Of course it was Jewel's horse was traded to get her that nigh to town, and in a sense it was the value of his horse Darl tried to burn up. But I thought more than once before we crossed the river and after, how it would be God's blessing if He did take her outen our hands and get shut of her in some clean way, and it seemed to me that when Jewel worked so to get her outen the river, he was going against God in a way, and then when Darl seen that it looked like one of us would have to do something, I can almost believe he done right in a way. But I don't reckon nothing excuses setting fire to a man's barn and endangering his stock and destroying his property. That's how I reckon a man is crazy. That's how he can't see eye to eye with other folks. And I reckon they ain't nothing else to do with him but what the most folks says is right.

But it's a shame, in a way. Folks seems to get away from the olden right teaching that says to drive the nails down and trim the edges well always like it was for your own use and comfort you were making it. It's like some folks has the smooth, pretty boards to build a court-house with and others don't have no more than rough lumber fitten to build a chicken coop. But it's better to build a tight chicken coop than a shoddy court-house, and when they both build shoddy or build well, neither because it's

one or tother is going to make a man feel the better not the worse.

So we went up the street, toward the square, and he said, "We better take Cash to the doctor first. We can leave him there and come back for him." That's it. It's because me and him was born close together, and it nigh ten years before Jewel and Dewey Dell and Vardaman begun to come along. I feel kin to them, all right, but I don't know. And me being the oldest, and thinking already the very thing that he done: I don't know.

Pa was looking at me, then at him, mumbling his mouth.

"Go on," I said. "We'll get it done first."

"She would want us all there," pa says.

"Let's take Cash to the doctor first," Darl said. "She'll wait. She's already waited nine days."

"You all don't know," pa says. "The somebody you was young with and you growed old in her and she growed old in you, seeing the old coming on and it was the one somebody you could hear say it don't matter and know it was the truth outen the hard world and all a man's grief and trials. You all don't know."

"We got the digging to do, too," I said.

"Armstid and Gillespie both told you to send word ahead," Darl said. "Don't you want to go to Peabody's now, Cash?"

"Go on," I said. "It feels right easy now. It's best to get things done in the right place."

"If it was just dug," pa says. "We forgot our spade, too."

"Yes," Darl said. "I'll go to the hardware store. We'll have to buy one."

"It'll cost money," pa says.

"Do you begrudge her it?" Darl says.

"Go on and get a spade," Jewel said. "Here, give me the money."

But pa didn't stop. "I reckon we can get a spade," he said. "I reckon there are Christians here." So Darl set still and we went on, with Jewel squatting on the tail gate, watching the back of Darl's head. He looked like one of these bulldogs, one of these dogs that don't bark none, squatting against the rope, watching the thing he was waiting to jump at.

He set that way all the time we was in front of Mrs. Bundren's house, hearing the music, watching the back of Darl's head with them hard white eyes of hisn.

The music was playing in the house. It was one of them graphophones. It was natural as a music-band.

"Do you want to go to Peabody's?" Darl said. "They can wait here and tell pa, and I'll drive you to Peabody's and come back for them."

"No," I said. It was better to get her underground, now we was this close, just waiting until pa borrowed the shovel. He drove along the street until we could hear the music.

"Maybe they got one here," he said. He pulled up at Mrs. Bundren's. It was like he knowed. Sometimes I think that if a working man could see work as far ahead as a lazy man can see laziness. So he stopped there like he knowed, before that little new house, where the music was. We waited there, hearing it. I believe I could have dickered Suratt down to five dollars on that one of his. It's a comfortable thing, music is. "Maybe they got one here," pa says.

"You want Jewel to go," Darl says, "or do you reckon I better?"

"I reckon I better," pa says. He got down and went up

the path and around the house to the back. The music stopped, then it started again.

"He'll get it, too," Darl said.

"Ay," I said. It was just like he knowed, like he could see through the walls and into the next ten minutes.

Only it was more than ten minutes. The music stopped and never commenced again for a good spell, where her and pa was talking at the back. We waited in the wagon.

"You let me take you back to Peabody's," Darl said.

"No," I said. "We'll get her underground."

"If he ever gets back," Jewel said. He began to cuss. He started to get down from the wagon. "I'm going," he said.

Then we saw pa coming back. He had two spades, coming around the house. He laid them in the wagon and got in and we went on. The music never started again. Pa was looking back at the house. He kind of lifted his hand a little and I saw the shade pulled back a little at the window and her face in it.

But the curiousest thing was Dewey Dell. It surprised me. I see all the while how folks could say he was queer, but that was the very reason couldn't nobody hold it personal. It was like he was outside of it too, same as you, and getting mad as it would be kind of like getting mad at a mud-puddle that splashed you when you stepped in it. And then I always kind of had a idea that him and Dewey Dell kind of knowed things betwixt them. If I'd 'a' said it was ere a one of us she liked better than ere a other, I'd 'a' said it was Darl. But when we got it filled and covered and drove out the gate and turned into the lane where them fellows was waiting, when they come out and come on him and he jerked back, it was Dewey Dell that was on him before even Jewel could get at him. And then I believed I knowed how Gillespie knowed about how his barn taken fire.

She hadn't said a word, hadn't even looked at him, but when them fellows told him what they wanted and that they had come to get him and he throwed back, she jumped on him like a wild cat so that one ot the fellows had to quit and hold her and her scratching and clawing at him like a wild cat, while the other one and pa and Jewel throwed Darl down and held him lying on his back, looking up at me.

"I thought you would have told me," he said. "I never thought you wouldn't have."

"Darl," I said. But he fought again, him and Jewel and the fellow, and the other one holding Dewey Dell and Vardaman yelling and Jewel saying,

"Kill him. Kill the son of a bitch."

It was bad so. It was bad. A fellow can't get away from a shoddy job. He can't do it. I tried to tell him, but he just said, "I thought you'd 'a' told me. It's not that I," he said, then he began to laugh. The other fellow pulled Jewel off of him and he sat there on the ground, laughing.

I tried to tell him. If I could have just moved, even set up. But I tried to tell him and he quit laughing, looking up at me.

"Do you want me to go?" he said.

"It'll be better for you," I said. "Down there it'll be quiet, with none of the bothering and such. It'll be better for you, Darl," I said.

"Better," he said. He began to laugh again. "Better," he said. He couldn't hardly say it for laughing. He sat on the ground and us watching him, laughing and laughing. It was bad. It was bad so. I be durn if I could see anything to laugh at. Because there just ain't nothing justifies the deliberate destruction of what a man has built with his own sweat and stored the fruit of his sweat into.

But I ain't so sho that ere a man has the right to say what is crazy and what ain't. It's like there was a fellow in every man that's done a-past the sanity or the insanity, that watches the sane and the insane doings of that man with the same horror and the same astonishment.

PEABODY

I SAID, "I RECKON A MAN IN A TIGHT MIGHT LET BILL Varner patch him up like a damn mule, but I be damned if the man that'd let Anse Bundren treat him with raw cement ain't got more spare legs than I have."

"They just aimed to ease hit some," he said.

"Aimed, hell," I said. "What in hell did Armstid mean by even letting them put you on that wagon again?"

"Hit was gittin' right noticeable," he said. "We never had time to wait." I just looked at him. "Hit never bothered me none," he said.

"Don't you lie there and try to tell me you rode six days on a wagon without springs, with a broken leg and it never bothered you."

"I never bothered me much," he said.

"You mean, it never bothered Anse much," I said. "No more than it bothered him to throw that poor devil down in the public street and handcuff him like a damn mur derer. Don't tell me. And don't tell me it ain't going to bother you to lose sixty-odd square inches of skin to get that concrete off. And don't tell me it ain't going to bother you to have to limp around on one short leg for the balance of your life—if you walk at all again. Concrete," I said. "God Amighty, why didn't Anse carry you to the nearest sawmill and stick your leg in the saw? That would have cured it. Then you all could have stuck his head into the saw and cured a whole family. . . . Where is Anse, anyway? What's he up to now?"

"He's takin' back them spades he borrowed," he said.

"That's right," I said. "Of course he'd have to borrow a spade to bury his wife with. Unless he could borrow a hole in the ground. Too bad you all didn't put him in it too. . . . Does that hurt?"

"Not to speak of," he said, and the sweat big as marbles running down his face and his face about the colour of blotting-paper.

"Course not," I said. "About next summer you can hobble around fine on this leg. Then it won't bother you, not to speak of . . . If you had anything you could call luck, you might say it was lucky this is the same leg you broke before," I said.

"Hit's what paw says," he said.

MACGOWAN

IT HAPPENED I AM BACK OF THE PRESCRIPTION CASE, POUR-
ing up some chocolate sauce, when Jody comes back
and says, "Say, Skeet, there's a woman up front that
wants to see the doctor and when I said What doctor
you want to see, she said she want to see the doctor that
works here and when I said There ain't any doctor works
here, she just stood there, looking back this way."

"What kind of a woman is it?" I says. "Tell her to go
upstairs to Alford's office."

"Country woman," he says.

"Send her to the court-house," I says. "Tell her all the
doctors have gone to Memphis to a Barbers' Convention."

"All right," he says, going away. "She looks pretty
good for a country girl," he says.

"Wait," I says. He waited and I went and peeped
through the crack. But I couldn't tell nothing except she
had a good leg against the light. "Is she young, you say?"
I says.

"She looks like a pretty hot mamma, for a country
girl," he says.

"Take this," I says, giving him the chocolate. I took
off my apron and went up there. She looked pretty good.
One of them black-eyed ones that look like she'd as
soon put a knife in you as not if you two-timed her. She
looked pretty good. There wasn't nobody else in the
store; it was dinner-time.

"What can I do for you?" I says.

"Are you the doctor?" she says.

"Sure," I says. She quit looking at me and was kind of looking around.

"Can we go back yonder?" she says.

It was just a quarter-past twelve, but I went and told Jody to kind of watch out and whistle if the old man come in sight, because he never got back before one.

"You better lay off of that," Jody says. "He'll fire your stern out of here so quick you can't wink."

"He don't never get back before one," I says. "You can see him go into the post-office. You keep your eye peeled, now, and give me a whistle."

"What you going to do?" he says.

"You keep your eye out. I'll tell you later."

"Ain't you going to give me no seconds on it?" he says.

"What the hell do you think this is?" I says; "a stud-farm? You watch out for him. I'm going into conference."

So I go on to the back. I stopped at the glass and smoothed my hair, then I went behind the prescription case, where she was waiting. She is looking at the medicine cabinet, then she looks at me.

"Now, madam," I says; "what is your trouble?"

"It's the female trouble," she says, watching me. "I got the money," she says.

"Ah," I says. "Have you got female troubles or do you want female troubles? If so, you come to the right doctor." Them country people. Half the time they don't know what they want, and the balance of the time they can't tell it to you. The clock said twenty past twelve.

"No," she says.

"No which?" I says.

"I ain't had it," she says. "That's it." She looked at me. "I got the money," she says.

So I knew what she was talking about.

"Oh," I says. "You got something in your belly you wish you didn't have." She looks at me. "You wish you had a little more or a little less, huh?"

"I got the money," she says. "He said I could git something at the drug-store for hit."

"Who said so?" I says.

"He did," she says, looking at me.

"You don't want to call no names," I says. "The one that put the acorn in your belly? He the one that told you?" She don't say nothing. "You ain't married, are you?" I says. I never saw no ring. But like as not, they ain't heard yet out there that they use rings.

"I got the money," she says. She showed it to me, tied up in her handkerchief: a ten spot.

"I'll swear you have," I says. "He give it to you?"

"Yes," she says.

"Which one?" I says. She looks at me. "Which one of them give it to you?"

"It ain't but one," she says. She looks at me.

"Go on," I says. She don't say nothing. The trouble about the cellar is, it ain't but one way out and that's back up the inside stairs. The clock says twenty-five to one. "A pretty girl like you," I says.

She looks at me. She begins to tie the money back up in the handkerchief. "Excuse me a minute," I says. I go around the prescription case. "Did you hear about that fellow sprained his ear?" I says. "After that he couldn't even hear a belch."

"You better get her out from back there before the old man comes," Jody says.

"If you'll stay up there in front where he pays you to stay, he won't catch nobody but me," I says.

He goes on, slow, toward the front. "What you doing to her, Skeet?" he says.

"I can't tell you," I says. "It wouldn't be ethical. You go on up there and watch."

"Say, Skeet," he says.

"Ah, go on," I says. "I ain't doing nothing but filling a prescription."

"He may not do nothing about that woman back there, but if he finds you monkeying with that prescription case, he'll kick your stern clean down them cellar stairs."

"My stern has been kicked by bigger bastards than him," I says. "Go back and watch out for him, now."

So I come back. The clock said fifteen to one. She is tying the money in the handkerchief. "You ain't the doctor," she says.

"Sure I am," I says. She watches me. "Is it because I look too young, or am I too handsome?" I says. "We used to have a bunch of old water-jointed doctors here," I says; "Jefferson used to be a kind of Old Doctors' Home for them. But business started falling off and folks stayed so well until one day they found out that the women wouldn't never get sick at all. So they run all the old doctors out and got us young good-looking ones that the women would like and then the women begun to get sick again and so business picked up. They're doing that all over the country. Hadn't you heard about it? Maybe it's because you ain't never needed a doctor."

"I need one now," she says.

"And you come to the right one," I says. "I already told you that."

"Have you got something for it?" she says. "I got the money."

"Well," I says, "of course a doctor has to learn all sorts

of things while he's learning to roll calomel; he can't help himself. But I don't know about your trouble."

"He told me I could get something. He told me I could get it at the drug-store."

"Did he tell you the name of it?" I says. "You better go back and ask him."

She quit looking at me, kind of turning the handkerchief in her hands. "I got to do something," she says.

"How bad do you want to do something?" I says. She looks at me. "Of course, a doctor learns all sorts of things folks don't think he knows. But he ain't supposed to tell all he knows. It's against the law."

Up front Jody says, "Skeet."

"Excuse me a minute," I says. I went up front. "Do you see him?" I says.

"Ain't you done yet?" he says. "Maybe you better come up here and watch and let me do that consulting."

"Maybe you'll lay a egg," I says. I come back. She is looking at me. "Of course you realize that I could be put in the penitentiary for doing what you want," I says. "I would lose my licence and then I'd have to go to work. You realize that?"

"I ain't got but ten dollars," she says. "I could bring the rest next month, maybe."

"Pooh," I says, "ten dollars? You see, I can't put no price on my knowledge and skill. Certainly not for no little paltry sawbuck."

She looks at me. She don't even blink. "What you want, then?"

The clock said four to one. So I decided I better get her out. "You guess three times and then I'll show you," I says.

She don't even blink her eyes. "I got to do something,"

she says. She looks behind her and around, then she looks toward the front. "Gimme the medicine first," she says.

"You mean, you're ready to right now?" I says. "Here?"

"Gimme the medicine first," she says.

So I took a graduated glass and kind of turned my back to her and picked out a bottle that looked all right, because a man that would keep poison setting around in a unlabelled bottle ought to be in jail, anyway. It smelled like turpentine. I poured some into the glass and give it to her. She smelled it, looking at me across the glass.

"Hit smells like turpentine," she says.

"Sure," I says. "That's just the beginning of the treatment. You come back at ten o'clock to-night and I'll give you the rest of it and perform the operation."

"Operation?" she says.

"It won't hurt you. You've had the same operation before. Ever hear about the hair of the dog?"

She looks at me. "Will it work?" she says.

"Sure it'll work. If you come back and get it."

So she drunk whatever it was without batting a eye, and went out. I went up front.

"Didn't you get it?" Jody says.

"Get what?" I says.

"Ah, come on," he says. "I ain't going to try to beat your time."

"Oh, her," I says. "She just wanted a little medicine. She's got a bad case of dysentery and she's a little ashamed about mentioning it with a stranger there."

It was my night, anyway, so I helped the old bastard check up and I got his hat on him and got him out of the store by eight-thirty. I went as far as the corner with him and watched him until he passed under two street lamps and went on out of sight. Then I come back to the store and waited until nine-thirty and turned out the front lights and locked the door and left just one light burning at the back, and I went back and put some talcum powder into six capsules and kind of cleared up the cellar and then I was all ready.

She come in just at ten, before the clock had done striking. I let her in and she come in, walking fast. I looked out the door, but there wasn't nobody but a boy in overalls sitting on the curb. "You want something?" I says. He never said nothing, just looking at me. I locked the door and turned off the light and went on back. She was waiting. She didn't look at me now.

"Where is it?" she said.

I gave her the box of capsules. She held the box in her hand, looking at the capsules.

"Are you sure it'll work?" she says.

"Sure," I says. "When you take the rest of the treatment."

"Where do I take it?" she says.

"Down in the cellar," I says.

VARDAMAN

Now it is wider and lighter, but the stores are dark because they have all gone home. The stores are dark, but the lights pass on the windows when we pass. The lights are in the trees around the court-house.

They roost in the trees, but the court-house is dark. The clock on it looks four ways, because it is not dark. The moon is not dark too. Not very dark. *Darl he went to Jackson is my brother Darl is my brother* Only it was over that way, shining on the track.

"Let's go that way, Dewey Dell," I say.

"What for?" Dewey Dell says. The track went shining around the window, it red on the track. But she said he would not sell it to the town boys. "But it will be there Christmas," Dewey Dell says. "You'll have to wait till then, when he brings it back."

Darl went to Jackson. Lots of people didn't go to Jackson. Darl is my brother. My brother is going to Jackson

While we walk the lights go around, roosting in the trees. On all sides it is the same. They go around the court-house and then you cannot see them. But you can see them in the black windows beyond. They have all gone home to bed except me and Dewey Dell.

Going on the train to Jackson. My brother

There is a light in the store, far back. In the window are two big glasses of soda-water, red and green. Two men could not drink them. Two mules could not. Two cows could not. *Darl*

A man comes to the door. He looks at Dewey Dell.

"You wait out here," Dewey Dell says.

"Why can't I come in?" I say. "I want to come in, too."

"You wait out here," she says.

"All right," I say.

Dewey Dell goes in.

Darl is my brother. Darl went crazy

The walk is harder than sitting on the ground. He is in the open door. He looks at me. "You want something?" he says. His head is slick. Jewel's head is slick sometimes.

Cash's head is not slick. *Darl he went to Jackson my Brother Darl* In the street he ate a banana. *Wouldn't you rather have bananas? Dewey Dell said. You wait till Christmas. It'll be there then. Then you can see it. So we are going to have some bananas. We are going to have a bag full, me and Dewey Dell.* He locks the door. Dewey Dell is inside. Then the light winks out.

He went to Jackson. He went crazy and went to Jackson both. Lots of people didn't go crazy. Pa and Cash and Jewel and Dewey Dell and me didn't go crazy. We never did go crazy. We didn't go to Jackson either. Darl

I hear the cow a long time, clopping on the street. Then she comes into the square. She goes across the square, her head down   clopping . She lows. There was nothing in the square before she lowed, but it wasn't empty. Now it is empty after she lowed. She goes on, clopping . She lows. *My brother is Darl. He went to Jackson on the train. He didn't go on the train to go crazy. He went crazy in our wagon. Darl* She had been in there a long time. And the cow is gone too. A long time. She has been in there longer than the cow was. But not as long as empty. *Darl is my brother. My brother Darl*

Dewey Dell comes out. She looks at me.

"Let's go around that way now," I say.

She looks at me. "It ain't going to work," she says. "That son of a bitch."

"What ain't going to work, Dewey Dell?"

"I just know it won't," she says. She is not looking at anything. "I just know it."

"Let's go that way," I say.

"We got to go back to the hotel. It's late. We got to slip back in."

"Can't we go by and see, anyway?"

"Hadn't you rather have bananas? Hadn't you rather?"

"All right." *My brother he went crazy and he went to Jackson too. Jackson is further away than crazy*

"It won't work," Dewey Dell says. "I just know it won't."

"What won't work?" I say. *He had to get on the train to go to Jackson. I have not been on the train, but Darl has been on the train. Darl. Darl is my brother. Darl. Darl*

DARL

DARL HAS GONE TO JACKSON. THEY PUT HIM ON THE train, laughing, down the long car laughing, the heads turning like the heads of owls when he passed. "What are you laughing at?" I said.

"Yes yes yes yes yes."

Two men put him on the train. They wore mismatched coats, bulging behind over their right hip pockets. Their necks were shaved to a hairline, as though the recent and simultaneous barbers had had a chalkline like Cash's. "Is it the pistols you're laughing at?" I said. "Why do you laugh?" I said. "Is it because you hate the sound of laughing?"

They pulled two seats together so Darl could sit by the window to laugh. One of them sat beside him, the other sat on the seat facing him, riding backward. One of them had to ride backward because the state's money had a face to each backside and a backside to each face, and they are riding on the state's money which is incest. A nickel has a woman on one side and a buffalo on the other; two faces and no back. I don't know what that is. Darl had a little spy-glass he got in France at the war. In it it had a woman and a pig with two backs and no face. I know what that is. "Is that why you are laughing, Darl?"

"Yes yes yes yes yes yes."

The wagon stands on the square, hitched, the mules motionless, the reins wrapped about the seat-spring, the back of the wagon toward the court-house. It looks no different from a hundred other wagons there; Jewel standing beside it and looking up the street like any other man in town that day, yet there is something different, distinctive. There is about it that unmistakable air of definite and imminent departure that trains have, perhaps due to the fact that Dewey Dell and Vardaman on the seat and Cash on a pallet in the wagon bed are eating bananas from a paper bag. "Is that why you are laughing, Darl?"

Darl is our brother, our brother Darl. Our brother Darl in a cage in Jackson where, his grimed hands lying light in the quiet interstices, looking out he foams.

"Yes yes yes yes yes yes yes yes."

DEWEY DELL

W HEN HE SAW THE MONEY I SAID, "IT'S NOT MY money, it doesn't belong to me."

"Whose is it, then?"

"It's Cora Tull's money. It's Mrs. Tull's. I sold the cakes for it."

"Ten dollars for two cakes?"

"Don't you touch it. It's not mine."

"You never had them cakes. It's a lie. It was them Sunday clothes you had in that package."

"Don't you touch it! If you take it you are a thief."

"My own daughter accuses me of being a thief. My own daughter."

"Pa. Pa."

"I have fed you and sheltered you. I give you love and care, yet my own daughter, the daughter of my dead wife, calls me a thief over her mother's grave."

"It's not mine, I tell you. If it was, God knows you could have it."

"Where did you get ten dollars?"

"Pa. Pa."

"You won't tell me. Did you come by it so shameful you dare not?"

"It's not mine, I tell you. Can't you understand it's not mine?"

"It's not like I wouldn't pay it back. But she calls her own father a thief."

"I can't, I tell you. I tell you it's not my money. God knows you could have it."

"I wouldn't take it. My own born daughter that has et my food for seventeen years, begrudges me the loan of ten dollars."

"It's not mine. I can't."

"Whose is it, then?"

"It was give to me. To buy something with."

"To buy what with?"

"Pa. Pa."

"It's just a loan. God knows, I hate for my blooden children to reproach me. But I give them what was mine without stint. Cheerful I give them, without stint. And now they deny me. Addie. It was lucky for you you died, Addie."

"Pa. Pa."

"God knows it is."

He took the money and went out.

CASH

SO WHEN WE STOPPED THERE TO BORROW THE SHOVELS we heard the graphophone playing in the house, and so when we got done with the shovels pa says, "I reckon I better take them back."

So we went back to the house. "We better take Cash on to Peabody's," Jewel said.

"It won't take but a minute," pa said. He got down from the wagon. The music was not playing now.

"Let Vardaman do it," Jewel said. "He can do it in half the time you can. Or here, you let me——"

"I reckon I better do it," pa says. "Long as it was me that borrowed them."

So we set in the wagon, but the music wasn't playing now. I reckon it's a good thing we ain't got ere a one of them. I reckon I wouldn't never get no work done a-tall for listening to it. I don't know if a little music ain't about the nicest thing a fellow can have. Seems like when he comes in tired of a night, it ain't nothing could rest him like having a little music played and him resting. I have seen them that shuts up like a hand-grip, with a handle and all, so a fellow can carry it with him wherever he wants.

"What you reckon he's doing?" Jewel says. "I could a toted them shovels back and forth ten times by now."

"Let him take his time," I said. "He ain't as spry as you, remember."

"Why didn't he let me take them back, then? We got to get your leg fixed up so we can start home tomorrow."

"We got plenty of time," I said. "I wonder what them machines costs on the instalment."

"Instalment of what?" Jewel said. "What you got to buy it with?"

"A fellow can't tell," I said. "I could 'a' bought that one from Suratt for five dollars, I believe."

And so pa come back and we went to Peabody's. While we was there pa said he was going to the barbershop and get a shave. And so that night he said he had some business to tend to, kind of looking away from us while he said it, with his hair combed wet and slick and smelling sweet with perfume, but I said leave him be; I wouldn't mind hearing a little more of that music myself.

And so next morning he was gone again, then he come back and told us get hitched up and ready to take out and he would meet us and when they was gone he said,

"I don't reckon you got no more money."

"Peabody just give me enough to pay the hotel with," I said. "We don't need nothing else, do we?"

"No," pa said; "no. We don't need nothing." He stood there, not looking at me.

"If it is something we got to have, I reckon maybe Peabody," I said.

"No," he said; "it ain't nothing else. You all wait for me at the corner."

So Jewel got the team and come for me and they fixed me a pallet in the wagon and we drove across the square to the corner where Pa said, and we was waiting there in the wagon, with Dewey Dell and Vardaman eating bananas, when we see them coming up the street. Pa was coming along with that kind of daresome and hang-dog look all at once like when he has been up to something he knows ma ain't going to like, carrying a grip in his hand, and Jewel says,

"Who's that?"

Then we see it wasn't the grip that made him look different; it was his face, and Jewel says, "He got them teeth."

It was a fact. It made him look a foot taller, kind of holding his head up, hangdog and proud too, and then we see her behind him, carrying the other grip—a kind of duck-shaped woman all dressed up, with them kind of hard-looking pop eyes like she was daring ere a man to say nothing. And there we set watching them, with Dewey Dell's and Vardaman's mouth half open and half-et bananas in their hands and her coming around from behind pa, looking at us like she dared ere a man. And then I see that the grip she was carrying was one of them little graphophones. It was for a fact, all shut up as pretty as a picture, and every time a new record would come from the mail order and us setting in the house in the winter, listening to it, I would think what a shame Darl couldn't be to enjoy it too. But it is better so for him. This world is not his world; this life his life.

"It's Cash and Jewel and Vardaman and Dewey Dell," pa says, kind of hangdog and proud too, with his teeth and all, even if he wouldn't look at us. "Meet Mrs. Bundren," he says.

The Best of the World's Best Books

COMPLETE LIST OF TITLES IN
THE MODERN LIBRARY

MODERN LIBRARY GIANTS

A series of sturdily bound and handsomely printed, full-sized library editions of books formerly available only in expensive sets. These volumes contain from 600 to 1,400 pages each.

THE MODERN LIBRARY GIANTS REPRESENT A
SELECTION OF THE WORLD'S GREATEST BOOKS

MISCELLANEOUS